# IN HER
# SIGHTS

## KATIE
## RUGGLE

sourcebooks
casablanca

Published by Sourcebooks Casablanca, an imprint of Sourcebooks, Inc.
P.O. Box 4410, Naperville, Illinois 60567-4410
(630) 961-3900
Fax: (630) 961-2168
sourcebooks.com

Printed and bound in the United States of America.
OPM 10 9 8 7 6 5 4 3 2 1

*For all my sisters*

# CHAPTER 1

"I'M HEADED TO THE PARK," MOLLY CALLED AS SHE LET THE screen door slam behind her. It slapped against the edge of the frame, too warped to close properly. She absently made a mental note to fix it later…along with the hundred other things that needed doing around the house.

"You want backup?" Charlie yelled back, and Molly resisted the urge to roll her eyes. Her sister would do anything to get out of paperwork, but Molly wasn't about to enable her, even if it would be nice to have someone along to help relieve the boredom.

"Nope, this should be easy-peasy."

"You're taking Warrant though, right?" Cara, Charlie's twin and the worrywart of the family, peered at Molly through the screen door.

Their enormous, hairy Great Pyrenees mix cocked his head when he heard his name. "Yes." Leash in hand, Molly allowed Warrant to tow her down the porch steps as she gave Cara a wave over her shoulder, wanting to get out of earshot before her sisters thought of any more questions. If Molly was delayed long enough, Charlie would somehow finagle her way into coming along, and that meant Molly would be stuck sorting her sister's expense reports. That prospect wouldn't be so bad, except that Charlie was terrible about taking care of her receipts. They were always sticky or stained or wrapped around chewed gum. *Nope*. Charlie could do her own expense report. It was a beautiful afternoon for a walk to the park, and Molly was going to enjoy it.

Warrant trotted at her side as they passed their neighbor's scarily perfect yard. Mr. Petra silently watched from his wide, immaculate porch, his narrow-eyed glare boring into her.

Baring her teeth in a wide smile, Molly waved. "Hey, Mr. P! Beautiful day, isn't it?"

As he continued to glower, Molly felt her forced smile shift to a real grin. Being passive-aggressively friendly to her sourpuss of a neighbor was oddly satisfying. She felt his disapproving glare follow her until she reached the end of their street and turned the corner. Warrant happily bumbled along next to her, although his broad, pink tongue was already hanging out of his mouth.

"We've gone a *block*," she said. "You can't be getting tired already."

Warrant just blinked his oblivious dark eyes at her, and she sighed.

"You're the laziest dog in the world. It's a good thing you're cute, or we wouldn't put up with your shenanigans." That last part was a lie. Molly and her sisters would put up with Warrant even if all of his fur fell out and he sprouted leathery, bat-like wings. They'd probably even get specially made sweaters with appropriately placed holes for his new appendages. She smiled at the mental image as she ran a hand over his silky-soft head.

The sun beamed down warmly on them as they walked, light filtering through the trees that lined the residential street. Langston was close enough to Denver—just an hour's drive from downtown to downtown if traffic was light—that commuters were snapping up new cookie-cutter homes on the northern edge of the small city as fast as they could be built. Set tucked against the foothills of the Rocky Mountains, the new suburbs had wide stretches of fresh sod and spindly saplings that cast barely any shade, but Molly's house was in the older, richer, southern part of town. That meant neighbors eyed her family's worn and comfortably raggedy property from their own perfectly restored Victorians with lush, Mr. P-approved lawns, but it also meant that the trees were old enough to spread their sheltering branches over the yards and quiet streets, protecting Molly and Warrant from the strong Colorado sun.

Although it was mid-September, it still looked—and felt—like summer. The only hint that fall had begun was the absence of kids running around at two thirty on a Tuesday afternoon. Despite Warrant's slowing pace, the mile-long walk went quickly, the peace of the quiet, warm day soothing Molly's too-busy brain.

After much coaxing and a minimal amount of dragging her increasingly lazy dog, Molly made it to the park. Only a handful of people were there, mostly parents watching their preschool-age kids play. Warrant perked up once the dog park came into view, but Molly towed him in the opposite direction toward an empty bench next to the swings, doing her best to pretend she couldn't see his sad look. She failed miserably.

"I know, Warrant." She sat and tried to ignore the guilt swamping her. "We need to make some money, though. You eat a lot, and it's not the cheap stuff, either. Your food is the equivalent of dog caviar, so

I don't think it's too much to ask for you to help out occasionally."

With a soul-deep sigh, he lay down next to the bench and rested his chin on his front paws. Molly turned her attention away from the dog and eyed the shops across the street. Her spot on the bench was the perfect vantage point.

She pulled her phone from her pocket and pretended that she wasn't watching the door next to the cute ice cream parlor. The apartment above the shop was leased by Maryann Cooper, who seemed to be a law-abiding, responsible citizen. The same couldn't be said about her younger brother, Donnie. He had a habit of taking things that didn't belong to him—like wallets and cell phones and the occasional car—and he hadn't shown up for his most recent court date.

Molly had a strong suspicion that Maryann knew where Donnie was hiding, and she would leave for her shift at the turkey-processing plant in an hour or so. Since Maryann had been dodging all of her calls and refusing to answer the door, Molly would have to take a more direct approach. She started playing a game on her phone to pass the time while keeping one eye on the apartment across the street, just in case Maryann decided to leave early. Warrant stretched out on his side and dozed, snoring softly.

After a peaceful half hour drifted by, Molly stood and stretched, knowing it was time to move closer to the ice cream shop. Warrant provided an excuse to hang out at the park without looking like a lurker—and he'd also proven to be an excellent conversation starter with people who wouldn't have given her the time of day if she'd tried approaching them alone—but having the dog along did require some additional planning. Warrant's top speed was a slow amble, so she had to allow enough time to get him through the park and across the street.

Before she could make her move, an all-too-familiar voice made her groan and plop back down in her seat.

"Molly Pax. Just the person I wanted to see." John Carmondy started rounding the bench but paused to rub Warrant behind the ears. The dog—traitor that he was—thumped his heavy tail against the ground and rolled over in a plea for belly scratches. To Warrant's obvious delight, John complied.

"John Carmondy. Just the person I *didn't* want to see." If she'd known that he was going to be at the park, she would've stopped and talked to Mr. P, or even helped Charlie with those sticky receipts. Molly sent a quick text and then slid her phone into her pocket. "Why are you here?"

Still crouched to pet Warrant, John grinned up at her. Her dog's back foot pedaled in the air as John found just the right spot. Molly wasn't surprised. She was well aware that the man knew exactly how to hit everyone's buttons. Too bad he seemed to take as much pleasure in pestering her as he did in playing with her dog. "Why am I at the park?" he asked. "Why does anyone go to the park on such a beautiful day?"

Across the street, Maryann slipped out of the door next to the ice cream shop and hurried toward her ancient Honda parked on the street. She was leaving early today. Molly watched her go, holding back a growl when she saw Maryann get in her car and pull away from the curb. There went her chance to talk to the bail-jumper's sister.

"You're such a happy dog, aren't you?" John cooed. "Not all crabby like your owner."

Molly rolled her eyes hard enough that she was surprised they didn't spin right out of her skull. "I'm not crabby." She hesitated, honesty pushing her to add, "Well, not to most people."

With a snort, John gave Warrant a final belly scratch before straightening to his full—and significant—height. Crossing over, he took the spot next to her on the bench, and Molly fought the urge to shift to give him more room. He was just so darn *huge*, with biceps as big as her head and thighs like muscled tree trunks. His ridiculously enormous body took up almost the entire bench. "I'm special, then?"

"Special's one word for it," she muttered. *Aggravating* was another. So were *flirty*, *distracting*, and *confusing*, although she wasn't about to admit to any of the last three. Forcing her brain back to the job at hand, she snuck another quick glance across the street. Even though Maryann had left, Molly kept a furtive eye on the shops as she pretended to watch the kids playing on the jungle gym. She hoped that her unwelcome companion would wander away if she ignored him.

"So...how've you been?"

Of course he didn't wander away. She should've known better. John Carmondy was as hard to get rid of as head lice—and twice as irksome. The fact that her pulse did a weird skittery hop of excitement every time she saw him just annoyed her more. Shooting an irritated glance his way, she saw he was gazing across the street at the ice cream shop, the corner of his mouth tucked in as if he was trying to hold back a grin. He wasn't fooling anyone, though. The deep crease of his dimple gave him away.

Her sigh sounded more like a groan. "Did you want something, or do you have some kind of daily annoyance quota you need to fill?"

When he laughed, she couldn't help but dart another quick look in his direction. The harsh lines of his face—the square jaw and dark, intense eyes and bumpy nose that had obviously been the target of a fist or two in the past—were softened by his full lips, the lush sweep of his long eyelashes, and that stupidly appealing dimple. Someone that attractive shouldn't be so incredibly irritating, but that was John Carmondy in a nutshell: ridiculously pretty and just as ridiculously obnoxious.

"Oh, Pax…such a jokester." He continued before she could protest that she was completely serious. "What's happening in your life? It's been a while since we last got together, and I want to know everything. That's what good friends do. They share thoughts and ideas and feelings with each other. So share, my good friend. Whatcha up to?" He turned toward her, slinging his arm over the back of the bench so that his enormous hand rested behind her. Although she tried to ignore it, she couldn't help but shiver. She tried to tell herself it was her imagination, but it felt like the heat from his arm was burning the skin of her back like a brand.

"First of all," she started, even as the adult in her brain told her not to encourage him, to just ignore him until he gave up and left, "I saw you only three days ago, when I grabbed that bail jumper from the hardware store."

"The one *I* tracked down? The one you stole while I was in the bathroom? *That* bail jumper?"

Ignoring his—accurate—comment, she continued. "Second, we're not friends, so there will be no sharing of any kind. Third, please go away."

She did her best to keep her gaze forward, but it was like her eyes had a mind of their own. In her peripheral vision, she saw him clutch at his chest dramatically. "How can you say we're not friends? We share all the time. Skips, jokes...we're even sharing a park bench right now. We're sharers, Pax. That's what we do."

"No, that's *not* what we do." *Quit encouraging him*, the smart part of her brain warned.

"We should share an office," he continued, proving she shouldn't have said anything. "I don't know why you're fighting this so hard. We would be incredible together. A dream team, you might say."

Losing the battle over her self-control, she turned her head to look. Instantly, she regretted it when her brain went blank at the sight of him. As annoying as he could be, even she had to admit that he was a beautiful, beautiful man. Tearing her gaze from his amused face, she scowled hard at the ice cream shop across the street, trying to regain her composure—and her ability to speak. "One of us would be dead within a week. The other would be in jail for murder."

"But think how much fun that first week would be. Totally worth it." His chuckle was low, with a growly undertone that made her shiver. *Don't be stupid*, that practical portion of her brain warned. This talk about killing each other and stealing skips and their mutual antagonism wasn't some weird, twisted version of flirting. He might enjoy riling her up, and he was most likely sincere about wanting her to work for him—she and her sisters were very good at what they did, after all—but he wasn't interested in her like that. He was just a very, very attractive guy who was used to getting what he wanted. When she refused his job offers and stole his skips and responded to his teasing with snark rather than utter adoration, he wanted her even more.

Heat rushed to her belly, even as she hurried to correct the thought. *Wants me to* work *for him, not wants me in any other way*.

Wrestling her mind away from that line of thinking before she could get even more flustered, she focused on the playground. A toddler who'd been playing on the base of the slide was swept up by her mom, and the two walked toward the ice cream shop. Even though it was the middle of the day, the place seemed to be doing a brisk business. An older couple entered the shop while a young woman in running clothes peered through the front window, as if tempted by the thought of a cone.

John chuckled and shifted on the bench, drawing her attention once again. "Has it only been three days since we saw each other last? It *feels* longer, probably because I missed this." From the corner of her eye, she saw him gesture back and forth between the two of them, and she had to swallow an amused snort. He was persistent, she'd give him that. When she didn't respond, he turned to follow her gaze, although his arm remained stretched behind her. "So…? Who are you hunting these days?"

And there it was…his true motivation. While she'd been dithering about whether he was actually flirting with her, he'd been focused on stealing her latest job. She gave herself a mental shake. When would she learn that John Carmondy was only interested in what benefited John Carmondy? "Who says I'm working? Why couldn't I just be walking my dog on a beautiful day?" Even as she spoke, she scolded herself for encouraging him. John was the human manifestation of *give an inch, take a mile*.

He laughed again in that low, husky way that she refused to think of as sexy. "Because you have that look you get when you're on the trail of a skip. You're a bloodhound, Miss Molly Pax, and you don't lift your nose from the ground until you find your target."

Sighing in a deeply exaggerated way, she stood, and he immediately followed suit. Of course it was too much to ask that she could lose him that easily. She was going to have to get creative. "As much as I would love to stay and listen to you compare me to a dog, Warrant and I have things to do."

Although Warrant got to his feet reluctantly, he perked up as she headed toward the dog park and walked willingly at her side.

"When are you going to come work for me, Pax?" John asked, catching up easily.

"Never ever." She paused and then added for good measure, "Ever."

"I offer a really good health insurance plan," he said in the tone of someone dangling candy in front of a toddler. The sad thing was that Molly would've been tempted by that…if this were anyone but John. She enjoyed being a bail recovery agent more than she'd ever expected, but the paperwork involved in owning a business was much less fun. There was no way she'd ever accept a job from John, though. Forget a week—she'd murder him before she completed her first *day*.

"Good for you." As they drew closer to the dog park's gate, Warrant trotted in front of her, eager to get inside. Molly's phone buzzed in her pocket, and she pulled it out to glance at the text. Showtime. Get over here. She held back a smile at the perfect timing. Sometimes things really did work out beautifully, even when John was sticking his nose where it didn't belong. "Here. Hold him a second."

She tossed the end of the leash to John, and he caught it automatically. Turning, she jogged toward the road. In front of the ice cream shop, the runner who'd been peering wistfully through the window now looked to be flirting with a scruffy-looking white guy in his midthirties.

As Molly paused by the side of the road to let a car pass, she typed Donald Cooper, ice cream shop on Walnut St. NOW and sent the text before glancing behind her. She couldn't hold back a smirk. John was trying to follow her, but Warrant had put on the brakes. He'd plopped his fluffy hundred-pound butt down in front of the dog park entrance and braced his front legs, refusing to move. *That's right, baby*, she thought gleefully. *Earn your expensive dog food*.

"Don't you want to go with your mama?" The distance between them made his voice faint, but Molly could still hear John's cajoling words. "I bet there's some bacon over there. Wouldn't you like some bacon? Mmm…salty and meaty?"

A laugh escaped Molly as she glanced at the text that had popped up on her phone.

On our way from Clayton and Fifth. ETA four minutes.

*Four minutes is doable*, she thought, jogging across the road while adopting her game face. "Felicity!" she said, the last syllable rising in a well-practiced squeal as she trotted over to the runner to give her an exuberant hug. "I thought that was you." Keeping an arm around Felicity's back, she turned toward the man who was not even trying to hide the way he was checking her out. She gave him a small smile that he returned with a leer.

"Are you two twins?" he asked.

"Just sisters," they chorused, before bursting into practiced giggles.

Molly kept her expression as dumb and happy as possible. "Who's this?"

"This," Felicity said, "is Donnie. I dropped my apartment key without realizing it, and he picked it up for me. The stupid tiny pocket in these shorts is useless." She flipped the waistband of her shorts over, revealing the small inside pocket and a smooth, bronze patch of hip. Donnie's gaze locked onto the exposed skin, and his eyes bugged out a little.

"That's so sweet of you, Donnie," Molly cooed.

"It's *so* sweet." Felicity tossed her glossy, dark hair over her shoulder, and Donnie's eyes followed the movement as he swallowed visibly.

"You should buy him some ice cream as a thank-you." Molly gave him an approving smile, carefully not looking over his shoulder. Surely four minutes had passed by now.

Pouting a little, Felicity said, "I'd love to, but I left all my money at home."

"I have money." Molly patted her pocket. "You can pay me back later, Fifi."

Felicity gave her a quick, covert glare at the hated nickname, but the expression disappeared as quickly as it arrived, replaced by a beaming smile. "Thanks, Moo!"

Hiding her grimace, Molly accepted that as well-deserved payback.

"I should…" Donnie trailed off as he glanced over his shoulder, his whole body going stiff as he saw the approaching sheriff's deputies. "Shit! Gotta go!"

He bolted.

"Wait!" Molly tried to grab his arm, but he slipped past her outstretched hand.

"Sorry, ladies!" he shouted over his shoulder. "You can buy me that ice cream some other time!"

Sharing an exasperated glance with her sister, Molly took off after him, Felicity close behind. "Way to be stealthy, Deputies!" she called back over her shoulder before focusing on the chase.

"Why do they always run?" Felicity grumbled as they sprinted past a Mexican restaurant followed by a bank, weaving between people who were trying to enjoy the early fall day. Donnie shoved through a group of young teens, ignoring their protests, and disappeared as the boys clustered back together. Molly muttered a breathless curse as she jumped into the road to skirt the group, not rude enough to knock the teens out of the way as Donnie had done.

"Hey!" one of the boys called, puffing out his narrow chest as he trotted after them. "What's the hurry? Stop and talk to us."

The others in the group laughed and made *oooh* noises. Mentally thanking the universe that she only had to deal with sisters, Molly didn't break stride as she barked out, "Get back to school!"

As Felicity choked back a laugh behind her, the boy deflated and returned to his hooting group. Molly barely noticed his retreat or her sister's amusement, completely focused on finding which direction Donnie had run. A yelp from a middle-aged man as he stumbled sideways caught her attention, and she dashed in his direction. Spotting the back of Donnie's blond head, she called out, "This way!" and took off after him again.

Up ahead, two moms faced each other, chatting as they leaned on their baby strollers, blocking the sidewalk completely. Molly sucked in a worried breath, concerned that Donnie would plow right through, sending the babies flying, but he went into the street to go around them. Molly started to do the same, but a garbage truck barreled toward her, and she returned to the safety of the sidewalk. She was going too fast to stop, so she jumped over the front wheels of the strollers.

Behind her, she heard Felicity calling apologies to the furiously shouting moms, but Molly focused on Donnie's back. He was fast, the slippery doofus.

"Why do they always run?" Felicity asked again as she lengthened her stride to pull level with Molly.

"Because they know they're going to jail?" Unlike her sister, Molly was already sucking air, and she cursed her love of pastries and hatred of exercise for the hundredth time. "At least…*you're* wearing…appropriate clothes."

"Could be worse," Felicity said as they chased Donnie across an empty lot. "You could be in a dress and heels, like when we crashed that wedding to bring in the maid of honor."

"True."

Donnie darted sideways, grabbing the edge of a recycling bin and pulling it down behind him.

"Someone's been watching too many movies!" Molly shouted at his back as she dodged around the tipped bin. "Are you going to run…through an open-air market next?"

Except for a frantic glance over his shoulder, Donnie didn't reply. He took a sharp left turn between two large Victorian houses, and Molly skidded in the dry dirt as she tried to follow. Her feet slid out from under her, sending her down to one knee and her hands. Tiny pebbles bit into her palms as she grunted, pushing herself back up to her feet without missing a beat.

The fall had only cost her a second or two, and she took off after Felicity. Determined to bring Donnie in, Molly increased her speed, her legs churning even faster until she started catching up to her sister. They wove through yards, skirting evergreens and even a cupid-bedecked fountain that looked much too tempting. Molly's lungs heaved with effort, her skin slick with sweat and gritty from salt and dust. She knew she was reaching the end of her endurance, so she pushed herself to go just a little bit faster, knowing that they had to bring down Donnie within the next few seconds or he would get away.

Her molars clicked together at the thought. There was no way she was going to let Donnie escape. Not after all of this. Her latest burst of speed shot her past Felicity, who glanced at her with a bared-teeth grin. The crazy woman loved foot chases. If Molly had any energy to spare, she would've rolled her eyes.

Instead, she focused on the sweat-soaked back of

Donnie's shirt. Digging deep, she slowly closed the gap between them until they were only ten feet apart. Giving her another hunted glance, he turned abruptly and headed for a six-foot wooden fence enclosing someone's backyard. Molly and Felicity groaned in unison.

"Not it," Molly said quickly, just before Felicity said it.

"But I'm in shorts and a sports bra!"

She sighed, her heaving lungs making it come out in an uneven rush. "Fine. I'll do it." Although Molly would much rather be the one who gave her sister a leg up rather than dropping into a stranger's backyard, Felicity had a point. Molly's T-shirt and capris were slightly more suited to hurdling a fence.

Donnie didn't slow down as he approached the wooden barricade, using his momentum to haul himself up the side. Driven by the intense desire to avoid doing the same, Molly scraped up the very last of her energy and surged forward, leaping up to latch her arms around his waist. Her weight unbalanced him, and his grip on the top of the boards slipped, sending them both tumbling to the ground.

Molly hit the sunbaked earth first, grunting as the air was driven out of her lungs from the force of the fall. Although she managed to twist slightly so that his entire weight didn't land on her, he'd still pinned her right arm and shoulder to the weedy ground. Then Felicity was flipping him over, and Molly was free of his weight.

Rolling over and pushing to her knees, Molly blinked a couple of times to orient herself. "You good?" she asked, and Felicity gave her a fierce grin. Her knee was pressing firmly into Donnie's spine, and she had a strong grip on his hand, using it to twist his arm behind his back. Donnie was swearing and muttering, his words muffled by the thick thatch of weeds his face was shoved into.

"Never better."

"I'm not," Donnie whined. "Who the hell *are* you?"

With a breathless chuckle, Molly stood up and did a quick inventory, checking for any injuries of her own. Although her shoulder was throbbing where Donnie had landed on it, she knew there was no major damage done. She'd just be bruised and sore for a few days.

The two deputies ran toward them, barely winded, and she raised her eyebrows. "You were slow on purpose, weren't you?"

"I'm admitting nothing." Maria winked at her as she and her partner, Darren, took over, allowing Felicity to climb off Donnie. "Just think of it as a measure of trust in you. We knew you'd run him down. You always get your guy."

"Besides," Darren said as he cuffed Donnie's hands behind his back, "this way you really feel like you earned the payout."

"I'm fine with not earning it," Felicity said, and Molly nodded in agreement. "If we'd ended up having to go over that fence, I would've been *annoyed*."

"I'll leave the acrobatics to you youngsters," Maria said, helping Donnie to his feet.

"Youngsters?" Molly exchanged a skeptical look with her sister. "What are you? Thirty?"

"Thirty-*two*."

Rolling her eyes, Molly fell in behind the trio as they headed back in the direction of the park. "Okay, Grandma."

"No one read me my rights." Donnie's voice was a

winded mix of complaint and triumph. "That's illegal. I'm going to sue you all."

"We're only required to let you know your Miranda rights if you're being questioned while in police custody," Maria explained with more patience than Molly could muster after that chase.

"*We* never have to read you your rights, dummy." From Felicity's gleeful tone, she had just about as much sympathy for Donnie as Molly did. "We're not cops."

"I can't believe you played me like that," Donnie whined from his spot between the two deputies. "That's why I don't trust chicks."

Darren gave him a look. "How were you not suspicious when they started paying attention to you? Those two are *way* out of your league."

Molly tuned out Donnie's indignant sputters and turned to her sister. "Thanks for getting here so fast after I texted. How'd you sneak away without Charlie tagging along?"

Felicity grinned. "I asked her to help me clean the garage. That's the one thing she hates more than paperwork. There's no way she'll go out to check if I'm in there. She'll be too worried that I'll make her help."

"Genius."

"Yep."

As they reached the ice cream shop, a shout from across the street caught Molly's attention. When she turned her head and saw John and Warrant, both looking equally stubborn and annoyed, she pressed her lips together to hold back a laugh.

"Talk about genius." Felicity sounded just as amused as Molly felt. "You finally figured out a way to ditch Carmondy. Nice one, Molls."

"Thanks. I just wish he'd give up on following me around and chase his own skips."

Her sister's eyebrows bobbed up and down comically. "I've told you about a thousand times why he's really always trailing after you."

"Not that again." Molly groaned. This was a regular joke that Felicity—all of her sisters, actually—teased her with, but it was as far from reality as it could possibly be. "He wants me to work for him. Since I keep refusing, he wants to steal my skips out from under me. That's all there is to it."

"He's in *loooove*," Felicity cooed, and Molly jabbed her sister in the side with her elbow. "How have you not realized this? He basically has cartoon hearts where his pupils should be whenever he looks at you."

"Hush." Even though Molly knew it wasn't true and that her sister was just trying to get a rise out of her, the running joke still made her squirm…mainly because the teeniest, tiniest, stupidest part of her felt a ridiculous surge of hope.

Although Felicity smirked at her, she did fall silent, to Molly's relief.

"Would you mind finishing up with Maria and Darren?" Molly asked. "I need to retrieve our dog."

"Sure." Felicity jogged to catch up with the deputies, who were ushering Donnie around the corner to where they must've parked their squad car.

"You're my favorite sister!" Molly called after Felicity before crossing the street. Her pace slowed as she neared John and Warrant, their twin accusing stares making her feel a bit guilty, even as she had to bite back a grin.

"Thank you for holding him," she said, taking the leash. "I just had to take care of something."

Instead of yelling about getting ditched, however, John's attention ran over her grass-and-dirt-stained clothes and settled on the scrape on her forearm. His eyes narrowed. "What happened?"

She flapped her hand to dismiss his concern. "I just didn't feel like climbing over a fence today."

"That makes no sense." He eyed her carefully, as if searching for other injuries. "You okay?"

"Of course. All in a day's work." She couldn't help smiling at him. No matter how aggravating John Carmondy was, it was kind of nice having someone worry about her.

She quickly nipped that thought in the bud. If she allowed herself to get mushy where John was concerned, he'd start stealing jobs from her left and right. Even worse, if she didn't stay on her guard around him, she'd end up agreeing to work for or with him, and one of them would surely end up dead in short order. It was important for their continued safety that she resist any urge to soften toward her biggest rival.

"You *are* hurt, aren't you?" His voice was full of concern as he took a half step closer, as though ready to administer first aid. Molly didn't find the idea of John's big hands on her as repugnant as she should have. In fact, the thought of him taking care of her, of letting her lean against his broad chest as he checked her scrapes and bruises was almost…nice.

*That* thought brought her back to reality, and she turned sharply away, tossing him a muttered "bye." That was why it was important to not let Felicity's insinuations take root in her brain. Molly had to be careful, since she had a bad habit of playing the sucker for a pair of puppy-dog eyes and a sob story. Although she'd been forced to develop a hard shell when she and her sisters started their bail recovery business, there was nothing she could do about her soft, marshmallowy center. She was pretty much stuck with that.

"Remember," she muttered as she strode toward the dog park, Warrant happily trundling along at her side now that he was finally, *finally* getting his way, "that way leads to death or prison."

"What?"

She turned her head to see that John had tagged along. His scowl had softened, and a corner of his mouth was even threatening to twitch upward again. "I was talking to Warrant."

"About death and prison?"

"He's a good listener."

"I'm sure he is." John matched his pace to hers, as if they were a couple taking their dog for a walk. Molly tried to speed up, but his long legs easily kept pace, and before long *she* was the one getting sweaty and breathless.

Slowing down again, she gave him an exasperated look. Since she had four younger sisters—and a mom who acted more like a kid than any of her offspring ever had—Molly knew her glare was on point. "Why are you still here?"

For some strange reason, that question banished the last of his scowl, and he grinned sunnily at her. There was no sign he'd ever been annoyed *or* concerned. "It's a beautiful day. Why wouldn't I want to spend it in the park?"

"This place is pretty big." She didn't believe for a second that he was following her around for the fun of it. John Carmondy wanted something from her. "Can't you spend this beautiful day in another part of it? One that's *away*?" She gestured in a broad circle, encompassing the entire park.

He chuckled. It was like he was incapable of being offended. "But it's nicest right here."

"It smells like dog poop right here." They reached the gate again, and she paused, wanting to chase John off before they entered the run. It was one thing for him to follow her around the park, but standing together, watching Warrant play, laughing over the dogs' antics... It all felt too dangerously intimate for her comfort. John wasn't her boyfriend. He wasn't even a friend. He was a rival and a skip-stealer, and Molly knew it was ill-advised to let him into the dog park with her. There was no way to watch some big hulk of a guy play with puppies and not turn to mush inside.

"All I smell is flowers." His grin widened, and Molly let her head fall back as she mentally swore at the sky.

"Fine." She opened the gate and followed Warrant through it. "But there will be no laughing. And *no* playing with puppies. Understand?" Unclipping Warrant's leash, she let him into the main part of the park. He immediately galumphed over to make friends with an overweight black Lab.

"Not really?" He sounded like he was about to disobey the first rule already.

She glanced at his bemused face and quickly turned away. She could already tell that this wasn't going to end well. There was going to be cuteness, and she was going to get mushy, and it was all going to end with someone's death.

He smiled, flashing that aggravatingly adorable dimple as he settled in next to her, and she had to admit…it wouldn't be the worst way to go.

# CHAPTER 2

MOLLY YAWNED AND BLINKED, TRYING TO CLEAR HER FUZZY eyesight. It didn't help. The spreadsheet's numbers still looked like someone had smeared Vaseline over the laptop screen. Letting out a huff of frustration that morphed into another yawn halfway through, she sat back in her chair and squinted at the clock on the microwave display.

"Almost one. No wonder I'm tired," she muttered, rolling her head to stretch out her tense neck muscles. Her right leg felt stiff, and she was dying to move it, but a snoozing Warrant was resting his huge head on her foot, and she didn't want to disturb the dog. She knew she should just go to bed and finish work in the morning, but it was almost impossible to get anything done while everyone else was awake. There were always distractions and crises to manage, as well as research to be done. It was good to be busy, to be offered almost too many jobs, but it was also tiring. The business was solidly established now, but Molly still hated to turn away work. Even though it wasn't exactly logical, she worried that everything would collapse underneath them if she paused to take a breath.

Glancing back at the screen, she grimaced. The numbers weren't any clearer than they'd been a minute ago.

Saving the file, she shut down the laptop. If she tried to finish it tonight, she'd just have to fix mistakes tomorrow.

The kitchen was dimly lit by the gentle glow from the light over the stove. The room was just large enough to fit the small table that Molly used as a desk. No matter how much she would've loved to have an office with a door she could use to shut out the hubbub, space was at a premium when six women shared one house. There were officially three bedrooms, although solitude-loving Norah had tucked a twin bed into what was supposed to be an upstairs sitting room and had appropriated the hall closet for her own use. Molly and Felicity shared one room, and the twins—Cara and Charlie—took another. It irked Molly that their mother, who contributed the least to the household expenses, had her own room.

Tapping her finger absently on the closed laptop, she frowned, knowing that she was going to have to have a conversation with her mom soon about paying her way or finding another place to live.

With a groan, she let her head tip forward to rest on the cool laptop lid. She dreaded the drama that conversation would cause. Molly'd had similar talks with her mom over the years—the first was when she was twelve—and Jane had always somehow wiggled out of her promises or negotiated more time or had such a fit that Molly had backed off. Lifting her head, she drew her shoulders back. Not this time. She was determined to stand strong.

The overhead light flickered on, making her blink from the glare. Warrant's snuffled snores cut off abruptly. He raised his head off of her foot when Jane swept into the kitchen as if Molly's thoughts had summoned her. Her tall, angular form was dressed in black skinny jeans and a dark, formfitting top, with her red hair pulled back in a severe bun.

"Molly!" Bending, Jane pressed a kiss to the crown of her head.

"Hey, Mom." Molly turned in her chair so she could examine Jane's outfit as her mother pulled a water bottle out of the fridge. "What's with the…look?"

"What?" Keeping the refrigerator door propped open with her hip, Jane took a long drink of water, screwed the cap back on, and returned it to the shelf before letting the fridge close again. Molly resisted the urge to ask her mom if she planned to air-condition the entire house via refrigerator. Even though Molly was only twenty-seven, being around Jane somehow made her feel like a cranky parent. "You don't like it?" Jane asked as she did a turn, as if modeling.

"It's very…cat-burglar chic, I guess." When Jane jerked around with a reproving look—presumably for her skeptical tone—Molly just shrugged. She was used to having her mom's disapproval. Molly was much too responsible to ever be the favorite. Usually, that was Felicity or Charlie, depending on Jane's whim, but they'd all learned not to allow their mom to play them off one another. They were sisters first—sisters who shared the misfortune of having an often irresponsible mother. "Where are you off to at one on a Wednesday morning?"

Jane flipped her hand as if the words smelled bad. The familiarity of the gesture caused Molly to blink. She did exactly the same thing when she wanted to change the subject. She immediately made a firm resolution to stop. "I have to ask my daughter for permission to go out?" Jane scoffed. "Don't forget who the mother is around here."

Unfortunately, Jane made it all too easy to do exactly that. Her words reminded Molly of her earlier thoughts. "Will you be back by tomorrow—this afternoon, I mean? I need to talk to you."

Smoothing her hair even though the strands were perfectly flat, Jane lifted her shoulders and let them drop. "Possibly. If the perfect opportunity to be spontaneous presents itself, I'm not going to pass it up. You're an adult now. You need to learn that you don't need your mom around all the time anymore."

Molly had to clench her jaw and count to fourteen before she trusted herself to speak semicivilly. "Text me if you're going to be gone more than a day so I don't have to start searching hospitals and jails."

With a light laugh—as if the suggestion was ridiculous and not a regular thing her kids'd had to do since they'd been much too young to be dealing with that nonsense—Jane headed for the door to the garage.

"Why are you going that way?" Molly asked, standing up, prepared to tackle her mom if necessary. There were hard lines, and her beloved Prius was one of them. "Your car is parked in the driveway."

"Oh!" Jane paused, her hand on the doorknob. "I thought we could swap for a few days. Yours gets better gas mileage, and mine's making this strange rattling sound every time I go over eighty."

There were so many things wrong with what her mother said that Molly couldn't decide where to start. She ended up going with a flat "No."

"Molly…" It was her stern mother voice, which had lost all of its power by the time Molly was a teenager.

"If you take my car, I'm going to report it stolen." Molly grabbed her backpack off the hook next to the door and rummaged through it, searching for the key fob that she always kept tucked in the front pocket. It wasn't there. Setting her backpack down with a solid thump, she held out her hand, maneuvering her body to block the garage door. "Keys."

"My car isn't safe right now." Jane tucked her fingers into her back pocket, but Molly knew that she was protecting her access to the keys rather than moving to pull them out and hand them over. "Do you really want your mother driving around Denver in a dangerous vehicle?"

Molly kept her hand outstretched, palm up expectantly. "Do you want your *daughter* driving around in a dangerous vehicle?"

Jane did that familiar sweep of her hand again, doubling Molly's resolution to remove the motion from her own repertoire. "You're in Langston. You don't need a car. Where would you need to go that you couldn't just walk to?"

"Work." Molly's tone was heavy with sarcasm, but her position in front of the door didn't waver. "I need to work, so that we can eat and have nice things like heat in the winter. The same work that often requires me to go to Denver to chase after skips or meet with bail-bond agents. Why don't you stay home tonight and take your car to the shop tomorrow morning?"

Dropping her chin, Jane peered at Molly through her lashes. "I can't afford to have it fixed. Can I borrow some money from you?"

"No." The response was immediate and unhesitating. "You know the rules. We let you live here, but you have to support yourself otherwise." Even though she didn't want to get into another drama-filled conversation so late at night, the words just popped out. "That's one of the things we need to talk about. You're supposed to be helping with utilities and groceries, but you haven't contributed in months." *More like years*, Molly thought, but she was trying to be a little tactful, at least. "I know you scammed some money from Cara last week. If you're not going to give that back to her, at least use it to fix your car."

Annoyance flickered over Jane's face, disappearing so quickly that Molly would've thought she'd imagined it if she didn't know her mom so well. Jane's expression morphed into something that somehow radiated sad guilt and martyrdom in equal measures. "I didn't *scam* my own daughter. Just because you're hard and suspicious doesn't mean you should bully your sister into being that way as well. Cara's sweet and caring, and there's nothing wrong with that."

It was difficult for Molly to resist the urge to roll her eyes. *Apparently, Cara's the favorite tonight*. "You're right. There's nothing wrong with being caring and sweet. There *is* something wrong with taking money that your daughter needs for school."

Shifting her weight, Jane jutted out one hip, her hands still tucked into her right back pocket—guarding the keys, Molly assumed. "If Cara doesn't have enough money for school, that's not on me. Maybe you should be paying her more for the work she does. You know she doesn't like this bounty-hunter nonsense. The least you can do is offer her a fair wage."

"Stop." The word came out with a snap that showed just how close Molly was to losing her temper. "We're not talking about this now…or ever, really. What we *are* talking about is how you're going to hand over my car keys right now."

Still Jane hesitated, and Molly knew her mom's mind was clicking away, trying to come up with a new plan to get what she wanted. Jane always had a plan B, and she consistently figured a dozen ways out of any trap. That was how she'd survived for almost fifty years when she'd been conning people out of money since she was old enough to bat her lashes and talk her way into getting an extra piece of candy—or, if that failed, just stealing it.

"Mom." Molly used the firm tone that Jane had tried on her. "Keys. Now. You know I won't hesitate to tackle you."

Her mom's mouth drew down in an unhappy frown. Molly tightened her jaw and didn't lower her arm or her gaze. After a tense few seconds, Jane dug out the keys and slapped them against Molly's extended palm.

"Thank you." Fighting not to let her relief show, Molly fisted her fingers around the key fob and dropped her arm to her side. She didn't move away from the door, holding her ground as her mom gave a dramatic huff and flounced into the living room—at least as much as someone wearing skintight cat-burglar gear could flounce. "Be safe," Molly called softly from her spot in the kitchen.

Jane's only response was to slam the front door behind her. Grimacing at the loud noise and the acrid taste the scene had left in her mouth, Molly leaned back against the garage door and waited for the inevitable sound of footsteps from the upper floor. Nails clicked against the ancient linoleum as Warrant crossed the kitchen to press against her legs. Grateful for the support, she rubbed behind his ears.

"Everything okay?" Norah was the first to pop her sleep-mussed head into the kitchen.

"Yeah." Holding up the key fob, Molly gave it a little shake. "Just preemptively stopping some grand theft auto."

"Mom?" Norah moved the rest of the way into the kitchen, tugging the hem of her oversize sleep shirt over her shorts. Cara and Charlie came into the kitchen just in time to hear Norah's question and immediately turned to head back to bed, Warrant following them. He knew Cara was a sucker and would let him sleep on her bed, even though he was notorious for taking over the entire thing.

Charlie's voice filtered back into the kitchen. "It was just Mom, Fifi. Go back to bed."

The sound of three sets of footsteps and one set of paws thumping up the stairs along with Felicity's grumbles—although Molly couldn't hear whether she was complaining about Jane's lack of courtesy or the hated nickname—gradually quieted. Molly turned her attention back to Norah, who still seemed to be waiting for an answer, even though it was obvious.

"Yeah, Mom tried to *trade* cars with me." Molly forced a smile for her sister. Although Norah was almost twenty-four, she looked younger, thanks to her usual anxious expression and the way her baggy pajamas overwhelmed her slight frame. Her medical alert bracelet hung around her wrist like a bangle, even though it was tightened to the smallest setting.

"Why did she need your car?" Norah asked.

Molly made a face as she moved over to her abandoned seat and plopped down in it. "Apparently, I'm not the mom, so I don't get to ask that."

The tension in Norah's face faded slightly as she settled on the other chair. "Did she sell her car again for cash?"

"No. It's just making an odd noise—or that's what she said, at least." Propping her elbow on the table and setting her chin in her hand, Molly arched her eyebrows at Norah. Her sister knew as well as Molly that their mom played fast and loose with the truth. "I'm guessing it's something else, like she dropped part of her burrito under the seat and it's starting to really stink."

Norah gave a small huff of a laugh, and Molly grinned, triumphant that she'd gotten her sister's anxiety to ease—at least temporarily. Not wanting her to dwell on where Jane was going or why she'd wanted Molly's car, since Norah always assumed the worst possible scenarios were true, Molly quickly changed the subject.

"I hate having conversations like that with Mom," she said, slumping forward even more to rest her cheek on her crossed arms. "I turn into this strict, mean, no-fun *rules, rules, rules* nun-teacher person who I kind of hate."

"You have to." Norah mirrored her position so they both had their heads down, facing each other. "If you don't set rules, then there will be no rules. *Mom* certainly isn't going to set any. And I don't hate your nun-teacher person. I find her reassuring."

"Not very fun, though."

"Fun has its place," Norah said seriously. "Without rules, fun can be really scary. Remember Mom's middle-of-the-night family dance parties that time Lono left for a few months?"

Molly grimaced. "Now I do. I've worked really hard to forget that mess. Thanks for the reminder, Norah."

Even though Molly had been teasing, Norah didn't smile as she played with her medical alert bracelet. "At least she stopped after I went to the hospital during the last one."

That erased the last bit of Molly's amusement. "I should've kept her from dragging you out of bed that night. I knew it would lead to an asthma attack. Back then, you had to nebulize after going up the stairs too fast."

"Not your fault." Releasing her bracelet, Norah gripped her own forearm. "She's the mom. You were, what? Nine?"

Molly forced the memory of that horrible night to the back of her mind. If she allowed herself to dwell on all the nightmares Jane had caused, she would get angry and bitter, and Norah would feel guilty about bringing it up. "I'm just glad your asthma's under control now. No ER visits in six years." Without raising her head, she lifted her hand for a high five. Norah smacked her palm lightly as they both started to smile at each other.

"Thanks, Moo. I wouldn't have made it without you."

"How did such an incredible person like you come from Mom and a guy nicknamed *POS*?" Molly asked. After Jane's second husband, Victor, had died, she'd been wild with grief. Impulsively, she'd married Dwayne "POS" Possin just long enough to get pregnant before divorcing him and remarrying her first husband, Lono. Jane's marriage to POS had been a short-lived mistake, but Molly was grateful for it. After all, Norah had been the result. "That's a genetic miracle right there."

"Hey!" Norah sat up straight. Even though she was obviously trying to sound indignant, a grin tugged at her lips. "She's your mom, too. Fifty percent of your genetic material came from her." She paused for a moment. "Though I have to admit that being half Lono is better than being half POS."

Stifling a sudden yawn, Molly stood and reached to pull Norah to her feet. "Well, POS must've had some good dormant material, because you turned out pretty perfect."

Although Norah rolled her eyes, she fought a smile, too. "Thanks, strict nun-teacher person."

Molly poked her sister in the side, just where she knew Norah was ticklish. "Maybe not completely perfect."

With a giggle, Norah bumped her with her painfully pointy elbow before heading up the stairs. As Molly followed, her thoughts turned back to her mom, and her smile faded. After the scene earlier, it was even more evident that they needed to have a serious conversation...one that might very well end with Molly having to kick her mother out of their house. Firming her jaw, she straightened her spine. It was past time Jane learned to stand on her own two feet and quit mooching off her kids.

As much as Molly dreaded the scene it would cause, she was going to evict her mom...for all of their sakes.

# CHAPTER 3

At the loud pounding, Molly buried her head under her pillow and whimpered. It felt like she'd just dozed off after lying exhausted but wide awake in bed, stewing about her mom, feeling the usual medley of guilt and resentment and annoyance that encounters with Jane always inspired in her. Now, her eyelids refused to open, her brain fuzzy and heavy with the need to sleep, but whoever was knocking on the door wasn't stopping. In fact, they were getting louder.

With a sound that was part growl and part pathetic whine, she lifted her head, prying her eyes open just enough to locate her phone where it sat on the bedside table. Even before she grabbed it, she knew it was much too early—barely dawn, judging by the dark-gray cast of the light filtering through her bedroom window.

"Are you serious?" she croaked when she finally saw the time. Apparently, the visitor *was* serious, because the pounding on the door continued. "Five fourteen in the morning?" She also noticed that she had a whole slew of texts and calls, several from unknown numbers, and she realized that she'd managed to sleep through all the notifications. The latest text was from her mom, and Molly climbed out of bed, now fully awake. Of course Jane was the reason someone was trying to break down their front door at dawn. *Of course.*

Suddenly, the knocking stopped, and the faint sound of voices—one male and one female—took its place. Someone else must've been faster getting out of bed than she'd been. Now that some of the resentment of being woken so early had faded, curiosity was worming its way into Molly's brain. She debated whether she should get dressed or not and finally decided not to miss any more of the action than she already had.

As she rushed downstairs, she skimmed through her new texts, and her apprehension grew at the same rate as her irritation. Her mom's messages were typical of Jane, starting two hours earlier and ending forty minutes ago.

> Need help. Car died. Pick me up in front of the parking ramp at 3rd and Josephine. Hurry.
> In Cherry Creek.
> Hurry.
> Why aren't you answering?
> I can't believe you're going to abandon me in my time of need!
> After refusing to let me use your car, too.
> You're a selfish child, Molly.
> I can't believe you're ignoring me.
> If you were in trouble, I'd immediately run to your rescue, no questions asked.

Pausing at the base of the stairs, Molly stared at her phone. Why had her mom been in Cherry Creek, an affluent section of Denver, at three in the morning? She kept reading but just got more and more confused with each text.

> I had to move. Now in front of the mall.
> This is your fault, you know.
> I need you to call Lono. He's ignoring me.
> He'll pick up if you call. You've always been his favorite.

Molly had to roll her eyes at that. Her dad was a smart guy, but he could be incredibly gullible when it came to Jane. After marrying and divorcing her twice, Lono had finally realized that he needed to put some space between himself and his ex-wife and moved back to Hawaii. Now he was married to someone else and had two small kids. Molly wasn't exactly sure what help he could've offered to Jane an hour ago. After all, it wasn't like he could swing by and pick her up when he lived a seven-hour plane trip away from Denver.

There were a few other texts from a different number, but Molly assumed Jane had switched to a friend's phone.

> Molly, call me.
> Call me. It's important.

"Molly." Cara's voice pulled her attention off the screen. When Molly glanced up, her gaze fell on the man hulking behind Cara, and she almost dropped her phone.

"Carmondy? What are you doing here?" she demanded, resisting the urge to tug her sleep shorts down to cover a little more thigh. The hem of her tank top barely reached her hips, so that wasn't much help. She now regretted her decision to stomp downstairs in her pajamas, and it irritated her that John could make her so self-conscious. With an effort, she kept her fingers away from her shorts and straightened her shoulders, even when she caught his gaze flicking down her bare legs ever so quickly before he focused on the phone in her hand.

"Your cell works, then?" he asked, the sarcastic edge to his words doubling her annoyance. Why was *he* peeved with *her*, when he was the one who'd shown up at her house at a completely unreasonable hour, pounding on the door just after she'd managed to fall asleep? To add insult to injury, Warrant was leaning against his legs, staring up at him with a look of complete hero-worship in his eyes. The way Carmondy was absently rubbing Warrant's ears made things even worse, since it was hard to be aggravated when he was making her dog so happy.

"Did you come over here and wake up the entire house just to ask that?"

"I wanted to tell you over the phone, but you never called or texted back." His voice rose in volume, still well below a shout, but it made Molly blink in surprise. Even when they'd sniped at each other, he'd always seemed secretly amused. She'd never heard him sound so irritated.

"You texted me?" She glanced down at the screen even as she realized that the texts from the unknown number—the ones she assumed were from her mom using a friend's phone—must've been John. It made sense, now that she thought about it. The terse texts were much too short, drama-light, and passive-aggression-free to have been from Jane. "How'd you get my number?"

His sigh rumbled out of him in a heavy gust. Apparently, he *was* all about the drama. "Finding people is sort of what I do for a living. The question should be…why don't you have *my* number?"

"Why would I have your number?" His offended expression almost made her laugh, but then she remembered how he'd just woken her up. "Carmondy. Why are you here?"

"What's going on?" Charlie somehow made the entire question a yawn as she shuffled down the last few steps. Behind her, Norah looked equally sleep-rumpled but was alert enough to look wary. Molly barely had a chance to wonder where Felicity was when her youngest sister jogged down the stairs, looking ridiculously wide awake—and avidly curious.

"I don't know yet," Molly answered. "Carmondy's too busy bitching about my refusal to figure out his locker combination so I could leave him notes after algebra."

There was a moment of silence as her sisters blinked at her.

"What?" Charlie finally asked.

Raising her hand to brush away her sisters' confusion, Molly remembered her vow from the night before and dropped her arm to her side. Just to make sure she wouldn't make any Jane-like gestures unconsciously, she grabbed her right hand in her left and held on tight. "Never mind. Carmondy's about to tell us all why he's here, banging on the door and waking innocent, hard-working bounty hunters." She gave him her best stern glare. "This better not just be you stepping up your recruiting game, because this is not the way to change my answer."

"Recruiting?" Felicity muttered. "Yeah, right."

Although Molly was tempted to make her sister explain exactly what she meant by that, she kept her mouth closed, knowing that it'd be too easy to get off track again, stealing even more of her precious sleep time. If she could get John out of the house in the next few minutes, she could get *maybe* an hour of sleep before she had to get up for good. With that motivation, she turned to John with an expectant look.

His gaze flicked over her sisters before returning to Molly. His hand left Warrant's head, and the Great Pyrenees gave him a disappointed look before trundling toward the dog door leading to the backyard. Watching Molly closely, John finally answered. "Your mom's in jail."

There was an instant chorus of groans. "Again?" Charlie sounded exactly how Molly felt—disappointed but not surprised in the least. Jane had gone to jail more often than she'd attended any of their school events, and they had all grown up knowing the ins and outs of the entire criminal process, from arrest to court. That was one reason Molly had chosen to start a bail recovery business. Since they knew all of the players involved already, it had been easy to step into the industry.

"No wonder she was blowing up my phone last night." Although she was pretty sure what the answer would be, she had to ask. "How'd you find out?"

"She texted me when she couldn't get ahold of you." He gave her phone another condemnatory glance. "Even your *mom* knows my number."

He sounded so uncharacteristically pouty that Molly couldn't hold back an eye roll. Normally, she'd try to be a little bit more polite, even with John Carmondy, but she was tired and it was early and she didn't really care if he saw her mocking him. "If I save your number in my phone, will you leave now?"

He looked startled. "That's it? Don't you want to know which jail?"

"Not really." She moved toward him, hoping to herd him out the door, but he didn't move, which meant that they were now standing uncomfortably close. John seemed even bigger than usual, which made sense, since his broad chest was only inches from her nose. If only he didn't smell so stupidly good, like leather and falling leaves and… Was that bubble gum? Only he could make the slight whiff of sugar and strawberries seem attractive.

If it had been anyone else, she would've backed up a step or two to reestablish her personal space, but this was John Carmondy, and she didn't want to give up any ground to him. Even though she knew she was being irrationally stubborn, she couldn't seem to help it. John brought out the teenager in her.

Cocking his head to the side, he looked down at her with a quizzical gaze. "Aren't you going to call her lawyer?"

"She likes to represent herself." That wasn't quite true, but Molly really didn't want to explain how her mom had fired or alienated every lawyer in Langston and the greater Denver area—possibly in all of Colorado. Jane was stuck with either using a public defender— who had an enormous grudge against her—or defending herself in court.

Still hopeful she might be able to get a little bit of sleep that morning, Molly plastered on the fakest of fake smiles. "Thanks for letting us know. It was very…

helpful of you." He didn't move, and it got harder for her to hold her attempt at a polite expression. "We don't want to keep you from your very early morning activities, so thanks again." Still, he didn't shift toward the door, and she seriously debated giving him a firm shove. The only reason she resisted was because she doubted it would have any effect. It was almost impossible to force a mountain into motion if he didn't want to go anywhere.

The silence dragged out, and even her sisters—who usually wouldn't stop talking long enough for her to hear herself think—didn't say a word. The awkward tension reached a painful intensity, but Molly refused to say one more thing. This was all on John now.

Finally—*finally*—he spoke. "Save my number."

"Sure." Her quick agreement must've made him suspicious about her sincerity, because he tipped his head down and to the side slightly, as if to study her in the haughtiest way possible. John was such a weird mix of irreverent and arrogant. His mercurial personality kept her constantly off guard, as she never knew what his reaction would be. Her usual ability to come up with four different contingency plans on the spot often failed when she was dealing with John—although her trick with Warrant had worked rather splendidly. Leaning to the side to peer around his bulk, she looked at Cara, who still stood between John and the door. Catching her sister's attention, Molly widened her eyes in a wordless plea.

Although she smirked slightly, Cara stepped up to help as she always did. "We appreciate you letting us know about Mom. Did you want some water or anything before you leave?"

*No!* Molly narrowed her eyes, shooting mental lasers and an *abort mission!* psychic warning that Cara either completely misinterpreted or ignored. By the tiny smile on her sister's face, Molly was pretty sure it was the latter. Most of the time, Cara was as sweet as a soon-to-be kindergarten teacher should be, but her devilish streak popped out occasionally—usually at the worst possible times.

As he looked back and forth between Molly and Cara, John's mouth flattened from irritation—or an attempt to hold back a smile. It irked Molly that she couldn't read him like she could most people. "No, but thanks for offering." His words felt pointed as he directed his gaze toward Molly, but she just shrugged. If he wanted her to give him refreshments, then he should show up at a decent hour—with a less cranky attitude.

"I'll get the door for you, then." Cara moved through the living room toward the front entry. After a final piercing look from John, which Molly met with a blandly polite smile of her own, he followed Cara to the door.

They stood quietly as the door closed behind him and Cara engaged the lock. Only after the low rumble of his car engine faded did someone speak.

"You're so mean to him." Of course it was Charlie. She usually couldn't go more than a few minutes without saying something snarky. "It's both hilarious and a little heartrending."

"Heartrending?" Molly knew she was in danger of being sucked down into one of Charlie's rabbit-hole conversations, but it was better than having to discuss the fact that their mom was in jail...again. "Don't feel bad for Carmondy. If he couldn't take it, he wouldn't always be popping up wherever I happen to be. What's heartrending is that I've gotten about two hours of sleep total." Even though she'd been hoping to be able to go back to bed, the conversation with John ensured that she'd be too wound up to sleep anymore. "If we're going to stay up, let's go into the kitchen. I need some coffee."

"Nope. No coffee. Water." Hurrying to make it to the kitchen first, Felicity started filling water bottles, keeping her body between Molly and the coffee maker. "Just because Mom's in jail again doesn't mean that you all can skip today's workout."

The chorus of groans that followed was louder than when John had told them that Jane had been arrested.

"But Fifi…" Charlie started, only to go silent when Felicity whipped out her fiercest glare.

"You get thirty extra seconds in plank position, just for calling me that." Thrusting a filled water bottle at Charlie, Felicity raked the others with a stern glance. "Anyone else want to whine?"

Molly really did, but she knew better. Although Felicity was normally easygoing, she took her role as family physical trainer seriously, transforming into a merciless drill sergeant for an hour or so every morning. As soon as they were done working out, she turned back into her normal sunny self as suddenly as if a switch had been flipped.

It wasn't just fear of extra torture that kept Molly from complaining, though. "We need this if we're going to be chasing down skips and wrestling them into submission."

Tentatively, Norah lifted her hand. "Since I'm on

research duty and won't be chasing or...wrestling anyone if I can help it...may I be excused?"

"Me too," Cara chimed in.

Felicity just glared silently at them until they both wilted and accepted the water bottles she held out. "Everyone benefits from exercise. I do this because I care about you. Tough love and all that. So go get changed and meet me on the back porch in five minutes. Don't make me come find you and drag you out there."

"It's not tough love," Charlie muttered, just loud enough for Molly to hear. "It's *mean* love."

Choking on laughter, Molly saw Felicity's suspicious gaze turn toward her and quickly swallowed her amusement, regaining her straight face with an effort. "Let's get this over with."

As she hurried up to her bedroom to change into workout clothes, she felt a secret wave of relief. Although she didn't admit it to her sisters, she was a tiny bit relieved that Felicity's torture would keep her from thinking about anything except the pain in her lungs and muscles for the next hour. This way, stewing about her mom ending up in jail again—and John Carmondy's front-row seat to their family's dysfunction—would have to wait...at least for a little while.

━━━━━━━━━━

Since Molly had been the last to finish their final sprint back to the house, she was stuck at the back of the line for the shower. By the time she was clean and dressed and walking back downstairs, the house was a lot quieter than it had been just a half hour earlier. Cara was the only one in the kitchen, sitting at the small table and talking on her cell phone, her open laptop perched on top of a stack of files.

Raising an eyebrow at Cara's sour expression, Molly made a beeline over to the coffee maker. *Finally*, she thought as she poured herself a mugful, sneaking in a sip even before she added her usual sugar and creamer. Although she made a face at the bitter taste, it was worth it. She could almost feel her exhausted brain cells perking up as the caffeine hit her system.

"I'll let her know," Cara said into her phone, still looking annoyed. The pinched expression looked strange on her sweet, girl-next-door face, with her round dimpled cheeks, wide brown eyes, and mile-long dark lashes. "Her answer isn't going to be any different than mine, though."

When Cara ended the call with a dramatic poke of her finger a few moments later, Molly gave her an exaggerated double-eyebrow lift over her mug in silent question.

"Barney." The way she said his name made it sound like it tasted bad. "One of his clients skipped, and he wants us to take the job. I've already told him no, but I promised I'd check with you."

"Barney?" Molly didn't even need to hear the details. Just knowing the name of the bail bond agent was enough. "No."

Cara's mouth curled up in a smug smile as she tapped out a text. From the satisfaction in her expression, she was taking great pleasure in turning Barney down. Molly didn't blame her. Not only was Barney an amoral slug of a man who would frame his own grandma for murder if it earned him a buck, but he was also condescending enough to make Molly want to punch him in the face every time they met. Even even-keeled Cara, who found *something* good in almost everyone, couldn't stand Barney.

Curiosity niggled at her, so she waited until Cara had finished her text before asking, "Who was his skip?"

"Edison Zarver."

Rearing back, Molly was shaking her head before Cara even got the last name out. "Sonny? Oh, hell no."

"Right?" Cara gave her phone a disapproving look, as if Barney were able to see her. "There's no amount of money in the world that'd be worth getting caught up in Sonny Z's mess."

Making a wordless sound of agreement, Molly pulled out the chair next to Cara's. Even a few years ago, when their business was brand new and they'd had to scramble for every possible job just to survive, they'd known enough to stay clear of Sonny. Now that they'd established themselves and paid off the mortgage, they weren't quite so desperate for work—and they definitely weren't desperate enough to go after *him*. "What less life-threatening jobs do we have lined up for the week?"

Working a couple of files out from under her laptop, Cara handed them over. "Take your pick. Charlie's already snagged the Nina Salas job, and Felicity's going with her to Thornton today as backup. I have to finish a paper for school, and then I'll take Fifi's place, and she can pick up another job."

Looking up from the first folder, Molly repeated, "Charlie took backup? Does she think there'll be trouble?"

Cara made a so-so gesture with her hand before stealing Molly's coffee mug and taking a sip. She made a *yuck* face. "Oh wow. That's gross. I always forget how sweet you make it." Despite her complaints, she took another sip and grimaced again at the taste. "No trouble expected. Since it'd take one of us a while to get there, Charlie wanted someone close by, just in case."

Reclaiming her mug, Molly held it to her chest protectively. "It's not *gross*. It's perfect." At Cara's skeptical grunt, Molly waved off her sister's criticism. "I'm glad Charlie's thinking ahead and showing some caution. Sometimes she acts so recklessly, it makes me think she's missing the fear gene."

"Yeah, although I think Felicity planted the idea of her coming along."

"Go, Fifi," Molly said approvingly. "She may be the baby of the family, but she's still smarter than the rest of us."

"And the most tactful…except when she's torturing us during workouts."

Holding up her coffee mug in a silent toast to her diplomatic—and only occasionally sadistic—little sister, Molly turned back to the file in front of her. "What's Norah working on?"

"She's doing some research on Hans Miller."

"Alone?" Molly frowned, surprised that Cara had let Norah go off by herself. Most of the time, talking to people's friends, families, coworkers, and landlords wasn't dangerous, but there was always a chance something might go wrong. Besides, Norah hated interacting with strangers…and acquaintances…and most people, really. Most of her contribution to their business was tech assistance.

"Settle down. It's internet research. She walked

Warrant to that coffee place she likes," Cara said, looking a little offended. "First of all, I'd never send her out on her own to talk to people she doesn't know, and second, she'd never do it even if I told her to."

"True. Sorry. I should've known both of those things. I don't think my brain is fully awake yet." She took another sip of coffee to hurry it along.

"So…" Cara's tone was tentative, and Molly's spine stiffened, but she kept her gaze on the papers in front of her. She knew what was coming. "About Mom. Don't you think we should find out where she's being held?"

"No." There was no give in her voice at all.

"Shouldn't we at least find out what she's done?"

With a negative grunt, Molly flipped over a sheet of paper with a little too much force. "I'm sure everyone we know will be all too gleeful to share that information. Look at how fast Carmondy ran over here to tell us she was picked up again." As soon as the words were out, she felt a lurch of guilt.

"He wasn't being spiteful," Cara said, echoing Molly's thoughts.

"I know." Molly sighed, hating this topic of conversation almost more than the previous one. Thinking about John Carmondy made her…twitchy and warm and fidgety. Needing to do something with her hands, she turned over another sheet and stared at it without seeing any of the words. "Why do we still have paper files, anyway?"

"Charlie hates to read anything on her phone."

Molly, relieved to be talking about something other than John Carmondy—or their mom—asked, "Why doesn't she use her laptop?"

"She broke it."

"No, not that one. The new one we ordered for her last month."

Cara gave her a look. "She broke it."

"The new one?" Molly's voice rose, ending in an indignant squeak. "She wrecked another laptop? How? When? Why didn't she tell me?"

"It was last week, and she didn't tell you because she's a chicken and didn't want to get in trouble. The only reason I know is that I saw the whole thing from my bedroom window. I tried to warn her, but she didn't hear me until it was too late."

"What happened?"

With a grimace, Cara explained. "She set it on the roof of her car and forgot it was there. It slid off, and she backed over it."

Leaning back in her chair, Molly stared at the ceiling for several long moments. "No more computers for Charlie."

"Strongly agree."

"She's already on phone probation. If she loses one more, she's getting a used, twenty-year-old flip phone."

Cara giggled at that. "She just gets really focused on tracking down skips and forgets to pay attention to other minor details."

"Uh-huh," Molly said dryly. "Minor details like expensive new computers and oodles of phones?"

"Exactly." One corner of Cara's mouth tucked in, showing off her dimple. It was the only indication of the smile that she was trying to hold back. Sometimes Molly marveled at how different Charlie and Cara were from each other. Although they were similar in looks, personality-wise they were pretty much opposites.

Molly blew out a long breath, reminding herself that she was lucky to be able to work with her sisters. As different as they were, each one contributed something that the business needed…despite the occasional destroyed laptop.

"Guess we're keeping the paper files, then."

Cara's snort was amused. "Seems like the cheapest way to go."

They fell quiet as Cara worked on her laptop and Molly skimmed over the contents of the files…or tried to, at least. Her brain wouldn't settle down, jumping from her mom's situation to John Carmondy and back until she finally slapped the top file closed, her hand smacking against the table loudly enough to make Cara jump.

"Sorry," Molly said sheepishly. Standing, she grabbed a file at random, put her coffee mug in the sink, and headed for the garage door, grabbing her backpack from a hook on the wall.

"I thought you were going to do paperwork today," Cara said. "You're not really dressed for chasing anyone. You need to pin that braid of yours up, or someone could use it as a handle. And that dress is no good. If you tackle someone, I guarantee you're going to be flashing your panties to God and the neighborhood."

Glancing down at her short sundress and sandals, Molly mentally debated whether to stay or head out, but she knew she'd be pacing the kitchen in minutes if she tried to focus on filing the business's quarterly taxes. The idea of putting on boots, jeans, and a heavier shirt didn't appeal, either. The day was already warm, and it wasn't even midmorning yet. It'd be way too hot for socks, much less denim.

"I promise to do my best to avoid any chasing,

tackling, or flashing of my goods." Making an X over her heart, she gave Cara a reassuring grin. "This is a new job. I'm just going to familiarize myself with the file and possibly check out the skip's neighborhood. At the very most, I'll chat with Sergeant Blake to see if she has any interesting tidbits she wants to pass on."

"Fine." Cara pursed her lips, somehow managing to look more like a kindly but stern schoolteacher than sour and prissy. "Don't come crying to me when you have skinned knees and a video of your granny panties is up on YouTube."

Molly tried for a sober expression, but she couldn't stop the grin that wanted to break out. When Cara sounded like a crabby auntie, it always made her laugh. "I make no promises about that, although I'll probably go crying to Norah instead, since *she'll* know how to get the video taken down." Pulling open the door to the garage, she gave Cara her best duck face over her shoulder and flipped her skirt up, showing a flash of underwear. "And I'll have you know I'm wearing my sexiest Wonder Woman panties, so I'd be proud to show them off on YouTube."

Cara didn't look impressed. "So, basically, you're wearing *nerd* granny panties."

"Pretty much, yeah." Automatically, Molly hit the button on the wall to open the overhead door while digging in the front pocket of her bag for her keys. The motor hummed as the door started to rise, filling the small garage with light, and two things hit her at the same time.

Her keys were missing from her backpack.

And the garage was empty.

# CHAPTER 4

"CARA!" MOLLY BURST BACK INTO THE KITCHEN. "WHAT car did Charlie and Felicity take?"

Her eyes wide and startled, Cara stared at her for a fraction of a second before answering. "Charlie's, I assume. Why?" Before Molly could wrestle her building rage down enough to answer, Cara's eyes got even bigger. "Oh, no. She didn't. She *couldn't*. She's in jail."

*She did.* Molly wasn't sure how their mother had managed it, but she—or one of her shady friends— had taken her car. No, Jane had *stolen* her car. Molly yanked out her cell phone and jabbed at the screen, her fingers shaking with anger and, although she didn't want to admit it, devastation that her own mother would do something like this to her. Why couldn't they have ended up with a nice mom, one who'd actually put food in the fridge rather than eating the groceries her kids had bought, one who'd helped her daughter pick out a car to buy rather than stealing her own child's hard-earned Prius?

"Who are you texting?" Cara asked, her voice tentative and shaky.

After hitting Send, Molly started a second text as she hurried through the living room. "Felicity and Norah. Charlie's car's gone, and I know that Norah walked, but

I just need to make sure that neither of them have mine before I report it."

Cara followed her to the window, where they both looked out at the empty driveway and street in front of the house. "Report it…stolen?"

Tearing her glare away from the spot where Jane's car had sat yesterday evening, Molly narrowed her eyes at Cara. "Yes. I'm reporting it stolen because she stole it. I told her I'd call it in if she took my car last night, and that's what I'm about to do. I'm done babying her. She's our *parent*, Cara. We've given her too many chances as it is."

She would've continued, but Cara held up her hands, palms out, as if blocking Molly's words from hitting her. "You're right." Cara didn't sound happy about it, but she didn't sound angry—at Molly, at least. "You should report it stolen. I'm just so used to covering for her, which doesn't help anything. It's just… Could it have been someone else?"

Her sister sounded so miserable that Molly wrapped an arm around her shoulders, but she didn't soften her next words. "Yeah, it probably was someone else—one of her shady buddies she convinced to take it." Molly's phone beeped with two incoming texts, and she checked the messages, her rage bubbling up again when both Felicity and Norah confirmed that they hadn't taken her car. With an angry flick of her thumb, she scrolled through her contacts until she reached Sergeant Taylor Blake's name.

After several rings, Molly was preparing to leave a voicemail when the sergeant finally answered brusquely. "Blake."

"Sergeant, it's Molly Pax."

"Pax." Blake's tone softened ever so slightly. For the hard-edged cop, that was the equivalent of anyone else gushing with sympathy. "Heard your mom fell off the straight and narrow again."

Hearing the blunt statement felt like a punch to the gut, but it was nothing if not true. "She has—in a big way. She's been in jail since very early this morning, but she's still managed to somehow steal my car."

There was the tiniest pause before the sergeant spoke again, her voice impartial and matter-of-fact. "You're sure it was her?"

"Positive." There was no doubt in Molly's mind that Jane had been the one behind her car's disappearance. "If it wasn't her, then she talked one of her friends into taking it and told them where I keep my keys. She tried to convince me to lend it to her last night, but I refused. Everyone was out of the house for a little over an hour this morning, from about quarter to six until seven. Otherwise, at least two people have been home since I last saw my car parked in the garage."

As she spoke, Molly examined the outside of the front door, looking for signs that the lock had been tampered with. There was nothing she could see that showed anyone had tried to break in. Closing and locking the front door behind her, she moved to check the garage door as well. Cara trailed after her like an apprehensive ghost.

"Anyone else have permission to drive it?"

"Sure, my sisters, but I've checked with all of them, and none have touched it." As much as she wanted to stay as professional and clinical-sounding as the sergeant, a thread of her anger snuck out. "They also aren't the ones who are going to need bail money over the next day or two."

The mention of money made her head snap up, and she rushed back to where she'd dropped her backpack on the kitchen counter. Yanking out her wallet, she quickly checked inside and bit back a snarl.

"All the cash in my purse—about eighty dollars— and our business ATM card are missing. I'm going to pass you over to Cara so she can answer your questions while I call my bank." She and Cara exchanged phones, and Molly hurried to find the bank's phone number. As the automated answering system's spiel began, she resisted the urge to sink down onto the kitchen floor and curl up in a ball.

She knew, deep in her gut, that this was only the tip of the iceberg. Things would only get worse from here.

―――――――――

"What's the total loss?" Even though Molly asked the question, she wasn't really sure she wanted the answer. Just a day ago, she'd been blissfully ignorant about what Jane had been planning, and she wished she could go back to that time...mainly so she could hide her keys and wallet somewhere that Jane or one of her felonious buddies would never find them. After spending hours trying to sort out the mess their mother had made, all five sisters had gathered around the dining room table to hash out the next steps of their damage-control plan.

Cara and Norah tipped their heads together, both

peering at the spreadsheet Norah had whipped up once she'd gotten home and been apprised of the situation. "Sergeant Blake filed the stolen vehicle and burglary report and put out a BOLO for your car, but it still hasn't been found. We've initiated the insurance claim," Norah said.

"The bank's canceled your card and started an investigation," Cara continued from where Norah had left off. "We'll probably be reimbursed for the purchases— fifteen hundred at Walmart and nine hundred at Tiny's Automotive Repair—but the business is out the four hundred withdrawn from the ATM this morning, plus the cash taken from your purse...and all the hassle and aggravation." Cara gave Molly a shaky attempt at a sympathetic smile. "It doesn't look like anything else is missing from the house—that we've noticed, at least."

"Okay." Inhaling a breath, Molly blew it out in a long sigh. "This is a four-hundred-and-eighty-dollar life lesson, then. I'm voting that we learn from this and never let Mom move back in, no matter how guilty she tries to make us feel. Who's with me?"

"I am." Norah was the first to agree. "We've given her too many chances and too much money already. We're the ones who paid off the mortgage on this house, and we should get to decide who stays here."

Charlie nodded vehemently. "Let's change the locks and pretend we're orphans—well, except for when Lono comes to visit."

Although it was more a huff of air than an actual laugh, it was the closest Molly had come to smiling since she'd discovered the theft of her car. "I like your plan." She held her fist out, and Charlie bumped it with hers. "Cara? What are your thoughts?" She braced to hear her sister defend their mom, ready to deflect the automatic guilt and stand strong. After Jane's latest stunt, Molly did not want her mother in their house—or their lives—anymore. She was done.

"We've let her stay too long already," Cara said, surprising Molly. "She's almost fifty and a mother of five grown kids. She needs to learn to make it on her own, without us propping her up."

Everyone looked at Felicity, who simply said, "Agreed. Mom's out of the house, even after she gets herself out of her current situation."

Despite the horrendous day she'd just had, Molly felt a slight easing of the tension banded around her lungs, making it easier to breathe. "Good. That's decided, at least. Now let's talk about work." Picking up the folders, she waved them at her sisters. "Until we get reimbursed by the bank, things are going to be tight. The more skips we can bring in, the less ramen we'll be eating."

"Do we need to reconsider taking Barney's job?" Cara asked with a preemptive wince.

Without having to consider the question, Molly immediately nixed it. "Tracking Sonny? Nope. We're not that desperate yet."

"Sonny?" Norah repeated, her eyebrows drawn together in confusion.

"Edison Zarver." Just saying the name made Molly's stomach twist. She'd only met him in person once at the courthouse, but his soulless eyes had left a definite impression—and not a positive one. "He skipped, so Barney's trying to convince us to track him down."

"Ugh." Charlie's screwed-up face showed exactly

how she felt about Sonny. "I'd rather eat ramen every day than get mixed up in Zarver's slimy business."

"That's basically what Cara told Barney when he called."

Her eyebrows shooting up, Charlie stared at her twin, looking impressed. "Really? You said that?"

Always meticulously honest, Cara rolled her eyes. "Not really."

"Pretty close." Molly refocused on what they'd been talking about before they'd gone off on their Sonny tangent. "Anyway, it's a no to Sonny, but all of these are yeses." She held up the folders and extended them toward her sisters. Felicity and Charlie each immediately took one, and Norah extended her hand but didn't touch the folders as she looked at Molly, her expression anxious.

"Do I need to help out more on the actual bounty-hunting front?" she asked, her tone telling Molly how very unappealing she found that thought.

"Thank you," Molly told her sincerely, giving her arm a squeeze, "but you stick with research and fixing our tech." Pausing, she shot Charlie a stern glare. "Whenever possible, that is. If someone, say, *runs over* her *brand-new* laptop with her *car*, then it's probably hopeless, and we won't judge you for not being able to fix it. We *will* judge the person who ran over her brand-new laptop with her car, however. We will judge *that* person harshly."

Norah appeared to be completely confused, but Charlie looked as guilty as Warrant when he was caught eating out of the garbage. Felicity's expression, on the other hand, was one of pure triumph.

"I *knew* it!" Felicity crowed, slapping the table with her open palm. "I asked where your laptop was, and you did that mumble-mumble thing you always do when you're trying to lie without really lying, and I knew you'd destroyed it somehow. Seriously, Charlie? You ran the poor thing over? Your innocent little laptop crushed? What is that? Your second new computer this year? Third?"

Charlie opened her mouth, but a heavy knock on the door interrupted her before she could defend herself. They all went still, their eyes wide as they looked around at each other. Even Warrant, who'd been napping under the table, using Cara's foot as a pillow this time, stuck his head out but stayed quiet. At the next even louder knock, Molly shook herself out of her apprehensive paralysis and stood up. Her sisters followed her lead, and she snorted as she eyed them.

"Are we answering the door as a group?" she asked, leading the way to the front door. From the sound of the footsteps behind her, it seemed that the answer was *yes*. Privately, she didn't mind the company. After everything that had happened with Jane, plus John Carmondy's unexpected arrival early that morning, she didn't mind having some backup—at least until their family's luck changed for the better.

As she unlocked the front door and pulled it open, she squinted against the low-hanging sun that was perched right above the mountain peaks and peered at the pair standing on the porch. She bit back a curse when she saw the police T-shirts and the badges clipped to their belts. She had enough fingerprint powder all over her kitchen and garage from Sergeant Blake's visit, thank you very much. Besides, she didn't have the energy to deal with more cops today.

One of her sisters didn't have her restraint. A low, drawn-out groan came from behind her—Felicity, if Molly wasn't mistaken.

"Hello, Officers." Molly plastered on a smile and flicked a glance at the logo on one of the men's shirts. *Denver Police*. No wonder their faces weren't familiar. She knew everyone at the Langston PD and the Gordon County Sheriff's Office, at least by sight. "Are you here for some follow-up on my stolen car?"

"No, and it's *Detectives* Mill"—he gestured toward his own chest—"and Bastien. We have a search warrant for this property," the younger one said as the older cop—Bastien—silently and unsmilingly handed her the paperwork.

"Search warrant?" Her polite smile froze as she pulled out the warrant and scanned it, trying to push away her confusion and growing panic in order to take in the legalese. She knew she needed to focus so she could carefully check the areas the warrant allowed the cops to legally search and what items they were looking for.

"Give it here," Cara said, plucking the paper from Molly's hands. Once again relieved that her sisters were backing her up, Molly returned her attention to the detectives waiting not too patiently to get into the house.

"What's all this about?" she asked. "Whatever our mom was arrested for this time, it can't be major enough to require a search." *Except that auto theft's pretty major*, Molly thought. However, she knew that her car wasn't hidden in her mom's room.

"The judge disagrees," Detective Mill snapped, and the two entered the house. Her mind whirling with thoughts about the best way to handle the situation, Molly stepped back out of their way.

Once they were in the living room, she was moving to close the door when she spotted three more vehicles pulling up in front of the house: two unmarked and one with DENVER CRIME SCENE UNIT printed on the side. The Villaneaus, a retired couple living across the street who were endlessly bitter that Molly's family had the house with national park access instead of them, stepped outside and settled on their front-porch swing to watch the action.

"Great," Molly muttered under her breath, and Felicity—the only one who hadn't followed the first two cops deeper inside—met her gaze with a look of mutual dread. "This is going to be a huge mess."

Felicity's mouth flattened into a thin line. "It already is."

Molly couldn't argue with that.

# CHAPTER 5

BY THE TIME THE COPS, DETECTIVES, AND CRIME SCENE UNIT had made their significant mess and left, twilight had given way to full darkness. Molly paced the dining room, too anxious and furious to sit still, and glared at her cell phone.

"Just call him," Charlie said for the tenth time, and Molly had to clench her teeth to keep from snapping something rude at her sister. "He's the only one left."

"I know." Taking a deep breath, Molly forced herself to stand still. She'd tried all of their other contacts, but no one knew anything—or if they did, they wouldn't share with her. This was their last possible source for information, and even this was a long shot. She just really didn't want to call this number. As soon as she did, she'd be opening a huge, family-sized can of worms.

There wasn't anyone else left to call, though, and they needed answers. After one more exhale that came out as a sigh, she tapped the number on her screen.

"What's wrong, Pax?" John Carmondy answered immediately, so she didn't even get a chance to prepare herself for hearing his bass voice.

"What'd she do?" It was rude to just blurt out the question. Molly knew that, but when was she ever polite to John? *When you need answers from him*, a smugly know-it-all voice in the back of her head reminded her. She hated that voice.

There was a pause, and Molly wondered if John was just as startled by her call as she'd been by his. She almost immediately dismissed the notion, since she was pretty sure John Carmondy wasn't taken off guard by *anything*. He could be neck-deep in swamp water with piranhas chewing on one leg and an alligator chomping on the other, and he'd still be as cool and calm as could be, cracking jokes and looking hot in a mud- and blood-smeared way.

*Focus*, she told herself sharply.

"I don't know if she's actually guilty," he started, and Molly rolled her eyes. Of course Jane was guilty of whatever bad thing she was accused of doing. Molly couldn't remember one time that her mom had been falsely accused. "But she was arrested for burglary and theft."

"Okay," Molly said slowly, processing the information. All four of her sisters were watching her with a silent, steady intensity, as if they were trying to hear the other side of the call, but Molly wasn't about to put the phone on speaker. That would pretty much guarantee embarrassment on her part, since she'd never had a conversation with John that didn't involve him teasing her about something. Even though he was unusually serious at the moment, she knew it was just a matter of time before he said something to make her squirm. Her sisters did not need any more ammunition when it came to giving her a hard time about him.

She forced her brain to focus again, but it was difficult. The hellish day had taken all of her energy, plus whatever she had in reserve. Her thoughts were spinning around uselessly, replaying all the worst parts of the past twenty-four hours. Meanwhile, her stomach twisted with the knowledge that what Jane had done was really, really bad.

Although it was true that burglary was on the more serious end of her mom's usual crimes, that didn't seem to explain the search warrant. Jane had incredibly quick and sticky fingers, and she'd been charged with theft before...many times. The attitude of the cops who'd just finished searching their house had been unusually serious and intense, though, and Molly could feel the difference between all of Jane's earlier criminal exploits and this one. Whatever their mom had done, it was big.

"What did she steal?"

"What was she accused of stealing, do you mean?" John asked.

Molly frowned, unable to read his tone. Was he scolding her for not believing in her mom or warning her to keep up the pretense that Jane was innocent? Either way, she didn't have time to try to parse the undercurrents of every word. "Sure. Let's go with that. What was she *accused* of stealing?"

There it was again, that strange pause. John Carmondy was not normally hesitant. In fact, he was usually as not-hesitant as a person could possibly be. It was bizarre.

"Jewelry," he finally said, which told her almost nothing but raised another thousand questions in her mind.

"Why are you being weird?" she burst out, not wanting to hear one more cautious, carefully worded answer from him. Her world was already topsy-turvy, and she didn't need John acting strangely on top of everything else. He was always so rocklike, so confident and steady. No matter that she often found it annoying—she needed that John now.

"I'm not being weird," he huffed, amusement threaded beneath his outrage, and she relaxed. That was more like the John Carmondy she knew and...didn't really love. She was reassured by this small return to normal, though.

"Yes, you are." She flipped her free hand impatiently. "Just tell me. What did Mom steal—besides my car? How big of a mess are my sisters and I in? We need to know, and your wishy-washy answers aren't helping."

Although he made a sound of protest when she called him *wishy-washy*, he didn't waste time contradicting her, for which she was grateful.

"She was arrested for breaking into Simone Pichet's hotel room and stealing a very valuable necklace."

"Thank you." Her words were sincere, since it was so nice having even that small bit of information. Moving the phone away from her mouth, she spoke to her sisters. "She stole Simone Pichet's necklace."

"Simone Pichet...isn't she that famous sculptor?" Felicity asked, and Molly gave a short nod. Even *she* knew of Simone Pichet's work, and Molly was fairly clueless when it came to art.

Norah immediately began tapping her laptop keys, and Molly felt a moment of gratitude that computers and electronic devices hadn't been listed in the search warrant. One of the detectives had tried to take Norah's laptop, but Cara had stopped him. If all of their computers and phones had been taken, everything would've been so much harder.

"*Allegedly*." John stressed the word, and Molly put the phone back to her ear. "She *allegedly* stole Simone Pichet's necklace."

"Knock it off, Carmondy. She stole it. She has never been falsely accused. Not once in her life. I stopped giving her the benefit of the doubt when I was eight, and I don't need you trying to make me feel guilty. All I need from you is information."

"You're right. I'm sorry. I didn't mean…" He trailed off. When he spoke again, his voice was brisk and businesslike. "She pled innocent during her first advisement this afternoon."

That new bit of information made Molly's belly lurch with a whole new type of dread. "She had her first advisement hearing? Did the judge set bail?"

This time when he paused before speaking, she wanted to jump through the phone to rip the words out of him. "Yes. Five hundred."

She blinked. "Five hundred? That's it?"

"Thousand," he clarified, and she froze in place. "Five hundred *thousand*."

Molly's lips were numb, but she somehow managed to ask, "Did she make bond?"

"Yes." John didn't sound happy.

A horrible thought occurred to her, making her stomach twist painfully. "Did *you—*"

"No!" There was no hesitation before his answer this time. "I wouldn't do that. How could you think that I'd…?" He took a harsh, audible breath and then went quiet for a moment before speaking again, more calmly this time, although a hard edge remained to his voice. "It was Barney."

She hadn't believed things could get worse, but they suddenly had. "Barney Thompson?"

Her sisters, who'd been clustered around Norah, all trying to see her laptop screen, whipped around as one to stare at Molly. All she could do was stare back.

"This…is bad," she finally said, and John barked out a humorless laugh.

"You could say that," he said.

She didn't say anything in response, her mind churning helplessly as she tried to think her way out of this horribly messy circus that Jane had dropped them into.

Finally, he asked, "What do you need from me?"

The question snapped her brain into sharp focus, even as the unexpected offer made a tiny part of her heart feel as tender as a bruise. "I'm not sure yet. Can I get back to you on that?"

"Anytime."

"Thank you." For the second time in a single conversation, she was thanking John Carmondy—and not sarcastically.

After she ended the call, she continued staring at her phone until Charlie demanded, "Well? What'd he say?"

Blinking, she looked at her sisters. "That was weird."

"What was?" Cara asked.

"Carmondy was actually…*nice*."

All four of her sisters exchanged amused looks.

"What?" Even as Molly asked, she knew she'd regret it.

Felicity snorted. "Please. He's always nice to you. It's *ridiculous* how nice that man is to you. You're the only one who's blind to it."

*Blind to what?* This time, Molly knew better than to

say the words out loud. Instead, she settled on a skeptical shake of her head and a subject change. "Mom's out."

"What? How?" Cara's forehead crinkled with confusion. "Who gave her the bail money? Did they sell your car already?"

Wincing at the thought of her beloved car sold to some shady dealer, Molly shook her head and cringed for an entirely different reason. "Barney wrote her bond."

"What?" her sisters chorused, and Molly couldn't blame them for their incredulity. After all, she'd been just as shocked. All but the most desperate avoided working with Barney. He was an untrustworthy shark who'd sell anyone out in a second if he'd make a dime off it. Her mother knew better than to jump into metaphorical bed with Barney—at least she should have. Molly rubbed her right eye, which was starting to twitch. Would the day's bad surprises ever stop?

"Did John say what she used as collateral?" Cara asked.

Kicking herself for not thinking to ask, Molly shook her head. "I didn't check. Sorry. I was thrown by the whole Barney thing."

Charlie huffed out a laugh that held no amusement. "Understandable. I mean...Barney? What was she thinking?"

Unable to give her sisters a satisfactory answer, Molly could only shrug and change the subject. "What'd you find out about Simone What's-Her-Face's necklace?"

Turning her laptop so that Molly could see the screen, Norah made a pained face. "Mom went big this time."

Bracing herself, Molly scanned the photo on the screen. She'd never been very interested in jewelry—even before she'd started chasing and tackling people on a regular basis—so the picture didn't make too much of an impression on her. The necklace looked intricate and extremely sparkly, set mostly with what appeared to be diamonds, interspersed with blue stones. A large, clear gem dangled from the lowest point of the collar. Even she knew, based on that rock alone, that the necklace had to have an exorbitant price tag.

She scanned the description below the photo, and her lungs stopped working. "Twelve *million*?" she wheezed. "Mom stole a necklace worth twelve million dollars?"

From the sober faces of her sisters, it was obvious that Molly hadn't read the price wrong. She let out a silent whistle as her stomach continued to try to eat itself. This was nothing like the lipstick Jane liked to sneak from the department-store makeup counter.

"She is in so much trouble."

"So are we." Cara's voice was flat as she gestured around the dining room. It hadn't gotten more than a cursory search, but other rooms of the house—especially Jane's bedroom—were a tossed mess. Even the storage boxes in the garage had been dug through, and the contents had been strewn everywhere. At least they hadn't dusted for prints again. The fingerprint powder that Sergeant Blake had left everywhere was a beast to clean up, Molly had found. "I take it the necklace wasn't found on Mom when she was arrested?"

Molly held up her hands in an *I don't know* gesture. "Sorry. I didn't ask Carmondy that. Want me to call him back?" She really didn't want to talk to him again so soon, mainly because their last conversation had put her severely off-balance in an unexpected way, and she'd had quite enough surprises for one day.

"Not yet," Cara said, to Molly's relief. "First, let's figure out what we know—and what we can find out on our own. Then you can talk to John to fill in the blanks."

"Okay." Molly took great pains to hide her inward grimace. It appeared that her next call to John was just delayed slightly, not canceled as she'd hoped. As soon as the thought popped into her head, she mentally scolded herself. She and her sisters had an entire *world* of problems that were a thousand times worse than her uncertainty around this new version of John. If she had to call him for more answers—even if she had to ask him for help—she was going to put her pride in the closet and do exactly what was necessary.

After all, their mom had just jumped into a canyon of trouble…and Molly had to do her best to make sure that she and her sisters weren't dragged into the abyss with her.

# CHAPTER 6

SHOVING OPEN THE DINGY GLASS DOOR TO BARNEY Thompson's bail-bond office, Molly very carefully hid any sign of disgust that wanted to creep into her expression. She didn't even make a face when she felt something sticky adhere the door handle to her palm, and she was quite proud of herself for that.

After spending the morning chasing down leads on Jane's case and getting nowhere, Molly hadn't been able to put off the visit to Barney's office any longer. She wasn't happy to have to talk to him—in fact, she'd rather sleep in a bed full of cockroaches than waste a minute with Barney Thompson—but he'd written Jane's bond, which meant he had information that Molly and her sisters didn't. Reminding herself that it wouldn't take long and then she could leave this hole-in-the-wall, she stepped into the reception area.

Barney's twentysomething son, Ashton, sat at a battered metal desk, his focus on his phone. Peeling her hand free with an inner shudder, Molly let the door close behind her. When Ashton didn't look up from the small screen, she pulled the door open again a few inches and closed it with a loud bang.

Reluctantly, he tore his gaze from his phone and let it flick over her. Immediately, he lost his disinterested expression as he gave her another more thorough visual examination. "Whoa. You're one of the hot Mexican bounty-hunter sisters. Which one are you again?"

It became harder for her to hold back her *ick* face, but she somehow managed to cling to her coolly polite smile. "I'm Molly Pax. Is your dad here?" She didn't bother correcting him about her nationality. After all, if it hadn't sunk in after Ashton's previous four encounters with her, then he was never going to get it.

"Yeah." He didn't take his gaze off her as he raised his voice to a yell. "Dad! There's a hottie here for you!"

"Thanks," she said dryly.

"No problem." Ashton leaned back, ignoring his chair's protesting squeal. "So…Mel. Whatcha doing later?"

"A lot of things." She started to correct him on her name, but stopped herself before she could. It'd probably be a good thing if he couldn't remember it.

Ashton opened his mouth again, and she braced to firmly shut him down. Luckily, the inner office door opened before he could say another word.

Barney peered into the reception area. When he spotted Molly, his scowl disappeared and his mouth curved up in a small grin. The smugness in his expression was almost enough to make her turn right around and leave his office, but then she reminded herself that he had information she needed. First, she'd learn more about what happened with Jane, and then she'd tell him—and his son—to shove it.

"Molly Pax." He looked like he was resisting the desire to rub his hands together, evil-villain style. A tall man with a broad frame, he might have been considered moderately handsome if a stranger saw him in a picture, but his personality had completely warped her perception to the point that just the sight of his florid, square-jawed face made her gag a little. "What a surprise to see you here." His almost giddy tone made it clear that he wasn't surprised at all.

"Molly?" Ashton repeated, frowning, before she could get her bubbling temper under control enough to respond. "Why'd you tell me your name was Mel?"

Ignoring the son, she focused on Barney, clinging to her mantra that she only had to deal with these two for a short time before she could leave them to their dingy, depressing office with its mysteriously sticky doorknobs. "Barney. It's been a while." She almost told him that it was nice to see him again, but she couldn't force out such a whopping lie.

"Too long. Too long." He made a flourishing gesture, extending his arm toward the inner office. "Come in, and we'll discuss business."

Molly had to force her feet to move. Everything in her gut was telling her to cut and run and find a different source of information, but she was already here—plus she'd already dealt with Ashton's sliminess. Surely she could survive his father's as well?

Inside the office, Barney waved her toward a straight-backed wooden chair in front of his desk as he took the seat behind it. That chair protested just as Ashton's had, and Molly had the whimsical thought that even the furniture was complaining about having to work with these two—or, more practically, Barney was just too cheap to buy new chairs.

"So…Molly." Leaning back, he steepled his fingers and put on what Molly was pretty sure was supposed to be his thoughtful expression, but it ended up making him look even blanker than normal. "Since you're here, I'm guessing you've decided to take the Sonny Zarver job after all." Before she could refute this, he continued, "Figured you'd come around eventually. It's a lot of money at stake."

Even though she was almost painfully tempted to punch the smug condescension off his face, she crossed her legs and linked her fingers together in her lap instead. "Actually, I'm not here because of Sonny. Our decision not to take that job stands."

His smarmy grin disappeared as quickly as if she'd really allowed herself to smack him. It was very satisfying to watch. Unfortunately, she could only enjoy it for a few seconds before he smiled again. This one was a little meaner-looking than the last, and a great deal colder. "You sure about that?" After moving the remains of a fast-food breakfast sandwich off a pile on his desk, he slid a large manila file from the top of the stack and opened it. He didn't look down at the contents, so she knew he was already well aware of what they said. Her stomach twisted and turned as she waited for him to drop whatever bomb he had on her head.

Instead of answering, she waited. When she didn't know all of the facts, the only thing running her mouth would do was get her in trouble. Barney loved to brag about his exploits, so she figured that he'd tell her everything if she just stayed quiet.

When she didn't respond, his mouth tightened, and he tapped his fingers against the contents of the folder. Molly resisted the urge to glance down at the papers in front of him to get a peek at whatever he was about to throw her way. Instead, she held his gaze and kept her face calm...at least she hoped she was projecting a placid facade. After the turmoil of the past couple of days, her nerves were starting to fray, and she worried that her tension would show through.

Finally, he spoke. "Your mother got herself into a shitload of trouble."

*Tell me something I don't know.* Rather than letting her snarky words escape, Molly limited herself to raising her eyebrows slightly.

His face darkened, growing even more flushed than his normal ruddy coloring. "I, being the nice guy that I am, helped her out when none of her kids bothered to show up."

"Why'd she pick you?" Molly asked, relieved that they were finally getting to some details about Jane's arrest and first advisement. "She's never used your services before, right?"

Studying her face closely, he leaned back again, drawing a complaining shriek from his chair. "That's right. I happened to be at the courthouse yesterday, and we ran into each other." His grin was an unnatural shade of white, bordering on blue, and she made a mental note to mention his disconcerting appearance to Felicity, who was addicted to tooth whitening. "She must've realized what she's been missing all these years."

Ignoring the gross sexual innuendo for the time being, Molly focused on the situation and what needed to be done. "But why you? Normally, she uses Gavin or Delia."

His gaze dropped as he gave an irritated shrug. It was just for a second before he refocused on her face, his gaze snapping back to meet hers, but it was long enough for her to know that he was about to lie. "No idea. Like I said, she probably just figured out that I'm the best."

"Uh-huh." Even to her own ears, her tone made it sound like Molly didn't believe a word he was saying... which was pretty accurate. "So, she didn't hit up Gavin and Delia first, but they turned her down?"

His face darkened again, this time to almost a plum color. "How would I know that?"

"Uh..." Molly gave him a "duh" look. "You all stand in the back of the courtroom, waiting to pounce on potential clients. Don't you guys talk?"

"Of course we talk, but we don't share client information." He huffed, sounding more offended than a guy who, the bail-bond gossip pipeline had it, had once accepted someone's kidney as a form of payment. Although Molly was ninety-nine percent sure the rumor was false, that one percent of doubt remained. It would've been enough to make her shy away from working with Barney—that and his utter creepiness.

From Barney's defensive attitude, Molly was fairly certain that he'd been Jane's last choice. The question that remained was why? If Barney had fronted a five-hundred-*thousand*-dollar bond, it had to have been worth it. Even with the proceeds from Molly's car and the stolen cash, Jane didn't have enough collateral to justify the risk.

A suspicion crept into her brain.

"Are you holding the stolen necklace for her?" she asked suddenly and bluntly, wanting to see his immediate reaction before he managed to think up a proper lie.

The baffled surprise that instantly crossed Barney's expression seemed sincere, however. "I wish." That sounded heartfelt, too. "If she'd given me the necklace, I would've happily written a bond for ten times Jane's bail." His face blanked, and it was almost comical how chagrined he looked at his own honesty. "Not that I would ever deal in stolen merchandise."

A snort escaped Molly at his sloppy attempt to regain the moral high ground—not that he'd ever had it in the first place. She quickly sobered, however. The mystery of why Barney had helped Jane still hadn't been solved. "What'd she use for collateral then?"

His slow, snakelike smile caused a shiver to zip along Molly's spine, and she instinctively stiffened, knowing that whatever was going to come out of Barney's mouth next would be very, very bad. Flipping through the pages in the folder, he pulled something out and slowly extended it toward her. Despite the trembling deep in her gut, her hand was steady as she accepted it.

As she glanced down at the heavy paper, comprehension struck with the force of a sledgehammer. She held the title to her house. The place where she and her sisters lived, the one that had been a breath away from foreclosure when Molly had taken over the mortgage payments at the age of eighteen, the mortgage that she and her sisters had managed to pay off just four months and three weeks ago. It was the house that Molly—that all of them except Jane—had almost killed themselves to save, working long hours chasing down every skip who had an arrest warrant out, no matter how dangerous or how small the bounty was.

"That isn't hers," she managed to say with numb lips

as she clutched the precious paper with both hands. "The house is ours. Not hers."

"Her name's on it." With a shrug, he reached over and plucked the title from her hands as easily and effortlessly as their mother had stolen the house out from under them.

"She refused to sign the paperwork to transfer the title." Molly watched, unable to look away as he tucked the title for *her* house back into the folder with a smug neatness that belied the mess of his office. How had her mom even gotten hold of the title? Molly kept it in a document safe in her room, and she'd never told Jane the combination.

Barney made a *tsk* sound. "That's too bad. Not my fault that you don't have your ducks in a row, though, is it?" Patting the closed folder, he widened his smile. "It's a great piece of property, worth twice the amount I'll have to pay when Jane forfeits her bail, even if the house is a wreck. There are only two other houses in Langston with national forest access, and they'd never sell. What should I do with it? Tear down that dump you live in and build fresh? Sell it to the hunting resort next door? I've heard that they've been trying to buy your place for years. So many options... It's a good problem to have."

Molly wasn't sure what emotions she was showing, but whatever they were, they seemed to make Barney very happy—giddy even. "If you ask very nicely, I might even consider keeping the place intact for a few months and rent it to you. I'm sure we could come to some sort of amicable agreement."

A fresh wave of anger flared inside her, burning away the numbness, and she almost levitated off her chair from the contained rage. The only thing that kept her from leaping across the desk and doing major damage to Barney's smarmy, stupid face was the clear glee in his expression. He wanted to upset her, wanted her to lose it, and she couldn't give him the satisfaction. With a huge effort of will, she smoothed her expression and sat back in her chair, fighting for a show of indifference.

"It doesn't matter." It did, it really did, but she somehow managed to say the words anyway. "You won't be taking the house. To forfeit her bail, she'd have to miss her next court date, and she always makes her court dates." Even though Jane found it impossible to stay on the right side of the law, she'd never skipped before.

"She's never missed a court date *yet*," Barney corrected, although the unpleasant joy in his eyes had faded. "Jane's only done petty stuff before. She's in a whole other world now, one that could get her twenty years or more in prison. I'm betting she's already halfway through New Mexico, never to return."

Although Molly had known that stealing the necklace was a more serious crime than her mom had ever committed before, she hadn't allowed herself to consider what that meant as far as sentencing went. Up until that point, Jane had done quite a few short stints in the county jail, paid a boatload of fines, and was almost constantly on probation. As much as Molly hated to admit it, Barney was right in this case. Jane had committed a crime that could easily put her in prison for the rest of her life.

Pushing away the mountain of anxiety that this thought brought on, she tried to focus on the most immediate need—making sure Barney didn't yank their house away from them.

"This is all speculation until her court date arrives. Personally, I believe that she'll show." Molly tried to hide her doubts. "The house is simply collateral right now, so you can't touch it."

His smile was more a baring of his teeth. "The law is that the bond is forfeited if she doesn't appear…or if she flees." He gave her a knowing look. "Have you seen her since her hearing yesterday?"

"No, but that's not surprising." Molly's heart was firing in quick strokes that echoed in her head, and she hoped he didn't see the worry building inside her. "She burned her bridges with us. Speaking of that, you don't happen to be holding my car as collateral as well?" When he hesitated, she narrowed her eyes and fixed him with her best basilisk glare. "For your sake, I hope not, since it's stolen and I know *that* title is under my name."

"Jane didn't bring me any car." There was a stiltedness to his phrasing, as if he was carefully avoiding a lie. Molly didn't know why he bothered trying to stay truthful. It wasn't like she believed a word out of his mouth anyway.

"Hmm." She put all of her skepticism in that one wordless sound as she got to her feet. Her heart was racing, and her feet twitched with the need to rush out of that dingy, depressing office and find her mom. As soon as he'd said *flee*, the word had clicked in her brain. Of course Jane was going to run. These consequences were bigger than any she'd ever had to face before. If she still had possession of the necklace, that almost guaranteed she'd skip out and relocate somewhere across the country.

"Wait," he said, reaching across the desk toward

her, as if he could hold her in her chair. Pulling back far enough that he couldn't touch her, Molly eyed his outstretched arm with distaste. Straightening again, he cleared his throat as he withdrew his hand. "We're not done discussing this yet."

"Sure we are." Before he could make another effort to grab her, she took several backward steps toward the door. "Shall I recap? Mom put a home she doesn't own up as collateral for her bond, and you're threatening to kick us out, even though she hasn't forfeited it."

His lips flapped slightly, as if he were trying to figure out how to spin it.

Instead of waiting for him to say anything else, Molly turned on her heel and headed for the inner office door. She had it open and was stepping through before he spoke again.

"I can be your friend or your enemy," he called after her. "I promise you won't like having me for an enemy."

As Ashton watched her curiously, she strode for the main door. "You need to cut down on all those mobster movies," she called over her shoulder. "Or at least pick better lines to steal."

She shoved her way outside, slamming the door closed on Ashton's laughter…and immediately ran into what felt like a wall.

# CHAPTER 7

BOUNCING OFF THE HARD CHEST IN FRONT OF HER, SHE started tumbling toward the ground, but two huge, mitt-sized hands caught her before she fell. Although she tended to avoid touching him—and had never run head-long into his massive body before—she instantly knew who she'd crashed into. Molly wasn't at all surprised. The way the last few days had been going, how could it be anyone but John Carmondy who'd witnessed her latest humiliation?

Once she regained her balance, she hesitated, even as the thinking part of her brain screamed at her to pull away. The feel of his fingers pressing into the flesh of her hips made her body temperature shoot up several degrees, but she told herself it was just residual rage from meeting with Barney…and then literally running into her occasionally helpful nemesis.

Gathering what brain cells remained, she finally took a step back. His hands fell from her hips after a short pause, making her wonder if he'd been reluctant to let her go. Immediately, she shook off that whole train of thought. Her brain must've been scrambled when her head hit his rock-hard pecs.

The distant sound of an emergency vehicle siren yanked her out of her weird, uncharacteristically moony fit. Barney's office was one of the few occupied spaces in the ratty strip mall, and the neighborhood was just as run-down and abandoned. She glanced over her shoulder at Barney's office door and then back at John as suspicion began creeping in.

"Why are you here?" she asked bluntly. Either he was following her or he was coming to see Barney, neither of which were positives. Her mind was in chaos, thanks to the revelations that had just been dumped on her, and she was just one wrong thought away from exploding in a fit of rage or breaking down in uncontrollable tears.

"I stopped by your house, and one of your sisters told me you were here."

Molly suddenly wished she were an only child. "Which sister?"

"The one that looks the most like you."

"Felicity," she growled. It had to be her. She was the one who shared Molly's dad, and both of them were spitting images of Lono. There would be retribution for siccing Carmondy on her. Right now, though, she needed to put some distance between her and Barney so she didn't charge in there and choke him until his stupid, smug face turned purple and he handed over the title to their house. A tiny part of her was shocked at the grim satisfaction that mental image gave her, but most of her was all for putting aside her usual anti-violence stance.

Skirting around John, Molly strode across the parking lot. The absence of her car caused a flare of fresh anger, but she pushed it back and turned in the direction of the bus stop. John, being John, quickly caught up and walked alongside her.

"Why'd you track me down?" she asked, although

the question lacked its usual heat. Her brain was too busy processing what she'd just found out and trying to come up with a plan so they didn't get evicted if—when—Jane decided not to show up in court.

"Why were you talking to Barney?" he countered rather than answering her question.

Two could play at that game. "Why is that any of your business?"

"You aren't going to go after Sonny Zarver, I hope."

Irritation surged through her at his stern tone. "Again, focus on your own situation, and I'll do the same."

"Molly…" He caught her arm, pulling her to a stop. "Sonny's dangerous. I know the bounty's big, but you don't want to get mixed up in his world. Money's worthless if you're dead."

Despite her resolution not to get sucked into conversation with John, she couldn't keep her response to a mere sideways glance as she tugged away and started walking again. "Why are you pushing this so hard? Are you hoping to bring in Sonny yourself?"

His face tightened, his mouth pulling into a straight line. His long legs easily kept pace with hers. "Of course not. I'm not that stupid."

That stung. She kept her gaze forward, focusing hard on the bus stop a half block away. "You think I am, though?"

"You're not stupid." There was no hesitation in his words. "But after what your mom did, I'm worried you might be getting desperate."

"Desperate." The word was forced between gritted teeth. The truth of it made it especially painful to hear. She needed to get away from John before she did something embarrassing—like burst into tears or admit that he was right. "Go away, Carmondy."

He made a frustrated sound. "You're taking this the wrong way. I'm trying to look out for you."

"Stop trying." She reached the bus-stop shelter and halted. "You don't need to look out for me. I have four sisters who do that already."

"At least let me give you a ride home." He pulled out his phone and tapped at the screen. Although she was curious, she refused to crane her neck to see what he was doing.

"No. I'll take the bus."

"You're going to be waiting hours." He held up his phone with the screen toward her so she could see the bus schedule. He was right.

Suddenly, all of the anger that had been filling her whooshed out like a balloon with a leak, leaving her limp and tired. She sagged against the side of the shelter. She hadn't felt so hopeless and desperate since she was twelve and the heat had been turned off in January because Jane hadn't paid the gas bill. So many times, Molly had come up with solutions and worked hard and thought she'd succeeded in making life better for her sisters, only to have her mom destroy everything Molly had just built with one casually selfish decision.

John's mention of Sonny Zarver reminded Molly that Barney wanted her to bring in that particular skip. Now that he had leverage on her and her family, she couldn't see how they could get out of taking the job. Molly needed to call Jeremy Tremaine, an attorney her mom had used for years until Jane had finally chased him off, as she eventually did all of her lawyers. Jeremy would know whether Barney really could take possession of the house before Jane's next court date if it appeared that she'd fled. Molly's stomach twisted and churned.

Gentle, enormous hands on her shoulders brought her out of her galloping thoughts, and she looked up to see that John was watching her intently. "Let me give you a ride home," he said. "Please."

Her knee-jerk reaction was to turn him down, but she hesitated before saying the words. Her options were limited. She could walk several miles back home or wait hours for the next bus or text Charlie for a ride. The last was her only real option, and it wasn't ideal. Charlie and Felicity were doing the rounds of Jane's friends, trying to find out where their mom had landed after leaving the Denver jail. They didn't need to come all the way back to Langston to give her a ride home, especially not when John was right here, offering her his taxi services, and the only thing stopping her from accepting was her pride.

"Okay," she said before she could reconsider.

His eyes widened briefly before he grinned, playing it off as if he'd always known she'd give in and take him up on his offer. Somehow, that brief startled moment made him seem less like a rival and more…*sweet*—a term she'd never thought she'd use in reference to John Carmondy.

Pushing away from the side of the bus shelter, she headed back toward the parking lot in front of Barney's office. The closer they got, the more her thoughts tangled and turned. They'd reached the edge of the lot, a scraggly hedge separating them from the few vehicles, when Molly put a hand on John's arm, silently bringing him to a halt. His forearm tightened under her light touch, and the movement, for some stupid reason, made her insides buzz like she'd swallowed a whole hive of bees.

Reminding herself firmly that this was not the time for any of that, she shoved those thoughts away and focused on the reason she'd stopped. Barney was bent over, retrieving something out of his car. John took his cue from her and went still, his gaze scanning the area as if he was searching out potential threats.

Although such careful perusal wasn't necessary in their current situation, she still appreciated it. Molly usually had to be the responsible and cautious one, so it was nice to have someone else to watch her back for once.

She watched Barney as he found whatever he was looking for and slammed his car door. As soon as he'd disappeared back into his office, Molly moved out from behind the hedge that had been giving them cover. "Thanks for letting me avoid him," she said, giving John a quick glance.

"No problem." He steered her toward his SUV with a hand hovering just over her lower back—not quite making contact, but near enough that she felt the heat of his palm. "I get it. If I can manage to *not* talk to Barney, I do it in a second."

Molly huffed out a laugh. "Me too—obviously. Plus, we just had a not-so-friendly conversation, so I didn't want to have to start that up again."

He studied her out of the corner of his eye in a way that shouldn't have been cute, since he was a huge, built, tough-as-nails bounty hunter, but it *was* cute—adorable, even. "Can I ask what you talked about?"

"You can ask, but I probably won't tell you." He seemed to accept that with just a small dip of his chin as he unlocked the doors and opened the front passenger side for her, so she relented. "You already know Barney wrote Jane's bond."

He didn't respond, just waited for her to continue, and she wondered how much of what she was about to tell him he already knew. John's network of informants put Molly and her sisters' connections to shame. He always seemed to have information before anyone else. It was a bit infuriating, and Molly secretly wished she had access to his sources. Today, though, there was something freeing about knowing that John already had all of the information she had—and probably more. She didn't have to hide anything about the case from him, since that would've been futile. It was a sign of how desperate she was to talk to someone about what was happening, someone who wasn't one of her sisters, since she had to protect them. John, though, could take care of himself.

Because of this, she started talking as soon as he circled the truck and climbed into the driver's seat. "She put the house up as collateral."

He shot her a quick but penetrating glance, and she wasn't sure whether that look meant he was surprised by the news or already knew and was just checking to see how she was taking it. Knowing John, it was the latter.

"It's my fault." The words started tumbling out more quickly, the relief of talking about it making her spill what she probably should've kept to herself. "I should've pushed Mom to transfer the title over to us rather than taking the drama-free route of just paying it off while it was still under her name. I never thought she'd yank it out from under us like this."

As she heard her words out loud, she realized how silly and naive she had been. Why had she assumed that Jane wouldn't grab any and all assets she could? When had her mom ever kept her sticky, greedy fingers off any source of money, no matter how sacred? If she hadn't cared if her kids had enough to eat or heat in the winter when they were small, why would she care if those same kids were suddenly homeless as adults?

"None of this is your fault," John said, sounding so sure that what he was saying was the absolute truth. The utter confidence of his words untied a sticky knot in Molly's chest, and her tight shoulders relaxed a fraction. "This is all on your mom."

"I was stupid," she admitted. "I didn't want to deal with a huge fight, so I put all of us in this situation. We could lose our house because I was too big of a weenis to insist she sign it over when we paid it off."

He made a sound somewhere between a cough and a choke. "Weenis?"

Molly gave him a stern look, trying very hard not to be charmed by the way his suppressed smile dug vertical grooves into his cheeks. "Focus, Carmondy. We're not twelve."

His expression turned offended, although amusement still lurked under the surface. "I'm not the one who said 'weenis.'"

Flipping her hand in a dismissive gesture, she resisted the urge to engage in an off-track conversation about nonsexist synonyms for *wimp*. She needed to concentrate on the issue of Barney's hold on their lives. She dug her cell phone from her pocket. "Whatever. I need to call Jeremy Tremaine."

Instantly, all humor was gone from John's expression, his face all hard angles and sharp glares. The change startled Molly enough that she almost dropped her phone before she reminded herself that it was just John. "Why?" he barked, making her stare at his etched profile.

"Because he'll know if Barney really can take our house before Mom's first court date if it looks like she's taken off." The words came out sounding more tentative than she would've liked, and she straightened her shoulders, refusing to let John intimidate her, even if he suddenly looked like an angry gargoyle. A *hot* angry gargoyle. She shifted in her seat, not liking her body's reaction to this oddly stern version of her usually easy-going rival.

"He threatened to do that?" Now John looked even angrier, although Molly could tell it wasn't directed at her this time. "Bastard." He sent her a glance that had a hint of apology in it. "Maybe I should've bonded her out. At least then you wouldn't have Barney threatening to take your house away."

His words make her stomach churn with a medley of emotions. As much as she hated that Barney had power over them, the thought of John accepting their house as collateral for Jane's bond made Molly feel sick. Even if he'd done it to keep Barney's grubby paws off their home, it still would've felt like a betrayal. "No," she said slowly, trying to work through the hundreds of emotions swamping her. "I don't want you involved in this mess." At his wry look, she gave a small, slightly apologetic shrug and amended her statement. "I don't want you involved any more than you already are, at least."

He gave a noncommittal grunt as he pulled up to

the curb in front of her house, and Molly refocused on finding Jeremy's number in her phone. Even though she knew she should go inside and then call, a large part of her was reluctant to leave John's vehicle. It felt safe and peaceful, a small oasis of protection where she could hide from the current insanity of her life.

Shaking off her thoughts, she found Jeremy's number and moved to tap it, only to be interrupted when John covered the screen with one of his giant hands. Raising her head, she glared at him, but it was tough to hold on to her anger when he wore such a sheepish expression.

"What are you doing?" she asked as frostily as possible.

"Don't call Tremaine," he said, and her spine stiffened into a steel rod at the command in his voice. He must've noticed, because he grimaced and gave her hand a clumsy pat before withdrawing. "Please. I'll find out if Barney can take your house before Jane's next court date."

"Why don't you want me to talk to Jeremy?" Her question was more curious than offended, since his insistence that she not call the attorney had sounded sincerely concerned.

He opened his mouth and then shut it again, as if debating internally what to say out loud. "I don't trust him."

Tapping her cell phone against her palm, she eyed John as she considered what to do. She already felt like she was depending on him too much. He felt like a rock in the churning sea of chaos that her life had turned into, and while all of her instincts promised that she could trust him, she didn't really *know* him that well. Working as a bounty hunter had shown her over and over again that she could only depend on her sisters, and now was definitely not the time for her to forget all the hard lessons she'd learned. "Who are you going to ask?" she finally said. "I'd rather not share this information with anyone else."

"I won't mention any names or specific details." Lifting his hand, he traced an X over his heart like he was eight years old, and she was torn between laughing and melting. He could be such a big dork sometimes. "If you ask Jeremy, he'll know right away that you're talking about Jane, but my contacts won't make the connection—not if I'm the one asking."

Although she paused again to consider his words, she already knew what her answer was going to be. "Okay." There was barely a hesitation before she spoke the next words. "Thank you." It was getting dangerously easy to thank John. She felt another twinge of apprehension that she was relying on him too much. Once she allowed him into her world, it would be hard to eject him. When he smiled, though—a truly happy and wide grin—she couldn't regret opening the door for him.

Now she could only hope that regret wouldn't come later.

# CHAPTER 8

A KNOCK ON THE DOOR INTERRUPTED MOLLY'S PERUSAL OF the Colorado criminal statutes. Completely caught up in the sentencing guidelines that may be Jane's future, she jumped at the sound. Warrant, on the other hand, didn't even lift his head off the floor where he was sprawled out over an air-conditioning vent. Instead, his tail thumped lazily a few times before he fell back asleep. The dog's reaction made Molly fairly certain of who was at the door.

As she stood up, she swallowed a groan at the feel of her spine popping back into place. Glancing at the clock, she saw that she'd been hunched over her laptop for most of the afternoon. It was no wonder her body was protesting.

After peeking through the peephole in the front door, she unlocked it and swung it open. "This is becoming a habit."

"What is?" John slipped past her, striding into the house as if he owned the place.

Making a face and pretending that she wasn't glad to see him, she closed and relocked the door. "You show-ing up on our doorstep uninvited."

"If you want me to leave, I can take this very valuable information and go." His voice was muffled. As Molly entered the kitchen, she saw that he'd crouched down next to Warrant and was rubbing the delighted dog's belly.

"No, it's fine. I needed a break anyway." Even though they were most likely going to be talking about Jane, John was still a good distraction from the mess her mom had made. "I take it you talked to your contact?"

"I did." After a final pat, John straightened to his significant height. Having him here in her kitchen, taking up most of the space and a good portion of the oxygen—especially without her sisters there as a buffer—made Molly feel overheated. She couldn't decide whether it was in a good way or a bad way. Shaking off her errant thoughts, she refocused on the important thing.

"What'd they say?" Her knees wobbled slightly from a mixture of exhaustion and anxiety, but she refused to sit down in the chair she'd abandoned when she'd answered the door. The only other seat in the room was too close to hers, and it was hard enough having this conversation without the prospect of John being pressed against her from knee to shoulder. She braced her palms on the table behind her and steeled herself for bad news.

"Barney's *technically* right, but Zorah—my lawyer contact—said she doubted a judge would rule that Jane had violated her bail conditions if she hadn't missed a court date yet."

The tight knot of Molly's stomach eased ever so slightly, and she had to lean back more heavily against the table. John must've caught the slight movement, since he took a step closer, his hands reaching toward her as if he was prepared to catch her before she fell. Luckily for her presence of mind, he stopped before he was close enough to touch.

"Maybe you should sit down."

Ignoring the suggestion, she stiffened her spine so she could remove her hands from the table behind her and stand unsupported. Now was not the time for her to get literally weak in the knees. She could collapse later—much later—once they'd figured out the situation and their house was safe from Barney's clutches. "I'm fine. So, we're good until her arraignment, then?"

"Preliminary hearing." The correction sounded oddly gentle, but she still winced at the reminder.

"Right. She gets a preliminary hearing, since she committed a felony." She paused as she fought off an overwhelming surge of anger and anxiety. "Several felonies. So…we have thirty days, then?"

"Thirty to forty-five, yeah." He was watching her closely from his spot just a few steps away. She didn't like him treating her as if she might break. It made her want to collapse into his arms and bawl, which wouldn't solve anything. She was the oldest of her sisters, and they were counting on her to lead them through this, just like she'd done during the many, many other messes Jane had thrown them into.

"Okay." Taking a deep breath, she held it until her brain spun a little, and then released it in a long, silent exhalation. "This is good news. It gives us time."

A heavy knock on the front door made her jerk back. For an irrational moment, she felt a gut-deep fear that Barney was there to toss them out of their home, but then logic reasserted itself. She'd just learned that they had at least a month to figure a way out of this. Whoever was at the door wasn't there to evict them…yet.

She belatedly started moving through the living

room, but John was there first, putting his significant bulk between her and the door. As she stared at his broad back, she blinked, more baffled than annoyed by his protective action.

"What are you doing?" she asked quietly as the knocking stopped.

"Let me see who it is first." His voice was just a low rumble, and she wanted to laugh at their whispers. As far as she knew, there was no reason to hide from their latest visitor, but they were both muttering quietly at each other.

"No. It's my house, dum-dum." Slipping around him, she hurried to the door, knowing that it had taken her long enough that whoever it was might have already left.

"'Dum-dum'?" he repeated, although he kept his words quiet. "Are you five?"

"Most people say I'm a solid ten, but beauty is in the eye of the beholder, I suppose." When she went up onto her tiptoes to peer through the peephole, there was a scratchy, clicking sound. She froze, her gaze dropping to the doorknob, watching in shocked disbelief as the dead bolt thumped open. It felt surreal. Someone had picked the lock—was breaking in—right in front of them.

Her heart pounding, she took a step back and stared as the knob began to turn, twisting slowly as the door eased open. Behind her, John swore creatively under his breath. Then she was plucked off her feet and tucked behind his massive bulk again, so he was blocking her view of the opening door. Before she could protest or move to help protect him, John surged forward. A startled squawk from an unknown male voice jolted Molly out of her shock. She shifted to the side just in time to see a blond stranger get plucked off his feet and yanked into the house. Slamming the door closed again, John pinned the intruder against it.

"Who are you?" John demanded, the menace underlying the question making the stranger flinch back as much as possible, given that he was already mashed against the door, his backpack squashed between his back and the wood. When the man didn't answer, John used his fistful of dress shirt to give him a solid shake.

"Stu...Stuart," the stranger stammered. "Stuart Powers." His last name cut off with a squeak as John jostled him again.

"What are you doing here?" Molly asked, figuring that since John had Stuart so conveniently in his grip, she should use the opportunity to question him. She was used to doing her own tackling, so this was a nice change. "Why did you break in?"

Stuart shot her a panicked glance from the corner of his eye. "I didn't *break in*..." he started, cutting off when John gave him another shake. "I didn't! The door was unlocked!"

Molly and John exchanged a look.

"Sure. It was unlocked after you picked it," Molly said with heavy sarcasm. "Why did you break in? What were you planning on taking?"

"Nothing!" The yelp was full of indignation, but Stuart's gaze flickered down for a fraction of a second, just long enough to tell Molly that the trespassing stranger was lying. "I go to school with Cara. I'm just dropping off some lecture notes she asked for."

"You picked the lock in order to leave lecture notes?" The skepticism in John's voice was thick, and Molly agreed with him. Stuart's story was weak and full of holes. "Try again."

"I did!" Stuart blinked rapidly, as if trying to think up a more plausible lie. "I mean, I didn't pick the lock. I don't even know how to do that. I was going to just leave the notes inside…"

Molly couldn't keep her eyes from rolling. "Let's skip over the fact that we *saw* you unlock the door and move on to the question of why you came all the way over here rather than just emailing or texting her your notes."

"I…uh…" He swallowed, and his Adam's apple bobbed with the effort. "I don't actually know her number."

Exchanging another glance with John, Molly sighed. "There's a student directory. At the least, you could've found her email address. Not only that, but she would've *given* you her contact info if she'd actually asked you to bring her your notes." She pulled her phone out of her pocket, and Stuart's eyes bugged out in obvious panic.

"Wait! Who are you calling?"

"Cara, first of all." She shot off a quick text. "If her answer is what I think it's going to be, then you're going to have to think of a new and more convincing story for the cops, Stu."

His face went even paler until his skin matched his light-blond eyebrows and lashes. A blue vein pulsed in his temple as they all waited in silence for Cara's return text. Before Molly's phone could beep, the knob twisted and shook as someone outside tried to open the door.

"Molly?" Charlie called. "Are you trying to be funny, or is the door stuck again?"

"Neither!" Molly raised her voice in order for her

sister to be able to hear her. "Carmondy has a wannabe burglar shoved against it."

There wasn't even a startled pause before Charlie spoke again. "Could he move him for a sec? Just long enough for me and Fifi to get inside?"

John half carried and half dragged Stuart over and pressed him against the wall next to the door. "You're clear!" John called, and the door immediately flew open.

"What's up?" Charlie asked, her eyes wide with interest as she spotted Stuart. "Does this have anything to do with…?" She paused, obviously not wanting to say *Mom*. "The issue that we were talking about earlier?"

Molly wasn't sure why she'd needed the nudge, but it was painfully obvious once Charlie had asked the question. "We're not sure yet, but it's likely. Blondie here picked the lock after we were delayed in answering the door."

"Delayed by what?" Felicity asked, following Charlie inside and closing the door behind them.

"Does it matter?" Molly asked, not able to keep the testiness out of her voice. They had someone break into their home, and her sister was worried about why it took them a couple extra minutes to answer the door?

"Not really, but I'm interested in hearing the answer." As she spoke, Felicity coolly eyed Stuart up and down.

"Me too." Of course Charlie had to chime in.

"John and I were discussing something and took a few minutes to get to the door."

"Discussing something?" Charlie sounded like she was about to laugh. "Is that a euphemism?"

Stuart's gaze was darting from person to person. "If you all want to talk about this in private, I'll just leave…" He trailed off as John's fist tightened around his shirt, holding him more firmly in place.

Knowing that John had their intruder under control, Molly focused on her sisters. "No. It's not a euphemism. We were literally talking, as in using our words to exchange ideas."

Felicity looked from Molly to John and then back again. "Did you find out something new? Something about Mo—ah…something about the case we're working on?"

Gesturing toward where Stuart dangled from John's grip, Molly said, "Let's take care of this first, and then I'll fill you in."

The door swung open again, forcing Felicity to jump out of the way before it smacked into her. This time, it was Cara who stood there. She took in the scene with outward calm, her eyebrows arching just slightly higher than normal as she stepped inside and closed the door behind her.

"What's going on?" she asked, her gaze jumping to John's grip on Stuart and then back to Molly.

"Do you know him?" Molly asked, rather than answering her sister's question.

Her forehead creasing in confusion, Cara frowned. "John? Of course I know him."

"No, the other one."

Cara studied Stuart carefully. When he opened his mouth, as if to prompt Cara's memory, Molly made a *zip-it* gesture across her lips. Stuart stayed silent.

"Maybe?" Cara finally said, squinting at him with her head tilted to the right. "He looks vaguely familiar, but that could be because he's pretty generic-looking. He looks like ninety percent of the guys at school." When Stuart let out a testy grunt, Cara grimaced apologetically. "No offense."

"You didn't ask him for a copy of his notes?"

"Definitely not."

It was enough confirmation for Molly, and she pulled out her phone again, this time calling Sergeant Blake.

Stuart's eyes got round as she held the phone to her ear. "What are you doing?" he asked.

"Calling the police." When he began to sputter, she held up her hand in an *I don't want to hear it* gesture. "If you don't want the cops called on you, then don't break into people's houses."

Blake's phone went to voicemail, so Molly hung up. Ignoring the newly hopeful look on Stuart's face, she called the number for dispatch. After she gave the basic details of what had happened, she ended the call. The minutes ticked by in silence. Her sisters gave her wide-eyed *What is going on* looks, but Molly could only mouth *later* and shrug slightly, not wanting to give Stuart any information that he didn't have before. Everything was pointing toward his break-in being related to Jane, and she wondered if Stuart was the one who had stolen her car and the business's bank card.

"Have you broken in here before today?" she asked abruptly, watching his expression carefully.

"No," he blurted out, before pulling his chin back in a flinch. "I mean, I didn't break in ever, including today."

Ignoring his attempt to cover his tracks, she considered his immediate denial. Although she could be wrong, and he could be an excellent liar, she was inclined to believe his automatic answer.

"Let's go outside and wait for the cops," she said. Having their house searched had made her feel raw and exposed and not at all inclined toward inviting law-enforcement officers inside. From John's comprehending glance and the way he immediately moved toward the door, dragging Stuart along with him, he understood exactly where she was coming from. Molly was struck again by the oddness of having John around, correctly interpreting her subtext and expressions, when just days ago she'd been doing her best to dodge him.

They trooped out onto the porch, the elderly boards groaning under their combined weight. Molly automatically added checking the porch floor to her endless to-do list before realizing that it might not even be her house in a few weeks. Quickly, she shook off the thought. They had a month—possibly more—to track down Jane and drag her to court. She couldn't act as if losing their house was inevitable. She and her sisters were smart and resourceful enough to track down their mom. That was their business, for Pete's sake.

A police squad car pulled up to the curb in front of her house, rescuing her from her thoughts. As two plainclothes officers got out of the vehicle, she had to bite back a groan. These were the same two who'd had the warrant to search her house—Bastien and... She couldn't think of the younger one's name. She was suddenly glad that they'd moved outside. Those two detectives had seen more than enough of the inside of her house. Why couldn't it have been Garcia or even Lieutenant Botha who'd responded to the call? The two detectives were from Denver, in Langston because of the necklace, so why were they responding to a call that was only peripherally related to the theft?

The two cops' expressions were guarded as they approached the porch. As Bastien took in the sight of John, all ripped muscles and ferocious expression, his hand drifted to rest on the butt of his Taser. Molly sensed, rather than saw, John stiffen, and she hurried to speak before something unnecessarily bad could happen.

"Hey, Detectives." She tried to put some cheer into her voice, but she was fairly sure she failed. "Thanks for coming. This one"—she tipped her head toward Stuart and then switched to pointing, wanting to make sure it was clear that she was referring to him and not John— "just broke into our house."

"A lot of these types of things keep happening to you," the younger detective—*Mill*, she thought, finally remembering his name—said with the flat intonation that held a wealth of suspicion. "Your car's stolen and now this. You might want to think about why that is."

Molly rested her hands on her hips, counting in her head so she didn't utter the tempting but unhelpful retort that immediately jumped to her lips. Instead she managed to ask politely, "Why are you here? Aren't you with DPD?"

Mill gave her a sour twist of a smile. "We're working out of Langston for the time being. When we heard this address, we offered to take the call. We're helpful like that."

*Helpful. Right.* Before she could come up with a tactful response, John shifted over, putting his body between her and Detective Mill as he thrust Stuart toward the cop.

"Here. I've been restraining him since he broke in, so he hasn't had a chance to dump his lockpicking tools yet. You'll want to search him before he does." Even though John's voice was polite, his words rang with a command that made Molly wince and brace for the detective's reaction. In her experience, cops reacted badly to having people tell them how to do their jobs—at least, they did when she was the one making suggestions.

"I've got him," Bastien said, escorting Stuart over to the squad car with a tight grip on his upper arm. Stuart immediately began speaking. Although Molly was too far away from the pair to make out what he was saying, she could see his arms waving dramatically, and she suspected that he'd come up with a new story in the time they'd been waiting for the cops to arrive.

Now that she had her irritation under control, Molly shifted over so that John was no longer blocking her view of Mill.

"So, what happened here…this time?" the detective asked. His slight emphasis on the last two words immediately topped off her annoyance levels again. She could feel John's assessing gaze on her, but she ignored it. Whatever the reason for his newly protective manner, she couldn't hide behind him while he dealt with all her problems.

"Stuart over there"—she jerked her chin toward him, noting that he was still gesticulating dramatically as he spoke to Bastien—"knocked on the front door about twenty minutes ago. When we didn't immediately answer, he picked the dead bolt and walked inside. He said that he was in a class with Cara and dropping off some notes she'd asked for, but…" Molly gestured toward Cara in an unspoken invitation to finish her sentence.

"I don't know him," Cara said immediately. "I definitely never asked him for notes."

Mill studied all of them, even though Felicity and Charlie had remained silent since the cops' arrival. "Why do you think he picked the lock?" he finally asked. "Isn't it more likely that the door was unlocked?"

Biting back the sarcastic response that wanted to escape, Molly said semicordially, "We watched the dead bolt turn."

Making a skeptical sound that brought Molly's restrained anger flaring to life, Mill eyed each of them again. She knew he was using silence to get them to talk from sheer discomfort, but she also knew it wouldn't work on any of them. They used the same trick when they were trying to track down skips. Even Cara had questioned her share of cagey friends and relatives of people who'd jumped bail. If Norah had been there, she might have broken into awkward chatter, but she also might have stayed frozen and silent. It was hard to predict how she'd react in social situations.

Several minutes ticked by quietly before Mill spoke again. "Why would someone break into your house?"

"Isn't that a question for Stuart?" Molly shot back, making the detective frown deeply.

"Why are you refusing to answer?"

"Oh, for God's sake..." Charlie muttered, drawing Mill's sharp attention.

"Were you going to add something?" he demanded, and Molly resisted rolling her eyes. Charlie didn't bother holding back her scorn.

"Why would I bother, when you've already made up your mind?" Crossing her arms over her chest,

Charlie leaned back against the doorframe. Normally, she tended to play up her innocent, girl-next-door look, using her dimples and wide Bambi eyes as a tool to get skips and sources to let down their guards and confide in her. Right now, however, her full lips were drawn into a tight frown, and her eyes were narrowed to slits. Molly knew just looking at her sister that she was *pissed*.

"Don't act like you're the innocent victims." Mill's lip was raised in a slight sneer as he gestured at all of them. "When you sleep with dogs and wake up with fleas, don't blame me when you're itching."

Molly blinked, torn between fury and laughter. She tightened her jaw so that neither escaped. Mill must've had *some* self-preservation, because he was moving away from the porch toward the pair by the squad car. "Stay here," he said, as if it weren't their house and they hadn't been the ones to call the police. Molly noticed that both the Villaneaus and Mr. P were on their porches now, watching the scene with a mixture of disdain and patronizing glee.

As they watched Mill join his partner and Stuart, John muttered something under his breath, the sound so low it came out as a rumbling growl.

Molly raised her eyebrows at him before turning back to the scene by the cop car. "Chill, papa bear," she said absently, trying to read Mill's lips as he spoke to Bastien.

At Charlie's choked laugh and Felicity's snort, Molly glanced over to see all of her sisters smirking at her. Even Cara looked to be fighting a smile.

"What?" she asked as her face got hot.

"Nothing." Of course it was Charlie who said it, in

a tone that made it obvious that *nothing* meant the very opposite. "Whatever sex games you like to play are between the two of you. I don't want to know."

"Speak for yourself." Felicity was obviously fighting— and failing—to keep a straight face. "I'm interested."

"Not me, especially since we should be concentrating on how they're letting Stuart go." Cara's tone went from wryly amused to flat, and Molly turned to see that her sister was right. Stuart was walking away from the squad car—no cuffs or even a ticket in evidence— heading toward a bright-green Jeep parked a half block away. When he saw them watching, he gave a jaunty wave. John swore under his breath, but Molly kept her comments to herself that time.

"Of course he drives a Jeep," Felicity said with tones of heavy loathing.

"What?" Charlie asked.

"I hate Jeeps."

"Why?"

"I just do. They're…gross."

"That's weird."

"It's *logical* and *right*."

"You're so strange."

Molly ignored her sisters' argument, concentrating on the two detectives as they headed for opposite sides of the squad car. "Is that it?" she called, unable to keep the sharp edge from her voice. "You're just letting him go after he broke into our home?"

"You really want to drag this out?" Mill yelled back, his words a challenge. "If you do, we can talk about the penalties for making a false statement to police."

From his spot next to his Jeep, Stuart let out a

mocking laugh, and it was Molly's turn to growl as she charged toward the car. She wasn't sure if she was planning on tackling Mill or Stuart, and she wasn't able to find out, since John grabbed her and swung around, putting himself between her and both of her targets.

"Carmondy," she gritted out between clenched teeth, "move."

"You won't win this one, Pax." His tone was surprisingly gentle, considering she was basically snarling at him. "Sometimes head-on doesn't work. We need to retreat and come at them from the side."

"Okay, Sun Tzu." Despite her mocking words, the initial flash of rage had faded, and she shifted back a half step so she wasn't right in John's face. "What's the battle plan, then?" He gave the slightest wince, and she narrowed her eyes at him. "You don't have one, do you?"

"Not yet. Genius takes time."

Even with all the bad things that were happening, that drew a short—but honestly amused—laugh from her. "Fine." She let out a long breath, expelling the last of her frustrated anger at the cops' mishandling of the situation. Turning to her sisters, she said, "I'll text Norah and tell her to come home. Time for another family meeting."

They trooped inside, John bringing up the rear. Although Molly arched an eyebrow at him, he gave her a blank-faced, steady look, and she dropped her silent objection with a shrug. Maybe he wasn't technically family, but John was a wily one with the potential to be helpful. She'd worry about getting too dependent on him later. Right now, the priority was to save their house— and figure out what the heck was going on—and for that, they'd need all the brains they could get.

# CHAPTER 9

NORAH HAD JUST WALKED IN THE DOOR WHEN CARA'S phone beeped. As she checked the screen, her nose wrinkled, and Molly knew exactly who was calling. No one except Barney got that bad a reaction from Cara.

"I can't wait until the month's over and someone else has to take his calls," she grumbled as she poked the screen with an angry finger.

John looked confused, so Molly explained, "Every month, we switch off whose phone gets the calls from our main business line. That way, no one has to give their cell number to clients or informants, and we only have to deal with the Barneys of the world every fifth month."

"Pax Bail Recovery. How can I help you?" Cara asked in a syrupy-sweet voice that made Charlie snicker. When Cara's gaze darted toward Molly, she immediately knew what Barney wanted, and she waved her hands, palms out, in a frantic effort to ward off the pass. From Cara's wicked smile, Molly knew it was a futile effort. "She *is* available. One moment, please."

When Cara tossed her the cell phone, Molly briefly considered dodging and letting it drop to the floor, but then she remembered that money was tight at the moment and they didn't need to be buying more phones. With a silent sigh, she raised Cara's cell to her ear.

"This is Molly."

"Molly Pax, my favorite soon-to-be tenant." Barney's smarmy voice immediately shot Molly's rage to maximum levels.

She fought to keep her voice level and slightly amused. "Haven't you heard the old saying about not counting your chickens before they skip their next court appearance?"

"I'm just counting the chickens that have already skipped town." The smugness in his tone didn't lessen.

Molly briefly debated whether she should let him know that she knew his threat was basically empty—at least for the next four to six weeks—and decided to tell him. She didn't want him to think that he had any power over them...at least not for another month. "Good luck finding a judge to go along with that. No one's going to rule to forfeit her bail until she misses a hearing."

He paused, and she wondered if he was taken aback by her calm comeback or if he was just plotting. "Maybe I'll just have to push to get her preliminary hearing moved up. The public defender assigned to her is Nancy Lehry, who just happens to owe me a favor."

It was Molly's turn to fall silent as she squeezed her eyes closed, as if she could shut out the truth along with her vision. Her lungs squeezed with a fresh jolt of panic, and she fought through it, knowing she needed to keep a calm head.

"All the judges love Nancy. She could easily call in a favor to get her client's hearing moved up." He paused, his glee an almost tangible thing. "Wasn't there some kerfuffle last time Nancy defended Jane? Hmm...let me think..."

Molly's molars met with a click. Everyone in Langston knew what had happened five years ago. She breathed through her nose, trying to bring her anger down to concealable levels, while Barney made a sound that could only be called a chortle.

"Oh, that's right! Jane and Nancy's son-in-law had a thing, didn't they? Things got messy. Nancy's daughter dumped her husband, even though she was going through chemo at the time and had a bunch of little crotch fruit running around. It's all coming back to me now." Only the grossest of men could've taken such pleasure in recounting something so terrible and life-destroying. True to form, Barney sounded positively joyful as he clicked his tongue with false concern. "That has to be awkward for Jane, having a woman who hates her as her attorney."

"I get it, Barney." Molly's voice came out with a gravelly edge, but it was the best she could do when her whole body ached to punch someone—either Barney or Jane, preferably. "What do you want?"

John made a wordless sound of protest, and she glanced away from him, only to find that all her sisters were staring at her as well. Molly didn't think anyone breathed while Barney took his sweet time to answer.

"I thought you'd never ask," he finally said, his voice sickeningly thick with satisfaction. "Just find Sonny and bring him back to jail, and I'll convince Nancy to let bygones be bygones...until Jane's preliminary hearing, at least."

Bitter acid churned in Molly's gut, but she knew she was trapped in a corner. Could Sonny Zarver be any worse than some of the sketchy skips they'd chased when the business was new, though? *So much worse*, a practical voice in her head warned, but she pushed it away. This had to be done. They'd get through it... hopefully. "If we do this, we get thirty percent, plus our usual expenses."

Barney let out a yelp that sounded like she'd just kicked him in a delicate place. "Thirty percent? That's twice the standard. I'm doing you a favor. You should just be happy you have a month to try to track down your felon of a mother."

"Thirty percent." She felt the muscles of her jaw lock into what Cara called her *mule face*. Her sisters knew when she got that look that Molly wasn't about to give in. "Plus expenses."

This time, he just made a pathetic bleat of a whine.

"If you want us to risk our lives by going after Sonny Zarver, then you're going to pay us thirty percent." She cringed at the gasps from her sisters when she said Sonny's name, and she very carefully didn't look at John. From the prickling feeling on her right cheek, he was shooting deadly eye lasers in her direction. She couldn't blame him. It was crazy to accept the Zarver job. There just wasn't any other choice if they wanted to keep their house—their only remaining connection to Victor Chavis, the twins' dad and the only one of Jane's husbands and boyfriends, besides Lono, who'd treated all the sisters like they were his children. The property had been in his family for four generations, and Molly hadn't almost killed herself to pay off the mortgage just to lose their home to Barney Thompson now.

"Twenty," Barney grumbled.

Clenching her jaw even tighter, she shook her head

despite knowing he couldn't see her. "Sonny beat his stepfather to death and then tried to do the same to his mother when she kicked him out. It was sheer luck that she managed to escape. Thirty plus expenses."

"Pax…" John's voice was a mere growl, and the sound shivered down her back and made her thighs tighten on air. Molly still didn't dare look at him. Her sisters were shifting in their chairs with nerves, except for Norah, who'd gone perfectly still except for the too-quick rise and fall of her chest. Shoving down her concern for her sister, Molly concentrated on the sound of Barney's huffing and puffing on the other end of the line instead.

"Fine." Barney spat out the word. "Thirty per-cent—*if* you bring him in within a month. If you don't, then I'll yank your house out from under you so fast your head'll spin."

"We'll get him." Although her calm tone was back, Molly didn't have any of the confidence she was projecting. How was she supposed to track and capture Sonny Zarver, of all people, within four weeks—all while they were searching for Jane and the necklace? It seemed impossible and hopeless, but she wasn't about to let Barney in on that information. "Will you write up the contract or should we?"

"I'll do it." Of course he would. She made a mental note to read through the small print several times to check for tricks. She'd have Cara check, too. Her sister was a whiz with contracts.

"Okay. Text me when it's ready. Bye." Without waiting for him to continue the conversation, she ended the call. There was too much to do for her to waste any more time listening to Barney.

Tossing the phone back in Cara's direction, Molly took a deep breath and met her sisters' appalled expressions.

"Didn't we *just* have this conversation?" John's voice was low and rough, raising goose bumps on Molly's arms for some reason she didn't want to think about. "I thought we agreed that it's suicide to chase after Zarver."

"I don't remember agreeing to that. You lectured, and I pretended to listen." For some reason, it was a hundred times harder to meet John's furious gaze than it had been to look at her sisters. The main reason for that was because she *knew* it was stupid to take the job. There just wasn't any other option right now, not if they wanted to have time to track down Jane. When John made a sound low in his throat and started to say something else, she snapped her head toward him and glared. "It's done. You don't get a say."

Although his glower was just as fierce as hers, he stayed quiet, and she was grateful for that small mercy. She didn't want to hear—especially from John—how idiotic she was being. Turning toward her sisters, she hid a wince. Maybe it wouldn't be from John, but she knew she was about to hear all about her poor life choices.

"Nancy Lehry is Mom's public defender," she blurted out before any of her sisters could say a word. "If I didn't agree to track down Sonny, Barney was going to have her push to move up the preliminary hearing."

"That would be bad," Charlie said, and Molly gave her a look. Of course it would be bad. They all knew that would be bad. Apparently ignoring Molly's silent *duh*, Charlie continued talking. "Fifi and I did the rounds. None of Mom's friends have seen her—or will admit to seeing her, at least—since she was released."

"So, if she's not staying here, and she's not at any of her usual crash spots…" Cara trailed off, but Molly didn't need her to finish to make the logical leap. Jane had skipped town, just like Barney had said she would.

A thick silence settled over them. Molly glanced around their group, seeing worry in her sisters' faces. Even John looked concerned under his stalwart poker face. The tension made her stomach twist, and she forced herself to think constructively. Wallowing in her anger and frustration and helplessness wouldn't save their house.

She clapped her hands together once, breaking the brittle quiet. "Okay. I'm on Sonny duty. Norah and Cara, see if you can get a lead on where Mom might've gone. She had her car fixed, so she either sold it or is driving it—same with my car." Her belly lurched again at the reminder that her beloved Prius was gone, but she pushed away the thought. There wasn't time for moping, no matter how much she'd loved her car. "Give any information you find to Felicity and Charlie." She looked at them. "You two are okay with chasing Mom down?"

Charlie scowled. "You can't go after Sonny Zarver on your own."

Before Molly could assure her sister that she'd be fine, John spoke. "She won't. I'll be with her."

"You will?" Startled, Molly turned to stare at John, but he was still wearing his serious—and expressionless—face, so she couldn't interpret what he was thinking.

"Yes."

Despite her inability to read his expression, she studied him for several moments. Even though she had no idea why he'd inserted himself into their lives and was offering to assist her in running down a skip he'd tried very hard to keep her away from, help was help, and she wasn't about to turn down his offer. "Okay," she finally said, deciding to ponder his motivation later when their lives were back on track. "John's with me, then. Are we all good?" She eyed her sisters, and they all made affirmative sounds or gestures. Only Cara looked torn, her lips pressed together as if she was holding back a torrent of words.

"Something wrong, Cara?" Molly asked.

"Should I drop out of school?" The words tumbled out too quickly, one on top of the other, as Cara refused to meet Molly's gaze. "Just for this semester, I mean. We just started, and I know you could use more help with trying to find Mom and Sonny and all the other jobs we need to take to keep our heads above water. I shouldn't be going to classes when all of you are working so hard to keep this house."

"No." Molly put as much force behind the word as she could. "You've already put off school too long, thanks to Mom taking your tuition money and you helping get the business going. You're not dropping out. Mom's not taking anything else away from us, not if I can help it."

From the way Warrant slunk under the table and Cara's eyes went wide, Molly realized that she must've looked and sounded rather ferocious. She took a breath to try to get her heart to stop pounding so hard.

"I mean it, Cara." Although her voice was calmer, it was no less resolute, and she could see that her other sisters agreed with her. "No more delays. You just have three semesters left and then student teaching. If you get off track now because of Mom's nonsense, you might never finish."

"Molly's right," Charlie said as Felicity and Norah nodded in agreement. "You need to stick this out. Otherwise, you're going to be eighty and still working as a bounty hunter and hating it just as much then as you do now."

"I don't *hate* it." Despite her words, Cara's tone was half-hearted, and Molly raised an eyebrow at her.

"You so hate it."

"As long as I don't have to tackle anyone, or get spit on, or sworn at, or hit on, or talk to mean people, then it's fine."

Charlie snorted a laugh. "That's pretty much my usual day."

"I like the research part," Cara protested, even though she was halfway to laughing as well. "Especially if it's just on the internet. *Especially* if it's internet research while I'm sitting on the patio at the coffee shop, drinking a cappuccino with Warrant sleeping under the table." Warrant shifted at the sound of his name before resettling flat on his side.

Norah gave a small smile. "That's my favorite part, too."

"Okay." Molly blew up her cheeks like a balloon and let her breath out with an audible *puff*. When John made an amused sound, she inwardly cringed at how goofily unattractive the face she'd just made must've looked, and then she immediately scolded herself for worrying whether John found her *attractive* when their world was currently imploding. "Now that we know that Cara's staying in school and everyone has their assignments, let's get to work."

Norah tentatively raised her hand.

Blinking at her sister, Molly resisted the urge to say something sarcastic and just said, "Yes?" instead.

"What about the jobs we were already working on before the...Mom thing happened?"

Molly grimaced. "Try to stay on them as much as possible, but finding Mom and getting her back here in time for her hearing are paramount. Sorry. It's going to be really busy and will almost definitely suck for a while, but we'll get through this."

Her sisters made unenthusiastic grumbles of agreement—although whether they agreed that they'd get through it or that things would suck was unclear— and Molly stood, her gaze finding John. He'd been quiet and stoic through most of the meeting, and his serious manner set her off-balance. She was used to a joking and devilishly teasing John, not this giant, somber statue leaning against her dining room wall.

"Ready for this?" she asked him.

His mouth twitched at the corner, just a tiny movement but enough to make him seem more like the John Carmondy she knew. "If I say no, will that change anything?"

"Not really."

"I figured." This time, his smile was more of a grimace. "Let's go find Zarver, then."

# CHAPTER 10

FINDING SONNY ZARVER WAS EASIER SAID THAN DONE. Molly tapped at her phone screen as she thought, trying to come up with the best plan. She realized that Norah and Cara had spoiled her with their research skills, always handing Molly a file filled with leads and background information for each skip she was tracking. She hadn't started from square zero in over a year.

Realizing that John hadn't started his SUV, even though they were both buckled in, she gave him an inquiring glance.

"What's next?" he asked.

The question took her by surprise. John had been doing that a lot lately, challenging assumptions about him she'd held on to since they'd first met. She'd figured that he'd want to lead, and that she would have to fight to get him to listen to her ideas, but he was just sitting there, waiting for her to tell him how they were going to run the show.

Her eyebrows lifted along with the corners of her mouth. She could work with *this* John Carmondy. "I'm starting from scratch on this one. Up until this point, I've always tried to avoid places where Sonny Zarver and his friends hang out."

He smiled back at her. "Me too."

"So much for that excellent plan." As he made a grunt of amused agreement, she thought about the next step. "Let's start at 200 Bluffside Road."

His gaze snapped to hers, and she took an odd satisfaction in surprising him. "The police station? Isn't that the only place we know is Sonny-free?"

She knew her smile was smug but didn't really care. "There's a sergeant there who owes me a favor."

John sent her another curious look but didn't say anything. He just started the SUV and eased it away from the curb. They traveled in silence for a while, and Molly shifted restlessly, missing her car and the control driving gave her. To distract herself, she pulled up her contacts on her phone and started skimming through them, checking for people with possible connections to Sonny. She narrowed it down to three and sent them each a text, asking if they had any information on Zarver's whereabouts.

Only one responded immediately. Are you crazy?? Why are you messing with him???

Molly must've made a face, because John asked, "What is it?"

"One of my contacts just confirming what a dumb thing we're doing," she said, just as a text from another person came in. NO! "Two of my contacts." There was another buzz from her phone, and she sighed. "All of them. They all think I'm insane for going after Sonny."

"Well…" He trailed off into silence as he pulled into the lot of the law enforcement center. He didn't need to finish his thought, though. Molly knew perfectly well that he considered this a suicide mission…and she didn't disagree.

She tried to mash down that feeling of impending doom as she hopped out of the SUV and headed for the front entrance, but she was only somewhat successful. Apprehension still tagged after her, nipping at her heels like a phantom sheepdog. John caught up to her easily, his huge form falling into step next to her, and she gave him a sideways glance. Despite the strange rivalry or whatever they'd had happening since they met, she had to admit that she was glad he was with her.

He pulled open the door for her, and she stepped inside. Only when she blinked in the brightness of the artificial lights did she realize how dark it had gotten outside. She almost ran into someone heading out the door, dodging out of the way at the last second before she crashed into them.

"Excuse me," she said automatically, a moment before she recognized Detective Mill, the ray of sunshine who'd been at her house that afternoon.

His gaze turned frigid, so she guessed that he'd just recognized her, too. "Back again? What happened *this* time?"

"Nothing to do with you." She always tried to have good relationships with the cops she dealt with in her work, but she was pretty sure that Mill would never be an ally. Besides, he and Bastien would be trotting back to Denver as soon as they wrapped up their case, so she let a bit of her snarky side show. "I won't keep you. I'm sure you have criminals you need to let loose to roam the streets and break into innocent people's houses."

"Innocent?" His tone was thick with sarcasm. "Right."

She was just thinking up a great comeback when a big hand on her lower back nudged her forward past Mill. Although she gave John a minor glare, she allowed him to usher her away from the aggravating cop. Mill muttered something not quite loud enough for her to make out before he shoved open the door and left the building. "What is his deal?" she asked under her breath.

"Who knows, but you're not going to gain anything by getting into a pissing match with him." John kept his hand on her back as they approached the desk sergeant, and Molly allowed it for a few seconds before shifting to the side. His touch disappeared, and she immediately missed the warmth and, even more, the feeling that John had her back.

Shaking off her distracting feelings, she stepped up to the window dividing the main reception area from the desk sergeant's domain. When she recognized who was on duty, she gave him a genuine smile of greeting. "Sergeant Garcia. What are you doing behind a desk? Did you hurt yourself again, or is your knee still giving you trouble?"

His return grin turned into a pained frown as he held up his left arm, showing her the plastic brace on his forearm. "I wish it were just my knee. Everyone's started calling me Sergeant Glass."

She winced sympathetically. "What happened?"

"Slid on some loose gravel and fell." Lowering his injured arm, he gave a shrug. "My wrist took the worst of it."

"At least you didn't land on your face. Protect the moneymaker, right?"

"That's right." He chuckled as his gaze flicked back and forth between Molly and John. "What's with the two of you? You working together now?"

It took some effort, but Molly resisted the urge to

glance at John as she answered. Instead, she kept her gaze locked on Garcia's face. "John's just helping me out with a tricky skip."

The sergeant went quiet for a few moments, still studying them as his expression sobered. "Hope that 'tricky skip' isn't a certain Mr. Zarver."

She made a face. "Are you psychic? Because that's not fair if you are."

"Mooollllly." He dragged out her name in an extended scolding whine before his voice returned to its usual tenor. "What are you thinking? Zarver's bad news. I like you. I don't want bad things to happen to you, but they will, if you hang around Zarver and his pals."

"I know." She did her best to not sound flippant or like she'd heard the same lecture a half-dozen times, even though she had. "I'll be careful. Besides…" She bumped John's meaty biceps with her shoulder, just then noticing that he'd moved very close to her. Although she gave him a funny look, she didn't move away. "Carmondy's on the case with me. I'll just leap behind him and use him for a shield when the bullets start flying."

The sergeant laughed as John gave her a look that was both censorious and wry.

The discussion about Sonny reminded Molly of why they were at the station. "Is Sergeant Blake in?"

"Hoping to mine her brain for nuggets of Sonny info?" Garcia asked with a wicked grin.

"Something like that." She lifted her hands in a *What can you do* motion.

"The answer's no. The sergeant—the *other* sergeant— is out for the rest of the week, and maybe longer. Her kid has chicken pox."

"Chicken pox?" A feeling of dread settled back into Molly's belly. No wonder she hadn't been able to get hold of Blake. Although she knew no one was to blame for a sick kid, she was tempted to throw a mini-tantrum. The loss of her key contact was going to hurt. "Don't parents vaccinate their kids for that now?"

"She did, and he still managed to catch it. Must be a mutant strain." Reaching out to the bottle of hand sanitizer sitting on his desk, Garcia pumped a generous amount into his palm and slicked it over his hands with great care.

Molly watched absently, her brain ticking over possible new plans. "You always know what's going on in Langston," she said, figuring she might as well give it a shot, even if Garcia was giving her a skeptical look as he de-germed his hands. "I don't suppose you could pass along some of Zarver's known associates, could you?"

"You know I can't give you that information." Garcia *tsk*ed at her, even as his grin threatened to break free. "Blake might whisper helpful things in your ear, but I'm not that kind of man." His huff sounded put-on, and he gave her a quick sideways look that gave her hope.

"If you do this, you'll be my favorite cop," she wheedled.

"Really?"

"Well, *one* of my favorites." Sergeant Blake had been too helpful over the years to be replaced thanks to one measly bout of chicken pox.

The door behind Garcia's desk swung open, and Lieutenant Botha stepped through. "Ms. Pax…and Mr. Carmondy," she said as Garcia straightened, his grin falling away. "To what do I owe this double bounty-hunter pleasure? Here to pump my sergeants for information?"

Placing her hand on her chest, Molly plastered on an appalled look when she really wanted to growl with irritation. Garcia had been so close to sharing before they were interrupted, and there was no way that Botha would spill any information. She loved rules and order too much for that. "As if I'd ever do that." She wished she had pearls to clutch. It would've added so much to her faux outrage. "I'm just helping you put the 'community' in 'community policing.'" At John's snort, she smothered the urge to elbow him.

The smooth skin between Botha's perfectly formed eyebrows puckered. "What does that even mean?"

"Just checking in, seeing how all of my cop friends are doing." She turned back to Garcia and gave him her best pleading-puppy expression. He rolled his eyes, but she pressed on, not wanting the visit to have been a total waste. "I'll make sure to visit that great bar you were telling me about. What was the name again?"

His sigh was audible, and Molly turned up the urgency in her wide eyes. "Dutch's," he mumbled as he shifted folders on his desk.

Hope lit in Molly's belly, causing it to untwist slightly. "Right. Thank you." She put a heavy emphasis on the last two words, which made Botha's brows draw even closer together as Garcia sent a hunted look toward Molly.

Now that she had *some* sort of lead, she gave the two cops a wave goodbye and headed for the door, John still sticking close to her side. Once they'd made it outside into the sodium-lit parking area, she grinned up at him. "So...Dutch's. It's a starting place, at least."

"Yeah. I wasn't sure that Garcia was going to come through for us, but you worked your magic."

She peered up at him, checking for any professional jealousy or insincerity. She didn't see any sign of it, though. "What was up with you in there? I would've never thought you could stay quiet for so long."

"You had it handled...well, until the lieutenant made her appearance, but I couldn't do anything to help that. It was just bad luck, and you still got a possible location from Garcia. Good job."

His praise made her too happy. She knew that was dangerous, to allow herself to fill with buoyant air every time he complimented her, but she couldn't seem to help it. "Thanks. I was worried when I heard that Blake's out for a while. She's the one who owes me a huge favor, so I get lots of useful tidbits from her."

Even in the dim light, John's eyes gleamed with curiosity. "What does she owe you for?"

She leaned in, as if she was about to share a huge secret. When he dipped his head down toward her, his attention laser-focused, she whispered, "It's a really wild story...and none of your business."

Trying not to laugh at his look of exaggerated disappointment, she strode to his SUV, needing to put a little distance between them so her brain would start working again. It was that stupid, slight hint of sugar and strawberry scent that did her in every time, which just made her more infuriated with that tiny, bitty part of her that *squeed* with excitement whenever he was close enough to get a whiff.

With a cough, Molly waited for him to beep open the doors, working equally hard at banishing the dangerous flickers of a Carmondy crush and focusing on the next step in tracking down Sonny Zarver. Just the thought of his name was enough to sober her, wiping away every giddy feeling and replacing it with dread.

By the time John was buckling himself into the driver's seat, Molly had a plan in place—or the start of one, at least.

"To Dutch's, then?" he asked, starting the SUV.

"We need to make a detour to my house first."

He turned left out of the parking lot. "Did you forget something?"

"Pants." She flicked at the hem of her sundress, and he shot a glance at her legs before quickly refocusing on the road. "Plus a few other things." She'd been in Dutch's once or twice, although she did her best to stay away from the hole-in-the-wall bar—which had always fit nicely with her previous plan of avoiding unnecessary danger. Just from those few visits, she knew she'd need some of her favorite on-the-job tools.

John cleared his throat. "Pants are probably a good idea. Dutch's is probably the only place you could get tetanus *and* hepatitis from sitting on one of their barstools."

Her lips pulled back in a disgusted grimace. "Thanks for that. I think I'll just stay standing, pants or no pants."

"Good idea."

He pulled into her driveway, and she hurried to get out of the SUV and jogged toward the front door, figuring that John would wait for her outside. When she heard the car door slam, she turned to see him following her, and she fixed him with a look.

"What are you doing?"

His eyebrows rose, matching hers, and his stride didn't slow until he stood right next to her on the front porch. "Getting you some pants."

"I don't exactly need your help with that." Despite her words, she unlocked the door and let him follow her inside. If she stopped every time they disagreed about something, they wouldn't get anything done. "I've been getting myself dressed for several years now."

His chuckle was low and had an odd note of heat, but she immediately dismissed the thought. If it was anything close to that, it was because he was just teasing her. Before he could say anything, the throaty grumble of a car engine turning over caught both of their attention.

The neighborhood was normally quiet—when they weren't getting their house searched by police and having random guys trying to break in. Since the hunting lodge's entrance was on the other side of the resort's property, the only occasional traffic was Mr. P's BMW sedan or the Villaneaus' grown daughter's minivan. Molly knew the sound and appearance of all her neighbors' vehicles. She was even familiar with all her neighbors' friends' and families' vehicles.

She didn't know this car.

She peered through the darkness, trying to make out the driver, but the car was sitting in the gloomy spot between two streetlights. The porch light above her was spotlighting her position and ruining her night vision, and she suddenly felt exposed. The dark interior of the strange vehicle seemed menacing, the unknown making the unseen driver a thousand times scarier than if she'd been able to make out the slightest details. All of the stories about Sonny's horrific misdeeds, both rumored and confirmed, rose in her mind, and her breath caught audibly.

"What's wrong?" John asked, his voice growly,

protective almost, as his gaze swept the street and immediately landed on the unknown car. "Who's that?"

The reminder of John's presence pulled her out of her imagination-fueled worry, and anger shoved out her feeling of vulnerability. "I don't know, but I'm going to find out." This was her neighborhood, her house. What right did this interloper have to make her feel hunted on her own front porch? As she surged down the steps and toward the car, intending to confront the driver, the headlights flashed on, blinding her even further. She hesitated, blinking away the bright haloes burned into her vision, and the car shot forward. The engine roared as the driver accelerated quickly, darting past her and leaving just the shrinking taillights and the acrid scent of burned rubber behind.

"I don't suppose you caught a plate number?" Even as she asked, Molly knew the answer would be no. There was no way that John had caught a glimpse of the license plate. With the glare of the headlights, all she'd been able to tell was that it'd been a four-door sedan.

"No." His voice came from right behind her, surprising her. She'd figured he'd stayed on the porch, but he must've followed during her impulsive attempt to confront the mystery car's driver.

Since the taillights had disappeared into the night, she turned and started back toward the house. John fell in beside her. "Any idea who that was? You didn't happen to get a peek at the driver, did you?" she asked.

"No to both." John's voice was tight with worry. "All I caught was that the car was a late-model Dodge Charger, dark blue or possibly green."

"Oh well." Molly brushed off her disappointment

and a lingering feeling of menace as she returned to the front door and opened it, waving John through into the house. "They weren't actually doing anything wrong, except being somewhat creepy." She had a hunch the cops—especially her two new Denver detective buddies—would've frowned on her doing a citizen's arrest for loitering. Still, with everything that had been happening, she knew better than to dismiss the incident completely. Besides, listening to her gut had kept her alive in a dangerous job over the past few years. If her instincts were telling her that something was off about that mystery car, she was going to listen.

Warrant greeted them, the lazy wag of his tail speeding up when he recognized John, who gave the dog's ruff a vigorous scratching. When John looked up and caught Molly's exasperated expression, he asked, "What?"

"Nothing," she grumbled, not wanting to admit that she was a little miffed that her dog was more excited to see Carmondy than he was to see her, the person who fed him. She *really* didn't want to admit that watching John loving on her dog was annoyingly endearing. Giving herself a mental shake, she started to automatically tell John to make himself at home, but then she caught herself and stuffed the words back down. He didn't need any encouragement to wedge himself even further into her life. Instead, as she headed for the stairs, she simply said, "I'll be right back."

On her way to go change, she saw the door to Norah's tiny bedroom was ajar and stuck her head in to see her sister in her usual position: sitting cross-legged on the bed, hunched over her laptop. Since Norah was obviously caught up in whatever was on her screen, Molly tapped her knuckles lightly against the doorjamb. Her efforts not to startle Norah weren't successful, since she jumped about a foot at the quiet knock.

"Molly! I didn't hear you come in." She straightened her laptop, which had toppled sideways when she'd startled. "You're back early. No luck?"

"Costume change and weapon collection," Molly explained. "Then we'll be heading back out again. All's quiet here?" Even as she kept her voice light, she thought about the car sitting within view of their house. Sometimes, she wished that Norah didn't get so caught up in her research. When she was really interested in what she was reading, the rest of the world disappeared.

"Yeah." Norah stretched her arms toward the ceiling, making her oversize sleep shirt bunch up around her shoulders. "Where's John? Did you ditch him already?"

"No. Not that it hasn't been tempting." The last part felt like a lie, and Molly hurried to change the subject before she did something ridiculous—like blush or explain that she'd been tempted by John, just not to *escape* him. "Is Cara in her room?"

"I think so." A small line appeared between Norah's eyebrows. "She said she had to run a few errands, but that was…" She glanced at the screen, as if checking the time. "An hour ago? Maybe? Sorry, I was caught up in this." As she gestured toward her laptop, worry tightened her features, and Molly hid her irrational concern for Cara being out alone under a reassuring smile.

"I'll check in with her before I leave. There was a car I didn't recognized parked outside, but they drove off as soon as I headed toward them. Did you hear anything?"

Norah's eyes widened. "No, nothing. Who do you think it was?"

Attempting to look unconcerned, Molly waved a deliberately careless hand. She wanted Norah to be watchful but not terrified, and that was a tough balance to achieve. "Probably just a lost tourist. Keep an eye out, though, just in case." Norah was beginning to look hunted, so Molly deliberately switched topics. "Any leads on where Mom might've gone?"

"I might've found her car at a dealership in Colorado Springs." The anxiety in Norah's expression eased as she spoke. "The VIN is off by a couple of numbers, but that could've just been because someone got sloppy entering it."

"Or the dealer suspected it might be stolen, so they're hoping to sell it before anyone tracks it down and they're left without their money or a car," Molly said.

Norah raised a shoulder in a shrug that Molly knew meant she agreed. "Felicity and Charlie are going to check it out tomorrow morning."

"Good job, researching genius." Moving into the room, Molly extended her fist. Norah bumped it while giving her a rare smile. "Any sign of my car?"

"Maybe." She fiddled with her laptop. "Nothing concrete enough to share yet."

"Okay." Shoving down her disappointment and antsy need to push for more answers, Molly moved to the doorway. If pressured, Norah would shut down, which wouldn't help anyone, but it was hard to be patient. "Text me if you need anything. Nice work so far. Don't stay up too late."

"I will, thanks, and I won't." The words sounded

distracted, as if Norah was already back in her research fog.

Molly backed out of the room, pulling the door mostly closed behind her, and ran into a solid form. Whirling around, she shoved away from the person she'd just run into, her fists automatically raising into a defensive position in front of her face. In that second, she recognized the man standing in her upstairs hallway, and her alarm faded—even as her annoyance increased.

"Carmondy," she hissed, dragging him away from Norah's room and into hers so she could yell at him without whispering. "What are you doing up here?"

His linebacker-worthy shoulders lifted and fell. "Just checking on you. I heard your voice but not what you were saying, and I thought you might be calling for me."

"Calling for you? *Calling* for you?" His look of innocence aggravated her even as she struggled not to find him amusing. It was the same reason she had a hard time training Warrant. Both the dog and John were too endearing for their own good, even when they were misbehaving. Biting back any hint of a smile, Molly gave him the sternest look she could manage. "Don't worry. If I ever call for you, you'll know."

"Good to know. Ready?" His gaze flickered down to her still bare legs before slowly making their way back up to her face. "Weren't you going to change?"

Ignoring his question, she rested her hands on her hips and stared at the ceiling, searching for patience. When she realized that none was forthcoming, she sighed heavily and met his eyes again. "Why do you have to be this way?"

"What way?"

The right words escaped her, so she waved her arms in a way that encompassed his whole huge form. "So… lurky. Happy and lurky."

His grin actually widened at that. "Thank you, but I think the phrase you're searching for is happy-go-*lucky*."

"No." Giving up, she dropped her backpack on the floor and headed for her closet. "That's not what I'm searching for. Now, get out."

"You sure you don't need any hel—?"

"Out." She emphasized the single-word command by pointing at the door. Even though he still wore his stupid grin, he obeyed, slipping out of the bedroom and closing the door behind him. Despite knowing that he was safely in the hall and did not, to the best of her knowledge, have X-ray vision, Molly still changed in a hurry, half expecting him to burst in with some half-assed excuse at any moment.

She managed to yank on her cargo pants and T-shirt uninterrupted, so she opened her nightstand drawer and picked through the contents. Since her pants provided multiple, easy-to-reach pockets, she decided to bring along a few more accessories than she normally did: a Taser, two folding knives, a pair of handcuffs, her lock-pick kit, a travel-sized pepper spray, and a few other handy odds and ends.

After twisting her hair into a braided bun at the base of her neck and checking to make sure her backpack had the usual first-aid kit and other essentials she needed when out chasing skips, she couldn't resist a quick glance in the mirror to make sure she looked okay. As soon as her eyes met her reflection, she looked away. What was she doing? This was a dangerous and important thing she needed to do, and she couldn't be getting distracted by her impromptu partner.

Turning resolutely toward the door, she shouldered her backpack and checked off all the items on her mental checklist. She was ready to go. As soon as she'd taken a single step toward the entrance to her room, the door swung open and Mr. Happy-and-Lurky stuck his face inside.

"Ready?"

"What's with your knocking deficiency?" she demanded, although most of the heat in her voice was gone. She was already learning to pick her battles with John, and they'd only been partners for a very short time—not even partners. It was more like they were acquaintances who'd stumbled over the same case... acquaintances who liked to bicker a lot. Recently, that bickering had felt like it bordered on flirting. Wrinkling her nose, Molly made a mental resolution to nip that in the bud. There'd be no living with her sisters if they found out that they'd been right all along about John Carmondy's more-than-friendly feelings toward her... not to mention her own confusing emotions.

"Sorry." He thumped his knuckles against the door-frame. "It's me, John Carmondy. Ready?"

She just rolled her eyes silently at him as she squeezed by him into the hall. Although she managed to squeak by with just the lightest brush of fabric and exposed skin, her traitorous pulse still thumped in double time from his proximity. "I'm just going to check in with Cara first."

The twins' bedroom door was closed, so she tapped on it, waiting to be invited in. When she was met with silence, she stuck her head in, taking in the unoccupied room. Backing out again, she closed the door behind her and typed a quick text to Cara, asking where she was and if she was okay. After a short pause, she sent a check-in message to Felicity and Charlie's phones, too. Everything that had happened was making Molly twitchy, and she didn't like not having her sisters safely within sight. It was silly, since they were just as proficient at taking care of themselves as Molly was—well, most of them, at least—but she still couldn't quiet the instinct to keep her younger sisters safe.

"Is she supposed to be home?" John asked, drawing her attention away from her phone. His expression had grown serious—worried, even—and she blinked at him, a little surprised by how much he seemed to care. Her phone's text alert sounded, pulling her out of her distracted thoughts. It was Felicity, confirming that both she and Charlie were fine—frustrated by a lack of leads, but otherwise fine. John shifted closer, reminding Molly that he'd asked a question about Cara.

Holding out one hand, she turned it side to side. "She's an adult, so she can go where she wants, but I just need to make sure she's okay. That car outside…" She let her voice trail off, not wanting to admit that she was spooked. Her phone beeped again, saving her from having to complete her thought. "She's fine." Molly frowned at the text. "Weirdly cagey, but fine."

"Weirdly cagey how?"

"She's not admitting where she is exactly." She typed as she spoke.

What animal would you be?

"What?" John asked. "That's a random question." He'd moved closer so he could read her phone. Without looking up at him, she put one hand in the middle of his chest and pushed until he took two steps back. Her fingers wanted to linger and explore the rock-solid planes of his upper torso, but she forced her hand to drop.

Panda bear. I'm FINE.

Although she was relieved at Cara's answer, Molly was still immensely curious about where her sister could be. Telling herself firmly that it was none of her business and, as she'd told John, Cara was an adult who could go wherever she wanted without having to explain herself to her nosy older sister, she pocketed her phone.

"Do we need to go save Cara?" John asked, and she shot him a sharp look. He'd asked so calmly, yet seriously, and was obviously fully prepared to mount a sister rescue mission if it was necessary. Her heart did a funny little skip, and she could feel her defenses against John Carmondy crumbling even more. How could she keep from liking him when he went all white knight in defense of her sisters?

"No. She answered the *Did your abductor take your phone and text for you?* question right, so she really is okay. I'm just not sure where she is. Let's head to Dutch's before I'm tempted to track her phone."

John looked a bit disappointed, making her think that he'd been hoping to do some tracking—or that he just wanted to put off their search for Sonny. He gestured toward the stairs, and Molly descended them in front of him. Normally, she liked to keep everyone who wasn't family—actually, everyone who wasn't her *sisters*—in her sights, since her years in bail recovery had taught her that she never could predict what panicked and desperate people would do. Strangely, she was comfortable with John behind her. For some reason, she trusted him to watch her back.

Surprised and a little discomfited by this realization, she glanced at him over her shoulder.

"What?" he asked.

"Nothing." It came out too quickly, and she hurried to face forward again, making a beeline for the front door.

"Now I really want to know." Laughter underscored his words, and she sighed soundlessly.

Unlocking and opening the front door, she didn't look at him as she walked outside. "Sometimes, Carmondy, *nothing* really means *nothing*."

Now she just had to convince herself. Despite her best efforts, her feelings toward John were starting to turn into a very scary and confusing *something*.

# CHAPTER 11

ALTHOUGH HE GRUMBLED, HE DIDN'T ASK AGAIN AS HE followed her out onto the porch, easing the screen door closed so it didn't smack against the jamb like it usually did. She scanned the street, looking for any suspicious people or vehicles. Except for John's SUV, the road and driveways were empty, the neighbors' cars tucked neatly away in their oversize garages. Molly relaxed a hair.

"I guess there *is* an upside to living in a Stepford neighborhood," she muttered, making John laugh.

"I've been wondering why you live here," he said, swinging his arm in a wide gesture that encompassed the entire area, from the pin-tucked lawns to the wrought-iron gate bordering the resort's property. "It doesn't seem to suit you."

"It belonged to Victor, the twins' dad and my favorite of the stepfathers. It's been in his family for decades." As she climbed into the front passenger seat of John's SUV, she wondered why she was sharing personal details with him. It might've been because she was still a little shell-shocked by the realization that she trusted him, or it could've been that he gave off the impression that she could tell him anything, and he'd keep her secrets safe.

Whatever the reason, she found herself spilling the whole—albeit abridged—story once he climbed into the driver's seat. "My mom and I moved in here when I was a baby, so I grew up in this house. After he died…" The word still stuck in her throat. She hadn't been kidding when she'd called him her favorite, even though he'd died when she was just a little kid. "After he died, Mom got the house, and we stayed here, even after she married again…twice."

John made a thoughtful sound as he backed out of the driveway, his headlights reflecting off the somewhat battered garage door. Now that they were talking about how she and her sisters didn't really fit in the neighborhood, the differences were more obvious, even under the cover of night. Despite her best efforts to keep up with repairs and maintenance, their house looked shabby and tired next to its polished and perfect neighbors. No wonder everyone in the area—from Mr. P and the Villaneaus to the owner of the hunting resort—had tried to buy it from them.

"I'm surprised Jane didn't sell it," John said. He winced slightly afterward, shooting her a sideways look as if checking to see if his comment had offended her.

Molly huffed a short laugh. There wasn't anything negative he could say about Jane that one or all of her daughters hadn't at least *thought*. "Me too. She did get a reverse mortgage on it and stopped making the payments, so it was really close to foreclosure. The bank would have it right now if I hadn't taken over paying the bills."

Again, he glanced at her quickly. "How old were you?"

"Too young." The topic was depressing her and

making her anxious at the same time, so she decided to change the subject. "What's the plan at Dutch's?"

"Plan?" He went with the abrupt switch in topics smoothly, and she appreciated his tact—or his short attention span. Either way, she breathed a relieved sigh and settled back in her seat as he pulled up to a red stoplight. "We need a plan?"

"Of course we need a plan." She frowned at his profile. "Several plans, if possible."

"Huh." He rubbed his jaw, the rasping sound of the heel of his hand against day-old beard stubble making her shiver. She wasn't sure if she liked the sound or not. It made her feel overly sensitive, like his rough cheek was brushing the delicate skin over her spine. The mental image immediately sent heat to her face and other places, and she tore her gaze away from him, focusing grimly at the now-green stoplight. "Why?" he asked as he accelerated. She liked how he drove, competent but not cocky, assertive but safe.

"Why? Because we need one! What do you do?" The heat in her cheeks began to gradually subside, although she still didn't want to risk looking directly at him. *He's like an eclipse*, she decided. It was utterly tempting to stare at him, but it was equally dangerous. Carefully keeping her gaze directed through the windshield, she tried to ignore the urge to watch him. "If you don't have a plan, do you just run in there willy-nilly and hope things work out?"

"There's no willy-nilly-ness." That was the John Carmondy she was most familiar with, his faux offense ruined by the amusement clear in his voice. "I just go with the flow."

"Go with the flow," she repeated flatly. "I don't like that plan. That's how you end up in the dumpster behind Dutch's, possibly missing some fingers or your tongue."

He winced, looking a little horrified as he pulled up to the curb and parked in the lot across the street from the bar. "Why would I be missing my tongue? How would a plan protect my tongue?"

"If you fail to plan, you plan to fail, and failing at Dutch's would be very bad."

"I still don't see how my fingers or tongue would be in danger."

She waved dismissively, remembered her vow to stop doing that, and sat on her hand. She wondered how many times she'd made that gesture without noticing and grimaced. Although she caught John's curious look as she tucked her fingers beneath her butt, she ignored it. "Arguing about it isn't going to get us anywhere. I have a plan. Let's go."

As she got out of the SUV, she pretended not to hear John's sputtering noises and bit back a smile. Once she closed the door, she didn't wait, but strode down the sidewalk toward Dutch's. Langston didn't really have an official *bad* part of town, but the area they were in was probably the least pleasant. Dutch's was in the industrial east end of Langston, surrounded by warehouses and gated yards enclosed by chain link and razor wire. The streets were dimly lit, the sodium lights spread thin, leaving deeply shadowed sections between the occasional pools of pale illumination.

The boxy buildings and narrow streets, as well as the way the rectangular shadows crept well past the curb into the lane, gave Molly a claustrophobic feel, and she quickened her pace. She didn't want to say it, but she was glad to have John with her. Although she would've hated to pull any of her sisters away from their work finding Jane, Molly would never have ventured into this neighborhood—and definitely not into Dutch's—alone. She was brave, but she wasn't stupid.

Before she'd gotten halfway down the block, John caught up with her. "So?" he asked.

"What?"

He huffed impatiently, and she had to hold back another grin. John's dramatic noises and gestures were unexpectedly endearing, not that she'd ever admit that to him. "What's the plan?"

"I thought you wanted to willy-nilly it."

"Not if *you* have a plan. If there's a plan, then I want to be part of the plan, and not just find out later that I was an unknowing part of someone else's machinations. I want to be part of the inner circle." He sketched a curved line in the air that encompassed both of them.

"Fine." She sighed, long and audibly, pretending as if she were horribly put-upon. "If Sonny's there, I'm going to text a couple of deputies to head this way. Then I'm going to get in his face and distract him while you come up behind and cuff him. We'll take him outside, put our backs to a wall, and wait for the cops to arrive and take him off our hands."

He was quiet for a few moments before he admitted, "That's not a bad plan."

"I'm an excellent plan maker." She wasn't going to be modest about one of her few solid skills. "I also have a plan B and a plan C in case something goes awry."

"Are you going to share with the class?"

They'd almost reached the door of the nondescript building, and a big, crabby-looking guy was watching them approach—the bouncer, Molly guessed. She lowered her voice. "Let's hope for plan A. Otherwise, just follow my lead."

Ignoring John's low groan, Molly pulled her ID from one of her many pockets and extended it to the waiting bouncer. Although he scowled at her, he accepted the driver's license, his gaze running over her in a way that wasn't sexual, as if he was evaluating the likelihood that she'd get into a fight. It was a welcome change and a cautiousness that Molly could rally behind, so she stood still and quiet as he finished his assessment. As he handed back her driver's license, he gave her the smallest, tightest dip of his chin, which she took as approval. Obviously, he couldn't tell that she tended to tackle people rather regularly.

He regarded John more sourly, and Molly couldn't blame the bouncer. After all, it was obvious that Carmondy would win whatever brawl he was involved in. For a moment, she wasn't sure if he'd be allowed in.

"Watch yourself," the bouncer finally grumbled, and Molly let out a silent breath of relief that she wouldn't have to go it alone. She slipped past him with John close behind her. Once she'd made it through the narrow entryway that seemed like a fire tragedy waiting to happen, she paused to examine the bar.

From the warehouse-like exterior, she'd expected something huge, but the main section of the bar wasn't very big. She couldn't exactly call it cozy, but she could see the entire space from her spot by the entry, even with the low mood lighting. The old-school rock music was loud but not breath-stealing-ly deafening like a club would be. The place was busy but not packed, and the crowd was…interesting. She saw some tatted and pierced twentysomethings, a handful of biker types in their sixties, a couple of hard-faced middle-aged guys in suits at a booth toward the back, and even a couple of people wearing cowboy hats.

"Eclectic place," John said in her ear, as if he'd read her mind.

"Yeah." She ignored the brush of his breath across her ear and the side of her neck, trying to stay focused on their objective. "Do you see him?"

"No."

On first scan, she didn't, either, and her heart sank at the death of plan A. It had been such a simple and pain-less plan, too. *On to plan B*. Straightening her shoulders, she moved toward the bar. Before she reached it, she caught a flash of movement in the corner of her eye. Swiveling her head around, she grabbed the briefest glimpse of Sonny Zarver before he disappeared down a hallway marked Bathrooms.

"There he is," John said, but she was already moving, weaving in and out of the crowd toward the spot where Sonny had disappeared. She didn't want to take the time to text the deputies, worried that he would slip away while she was busy on the phone. John would just have to sit on him while they waited for the cops to arrive. The tiny smile that touched her mouth at the mental image disappeared quickly as the patrons seemed to pack in tighter around her. Over the sound of the music, there was a muttering rumble, and Molly increased her speed, elbowing her way through the thickening crowd.

From the glares and sneers being directed her way, she figured this group must be Sonny fans, and the sooner she and John could get out of Dutch's, the better.

One of the bikers, a guy almost as big as John, stepped into Molly's path, bringing her to an abrupt halt. With an impatient sound, she tried to skirt around him, but he shifted, blocking her again.

"Move," she demanded impatiently, locking away the slight tremor of nerves that wanted to make her fingers shake, and the biker narrowed his eyes at her. With him right in front of her and others pressing closer on all sides, Molly felt as if the oxygen in the bar had thinned, and she fought to keep any sign of her growing unease from showing. Although she normally wasn't claustrophobic, the tension of the crowd, the sour smell of alcohol and anger, seemed to shrink the space. It was too hot, too close. A tickling drop of sweat ran down her lower back.

Before the stranger could say anything, John leaned over her shoulder so that his face was just inches from the biker's. Molly suddenly felt as if she could take a full breath again. Although John was just slightly taller than the other guy, he managed to loom over him, his expression so ferocious that even Molly had to stop herself from shying away from him, even as she felt the urge to move closer.

The stranger hesitated, his gaze flicking between Molly and John, and she took the opportunity to swerve around his bulk and head for the spot where she'd last seen Sonny. Although it was too loud in the bar to hear anyone's footsteps, she could feel John at her back, a wall of safety protecting her from the hostile patrons.

He'd apparently gotten away from the biker without an unpleasant altercation.

The crowd had massed around the entrance to the bathroom hallway, and Molly muttered rude things under her breath as she worked her way through the throng. She wasn't sure if the hostile glares she was receiving were because she was chasing Sonny or because she was throwing a thousand fouls worth of elbows. She didn't care either way, still pressing forward, needing to get clear of the crowd.

A hand on her arm had her swinging around, fist clenched and ready to swing, when she realized that John had her in his grip. She didn't punch him, but she stayed tense, the aggression of the bar patrons putting her on edge. In just the few seconds she'd stopped pushing forward through the crowd, they'd closed in, one woman even getting close enough to step hard on her foot. Mentally thanking her steel-toed boots, Molly shoved the woman away as John tugged her behind him.

With Carmondy in front, using his significant bulk to clear a path, they moved much more quickly until they reached the hallway where Sonny had disappeared. There were two bathrooms and an emergency-only exit that warned an alarm would sound if the door was opened. Molly was glad to see it, since that meant Sonny had to be in one of the bathrooms. Even with the loud music and the angry mutters of the patrons, she would've heard the fire alarm if Sonny had left through that exit.

"Thanks," Molly said to John once they'd left the worst of the crowd behind. As soon as the press of hostile strangers lightened, her heart rate slowed, and she could take deeper breaths. "Now I know what it'd be like to be mobbed by zombies." As John chuckled, she felt herself relax slightly, comforted by the warm, familiar sound, and gestured toward the women's bathroom. "Check the men's, and I'll look in here."

He nodded and turned toward the men's room as she shoved open the door to the women's. She entered cautiously, worried that a smaller—but just as angry—crowd of women would be waiting to poke her eyes out with their stilettos or stomp her into the tile with their motorcycle boots. To her relief, the bathroom seemed empty. As the door swung shut, muffling the music from the bar, she eyed the dingy space. Her boots tapped against the worn tiles, her gaze taking in the shadowed stalls and the crack that ran up the dirty, tarnished mirror. She glanced back at the door, tense at the possibility of someone following her into the small room. She could usually hold her own, but there were a lot of people right outside the bathroom who were obviously on Sonny's side, and she couldn't fight off an entire mob by herself.

Reaching out, Molly shoved the first stall door open, using a little too much force. The door banged into the partition, making her jump and then feel like an idiot for scaring herself. Shifting to the second stall, she pushed on it more gently this time. The door swung open, revealing a second empty stall, and she exhaled hard, her shoulders relaxing slightly. As she peered around the bathroom again without finding any possible hiding places, she laughed at herself. This search for Sonny was making her ridiculously jumpy.

Cautiously, she cracked the door to the hallway, finding it empty. As she slipped out, the other bathroom door swung open, and she pivoted around to face it, automatically falling into a defensive position. When she realized it was John, she straightened, her fists returning to her sides.

"Nothing?" she asked, even though it was obvious he wasn't dragging a full-grown man behind him.

"Empty."

They both turned toward the exit door. "The alarm must be disabled," Molly said as she hurried over. Despite her certainty, she held her breath as she shoved against the release bar, ready for the piercing squeal of the fire alarm. The door swung open silently, and she stuck her head outside.

The chilly air brushed against her damp face, making her realize how warm the bar was. She peered down the dim alley, checking both directions. Except for the dumpster that she'd warned John about, the narrow lane was empty. Frustration rose in her chest, squeezing her lungs. Sonny'd had too much time to get away. The crowd had succeeded in giving him enough of a head start to escape. Without a direction, Molly knew they had no hope of finding him.

John made an irritated sound, and Molly turned to meet his gaze. "I know. It sucks. At least we know he hasn't left town…yet. Should we go back and see what we can pry out of the zombies? Someone has to know where he's been crashing."

He looked unhappy about this idea. "That's a pretty hostile bunch. You shouldn't go back in there."

Although a big part of her bristled at the implication that she couldn't take care of herself, an even bigger part was relieved. She didn't want to question the bar patrons, and John was giving her an out. She'd be an idiot to insist on endangering them for a slight chance that someone in the crowd was willing to talk.

Letting out a disappointed huff of air, she stepped into the alley. When John didn't immediately follow, she turned to raise a questioning eyebrow. "You weren't planning on staying, were you?" Her stomach churned with concern at the thought of him alone in Dutch's. Sure, he was a strong guy, but even he couldn't fight off dozens of people if they meant him harm. Who knew how many were armed, too. The bouncer hadn't checked the two of them for weapons, and they weren't even regulars.

"No." John finally followed her out, and she released the door so it swung shut behind him. "I was just surprised you didn't insist on staying."

She shrugged, not wanting to admit that she'd considered it out of foolish pride, even though it had just been for a moment or two. "I have a greater sense of self-preservation than that."

"I..." Whatever he had been about to say was lost when his voice trailed off, his eyes locked on the back of a neighboring building. Molly followed his gaze to a door that was cracked open just an inch or two. Turning her head, she exchanged a speaking look with John, and they both moved quietly toward the slightly open door.

"You armed?" he asked so quietly that she could barely hear him.

"Depends how you define arms." Slipping her Taser from her pants pocket, she held it at her side. "You?"

"No gun." His gaze stayed fixed on the dark gap between the door and the frame as they moved closer to the building. "I do have arms, though."

She was pretty sure he flexed, although her attention, like his, was focused on the slightly open door. A touch of amusement ran through her, but it was quickly swallowed by apprehension. Who knew what kind of danger hid in the shadows of the warehouse?

When they were just a few feet from the door, Molly reached her free hand toward the edge, intending to push it open, but there was suddenly a huge man in her way. With a glare at the broad back in front of her, blocking her way and even her view of the entry, she dodged around him, giving him a sharp elbow in the side. Even if he was just trying to be chivalrous, it was still a ridiculous thing to do.

Easing the door open, she took a cautious step inside, grateful for John's watchful presence at her back. The murky ambient light illuminated the interior just enough to see shadows and forms. Dust and the lingering hint of old chemicals prickled her nose. Before she could take a second step, a darting movement caught her attention. Molly sucked in a startled breath and spun to face the threat, her entire focus on who—or what—was in the dark space with them. Before she could race after whoever it was, the world behind them lit up, whiting out her vision. She didn't have time to think or plan or even duck before a ferocious *boom* sounded, so loud that she felt it through her entire body.

*John!* her brain screamed, even as she knew it was too late to help him. The explosion had already sent her flying forward, weightless, from the force of the blast.

# CHAPTER 12

THE FLASH OF LIGHT AND CRASHING *BOOM* OF THE EXPLO-
sion blinded and deafened Molly as she flew through the
air, the sudden, unexpected shock of it stealing her ability to think. The floor came flying up to meet her face,
and she automatically executed a dive roll. Her palms
connected with the gritty concrete floor as she tucked
her head and curled her body, letting her momentum
carry her through the somersault and onto her feet. A
tiny, functioning portion of her brain thanked Felicity for
forcing them to practice tumbling moves over and over
until the motions were burned into her muscle memory.

She crouched for a fraction of a second, not sure what
was happening and disoriented by the flickering, changing lights and smoky smell. A crashing sound next to her
jerked her out of her frozen paralysis. Twisting around,
lifting her fists instinctively in front of her face, she saw
John sprawled on the floor, wooden pallets scattered
around him. Apparently, he hadn't landed as gracefully
as she had.

Before she even thought about moving, she was
already rushing to crouch next to John's large, motion-
less form. Her heart thudded with dread as she took in his
closed eyes and limp body. He was normally so strong
and dynamic that it was horribly wrong seeing him lying

there so still. With a hand that trembled despite her best attempt at staying calm, she reached to check his pulse. Before her fingers could touch his skin, his eyes blinked open, and relief poured through her in a dizzying rush. His eyes went from fuzzy to sharp, focusing on Molly.

Realizing that her hand was still outstretched, reaching for his neck, she dropped her arm to her side. "Are you okay?" she asked.

"Yeah." The answer was more of a grunt than a word as he pushed up into a seated position, his gaze never leaving her. "What about you? Are you hurt?"

"I'm fine." Resisting the urge to help him, she kept her hands to herself with a great deal of effort. She watched him as he moved, taking in the flash of a grimace before he smoothed his expression into neutral blankness. Even when he was obviously in pain, he kept his attention locked on her, his gaze roaming her body as if checking to make sure that she'd been telling the truth about not being injured.

His concern warmed a part of her, even as her own worry had her fighting the need to hold him upright as she checked for hidden injuries. Only when she'd reassured herself that he wasn't going to fall over unconscious or start spurting blood from some yet-unnoticed wound did she stand and turn toward the open door.

The alley and the back of Dutch's could be seen, since the door had swung open completely when the explosion had sent Molly and John flying. Some debris and remaining parts of the bar's back wall were burning sluggishly, illuminating the blackened hole leading into the men's bathroom. Water sprayed from broken and twisted pipes, hitting some of the flames with a hiss of steam. Curious faces peered at her through the new hole in the wall, and she could hear the excited chatter of the bar residents. From the lack of panic, she assumed that no one in Dutch's had been seriously hurt by the blast.

At the faint sound of sirens, she glanced back at John, who'd gotten to his feet. He appeared to be relatively steady, so she closed the door leading to the alley, shutting out the view of the damaged bar. They'd had enough encounters with law enforcement for one day. Besides, there was someone else in the building. She'd seen a movement just seconds before the explosion. If they could track down Sonny Zarver after all, it would make braving the hostile bar crowd and the explosion worth it. They needed to show something for this hellacious night. The toe of her boot hit something that skittered across the floor. She frowned at it until she realized it was a piece of her Taser. The rest of its remains were scattered across the corridor, and she sighed. It had been her favorite.

As she moved past John, he lifted his eyebrows in a quizzical look but didn't question her. Instead, he fell in behind her as she moved down the hallway. His lack of argument made her wonder if he'd hit his head. It wasn't like him to obey passively. She gave him another sharp look over her shoulder. His eyes seemed clear and focused, and he appeared to be walking in a straight line. Concentrating on making her way deeper into the building, Molly forced herself to quit obsessing over John's possible injuries. If Sonny was still in the building, their lives could depend on her not being distracted.

She followed the scuffs on the dusty floor, careful to keep an eye out for any sounds or movements and once again grateful for John's strong presence at her back. The sirens were growing loud enough to be heard inside the closed-up warehouse, and Molly frowned as she moved carefully along the hallway. The emergency vehicles were making it hard to hear if someone else was sneaking up on them. If Sonny was around the next corner, she wanted some advance warning.

A hand settled on her shoulder, making her jump in the split second before she recognized the touch as John's. He nudged her to the right, pointing over her shoulder with his other hand, and she immediately saw that the tracks they were following had indeed turned. She gave the hand still resting on her shoulder a pat in thanks as she switched directions.

The footprints led to a boarded-up window, the broken panes of glass all replaced by sheets of plywood. She pressed and tried to wiggle the boards, but everything was tightly secured. Frowning, she turned toward John, confused by how Sonny—or whoever they'd been following—could have gotten through this particular window.

Before she could voice her thoughts, a shadow moved behind John, catching her attention. The figure lifted a long, thin shape high above his head, and time seemed to freeze as she stared at the menacing threat. Sucking in a harsh breath, Molly knotted her fists in the front of John's shirt and threw herself back, dragging him along with her. Her back hit the concrete floor hard, knocking the wind out of her. John followed her down, his bulk tumbling toward her, and she stiffened, preparing for the sure-to-be-painful impact. When it didn't come, she opened her eyes to see that he'd caught his weight on his hands braced on either side of her body. For a fraction of a second, they both froze, his chest pressing against her just hard enough to make her feel protected.

She sucked in shallow breaths, her heart racing from danger and—as poorly timed as it was—John's unexpected proximity. The moment was gone in less than a blink as John grabbed her and rolled. Startled, she went with it, twisting out of the way just as the end of a two-by-four came crashing down where their heads had been. As soon as they were clear, John was on his feet, chasing their attacker back down the hallway. John glanced back over his shoulder, and Molly waved him on, still unable to take a deep enough breath to speak. Although he frowned, his concern evident even in the frantic moment, he followed her silent direction and continued his pursuit.

Pulling herself into a sitting position, Molly shuffled over until she was propped against a wall. She didn't want anyone sneaking up behind her, in case Sonny—or whoever had tried to bash their heads in—wasn't alone. Once her shoulder blades were pressed securely against the wall, she focused on getting her breath back.

As soon as she was breathing semi-normally again, she pushed to her feet and headed after John. Now that they were separated, the silent emptiness of the corridors seemed especially spooky, and the echo of Molly's boots against the concrete floor sounded much too loud to her own ears. She quieted her footsteps and resisted the urge to call out to John. He could very well have chased his quarry right out of the building and down the alley, and she didn't want to announce her presence to anyone else who might be lurking in the dark.

The stacks of boxes and pallets absorbed the sounds of her footsteps, somehow making the warehouse seem even eerier than if the space had echoed. It made her feel as if anyone could be creeping up on her or waiting in the shadows just ahead, preparing to grab her as she walked by. Her pace slowed as she peered into the dark corners, finding imaginary menacing figures in every innocuous shape.

A clang rang out, and Molly's muscles tensed as her body prepared for a fight, before she realized that her foot had hit a discarded scrap of metal, sending it spinning to hit the wall. Her shoulders lowered slightly, but her hands didn't drop to her sides. Instead, she walked with her fists raised, ready to take on whatever was hiding in the darkness. One of the shadows detached from the others, and she rocked back, hissing as she sucked in a reverse gasp. Her body automatically fell into a defensive position as the towering figure stepped closer, looking huge and dangerous in silhouette.

"It's just me." John's voice was low but immediately recognizable as his, and all of the tension drained out of her, leaving her feeling almost too limp to stand. He stepped closer, and her gaze ran over his face. She felt enormously grateful to see those familiar features.

"Lost him?" she asked. Although her voice was quiet, it still seemed too loud, echoing through the empty space.

"Yeah." John grimaced. "He's fast. By the time I realized he wasn't in front of me anymore, he was long gone."

Molly sighed, partly in disappointment, and partly from sheer exhaustion. After multiple adrenaline rushes in such a short time, her body was calling it quits. Turning, she headed toward the front of the building.

The shadows and the missing skip were still out there, however, reminding her that she couldn't relax yet. The threat wasn't eliminated.

"Where are you going?" John asked softly, falling in beside her. He appeared to be in better shape than her tired self, his eyes alert and his head turning from side to side as he kept a lookout for possible danger. There was tension to his muscles, like he was prepared to take on whatever emerged from those menacing shadows. Having John on guard allowed her to shift out of alert mode, and she let him check for danger as she focused on finding their way out.

"A front exit...hopefully." Molly hid a shiver that ran through her as she stared into the murky dimness in front of them. If it led to another dead end... The last thing she wanted was to get lost in a creepy abandoned warehouse where they'd both nearly been killed.

John made a wordless sound of comprehension, his intense alertness making it clear that he was just as eager to escape the building as she was. They moved quickly but cautiously in mutual silence, John's head still swiveling and his gaze sharp. Molly was beginning to feel like she was trying to walk through slowly setting cement, and she started to despair that they'd ever find a way out of this gloomy, spooky warehouse.

They turned yet another corner, and Molly's stomach gave a tiny jump of excitement when she saw a double door—that wasn't chained shut. As they drew closer and she glimpsed the battered and unlit Exit sign above the door, she almost burst into tears of sheer relief. Luckily, she managed to drag the remains of her will together and keep her exhausted emotions in check...just barely.

John eased one side open as she pushed the release bar on the other, opening it a few inches and checking the area in front of the building. All looked still, the empty street feeling almost welcoming after the crowded, shadowed warehouse, so she slipped out and fell into step with John.

As they passed the space between the warehouse and the neighboring building, they both glanced at the spectacle taking place at the back of Dutch's. Emergency lights flashed, and someone—the firefighters, most likely—had set up bright-white floodlights that made the area glow like a beacon. There were cops all over, as well as a growing crowd of onlookers, and John gave an audible sigh.

"Guess that means I won't be picking up my car until tomorrow morning," he said a bit mournfully as they continued down the street.

"It'd be best, unless you want to explain why we're not bombing suspects tonight. Personally, I'd rather drag my tired ass home and then hash it out with Langston PD tomorrow if we have to."

From the sound he made, John did not want to stick around to explain things to the cops, either.

"Let's get the car tomorrow morning. If the cops notice it in the lot and run the plates, you could just say that you had too much to drink, so you called for a ride long before the bar exploded." Molly felt a slight pang of guilt for getting him into this mess, so of course she overcompensated to try to make up for it. "You can stay at my house tonight, if you like."

She immediately felt his gaze on the side of her face, but she kept her eyes focused firmly forward, even as she felt goose bumps prickle her skin at the realization that she'd just invited John Carmondy to a sleepover.

When he didn't respond, she rushed to add, "The buses pretty much stop running at ten, but we could get a ride for you. If Charlie's back, I can use her car, or we could get a Lyft." Babble threatened to spill over, so she clamped her lips together and forced herself to wait for John to respond.

"I'll stay at your house."

She cocked her head as she studied him, unable to read his expressionless face and even tone. "Okay." Now that the sleepover was confirmed, panicked thoughts started working their way in. Jane's room was still a disaster area, her mattress sliced to ribbons, so that wouldn't work for a guest room. He couldn't stay in the twins' room or with her and Fifi or in Norah's tiny cave, so he'd have to go on the couch. Her shoulders relaxed a little after she came up with a solution that didn't involve John bunking with *her*.

The thought of her sisters reminded her that she hadn't checked on them in a while, and she pulled out her phone to see a couple of text messages had come through during the excitement in the warehouse.

"Everything okay?" John asked as she read them and typed a response.

"Charlie and Fifi want to keep following a lead on Mom, so they'll be gone for a few days." Although she kept her voice casual, her heart did the funny little squeeze and hop it always did when any of her sisters were out chasing a skip without her.

Somehow, John must've caught on to something in her tone, because he looked at her sharply. "What's wrong?"

"Nothing." When he narrowed his eyes at her, like he thought she was prevaricating, she waved a hand. "I'm just being an overly concerned big sister, that's all." She dropped her phone back in one of her pants pockets. "I do this every time they head out on their own. It's like I forget that they're adults—*capable* adults."

"Understandable, since it sounds like you pretty much raised them." Even though John's voice was relaxed, Molly noticed that he was still keeping a close eye on their surroundings, from the shadows between the buildings to the occasional vehicle that rolled past. She was grateful that he was alert, since she knew she was too tired and fuzzy-headed to notice anyone unless they ran up and screamed in her face. Shifting closer to John, she took reassurance in the brush of his sleeve against hers, a reminder that there was another capable adult present who would allow her to be off her game for once.

He glanced at her curiously, reminding her that they were having a conversation. "Hmm? Oh, right. Yeah, I guess I did act like the mom…even to Jane." When the mention of her mother didn't dredge up the usual vivid anger, Molly knew she really was exhausted. She yawned widely.

"Tired?" he asked.

"Adrenaline crash." The conversation faded, and Molly fought to keep her eyes from closing. When they finally turned onto her street, she'd never been so grateful to see her neighbors' ultra-neat lawns. Even as exhausted as she was, she still checked to see if there were any mysterious vehicles parked beside the curb, but the road was empty. A knot in her stomach unwound at this small mercy. She didn't think she had it in her to chase after another strange, lurking vehicle, not until she'd had a good night's sleep.

As she crossed the yard and climbed the porch steps, she woke up a little as she peered into the shadows. As Stuart's unwelcome visit had proved, all the wrong people knew—or would soon find out—about Jane's theft and subsequent arrest, and they'd be descending on the house like felonious vultures. She huffed a laugh, drawing John's curious gaze.

"Maybe we should hang a sign on the door, telling everyone that the necklace isn't here," she said. "That might cut down on the number of opportunists trying to break in."

John made a noncommittal sound in the back of his throat. "Are you sure it's not?"

Instantly, all of Molly's hackles were up as she turned to face him. Of course he had an ulterior motive. What else would explain how he went from trying to steal her skips out from under her to Mr. Helpful Backup Man? She squashed a rush of hurt that made her insides as tender as a bruise and stoked her anger instead. Since she was two steps higher than John, their eyes were almost level, and she used that unusual advantage to put extra power behind her glare. "Why are you asking? Is all this a scheme to get your hands on the necklace?"

His eyes widened as his hands came up, palms facing her, as if he were warding her off. "Whoa. No, of course not."

"Uh-huh." Crossing her arms, she didn't break their stare, even though she was pretty sure she saw a flash of hurt flicker over his face. She steeled her spine, reminding herself that he was a good actor. There was no reason her distrust should injure his feelings. Besides, she'd said things that were a lot meaner than that before, and he'd simply grinned and let her insults roll right off his back. "If you're not hunting for the necklace, than what's all this about?" She gestured broadly, indicating everything that had just happened to them.

"What's *what* about?" His already deep voice lowered even more, until it came out in a rumbly growl that made her shiver. What was it about John Carmondy that he could turn her legs to jelly just by talking? There was something very wrong with her. His annoyed tone shouldn't affect her this way. "Me being nice? You think I can't be a decent person without having an ulterior motive? Good to know exactly what you think of me."

"Why wouldn't I think that? When have you ever done anything for the sake of being 'nice'?"

"I'm always trying to help; you just never accept it!"

Molly made a scoffing sound. "When have you tried to help—before this whole mess started, I mean?"

"All. The. Time." His eyes were narrowed, and his mouth was set in a grim line. Molly was trying very hard not to get distracted by how aggravatingly attractive he looked when he was angry. "That skip who tried to jump you at the gas station in Franktown? Then there was the one whose mother chased after you with a hammer. *And* the guy who started throwing bottles of organic olive oil at you when you cornered him in Whole Foods. Any of these ringing a bell?"

The annoying thing was that they did ring a bell— all sorts of bells, actually. Each time, Molly had assumed that John just happened to be in the right place at the right time to help, thanks to him chasing her skips. She grimaced, feeling the first tentacles of guilt snaking through her. It was getting clearer and clearer that her sisters had been—obnoxiously—right. Molly had been oblivious. "I thought you just wanted to steal jobs from me."

His expression softened minutely. She wouldn't have noticed if she hadn't been staring at him, just inches from his face. Sometime during the argument, without realizing it, she'd moved closer to him... *really* close. "Well, that *was* a fun side benefit, but you started it."

Molly sucked in a breath, bracing herself to apologize, but the front door swung open before she could get any of the words out. She turned around to see Cara leaning against the doorjamb, wearing her sleep shorts and a tank, her dark-brown hair rumpled from moving restlessly against a pillow. "If the two of you get any louder, Mr. P is going to call the cops again."

Seeing her sister's sleepy face instantly drained all of Molly's adrenaline, her utter exhaustion waiting to take its place. "Ugh. Sorry. C'mon, let's go in." She directed her words to both John and Cara.

Cara took a step back, swinging the door open wide to allow them room to enter, but John gestured for Molly to go in first. His expression was mostly wiped clear, but she could tell there were storm clouds hiding behind his neutral visage. He didn't immediately follow her in, and Molly turned around to look at him. Their gazes snagged and held, making her pause as she tried to read his thoughts. She was a little overwhelmed by the knowledge that he'd been trailing after her this whole time with the intent of keeping her safe, rather than—well, in addition to—wanting to steal her skips. Her expression must've shown her remorse because, with a sigh that she couldn't interpret any more than she could read his expression, he lost more of his tension and stepped inside.

Molly found herself exhaling a relieved breath, not knowing exactly what had just happened, but glad that it had ended the way it had. If he'd stomped off into the night, she would've felt unsettled and antsy and, she admitted grudgingly, she would've worried about him until she'd heard that he'd gotten home safely. Even though he was a grown man with a cell phone and a brain who was perfectly capable of getting from one side of their small town to the other, she still would've been concerned.

As a fill-in mom, she couldn't help it. Worrying was what she did. Besides, now that he was neck-deep in the mess her mom had created, he was in as much danger as she and her sisters were. Even though John had willingly helped out, fully knowing what he was getting himself into, Molly couldn't help but feel guilty—and grateful— that he'd made that sacrifice.

As they entered the living room, her gaze was caught by the rumpled blanket on the couch. "Were you sleeping down here?"

"I was," Cara confirmed mid-yawn. "I sleep like the dead, but I figured if I was down here, I'd wake up if Stuart came back and tried breaking in again. Now that you're here, I'm going up to my bed. That couch is the worst. It feels like a bunch of rocks covered in upholstery."

Carefully avoiding John's gaze, Molly made a *hmm* sound. "Once all of this is over and we have some spare cash again, we're getting an alarm system." She very deliberately didn't mention that they might not be living in that house after everything was said and done.

Cara offered a good-night wave and climbed the stairs as John turned toward Molly. Reluctantly, knowing he was about to complain about sleeping on the couch made of rocks, she met his gaze.

"You need that alarm system sooner rather than later," he said, proving that she hadn't actually known what he was going to say after all. "I know someone who'll do it at cost."

"You know a lot of someones," she said absently, staring at the couch as her conscience fought with her caution. "It's handy." Her conscience won, and she waved him past the sofa and toward the stairs. "Come on upstairs. No sense in you sleeping on a rock mattress when there's a free bed."

He didn't protest. As he climbed the stairs behind her, he said, "I do know a lot of someones. You should take advantage of that. Unless you think I'm offering just so that I have another chance to search for the necklace."

She tried unsuccessfully to hold back a laugh, and her attempt to restrain herself turned it into a snort.

"What?" he asked, sounding torn between huffiness and reluctant amusement.

"You're…" She almost told him that he was cute when he pouted, but she swallowed the words at the last minute. Instead, she cleared her throat and scrambled to think of replacement words, ones that wouldn't sound so much like flirting. "Nothing. Don't mind me. I think I'm so tired I'm getting delirious."

"Bed, then." His huge hand touched her back ever so lightly, as if to help support her as she walked, and her skin instantly warmed. She knew she should pull away rather than soak up the contact, but it felt too good. Besides, she still felt a residual smidgen of guilt for so quickly assuming his motives were selfish when he'd saved her life at least once that night.

When she reached the bedroom, her hand hesitated on the doorknob for a moment before she turned it. It felt strange inviting John Carmondy into her room when she'd never thought about him except with irritation— and perhaps the tiniest bit of objective lust—until a few days ago. Now, she was trusting him to watch her back...well, mostly trusting him.

As her thoughts tumbled around, trying to figure out how she felt about her changing relationship with John, he stepped into her room, instantly shrinking it to dollhouse size.

Desperately trying to get her thoughts back in order, Molly cleared her throat as she worked out the best arrangement. She didn't feel right about offering up Felicity's bed to a random guy—not that John was acting like a random anything these days. "You can have mine." She waved toward the right side of the room, relieved that she at least had a full-size bed. It would've been mortifying if she and Felicity had kid-sized bunkbeds or something. Besides, there was no way that John's height and muscular bulk would've fit in a twin. Shaking away that slightly ridiculous mental picture, she forced herself to focus on what needed doing. "Hang on. Let me get you some clean sheets."

His eyebrow and the corner of his mouth rose at the same time, giving him that familiar devilish look that signaled he was about to tease her. "Yours are...*dirty*, then?" The emphasis he put on *dirty* gave a whole new meaning to the word.

"No." She was too tired to not get flustered, and that annoyed her. Normally, she prided herself on coolly volleying back whatever John served to her, but it had been a long day—several long days, in fact—and she could feel her face heat with a flush. "Not *dirty* dirty. I changed them a few days ago. Just, you know, sluffed skin cells and a few stray hairs, that sort of thing." Okay, she needed to stop talking immediately. Unfortunately, her mouth wasn't getting the message. "Nights have been cool recently, so I haven't been sweating, but the sheets probably still smell like me."

His smirk slowly grew until it was a full grin as he eyed her bed with more lasciviousness than it really deserved. "I'll use these sheets."

"But—" She took a step toward her bed, suddenly feeling all sorts of weird about John spending the night wrapped in sheets that she'd rolled around in. It was strangely hot, and that made her squirm.

Before she could strip the bed or finish her objection, he'd maneuvered himself in front of her, blocking her access. If she took even a half step closer, they would be touching. "I'll be fine," he said. Although the words were reassuring, there was a deeper timbre to his voice that definitely was not. "Where's the bathroom?"

"All the way down the hall," she answered automatically, her brain caught up in the overwhelming proximity of him. "Last door on the left. Why do you smell like bubble gum?"

He blinked. "I do not."

"You do."

"I do not smell like bubble gum. I'm not a sticky six-year-old."

Suddenly realizing the ridiculousness of their argument, she shifted back and mentally changed gears. "Fine. You don't smell like bubble gum, even though you really do. Hurry up in the bathroom. As soon as you're done, I want to take a shower. Dutch's and that empty warehouse left a film of grossness on me."

He scowled at her, looking like he was dying to continue their discussion, but he clamped his mouth closed with a tight nod and moved to the door instead. At the last second before he disappeared down the hall, he turned back toward her. "Leave those sheets on," he said, a trace of his usual smirk back in place.

He waited, so she held her hands up in the universal *I won't do anything* gesture. "Fine. If you want to sleep in my stink, I'm not going to stop you."

"I do." He gave her a wink—which should've looked stupid, but because it was John, turned out stupid *hot* instead—and headed to the bathroom.

As soon as he was out of sight, Molly let out a deep breath and started to sink down onto Felicity's bed. The squishy mattress called to her, tempting her to lie down and close her eyes, just for a moment. With a groan, she forced herself to stand again. Once she was down, she'd be out like a light, and she'd been telling the truth about needing to wash off this terrible night.

She headed out into the hall, figuring that she might as well check on Norah while she was attempting to stay awake. Cracking her sister's door, she saw that her room was lit by dim blue light from her sister's computer screen. Molly knocked softly, pushing open the door the rest of the way when Norah made a quiet sound that she took as an invitation to enter. Norah was sitting on her narrow bed, her legs curled underneath her and her laptop open. The rest of her bed was taken up by a snoring Warrant. Norah's face was bathed in the bluish light from the screen, making her look even paler than usual. Even though Molly knew it was just an illusion, she still couldn't stand to see her sister look so sickly. It reminded her too vividly of the many emergency-room visits when they were younger and Norah's asthma wasn't controlled. Molly flicked on the floor lamp to its lowest setting, bathing the tiny room with warm yellow light, and Norah instantly looked healthier.

"I know we need to find Mom as soon as possible," Molly said, leaning on the dresser. She was tempted to plop down on the bed next to her sister, but she knew it'd be just as easy to fall asleep here as it would be in Felicity's bed. Besides, the thought of waking Warrant and getting him to move was too much effort at the moment. "That doesn't mean you can't take a few hours off to sleep."

Norah finally glanced up to meet Molly's gaze. "I know. I just keep falling down research rabbit holes."

"I get it. Find out anything interesting?"

"Maybe." Norah's voice was hesitant, cautious as always, and Molly knew not to push. Her sister never liked to share information until after she'd confirmed and reconfirmed her facts.

"John's staying over tonight."

That caught Norah's attention. "He is? With you?"

"Uh…no." She hated that she'd hesitated on her answer, but the mental image that had sprung up in her head had been very distracting—and, despite knowing it was a bad idea, very tempting. "We had to slip away after Dutch's exploded."

"*Exploded?*" Norah stared at her, eyes wide, her ignored laptop tilting to the side.

"No one was hurt." After pausing, Molly corrected herself. "I'm pretty sure no one was hurt. We were out of the building at that point. You might want to add getting the police and fire department reports to your to-do list, though."

"Okay. You're not hurt? What about John?"

"I'm fine. John's a little banged up, but I did a beautifully executed dive roll. You should've seen it." Now that the sense of urgency and danger had faded, she wished that move had been recorded.

Norah's small smile disappeared a moment after it touched her lips. "You need to be careful, especially when you're dealing with Sonny Zarver."

"I know, and I will." Molly made the words a solemn promise.

From Norah's nod, she understood and accepted it as such.

"Don't forget to sleep." Straightening from her leaning position, Molly turned off the light and slipped into the hall before sticking her head back in. "All the rabbit holes will still be there tomorrow, and everything will probably make more sense."

Although Norah made a sound of agreement, it was absentminded, and her attention was completely focused on her screen again.

"Good night." Molly pulled her sister's door closed as she withdrew, knowing that all the well-intentioned nagging in the world wouldn't get Norah in bed any sooner. She'd finish when she was done researching, and then she'd sleep until noon.

Turning away from Norah's bedroom door, Molly found herself face to bare chest with John. She couldn't stop herself from taking in the broad, muscular expanse before resolutely tipping her head back to meet his gaze. She wasn't sure why she'd thought that looking up would be any less distracting. His beautiful face— with his mile-long dark lashes and full mouth and those tempting dimples—was just as drool-worthy as the hard planes of his chest. He, of course, noticed her looking, and his teasing grin was fully in place.

"See something you like?" he asked, flexing.

She'd already given herself away, but she refused to pump up his ego. It was big enough as it was. She couldn't bring herself to lie outright, though, so she simply raised one of her shoulders in a half shrug. "Eh."

Despite her put-on indifference, his smile grew wider. "Don't pretend like all this"—he made circles in front of his body—"doesn't flip your lust switch."

"What?" She laughed. How could she not? "That makes absolutely no sense. And you don't flip *any* of my switches." Despite pretending to be completely immune to his hotness, she couldn't keep her gaze from straying downward. He was just so perfect and so close and so shirtless.

Her amusement disappeared in a second when she noticed a huge bruise blooming along his side. Moving closer, she grasped his wrist and lifted his arm up and out of the way so she could see his injury. Although she felt him go still from surprise, he allowed her to shift his arm and peer at the dark-red contusion. With her free hand, she traced her fingertips very gently over the area. It was hot and swollen, and she knew it had to hurt. As he sucked in an audible breath, his skin jumping under her touch, she quickly pulled her hand away.

"Sorry. That's a nasty bruise. Are your ribs okay?" The bruise started beneath his lowest rib, but she still pressed against them to make sure.

He cleared his throat, but his voice still came out huskier than normal. "They're fine, but you're welcome to continue your examination. I can point out some other painfully swollen spots for you to examine."

Rolling her eyes, although less dramatically than she usually did, since he was honestly hurt, Molly carefully lowered his arm to his side. Releasing her grip on his wrist, she took a step back, not willing to admit that the idea of running her hands all over him was surprisingly tempting. "If you're back to flirting, then you're not going to die."

"Just feels like it sometimes," he muttered under his breath.

"What?"

"Nothing." His grin was back, but she thought it looked strained. No wonder, since he must be as exhausted as she was, and he was bruised and sore on top of that.

"Go to bed. I'm going to shower and then I'll join you." When John's smile widened into something she could only describe as wolfish, she realized her mistake. "As in join you in sleep, not join you in bed." Turning on her heel so he couldn't see the way her face flushed bright red, judging by the heat in her cheeks, Molly headed for the bathroom. She needed to get clean and then go to sleep. If she was unconscious, she wouldn't keep saying embarrassing things.

It was only after her shower, when she was damp and naked under her towel, dirty clothes tucked into the hamper, that she realized her mistake. She'd forgotten to bring pajamas into the bathroom with her. Now, she was going to have to waltz into her room, where John was, in just a towel, and dig through her dresser drawers... which of course were the bottom two. She could imagine the picture she was going to present, her towel-clad body bent over with her butt in the air as she dug for some clean underwear.

She sighed silently, jerking open the door with resigned resolve. Hopefully, John was fully asleep and would miss the show. With her luck, though, that was unlikely. Her only other option was to sleep naked, and that seemed even more ill-advised when sharing a bedroom with John Carmondy.

"How'd you end up in this situation?" she muttered to herself as she made her way down the hall toward her room. Tucking the towel around her torso a little more securely, she shoved open the door before she could annoy herself by hesitating.

The lights were on, making it easy to see that the room was empty. Molly paused, trying to figure out where John had disappeared to, but then reminded herself that she needed to take advantage of his absence to get less naked. She dressed in record time, yanking on the first pair of panties and sleep shorts she put her hands on. The first two tank tops were discarded because they were too tight, but the third was a loose winner.

Once she was no longer wearing only a towel and John still hadn't reappeared, she realized she was breathing hard with exertion and felt a little ridiculous for the urgency she'd felt just moments earlier. Her second thought was curiosity about where he'd gone. Knowing that she wouldn't be able to sleep with John roaming the house, possibly finding out personal and embarrassing things about her, she left her room to hunt him down.

He wasn't anywhere on the second level. She'd even peeked into the twins' room, finding only a heavily sleeping Cara. As she descended the stairs, she realized that she was tiptoeing and mentally scolded herself for being so tentative. She was a big, bad bounty hunter, for Pete's sake. She should be stomping down the stairs in steel-toed boots and leather pants, not sneaking along on bare feet with rainbow-colored toenails.

Despite her mental lecture, she jumped a foot when a huge form separated from the shadows cloaking the kitchen entrance. "Sorry," she said once she'd recovered her composure and realized that it was just John. "I should've asked if you were hungry when we got home. I hope you helped yourself to whatever you found in there."

His teeth flashed white in the dim light. "Thanks, but I'm not hungry. I was just making sure everything was secured." The humor left his voice as he added, "I'll get my buddy over here to install a security system first thing tomorrow."

Molly was about to protest that they didn't need the help, but she swallowed the words. At this moment, they *did* need the help, and her prideful objections wouldn't do anything to keep her family safe. Besides, John did owe her for the bounties she'd missed out on when he'd stolen skips out from under her nose. She ignored the voice in her head that reminded her that she'd pilfered more out from under *his* nose than he'd ever dreamed about taking from her. "Thanks," she replied belatedly. Taking a deep breath, she said something that she knew—just *knew*—was going to come back and bite her hard in the ass. "I'll owe you one."

That Cheshire cat grin showed up again. "Oh? That'll be fun."

"No." She huffed, turning toward the stairs to hide the way her mouth wanted to twitch up at the corners. *Stupid John Carmondy and his stupid infectious smiles.* "That won't be fun. Not at all."

# CHAPTER 13

"Pax. Pax, wake up."

She tried burrowing deeper into her pillow, tugging her covers up around her ears in a futile attempt to block the voice invading her dreams. Unfortunately, John didn't stop. "Pax, get up!"

She groaned into her pillow. It was still dark, for Pete's sake. Was this her punishment for being a bad person? Was karma going to send him to her every morning to rudely wake her at an ungodly hour until she'd made amends for whatever horrible thing she'd done? What could her sin have been to be bad enough to call for this miserable a penance?

"Someone's trying to break in," John whispered.

All traces of her lingering sleepy haze immediately evaporated. She was out of bed in an instant, moving so quickly that she almost crashed into John. Turning, she pulled a Taser out of the nightstand. As she bent to grab the weapon, she heard John make an indistinct sound, but his expression was bland by the time she'd straightened and turned to face him.

"Let's go," she said, ignoring his weirdness for now. There'd be time enough to try to solve the puzzle that was John Carmondy when they didn't have a burglar at their door. Without waiting for a response, she charged for the hallway.

John followed her, but when they reached the top of the stairs, he moved in front of her. Making a barely audible sound of protest, she poked him in the back. He ignored it and moved silently down the stairs. Although she could see the readiness in his movements, his hands were by his sides, empty of any kind of weapon, and she frowned, wishing she'd grabbed the second Taser. Tapping his hand lightly, she offered him the one she did have. Giving it a surprised glance, he waved it off with a smile of thanks. She withdrew, determined to do her best to save the crazy, unprepared man from any danger.

When they reached the bottom of the stairs, he slipped through the living room, a silent shadow. She was amazed again how agile and coordinated he was for such a big man. Molly was pretty sure she was klutzier than he was, and she was half his size. As he made his way toward the front door, she realized that she was following behind him like a scared kid, rather than acting like the badass she was—a badass with a Taser, at that. Rolling her eyes at herself, she peeled off, heading for the kitchen.

Before she managed to get a few steps away from John, he caught her wrist, tugging her gently back into place behind him. Knowing that she couldn't win a tug-of-war between them, she acquiesced…at least until he released her and refocused in front of him. As soon as her wrist was free, she slipped away, moving quickly, expecting and dodging his grab for her. Ignoring his low growl of annoyance, she headed for the kitchen, planning the lecture she was going to give him when they didn't have to be quiet anymore.

In the kitchen, shadows draped over the familiar

room, turning the innocent appliances and counters into menacing shapes. Attempting to ignore the unease creeping into her mind, she briskly moved past the threshold, telling herself she was being ridiculous. There was no reason to be scared of her own kitchen.

As she passed the pantry, the door flew open, hitting the wall with a bang that made her jump into the air like a startled cat. A shadow detached itself from the darkness of the small room and lunged for her. Her arm started to rise so that she could deploy the Taser, but it was too late. The attacker was already on her.

Strong arms wrapped around her as they both toppled to the floor. Molly hit first with a grunt, the Taser flying out of her grip. The weight of the burglar knocked the air out of her lungs, preventing her from calling out to John. She could only hope that he heard them struggling. After a split second of shock, she started to fight.

With the heavy form on her, her range of motion was limited, but she managed to get her right arm free. Craning her neck, she tried to make out who was on top of her, but all she could see was the bulky chest and jowly neck of the man who had her pinned. Making a fist, she punched him in the upper chest.

With her target so close, the hit was weak and off-center, but it did its job. The intruder reared back, lifting off enough for her to take aim at his throat. That punch was strong enough to make him choke. Grabbing his injured neck with both hands, he rolled to the side and wheezed for air.

Scrambling to her feet, Molly backed up several steps so she wasn't within reach. Her foot hit something, sending it sliding across the floor. A quick glance showed that it was her Taser, and she grabbed it, pointing it toward the intruder just as John charged into the kitchen, dragging a cuffed man behind him.

"Hit the lights, would you?" Although Molly strove for a conversational tone, her breath was still coming in short gasps.

John obliged, flicking the switch to turn on the overhead fixture. The brightness made Molly blink rapidly until her eyes adjusted. As soon as they did, she recognized the man lying on the floor, still clutching his throat.

"Sanders, you opportunistic slug." She resisted the urge to kick him, mostly because she knew it would hurt her bare foot more. "What do you think you're doing?" Even as she asked, she knew exactly what he was doing.

"Not doing anything." Sanders's voice was hoarse, and Molly could not find it in her to be at all sorry she'd punched him in the throat. "Jane told us to stop by whenever we want."

"An open invitation," the cuffed man John had a grip on added.

Molly eyed him. "Of course. Eddie Cord. Why am I not surprised to see you following Sanders around like a fuzzy little duckling?"

Cord narrowed his eyes at her, but his glare was just about as scary as the aforementioned baby duck. "I don't follow him around. We're partners."

"Partners in what? Dumbassery?" John asked.

Molly grinned at him, raising her hand not holding the Taser in the air. "Nice one."

Although he wasn't in reaching distance, he gave her an air high-five. "Thanks."

Ignoring the warm feeling that hummed through

her, she lowered her hand and focused on the intruders. "This is not Jane's house anymore, so consider that 'open invitation' revoked."

Sanders's lips drew back in a sneer. "Can't just say it's your house and make it so. I'm going to have to hear it straight from Jane."

Cord sniggered, and Molly fought the urge to tase them both. "Nope. It's my house because it is. The cops will agree with me." She'd expected that the mention of the police would make Sanders and Cord fall into line, but they just exchanged a smirk. She had the random thought that John was the only person who could make that expression look good.

"Not what I heard," Sanders said mockingly. "*I* heard they let the last guy who broke in walk."

*Stuart.* The name was a growl in her head. Molly wished the blabby weasel was here, so that she could tase him, too. She mentally added *punching Stuart in his smug, burglarizing face* onto her mental bucket list.

"You should be less concerned with what the cops did *then*," John said, his bass voice rumbling a warning, "and more concerned about what we're going to do *now*."

The two intruders stopped smirking as fear flashed in their eyes.

Molly was perfectly happy to play bad cop and badder cop with John. "That's better. Now tell us what you're doing here."

"Told you," Sanders muttered, his gaze darting away from her. "Jane asked us to pick up something."

"Yeah." Cord jumped in, nodding in such an exaggerated way that he looked like a bobblehead doll. "Jane asked us to come here and get…something."

Meeting John's exasperated gaze, Molly made a *Can you believe these guys?* face. Although his snort was amused, she noticed that John didn't loosen his grip on Cord. Her gaze fell to the smaller man's wrists, and she frowned, wondering where John had gotten the handcuffs. She glanced at his bare torso and down to the pants he must've yanked on in a hurry. Like hers, they had bunches of pockets. Shifting her gaze to meet his eyes, not allowing herself to linger on an expanse of brown, bare, obnoxiously beautiful chest on the way, she raised her eyebrows.

"You just happened to have cuffs on you?"

The corners of his mouth tucked in as he held back a smile, his dimple revealing his true amusement. "Never leave home without them."

"Always prepared, Boy Scout?"

"Always."

"If you two are going to flirt, can we leave?" Sanders asked, bringing Molly's attention back to him. He'd propped himself up on his elbows, and she knew she either had to cuff him or let him go soon. Letting him sit unrestrained on the floor was just asking for trouble.

"Once you tell us why you're really here," she said crisply, "you'll be able to leave. So spill."

Sanders clamped his lips together, pretending to zip them in a dramatic gesture. She allowed her smirk to emerge, looking away from Sanders in a dismissive gesture that meant she didn't need him, not when Cord was just dying to give away the entire game.

Letting her smile widen, she focused on the cuffed man. "So, Eddie... Jane must trust you a lot to give you a key to the house."

"Key?" The blank look he gave her spoke volumes. "What key? We don't have a key."

She put on her best confused expression. "How'd you get in, then?"

"Picked the lo—"

"Okay!" Sanders's roar drowned out Cord's confession. "I want to call my lawyer."

Meeting John's eyes, Molly burst into laughter. "Your lawyer? I don't think so." She sobered abruptly and put her face right in Sanders's, forcing away the thought that she was close enough for him to grab. "You're going to wish you were with the cops by the time we finish with you."

He flinched, and she barely kept herself from giving a triumphant grin. She knew she was not traditionally intimidating, but it was nice that she could hold the illusion for a while. Despite her glee, she did shift back out of reach, just in case. Giving Sanders her most ferocious glare, she turned back to Cord.

"Why'd you break in, Eddie?" she demanded, her words coming out as harshly as she could manage. "What's so valuable in here that you'd risk serving time?" She waved a hand at the contents of her kitchen with real bewilderment. As beloved as everything was to her and her sisters, there was no point in stealing what was worthless junk to anyone else.

"The neckla—"

"Eddie!" Sanders howled. Molly was tempted to gag him, or maybe kick him in the teeth so he'd be quiet for a few seconds.

"The necklace that Jane stole?" she asked Cord, ignoring his sputtering business partner. "Why would you think it was here?"

"That's where Zach Fridley said he put it."

*Zach Fridley?* It made all sorts of creepy sense. This was why the weasel Stuart had tried to break in, and why Cord and Sanders were currently in her kitchen. Zach was Jane's oldest and most loyal friend—and the one she got into the most trouble with. He'd do anything for her, including breaking into her house and hiding a priceless stolen necklace…and then blabbing about it.

This explained their recent rash of attempted break-ins…and meant that more would be coming—a lot more.

Swallowing a groan, she flicked a look at John. Judging by his grim expression, he'd come to the same conclusion. Keeping a firm grip on Cord with one hand, John waved at Sanders where he was still sprawled on the floor.

"Let's go," John said, and Molly's gaze turned startled. Why was he kicking them out when she hadn't finished the interrogation? Even though she'd mostly decided not to file a police report, the least John could've done was to check with her before he started tossing burglars out on the street willy-nilly.

"Hang on," she said in her best commanding voice, the one that made all her sisters freeze in place. It worked just as well on the two intruders. Even John gave her his attention. "Have you talked to Jane since she was arrested?"

The two men glanced at each other before Sanders answered. "No."

Despite the way he held her gaze, she wasn't sure if she believed him. Figuring that she wouldn't be able to glare the truth out of him, she flicked her fingers at him in a *let's go* motion. As soon as he stood, she said, "Turn around, hands up against the wall, legs spread."

"Seriously?" he complained, but she just lifted her Taser a little higher. He must've been able to read how delighted she would be to send a painful amount of electricity through him, because he turned and flattened his hands on the wall. Once he was in position, she tucked the Taser into the waistband of her sleep shorts and patted him down.

Once everything from his pockets was piled on the counter—including her new bank card, to her great annoyance—she shifted back slightly. "Put your right arm behind your back."

Grumbling, he obeyed, and she grabbed his thumb, using it to crank his arm up toward his shoulder blades. "Ready?" she asked John, who'd been searching Cord.

He nodded and gestured with the hand not holding on to his captive. "Ladies first."

"Thank you, Carmondy." She left the kitchen, shoving Sanders in front of her. "He's so polite. There just aren't that many people with manners left, are there?" When Sanders didn't respond, she cranked his arm even higher, making him yelp and go up on his tiptoes to relieve the pressure. "Are there?"

"I don't know," he said sulkily, and she gave his thumb an extra twist, making him swear. "Stop it! No, no one has manners anymore! Happy?"

"Not really." She did ease off on his arm, however. "I'd be happy to be sleeping right now, not escorting your sorry ass out of my house…the house that you just broke into."

He grumbled under his breath as she yanked open the door and shoved him onto the porch. The screen door swung shut behind them, and John timed it just right so that it smacked Cord in the face. Molly gave John an approving nod, making him grin back at her.

As she escorted Sanders across the lawn, she saw an SUV parked in front of Mr. P's house, and she felt a hint of evil glee rise inside her. "Is that yours?" she asked. At Sanders's affirmative grunt, she turned her head slightly to aim her next question at John. "Any chance you have a pointy tool of some sort in one of your pockets?"

"I do." He surged ahead of her, pushing Cord to move more quickly toward the SUV. When they reached it, John pulled what appeared to be a multi-tool out of his pocket. Before either Cord or Sanders could protest, John punctured the front left tire before striding toward the rear.

"What?" Sanders caught on too late as air hissed noisily out of the second punctured tire. "Stop! I'm going to kick your—" He lunged forward, but Molly kept hold of his thumb, giving it an extra upward yank to remind him that he was still restrained. "Ow! Bitch, let me go!"

"No, bitch." Her tone was mild, considering her lack of sleep and the events of the night, but she'd found John's slashing all four of the getaway vehicle's tires very cathartic. Raising her voice slightly, she said to John, "That was very nice. Thank you."

He dipped his head in an ironic almost-bow. "My pleasure." Pulling a handcuff key from one of his pockets, he freed Cord and gave him a strong nudge away from Molly and the house. "Off you go. You're free. Fly, little goose. Fly!"

Cord gave one last mournful look at the disabled SUV and Sanders before hurrying away from them.

John smiled broadly, making Molly give a snort

of amusement. "You're such a weirdo." She shoved Sanders away from her, grabbing the Taser from her waistband in the same motion so it was pointed at him before he even turned around. Giving him an insincere smile, she flapped her free hand in a shooing motion. "Better get moving. It's a long way to the bus stop."

"I need my phone back." He eyed the Taser, as if trying to decide whether or not he could tackle her before she could deploy it.

John moved to her side, but she kept her attention focused on Sanders. He was angry and embarrassed, and she didn't trust that he'd choose to follow the most reasonable path. "Maybe you should've thought about that before you broke into my house. Now, shoo."

He started to argue, but John shifted forward. It was a slight move, but it was enough to make Sanders jump back. With a final glare that Molly assumed was supposed to promise retribution, Sanders grudgingly turned and strode off after Cord. Without taking her eyes off the retreating duo, Molly gave an audible sigh.

"Why don't the bad guys ever quail in my presence like that?" she asked idly.

Even with her focus on Sanders and Cord, she knew he was eyeing her with amusement. "Maybe because I'm twice your height and weight?"

She waved a hand, dismissing that, and then remembered that she'd vowed to quit imitating Jane's gesture. "You're not twice my height."

"Close enough."

"No. Not close enough. You're like six inches taller than me." As Sanders rounded the corner and disappeared, she turned to face him. When she tilted her head

back to look at his grinning face, she realized that esti-
mate might've been low. "Fine. Ten inches, tops."

"That's what she said."

It was almost impossible to hold back her laugh at
that, but somehow she managed. Elbowing him in the
side, she turned her face to hide her struggle to contain
her amusement. As she did, she saw Mr. P's lights come
on, and her desire to laugh deserted her completely.
Instead, she groaned.

"What?" John asked, following her gaze.

As if in answer, Mr. P's front door swung open.
Grabbing John's arm, Molly hustled back toward her
house, towing him behind her. He went willingly, not
even laughing as her pace picked up until they were
practically sprinting toward her front porch. Only when
they were inside did she let out a relieved breath.

John, of course, was laughing at her. "Why did we
just run away from your elderly neighbor?"

"He's not really elderly. He just acts like it." Molly
knew that she was dodging the question, and the way
that John's eyebrows climbed higher on his forehead
told her that he knew it, too. "Fine. I didn't want to deal
with Mr. P tonight. I'll need more sleep before I can
listen to his complaining and stay civil. A *lot* more sleep.
And maybe some wine."

Chuckling quietly, John ushered her to the stairs. "I
can't help with the wine, but we can get some more sleep."

"Unless someone else breaks in," she grumbled,
making a serious effort to keep her feet quiet. She was
extremely tempted to stomp up the steps like a toddler
in the midst of a tantrum, but Cara and Norah—and
Warrant—had somehow miraculously managed to keep

sleeping through all the commotion earlier. She didn't want to wake them now and have to explain everything that had happened. All she wanted was to sleep, uninterrupted by sisters or dogs or burglars.

"True." John sounded quite a bit more nonchalant about the idea than she felt. "Burglarizing your house seems to have become a trend recently."

Making a sour face, she waved John toward her room before peeking in at Cara and Norah. Both were still down for the count, although how Norah could sleep clinging to the edge of her narrow bed while mattress-hog Warrant pressed huge feet into her back was a mystery.

Molly softly closed Norah's bedroom door before turning around to find John waiting for her. The sight of him there, so steady and strong, sent a sense of comfort sweeping through her, pushing away her exhaustion and stress. She froze, caught in a strange moment of wondering if this was what it would be like to have a partner, someone who could have her back and prop her up when the weight of taking care of her family got unbearably heavy. It was an addictive, incredible feeling to have support, and she knew she had to be careful. He wasn't here forever, just the night, and it would be stupid of her to start leaning on him. When he inevitably disappeared, she'd fall.

He eyed her curiously. "What?" he asked, his voice low.

Shaking off the longing for that moment to be a permanent reality, she brushed past him without speaking. She stayed silent, worried that something desperate and needy might slip out if she said anything. *Sleep.* She needed sleep to rebuild her walls and organize her thoughts, to tuck her hungry emotions back far enough that no one else could see them.

"What was that look?" John pressed as soon as they were in her room. He closed the door with a firm click that almost made her jump with its intimate finality.

"What look? There was no look." She didn't care that it was a lie. There was no way she could deal with an emotional discussion with John Carmondy right now. Meeting his gaze, she hoped desperately that he'd let it go.

His expression said clearly that he didn't believe her, but—miracle of miracles—he did let it go and shimmied out of clothes until he was just in his underwear.

"Whoa!" She spun around to face the wall, but it was too late. The image of mostly naked John was burned into her brain. "Give me a little warning next time."

"Next time?" The words were filled with laughter, and she remembered why she always had to fight the urge to shove him. "Aw, Pax. Is that your way of inviting me over for future sleepovers? An open invitation to turn any night into coed night, shall we say?"

"No." Her tone was harsh, but she knew the importance of making her answer very clear, or he'd be dropping in all the time, acting like her bedroom was his own. "Let's not say that."

Despite her denial, he chuckled softly. A pillow collided with the back of her head, and she made a strange squeaking sound of surprise as she automatically caught it. Whirling around, she chucked the pillow back at him, trying her best to not let her gaze slip below his neck. It wasn't easy.

"Good *night*, Carmondy," she said, keeping her voice stern with a great deal of effort, but exhaustion pulled at her, and she gave up the effort. "Or morning, or whatever."

"Good night, Pax." He still sounded amused and strangely affectionate, his voice making a happy shiver run down her spine. "I like sleeping with you even more than working with you. This is the start of a beautiful…partnership."

She wasn't sure why he'd paused, but her thoughts were bouncing around, refusing to settle down and analyze his motives. Responding with a grunt, she ignored his laugh and got ready for bed for the second time in too short a span.

"I knew this would be fun," he said, apparently ignoring her wordless hint to be quiet and let her sleep. "Didn't expect to like it so much, though."

He went quiet as her thoughts spun wildly. Forget the fact that her house had been burglarized three times in the past few days. The real danger to her—to her heart and happiness—was sprawled on the bed right across the room. All of her efforts to focus on her mom's case or even just to empty her mind so that she could sleep failed.

It seemed that John Carmondy hadn't just taken over her bed. He'd seemed to have taken over her brain, too.

# CHAPTER 14

LATER THAT MORNING, MOLLY WAS UNCOMFORTABLE. SHE was also annoyed with herself, because the reason she was uncomfortable was that things were *too* comfortable. Both her sisters were gone and John was already up by the time Molly dragged herself out of bed, and he'd wordlessly handed her a giant mug of coffee as soon as she'd entered the kitchen.

She, in turn, had made eggs and toast, while he'd cut up some fruit with only the slightest wistful mumbling about her lack of protein shakes. Warrant had curled up around her feet as she'd cooked, but she knew it wasn't because he loved her the best. If John had been making the eggs, Warrant would've been cozying up to him instead. After they'd eaten and washed up, moving with the synchronization of a couple who'd been living together for forty years, she was both fully unnerved and grateful for the few moments of peace.

"Desmond'll be here around noon to install a security system. What's the plan until then?" John asked once the kitchen was clean.

"We need to pick up your car from the lot by Dutch's before it's towed." Too restless to sit in her usual spot at her improvised desk, Molly leaned against the counter, drumming her fingertips against the lower cupboards while resisting the urge to pace. After a little bit of sleep and a whole lot of caffeine, she was ready to do something physical, like chase down and tackle a skip, but she had to find the guy first. It was frustrating.

"And after that?"

A tiny thread of guilt jabbed into her. "Are you sure you want to be involved in this whole mess?" She waved her arms, broadly indicating the house and everything that went along with it—her sisters and mom and Sonny Zarver and Barney and all the less-than-stellar characters who clung like leeches to the latter three.

"Are you kidding?" Dimple on full display, he mirrored her stance, leaning against the wall across from her. "Explosions? Tracking skips through abandoned warehouses? Exploring the underbelly of Langston society? This is why I became a bounty hunter."

Rolling her eyes, she decided she believed just about a quarter of his enthusiasm. After all, he could've found all that chasing his own skips and not had to deal with all of the nonsense that was part of Pax Bail Recovery at the moment. "Fine. It's your funeral." She paused. "Hopefully not literally."

"It's so sweet that you don't want me to die."

"That changes moment to moment," she said honestly. Instead of looking offended, John just laughed. Of course he found that funny.

They decided to walk to Dutch's. It was far enough that Molly left Warrant at home, knowing that John would end up having to carry the dog over his shoulders like a shepherd with a huge, fluffy sheep. As Molly and John passed the burglar's disabled SUV, a flatbed tow truck pulled up in front of it. She couldn't hold back a smile. Either Sanders and Cord had called for help bright and early that morning, or Mr. P couldn't stand having the vehicle sitting at his curb for even an hour or two in daylight. She was almost certain it was the latter.

Molly hummed quietly as they turned the corner at the end of her street, glad that Sanders and Cord had to deal with the headache of retrieving their car from the impound lot and weirdly happy to be walking. Even though she'd never admit it to Felicity, she missed starting the day with a sister-run boot-camp torture session. Without it, she felt lazy and slow, like she still had one foot in bed. The walk to the bar woke her up, knocking the sleepiness out of her and kicking her brain into gear.

"What are you going to do about Zach Fridley?" John asked.

A little startled at his apparent mind-reading skills, Molly met his gaze and then lifted one shoulder, more in indecision than apathy. "I'm torn. Since Sergeant Blake is out, I don't think just turning over his name to Detectives Hostile and Hostile-er is going to do anything unless I hand over a mountain of evidence against him at the same time." Although she didn't say it, even if she did have that evidence, she didn't trust those two cops enough to turn it over to them.

"Isn't there someone else you could deal with?"

Mentally paging through the cops at Langston's small department, she shook her head. "None that I know well enough to trust. Mostly I deal with the sheriff's department, since they run the jail. The only time I deal with Langston PD is when Mom does something squirrelly or if I need information and Blake isn't available."

"Like now."

"Like now," she agreed, although she grimaced at the sergeant's bad timing. "This is too important to hand off to some random officer I don't know."

John made an absent sound of agreement, as if his brain was working just as hard as hers. Molly was glad to have him on her team. As annoying as he could be, he was also extremely clever, and she'd had to be at the very tip-top of her game in order to steal a skip out from under him. In fact, she'd wondered a time or two whether those thefts had been too easy. Shooting him a suspicious sideways glance, she ran the possibility through her mind.

"What?" he asked, already blinking guileless, heavily lashed eyes at her.

"Did you let me steal your skips?" she asked baldly. Not only did she want to know the answer, but the distraction from her current, more critical issues was a relief.

Those eyelashes dropped for a long moment before they rose again. "Why would I do that?"

"I don't know." Her eyes narrowed. "Why *would* you do that?"

Before she could respond, he waved a hand, dismissing all future arguments with the same gesture that her mom—and Molly, despite her best efforts—used. Apparently, it was contagious. "Anyway, let's get back to talking about Zach. If you're not going to the cops with this, how are you going to shut him down? He most likely has your car—if he hasn't sold it—and he's telling everyone and their mother that you have the necklace. That's not good, unless you enjoyed our late-night visit with Sanders and Cord."

"I did not enjoy it one bit." Molly paused, considering

her words. "Okay, so maybe I enjoyed it a little when you slashed their tires."

"Yeah." His smile was just nostalgic enough to be amusing. "That was nice, wasn't it?"

"Very satisfying." When his eyebrows did that funny waggle thing that they did, she wanted to kick herself for using the word *satisfying* while talking with John, of all people. With a great effort, she brushed off her embarrassment and pulled herself out of the conversational rabbit hole. "Back to Zach, I texted Fifi and Charlie this morning, letting them know about him. Mom's mess is their deal, and Sonny Zarver is mine. Sonny is what we need to concentrate on." As soon as the words escaped, she realized how easily the *we* had slipped out, as if their team of two was an actual unbreakable thing now.

"Right." John still sounded concerned. "Sonny. Just for curiosity's sake, when's your sergeant friend getting back? Any update?"

"No," she answered gloomily. "Her kid must still be down with that mutant strain of chicken pox."

"That's too bad."

"It really is."

"Okay!" As they turned the corner just a few blocks from Dutch's, John clapped his hands together once and then dusted them off, as if physically removing any trace of disappointment. "The sisters are handling Zach. We'll get my car, bring Sonny in, and make it back to your house in time to meet Desmond to get your security system installed."

"Just like that?" she asked dubiously.

"Hopefully, we'll have time to fit some lunch in there, too."

She blinked at him and then laughed, shaking her head slightly even as her chest warmed. "You're nuts, but at least you're optimistic."

He gave her a crooked smile that said he accepted both those things as true before focusing on Dutch's. She followed his gaze, and the sight of the bar sobered her. John's car wasn't the only one parked in the lot across the street, and there were two vehicles in the bar parking lot, but neither was a marked police car. In fact, the only sign that there'd been any incident the night before was a broken strand of yellow police tape hanging next to the entrance.

As John made a beeline for his car, Molly headed toward the back of the bar. Once he noticed she wasn't following him, he changed course and jogged after her. In the daylight, the damaged portion of the building looked both worse and, at the same time, not as bad as it'd appeared the night before. Most of the back bathroom wall was missing, but the rest of the structure appeared sound—at least to her non-engineer eye.

On this side of the building, more of the police tape remained, but Molly ignored it as she picked her way through the scattered rubble that used to be a concrete-block wall.

"It felt worse than it looks," John said, apparently reading her mind once again.

"Yeah. I think it was meant to be a distraction rather than to be destructive." Crouching down, she examined the blackened base of the damaged wall. "Although the bar owner probably wouldn't agree with me."

"What wouldn't I agree with?" a rough voice demanded, and Molly hurried to stand.

"That it could've been worse," John said easily,

although he shifted to put his body between her and the newcomer.

The woman scoffed, even as Molly straightened and stepped to the side, so that she could see the other person without John's ridiculously enormous form in the way. When she finally got a good look, Molly recognized her as the bar owner, Yolanda.

"It's bad enough." She smoothed a flat hand over her reddish-blond hair. Her lips were drawn down tightly, emphasizing the wrinkles along her top lip and at the corners of her mouth. "Have to close down for a few days, which means that the two of you shouldn't be here."

"We were just picking up our car from the lot across the street and got curious," Molly said, trying to borrow John's look of wide-eyed innocence. "How'd this happen? Do you know?"

Yolanda's eyes narrowed. "That black car's yours?"

"Yes." Molly kept her gaze from sliding over to meet John's.

"You're the bounty hunters, then?" From the way the woman practically vibrated with growing fury, Molly knew that keeping her mouth shut was the safest option. Even without confirmation, Yolanda waved an angry hand toward the hole in the bathroom wall. "This is your fault!"

Clearing his throat, John inched in front of Molly again. "Since we weren't the ones who blew a hole in your bar, I'm thinking you're blaming the wrong people."

"*You* were the ones chasing Sonny! If you hadn't showed up, he wouldn't have had to run."

Molly peered around John, not minding having a physical barrier between them, since Yolanda was basically trying to kill Molly with her eye lasers. "Was Sonny the one who did this?" She pointed at the charred hole.

Yolanda took a deep breath, and Molly braced for lots of yelling, but her words came out in an angry growl instead. "Leave. Now."

"See, the problem is that this is the only place we know where Sonny is sure to show up eventually," Molly said in what she hoped was a reasonable tone. "If you tell us another place we could find Sonny, we won't have to come back here." She paused, giving Yolanda her most serious, determined face. "Every night."

"Are you threatening me?" Yolanda bristled and took a step forward. John made a sound in the back of his throat and seemed to grow another two inches, and she stopped her advance, an apprehensive look flashing across her face.

It was amazing how much more secure Molly felt when she had a man-shaped blockade between her and a pissed-off informant. "Not a threat. It's a promise to give you our patronage. Every night for weeks. Months even, if necessary. It'll be a win-win. We'll buy a beer or two, and I bet we'll find a *lot* of other bail jumpers while we wait for Sonny to show up."

"Fishing in a barrel." Despite his looming, tension-filled posture, John's voice sounded light and amused.

"Exactly!" Molly gave his back an approving pat. "I like this idea. Never mind about giving us an address for Sonny. We'll just wait for him here."

"I'll have you tossed out." There was a barely audible quiver in Yolanda's voice, and Molly felt a surge of triumph. This might actually work.

She gave a mocking laugh as she pointed at John.

"You're going to have *him* thrown out? Good luck with that. He's at least a three-bouncer job, and that's not factoring in his MMA training." Leaning around him so she could get a little closer to the bar owner, she stage-whispered, "His cage name was Rampage."

Because John was so close to her, she felt his tiny jerk of surprise, and she poked him to make sure he didn't start laughing and ruin his faux notoriety.

Yolanda's mouth drew even tighter, until her lips met in a sour pucker. "Sonny's staying with Tick Caruso's mother. Don't know the address, but it's on Westpeak Road, the blue house across from the old church. Now leave, and don't ever come back to my bar." With that, she spun around and stomped toward the back door.

Molly waited until the woman was inside and out of sight before stepping out from behind her John-shaped wall.

"Why didn't she just walk inside through the hole?" he asked, waving toward the damaged wall, and Molly bit back a laugh, only a tiny snort of amusement escaping.

Giving him a light push toward the corner of the building, she kept her mouth shut, not wanting to get overconfident before they were safely driving away. Who knew what could be heard through the hole in the wall?

Once they were in the car and turning out of the lot, Molly held up her fist. John flinched theatrically, and she gave his shoulder a chiding shove. "Don't leave me hanging, Carmondy. I'm celebrating our stunning team-work back there."

With a grin, he bumped her fist with his giant hand. "Agreed. I knew we'd be great together. Why haven't you come to work for me yet?"

"Because I'd kill you in a matter of days," she said matter-of-factly, even as she wondered if her long-held excuse was accurate. After all, she'd spent almost every second with him over the past couple of days and she didn't have any homicidal urges. In fact, she was feeling almost…warm and mushy inside. Dismissing that as the residual high of getting a potential location for Sonny, she was distracted when John turned south rather than north toward Westpeak Road. "Uh…aren't we going to pick up Sonny? We're on a tight schedule if we want to get this wrapped up before noon." As silly as that had seemed just a half hour earlier, now it felt almost possible that they'd be able to bring Sonny in soon.

"I need to swing by my place and change into some clean clothes," he said, catching her full attention. Even though he'd just spent the night at her house—in her *room*—it still seemed like an intimate thing to see where he lived and what his furniture looked like and if he left dishes in the sink. She'd soon find out if he was the kind of man who forgot to put the cap back on the toothpaste. She blinked rapidly several times, trying to come to grips with that knowledge. She must've been quiet too long, because he shot her a questioning look. "I'll be quick."

If he just ran in, maybe she could stay in the car? The thought was both a relief and a letdown, and she forced her brain to quit obsessing over such a silly thing. "Oh, that's fine. Sorry. I was just thinking about something else. Someone else. Sonny, to be exact—well, more thinking about what the best plan would be to bring him in, but…yeah." What was she doing? Molly never babbled—well, hardly ever. Why was she falling to ridiculously jittery pieces at the thought of seeing John's toilet? "Ugh." She rubbed her face. "I need more sleep."

He chuckled, and it sounded so normal that she relaxed, relieved that her weirdness hadn't fazed him. "I'm feeling you on that. So what have you decided?"

For a paralyzed second, she couldn't distinguish between her thoughts and what she'd just said aloud, but then she managed to sort out her answer. "Nothing concrete yet. We'll need to go in quickly, before he can rig up any explosions."

"Unless he already rigged them up, proactively."

She made a face, knowing that John was right. "That is likely, isn't it? Poor mother of Tick. Her house is probably going to have an extra hole or two by the time we get our hands on Sonny."

"Mother of Tick sounds like a prayer…or a curse word."

"I'm sure we'll be using both before this is done." She sighed, trying to get her thoughts in order. They needed a plan, a good one, or they'd end up getting exploded along with Mother of Tick's house.

Making a sound of agreement, John pulled up to the curb and turned off the car. Curious and still a little apprehensive about the whole home visit, Molly peered out her window at the adorable little brick house. "This is yours?" she asked, opening her door automatically before catching herself. "Did you want me to stay in the car?" Contrarily, now that she'd seen the outside of John's home, she was intensely interested in seeing the inside as well.

"Like a neglected dog?" he asked. Before she could decide whether that had been rude or not, he continued. "C'mon. Let's get inside."

As she climbed out of the car, she decided that she couldn't let his comment go. "A neglected dog?" she repeated, her tone chilly enough to make him wince.

"I said I *wouldn't* leave you in the car," he explained, his expressive hands making circles as he tried to think of the right words. "I wasn't calling you a dog or anything. I was saying that would make *me* a terrible owner—er…I mean, person—if I left you here to die in the heat of a closed-up car. See?" He grimaced, obviously knowing that he'd mucked up the explanation.

Clucking her tongue disapprovingly, she walked ahead of him to the adorable house, holding back her smile and letting him stew in his own awkwardness. It was rare to see John so flustered, and she wanted to squeeze every last drop of enjoyment out of the moment.

"Molly…" He drew out her name, sounding so tortured that she was tempted to relent. When he grabbed her hand and tugged her around, she stared at their interlocked fingers. Was John actually holding her hand? "I'm sorry. I didn't mean to even imply that you were a dog or had any characteristics that could, in the tiniest way, ever be considered canine. *I'm* the useless, socially impaired mutt who manages to say exactly the wrong thing to you every single time."

That made it impossible to hold back her laughter.

"Oh, good." He sounded tentatively relieved as he squeezed her hand. She hated to admit it, but the press of his large, warm palm against hers felt comforting and really, really nice. "Does this mean you don't want to rip my face off?"

"Yeah." She stepped to the side, surprised at how reluctant she was to untangle her fingers from his so

he could unlock his front door. From the way his grip
tightened for a moment before he released her, he felt
the same way. "For now. I imagine it won't last too
long, though."

"I'll take a temporary truce." He held the door open
for her. It was curved at the top, making her think of
hobbit houses, even though it was a full-size entrance,
big enough even for John's significant height.

Stepping inside, she pulled off her boots while looking around. The place smelled like lemons and fresh
wood, and she mentally rearranged all of her precon-
ceived notions about John and what type of house he'd
have. The hardwood floors were scarred from decades
of use but clean, and the light that filled the space didn't
catch on any dust motes floating in the air. She felt a
sudden rush of self-consciousness for her own rather
battered house. Usually, she and her sisters were too
busy working to do more than the bare minimum of
housecleaning, except when Cara had some stress to
work out at two in the morning. Even without seeing the
rest of the place, she knew for certain that his bathroom
would be spotlessly clean.

John had gone quiet and was eyeing her carefully as
she looked around. A flash of vulnerability peeked out
around his standard expression, and she realized that he
cared what she thought of his home. It reminded her of
how intimate it had felt when he'd seen her living space,
and it dawned on her that it worked the other way, too.
Watching her take in his home for the first time had to
be nerve-racking for him.

Feeling sympathetic, she offered the first compliment
that came to mind. "It's so much cleaner than I expected."

He blinked, appearing torn between offense and laughter. "What do you mean? Did you think I'd have a dirty house? Do I give off hoarder vibes?" His face dropped with obvious horror. "Do I *smell*?" Ducking his head, he raised his arm and sniffed.

"You don't smell." Since that wasn't technically true, as she couldn't get his addictive scent out of her mind, she amended her words. "Bad. You don't smell bad."

Eyeing her suspiciously, he took a whiff of his other armpit. "If I don't stink, why did you hesitate just now?"

She was not about to venture into that mess of an explanation, since it would only lead to extreme embarrassment. Instead, she rolled her eyes and gave him her best impatient look. "I didn't. Were you going to change clothes?"

Tossing his arms up dramatically, his expression one of complete indignation, he pinned her with an accusing glare. "If I don't smell, why are you suddenly so insistent that I change?"

"Ugh. Drama queen. That's why we came here, remember?"

Although he lowered his arms, he didn't look completely placated. "Right. I'll go change." He was halfway up the stairs as he muttered, "After I shower."

She debated whether to shout something impatient after him, but she was actually glad he was taking a few minutes longer than expected, since she was dying to explore the rest of his house. "Take your time," she said sweetly—*too* sweetly, judging by the way he halted and turned his head to eye her suspiciously. Widening her eyes, she returned his look with her best innocent one, and he finally turned to climb the rest of the stairs.

Once he was out of sight, she slipped through the first entryway on her left into his living room. Although the large flat-screen TV did have a spot of honor over a fireplace, it was still a cozy room with many more books than she'd expected. She'd already known that John was a smart guy, but he always seemed to be moving. It was hard wrapping her brain around the image of him spending a quiet evening reading, rather than being out at sketchy bars, knocking bail jumpers' heads together.

Resisting the urge to start examining titles—since she knew perfectly well that she'd never leave if she did—she moved into the dining room. The rooms were on the smaller side, but the lofted ceilings made up for it, keeping the house from feeling claustrophobic. It was cozy and adorable and, strangely enough, it suited John.

As she walked into the kitchen, she realized that the rooms made a circle, starting and ending at the entryway. Despite the age of the house, every room was freshly painted in currently trendy and warm colors, and all the furniture was newish and looked comfortable. He'd kept some of the vintage details, like the leaded windows and glass doorknobs, so that the place didn't seem completely modern. Although her house—the one she grew up in and that she was chasing Sonny Zarver in order to keep—was unquestionably her very favorite place to be, she knew immediately that John's house could quickly become a second favorite.

"Not that there's any reason to be here after we bring Sonny in," she told herself sternly, peeking into what appeared to be a study. This room was full of books, too. They covered two walls, making the small room feel even tinier. On the desk were a laptop and a tidy pile of folders. Quashing the temptation to peek inside those manila jackets and possibly get a glimpse of his active cases, she withdrew from the room. As much as she enjoyed stealing skips out from under John's nose, sneaking a glance at his folders after he'd invited her into his home would feel like cheating.

She made her way back to the entry and sat on a cute wooden bench next to the oversize hobbit door. Although she felt twitchy and wanted to pace, she forced herself to stay seated. Since she didn't want to think about how much she liked John's house and how much she was starting to *really* like the house's owner, she turned her mind to the skip they were chasing.

By the time John returned, freshly scrubbed and still smelling just the slightest bit like bubble gum, she'd come up with four and a half potential plans to get Sonny in custody without Tick's poor mother having her house explode.

"Ready?" he asked as she popped up off the bench.

"Yep. Plan number five is missing the back half, but the first four are fairly solid." She hurried out of the house in front of him, staying out of range so she could keep her body's reactions in hand.

Her efforts to put some distance between them were for naught, since he caught up with her outside. In just a couple of his long strides, he was right next to her, and her senses were overwhelmed by his sheer John Carmondy deliciousness. "You have four plans?"

"Almost five." If she was being honest, however, the parts missing from her fifth plan were fairly critical. "Personally, I like plan number two the best."

"What is plan number two?" They reached his car,

and John opened the passenger door for her. Although she gave him a sideways glance, she swallowed her snarky question about whether they were on a date. Instead of giving him a hard time, she slid into her seat and tried not to feel weird about the whole thing as he closed her door and circled around to the driver's side. Once he was in his seat, he started the engine and then turned toward her expectantly.

"You're actually up for making a plan this time, rather than just winging it?" she asked.

With a crooked smile, he raised his hands palms up in a *What can you do?* gesture. "Seems like it'd be a waste of four good plans if we don't use them, now that you've thought them up and all."

"In that case, head to Mother Tick's house, and I'll tell you on the way."

# CHAPTER 15

"I STILL LIKE PLAN NUMBER FIVE THE BEST," JOHN complained as he parked in the grocery-store lot a block from Mother Tick's house.

"Four and a half," Molly corrected, not for the first time. "It has huge gaping holes in it. So much could go wrong."

"I think that's why I like it—there's so much room for improvisation."

Giving him a look, she opened her door. "Improvisation is fine when a plan goes sideways, but it's better to at least start out with a solid plan…like plan number two."

"You just want to be pretend-married to me."

"Yeah, that's it," she said dryly as she stretched and tried to surreptitiously check out the house. "I made that very wish when I blew out the candles on my cake at my last birthday. *I wish more than anything that I could pretend to be married to Carmondy*." As he walked over to join her, she gave him a poke in the side. It must've been a ticklish spot, because he jumped and swatted her finger away. "Doofus. Why would anyone wish that?"

His expression showed exaggerated offense. "I, for one, would love to be fake-married to you."

Even though she knew he was teasing, and she'd just

been playing along, his words took her off guard. She went quiet for a beat, too flustered to respond.

"Pax?"

"Sorry." She shook off the strange moment, silently commanding her feelings to knock it off and quit being weird. Grabbing on to the first excuse she could think of, she stared at Tick's mother's house. "Thought I saw something move. So…plan two, then?"

"Fine." Although he grumbled, it was good-natured, and she knew his complaints were more to get her wound up than because he had any serious objections. "Just to make your birthday wish come true."

Inwardly, she felt that strange little swoop of her stomach, similar to how it felt on an airplane during turbulence, but she managed to keep her composure. "I'll be forever grateful," she said absently, checking out the area around the house as her mind concentrated on what she needed to do. Her focus was blown to bits when his huge hand grabbed hers.

"What?" she said, staring down at their linked fingers. His mitt was so big that hers had almost completely disappeared. "What?" If she hadn't been so thrown off, she would've been embarrassed by her confused response.

"Ready, Wife?" he asked. The way he gently squeezed her hand and smiled crookedly at her made it hard to remember that he was just playacting.

She was forced to clear her throat before she could get any words out. "Never call me that again, or I'll have to hurt you. And yes, I'm ready."

By his snort, he wasn't at all bothered by her threat. They strolled toward the house, and Molly tried to keep her expression guileless even as she scanned the area for Sonny—or any possible threats. Her heart rate picked up again, although this time it was at the thought of Tick's mom's house exploding in a ball of flame.

"Okay?" John asked as if he was able to hear her heart accelerate...or maybe her fingers were digging into his hand so tightly it had become painful.

She made an effort to loosen her grip. "Yeah. Just hoping we don't get blown up." Her mind flashed to the events of the previous night. "Again."

With a wince, he gave her hand a reassuring squeeze, even as he said something that wasn't reassuring at all. "Just remember to run if you think a bomb might go off."

"If I *think* a bomb might go off?" Realizing that she'd gotten a bit loud, she lowered her voice to a hiss. "How am I supposed to tell if a bomb's about to explode? A ticking clock like in a cartoon?"

He actually grinned at that. "Ah, the old ticking clock. It makes it so easy to identify a bomb. It even tells you how much time you have to run."

There were a lot of things she would've liked to say in response to that, but they'd reached the front yard, so she stayed quiet and forced a smile instead. As they climbed the worn steps to the front door, she let out a deep breath and focused on what they were doing. She could argue nonsense with John later. Right now, they had a bail jumper to catch.

He pounded on the door, and she shot him a warning look, even as she sighed in exasperation.

"What?" he asked softly.

"Why not just shout *police* while you're at it?" she muttered, keeping her gaze on the closed front door.

"Because that would be dumb, Pax."

"You know what's dumb, Carmondy?" Her voice was rising again. "Your cop knock."

"Cop knock?" He examined his meaty fist. "I do not have a cop knock."

"Yes, you do. It's more cop-knocky than a regular cop's knock. It's like you slammed an entire ham against the door multiple times."

Giving a dramatic gasp, he held his fist to his chest. "That's so not true. A ham hitting the door would make a wet, fleshy sound." His dimple flashed.

She threw up her hands, even as she made sure to keep her voice low. "Sonny probably took off through a back window when he heard that cop knock of yours."

"Back window?" Dropping his melodramatic posture, he cocked his head with true interest. "Why not the back door?"

"There is no back door."

"How do you know that?" There was no doubt in his tone, just curiosity, and it gave Molly a warm, mushy feeling inside to know that he trusted that she was right.

"Norah found the house floor plan online. The landlord posted them when he was advertising the place before Mother Tick rented it."

"Huh. When did you talk to Norah?"

"I texted her while you were in the shower." The door cracked open, and Molly prepared to chase if it was Sonny and he decided to run, but the person standing on the other side of the small opening was a woman in her fifties who, from what Molly could tell, did not look inclined toward sprinting. "Hello!"

"Can I help you?" The woman seemed a little

suspicious, but not immediately hostile. Molly could work with that.

She widened her smile and gave her words a breathy, bubbly quality. "I'm so sorry to bother you, but I'm Molly, and this is my husband, John. We're from Denver, but we're thinking about buying that church, and I wanted to get the opinion of someone who was really part of the neighborhood, you know?"

The woman—Mother Tick, Molly assumed—blinked several times, even as she opened the door a little wider.

"We just have a few questions about the area and the people... Would you mind?" Molly took a step closer, and Mother Tick fell back a step, swinging the door wider.

"Why would you buy that mess?" the woman asked, waving toward the dilapidated, vacant church.

"My husband's a pastor, you see, and we both love projects." Molly felt John's fingers twitch when she assigned him his new career. "The building is actually wonderful, and so full of history. The structure is solid; it just needs a coat of paint or two."

All three of them looked at the boarded-up church, which appeared to be leaning to the side.

"Anyway!" Molly said quickly in a bright voice. "What do you say? Could we ask you a few questions? It won't take long at all, and it'll help us so much with our decision."

From the way Mother Tick's mouth drew down at the corners as she studied them dubiously, Molly was sure that plan two was a bust. They were about to get the door slammed in their faces, and she knew that John would insist on trying half-assed plan four and a half next.

"Fine." To Molly's quickly hidden shock, Mother Tick swung the door open and waved them in. "I can't take too much time, though. My son'll be home soon, and he'll need his lunch."

"You have a son?" Molly hurried into the house before the offer could be rescinded. "How old is he?"

"Oh, he's grown." Mother Tick led them into a dimly lit living room. "He still loves his mom's cooking, though."

"I'm sure he does." Taking in the heavy, closed drapes that cut off almost all natural light, Molly couldn't keep herself from sending John a quick, bug-eyed look. The single floor lamp struggled to illuminate the space, providing just enough light to show an orange shag carpet and a floral couch. Squinting into the shadows coating the walls, Molly nearly recoiled when she caught a glimpse of glassy eyes staring at her. As her vision adjusted from the sunny outdoors to the dim interior, she realized that the walls were covered with taxidermy animal heads. "Oh…my. Do you hunt?"

John gave a slight cough into his fist to hide an obvious laugh. Smiling at Mother Tick, Molly resisted the urge to kick him on the ankle. If he kept that up, he was going to set her off, too. She sat down on the floral couch and was immediately swallowed up. Using John's grip on her hand as leverage, she pulled herself out of the enveloping sofa cushion and perched on the edge, where she was in less danger of being eaten by the furniture.

"No. That was my ex-husband." To Molly's relief, Mother Tick seemed oblivious to John's amusement, even though his dimple was in full appearance. He settled next to Molly, without giving up his grip on her hand. She didn't mind. It was oddly reassuring to hang on to him, especially in this strange, dark house where Sonny was likely lurking. "I only kept those after the divorce because he loved those nasty things so much, and I wanted to piss him off."

"Oh. Okay." Molly blinked. "Do you live here alone, then?"

When Mother Tick's expression closed, showing the suspicion Molly had thought they'd put aside once they'd been invited in, she hurried to smooth things over.

"It's such a beautiful, big house." Molly looked around, acting as if she could see much of anything in the low light. "But I'm sure the upkeep takes up a great deal of your time. That's one reason we're hesitating on buying the church; we're worried that it'll be a money pit."

Mother Tick's sour expression eased, and Molly gave a silent sigh of relief.

"If we do become neighbors," John chimed in, "we'll be happy to help you with the lawn and other things like that."

"Thank you. Sky is supposed to do all of that for me, but he gets busy and things slip his mind."

"Sky?" Molly echoed, confused.

"My son."

"Oh! Right." Molly avoided meeting John's gaze again, since she was already on the edge of laughter. How did someone go from the name *Sky* to the nickname *Tick*? They were both found in nature, but that was about the extent of the similarities. "He does live with you, then."

Mother Tick gave the smallest nod of agreement. "Just until he clears his record and can apply for a concealed weapon permit. After that, he can get a good security job."

Molly swallowed a snarky reply, offering a smile and a nod instead. "That sounds like a solid plan."

"Do you think he'd be interested in helping remodel the church?" John asked, and Molly gave his hand a squeeze. They worked well as a team. "We're going to need a lot of hands on deck, but we'll pay generously."

Mother Tick straightened with interest. "Well, I can't answer for him, but I'll pass that along to him."

"And his friends," Molly added quickly. "If he has some that are good with a hammer. We'll be new to town, so we'll need to rely on you to let us know who we should trust."

"Of course." Mother Tick looked pleased.

"So!" Molly broadened her sunny grin as she looked at the other woman. "Questions. How are the crime levels in this neighborhood? Do you have a lot of problems?"

"No, I don't, but that doesn't mean you won't. My Sky has contacts, and he makes sure I'm safe."

"Contacts?" Molly tried to sound hopeful, and not like she was going into interrogation mode. "Is there someone we should talk to? We'd like to get along with our new neighbors and parishioners, so any help you could give us would be welcome."

Mother Tick pursed her lips, eyeing them. It was fairly evident that her desire to brag about her inside knowledge was quickly overwhelming her caution. Wanting to encourage this, Molly widened her eyes and leaned forward slightly, as if she couldn't wait to hear what the other woman had to say.

"My son's friend might be able to help you," she said with a show of reluctance that was overridden by her obvious glee. "Sonny Zarver."

"Sonny Zarver." John pulled a pen and a small note-book out of one of his many pockets and jotted that down. "Where can we find him, do you know?"

Mother Tick looked startled by the question, and Molly held her breath, hoping that they hadn't spooked her. Molly plastered on her best pastor's wife smile and nudged John, who beamed kindly at Tick's mom as well. After a moment, she relaxed slightly, and Molly followed suit.

"He's been staying here, actually," Mother Tick said, and Molly forced down her excitement, keeping her expression blandly interested with a great deal of effort. They were so close.

"Oh?" Her fingers tightened on John's hand, needing an outlet to let out her nervous glee. When she heard him grunt, Molly relaxed her grip, giving his fingers the slightest light squeeze in apology. "Is he here now?"

"I think so." Mother Tick frowned, but it was more uncertain than suspicious this time. "Although I haven't heard anything from his room yet today." All three of them glanced at the ceiling, and Molly stopped herself before she could squirm. Their target was so close, just some wooden studs and plaster separating them from a huge bounty and a chance to keep her and her sisters' home. "He keeps rather...odd hours." The downturn of the woman's lips lightened, changing to a proud smile. "Sky, on the other hand... You could set a clock by him." Her gaze darted to a gold clock sitting on the table, just as it chimed the three-quarter hour.

*No time to waste*, Molly thought as she twitched, finally giving in to her urge to wriggle around. "I'm so sorry," she said, ducking her head in pretend bashfulness.

"We haven't told many people yet, but you've been so kind…" She shot a look at John, who smiled at her even as he silently asked what she was about to do. This part hadn't exactly been ironed out before they'd knocked on Mother Tick's door. "We're expecting our first."

Pressing her hand to her belly, low down where period cramps were centered every month, Molly let her smile stretch, trying to show all of the sappiness and none of the horror that came with the idea of being pregnant. "Unfortunately, this little bean is parked directly on my bladder. Would you mind if I used your bathroom?" When Mother Tick hesitated, Molly bit her lower lip, trying her best to look both embarrassed and in urgent need of the facilities.

"Very well," Mother Tick finally huffed, waving at the dim archway that led away from the front door. "Second door on your left."

"Thank you," Molly gushed, slipping her hand out of John's and instantly feeling the loss.

"Do you need any help, sweetness?" John asked her, and she barely kept herself from throwing him an eye-rolling *Why would I need help to pee?* look, giving him a gritted-teeth smile over her shoulder instead.

"I'll be fine, dumpling." She turned toward Mother Tick, whose eyes had narrowed again at his offer, and gave a small, isn't-he-sweet laugh. "Overprotective first-time daddy," she said in a stage whisper before throwing John a kiss. The dork actually pretended to catch it and pressed it to his heart, which was both ridiculous and, at the same time, gave her a warm feeling in her chest.

She hurried toward the hallway before John could do

anything else. The bathroom door was open, so Molly turned on both the light and the exhaust fan, the latter to hopefully hide any noises that she should be making. The door locked with a simple push button on the knob, so she engaged it before pulling the door closed while she was still in the hallway.

Not wanting to waste any time—since who knew what John was saying in the living room—Molly slipped deeper into the dark house. Although she knew from what Mother Tick had said that the room Sonny was staying in was upstairs, she pulled a small flashlight out of her pants pocket and peeked into the next room, which looked like a rarely used study. Once she saw no one was inside, she moved to the next doorway.

She hated to waste her limited time checking rooms, but Molly didn't want to be ambushed from behind. Her hope of simply grabbing Sonny and calling in a sheriff's department pickup had died the night before, when he'd blown a hole in a bathroom wall to escape from them. This would most likely be messy, but she was determined that this one bail jumper would not stand in the way of her keeping her family's home.

Stepping into the kitchen, she made a face as she looked around. Even in this room, curtains were pulled over the window above the sink, turning what should've been a bright and open kitchen into an eerie space. The counters and cupboards were obscured in the gloom, which blackened the space underneath the small table. Even her small light somehow made things worse, illuminating just a small area, but leaving the rest of the room shrouded in shadows.

The beam of the flashlight settled on a narrow,

closed door across the room, and she moved toward it. According to the floor plans Norah had found, that should lead to the stairs to the second level. She moved quickly, wanting to get out of the haunted kitchen as soon as possible, and her hip bumped against the edge of a metal chair, making it rattle as it slid a few inches across the scarred linoleum floor.

Molly froze, listening for any sound indicating that the residents of the house had heard, but the low rumble of John's voice and Mother Tick's higher-pitched responses didn't change. There was no movement on the second floor—at least not that Molly could hear—so she finished crossing the kitchen, taking care not to bump into anything else.

The knob felt cold in her grip, and she shivered as she turned it. *Don't let this spooky, dark house freak you out*, the practical part of her brain warned. Straightening her shoulders, she pulled the door open, revealing a narrow, steep flight of stairs that climbed into an even deeper darkness above.

*What do these people have against natural light—or any light, for that matter?* Molly wondered. She kept her flashlight low as she climbed, wincing at every squeak and crack of the steps under her weight. Reaching the top, she started to place her foot down, then froze at the faintest hint of pressure against her shin.

As she looked down, pointing the tiny flashlight at her feet, she saw the shine of a silver wire stretching across the top step about eight inches off the floor. Carefully stepping over the trip wire, she hoped that the slight tug hadn't been enough to trigger whatever it was connected to. Her heart thundered in her chest at the close call, and she wanted more than anything to run back down the stairs, grab John, and leave this spooky, dark house and all of its booby traps behind. They could go home and take Warrant for a nice walk in the national forest behind her house before making dinner with her sisters, all of them happily mashed into the tiny kitchen together.

The only problem was that if she didn't bring in Sonny Zarver, that house wouldn't be hers for much longer.

Resolved, she crept forward down a short hallway. There were three doors, one on either side and the last one straight ahead. She paused to listen, hoping to get a hint as to which one Sonny was in, but there was only silence. Unable to hear John or Mother Tick anymore, she suddenly felt very alone. As she shifted, the board under her feet gave a soft creak, and she went still for a long moment, fully expecting one of the three doors to bang open, revealing a murderous Sonny intent on keeping his freedom. Nothing moved. It felt as if even the house was holding its breath.

Knowing that the longer she hesitated, the greater the chance of them all being blown to pieces, Molly picked the door on her left at random. It was locked. *Of course it is.* She quickly ran through her options, deciding that picking the lock would be a last resort, since it would take more precious time than she wanted to spare and, although not especially noisy, the small sounds could easily catch Sonny's attention.

While she was deciding this, she checked the handle of the door on the right. To her surprise, it turned easily under her fingers. Standing to the side, she pushed it open, her muscles tensed, ready to fling herself out of the way. There was a slight resistance, and she shoved harder. There was a solid click as the door suddenly flew open completely, banging against the wall.

The room was shabby and messy, with a mattress on the floor and clothes and belongings strewn across everything. A blanket covered one window, but the other was wide open, the covering hanging limply to the side. Blinking against the unexpected brightness, Molly only vaguely noticed the untidy details, her focus fixed on the hand grenade rolling to a stop against the base of a pressboard dresser. The pin was missing, and the knowledge hit her in that split second that it was hanging on the door she'd just swung open.

She'd just activated a grenade.

This was bad. Very, very bad.

# CHAPTER 16

Without stopping to come up with a plan, Molly turned and bolted, hurdling the trip wire at the top of the stairs and getting all the way down the steps before her thinking brain engaged again. Blasting through the door at the bottom of the steps, she yelled, "Out! Get out!"

Tearing down the hallway, she saw John running across the living room toward her. There was no sign of Mother Tick.

"What are you doing?" Molly shrieked, not slowing down. "Go! Out! Grenade!"

His eyes widened, but instead of immediately hightailing it out of there, he waited until she flew past him and then tucked himself in behind her. *Stupid, chivalrous ass!* she yelled in her head, not wanting to waste the oxygen she needed for sprinting. She could scold him later for his lack of self-preservation…if they managed to not get blown up, that was.

As they neared the open front door, everything felt like it had slowed down to a nightmare pace. Fighting the need to look behind her to check on John, Molly forced her legs to move faster as she reached toward the doorframe, as if she could pull it closer to them if only she could reach it.

She wasn't fast enough.

A loud rumbling *bang!* made her duck and cover her head with both arms. Her heart caught as she turned toward John, instinctively moving to protect him from damage. Plaster dust rained down on them, interspersed with several louder crashes as pieces of the ceiling fell. John pushed her back, grunting as a chunk of plaster caught him on the shoulder. Blinking the dust out of her eyes, Molly moved to check if he was seriously hurt, but he turned her bodily around and pressed her through the open door and across the porch. They didn't stop until they were on the lawn.

Pulling her to a halt, John frantically checked her over, his hands moving gently along her arms and torso. "Does anything hurt? Do you need an ambulance?"

"John." She grabbed his fingers, stopping his inspection until he met her gaze. "I'm fine. You're the one who was hit. How's your shoulder?"

He glanced at it as if he'd forgotten. Molly hadn't forgotten. She'd be seeing that moment in her nightmares for a long time. "It's fine," he said, his voice calmer, shrugging that shoulder as if to prove that he was okay.

"Good." Relief that he wasn't seriously hurt rushed through her. Brushing small chunks of plaster out of her hair, she glanced over at Mother Tick by the curb, talking on her cell phone. Molly groaned.

"What's wrong?" John eyed her carefully up and down. "Are you sure you're not hurt?"

"Positive. That wasn't an I'm-in-pain sound. That was a she's-calling-the-cops-so-we'll-be-stuck-here-for-hours-answering-questions groan."

"What happened?" Mother Tick called out to them, the cell phone still at her ear. "Where's Sonny? Didn't he make it out? Someone needs to check on him." By the way she planted her feet and looked at John and Molly accusingly, that *someone* was not going to be Mother Tick.

Molly opened her mouth to say that Mr. Booby Trap could just deal with the consequences until the cops and firefighters arrived, but then she changed her mind before the words could make it out. "I'll go," she said sweetly instead.

"No, I'll go." John shifted so he stood between her and the house. "Think of the *baby*."

Instead of arguing, she just dodged around him, grabbing his hand on the way. "We'll both go and watch out for each other. The baby will need both its parents." She could feel his tension, and she knew he was going to try to prevent her from going back in the house. This was a prime opportunity to search through Sonny's things...what was left of them. As soon as they were out of Mother Tick's earshot, she muttered, "You need my help. I know where at least one of the trip wires is."

That shut him up until they were back inside, eyeing the damaged ceiling. Although there were chunks of plaster missing, and the light fixture hung askew, wires showing on one side, it didn't appear that the whole thing was going to come crashing down on their heads.

"I really don't want you coming up there," John grumbled, his gaze still fixed on the pockmarked ceiling. "It's not safe."

Molly snorted and moved toward the hallway. "If I only did what was *safe*, I'd never have started a bail recovery business. I'd have started a...safe-making business." She chuckled at her own stupid pun, needing to relieve the nervous tension. She knew it wasn't smart to wander around a house after a grenade had gone off, but this was Sonny Zarver's last place of residence, and he hadn't had a chance to clean it out yet. It was a golden opportunity.

As they headed toward the kitchen, Molly pulled out her flashlight. The short time she'd spent outside had ruined her night vision, and the house seemed even gloomier than before. She automatically checked rooms as they passed, noticing that John had his own flashlight in hand and was doing the same thing. For some reason, this similarity in their methods made her smile before she ordered her brain to focus on the potentially dangerous task ahead.

A loud crash came from upstairs as they moved through the kitchen, and Molly glanced back at John. He gave her a grim look and took the lead up the stairs.

"Trip wire at the top, close to the floor," she whispered.

His glance back at her was quick but telling. "You couldn't have just told me where it was instead of insisting on coming along?"

Even though he couldn't see her, she shrugged. "You might've missed something."

He muttered under his breath, too softly for her to hear.

Although she wanted to say something else, she stayed quiet as they reached the top of the stairs. Instead of stepping over the trip wire, John pulled a small pair of wire cutters out of his pocket and snipped the line.

*Good idea.* She patted him on the back in approval. There were going to be a lot of innocent first responders tromping through in ten minutes or so, and it was better that they didn't blow themselves up by accident. When

John turned, his eyebrows lifted in question, she just gave him a thumbs-up.

They moved toward the doors again, and Molly pointed at the one on the right, even though it was obvious where the explosion had occurred. The door was still wide open after her mad dash to escape, and shrapnel had peppered the wall and door across the hall from Sonny's room. Although there was a slight haze of smoke, the room wasn't the smoldering pit she'd expected. The glass from the uncovered window littered the floor, but otherwise all the mess was the same as before the explosion.

"Concussion grenade?" she asked, stepping cautiously into the space.

John caught her arm, tugging her back as he slid in front of her. That seemed to becoming a habit on his part. "Most likely. Be careful, though. In an old house like this, it still could've done damage."

The faint wail of an emergency siren drifted in through the open window, reminding Molly that they were short on time. "I'll search in here. Go break down the other two doors and see why they're locked. I'm guessing Sonny did that to slow down anyone who's searching for him, but there might be something useful. Be careful, though. Apparently, Sonny loves his booby traps."

John's eyebrows lifted. "Break them down? Look at you, Miss Demolition."

She gave a small shrug, even as she internally preened a little at the admiration in his voice. "Mother Tick can't get mad about the damage. She pretty much demanded that we search for Sonny."

Although he snorted, he moved back to the door. "Fine, but you be careful, too."

"I will." She made shooing motions. "Go kick some doors in. You know you want to."

His grin made her stomach swoop and dive. "Not every day I get to kick a door in…at least without getting yelled at after."

As he left the room, she immediately started searching, moving methodically from one side to the next, looking in the heating vents and air returns and checking for spots on the wall that appeared to have been recently restored. The floor creaked alarmingly under her feet, but it held.

She was checking the mattress for openings when the first *bang* of John's boot hitting a door sounded, and she closed her eyes, waiting for another explosion. After she counted to twenty, she let out her breath in a rush and opened her eyes again. She resumed her search, checking the floor for any loose boards or bigger-than-normal gaps. Sonny was apparently a terrible housekeeper. Dust—regular dust, along with the plaster—coated everything. Making a face, she slapped her dirty hands across her pants, but that didn't help much.

At the sound of another door being kicked in, Molly started to count again, although she didn't pause her search that time. Quickly, she reached the opposite side of the room without finding anything except clothes and other uninteresting personal items. She'd even rummaged through the pockets of all of his pants and jackets that she'd found strewn around. It wasn't pleasant. Sonny seemed to have the same aversion to doing laundry as he had for dusting. The closet was completely empty.

Running a hand over the top of her head to remove a spiderweb, she grimaced at the grainy feel of plaster dust coating her hair. She looked around the room, trying to figure out what she'd missed. There was no way that Sonny could've known they were coming, so he would've had to leave in a hurry. A glance out the window told her that he must've climbed down the rickety trellis or somehow scaled the smooth siding down to the ground or up to the roof. Either way, he would've only had time to grab the most important things—wallet and phone and possibly a laptop—and run.

Her gaze settled on an electrical outlet. It was strangely clean and dust-free compared to the rest of the room. When she looked at it more closely, she saw that the plate had a fresh coating of paint that didn't match the dingy walls. The plate around the light switch had been newly painted as well. A loud wail of a siren pulled her attention away from the outlet. They were getting much louder; the emergency vehicles couldn't be more than a half mile away by now. Stepping into the hall, she called out to John. "Can I use your flathead screwdriver?"

He popped out of the room directly across from the stairs and tossed her his multi-tool. "Be quick. We probably have three minutes before the firefighters will be tossing us over their shoulders and carrying us outside."

"Ooh...sounds hot." She winked and rushed back into Sonny's room, smiling at John's startled bark of laughter. She unscrewed the plate around the first outlet, but it was empty. The sirens grew deafeningly loud before shutting off completely, and Molly rushed to the light switch. Because the plate had been painted over, the screw didn't want to turn.

"C'mon…c'mon…" she muttered. The screw finally gave, and she hurried to twist it out. Heavy boots pounded on the stairs as she dropped the plate onto the floor and peered into the opening. Her heart gave a jump as she spotted the top of a small cell phone, and she slid it out just as the boots reached the top of the stairs. Dropping the phone and John's multi-tool into her pocket, she turned toward the doorway just as the first firefighter appeared.

"Are you okay, miss?" he asked, and she smiled as she walked toward him, her newly found evidence bumping against her leg.

"Yes, I'm fine." She joined him in the hallway just as John came out of the room across from hers.

"Sonny's not in here, either," he announced. "He must've left earlier without Mother Ti—uh, Sky's mom hearing."

Nervous giggles fueled by adrenaline threatened to bubble out of Molly, but she forced her expression to stay serious.

"The two of you shouldn't be up here." The firefighter, a very attractive black man, frowned at them disapprovingly as more of his colleagues moved around them, looking for the explosion site.

"Sorry, sir, but we had to check if someone was trapped up here." She grabbed John's hand. "We couldn't have lived with ourselves if someone died when we could've helped."

The firefighter's frown lightened slightly, although his tone remained scolding. "The next time there's an explosion of any kind, stay outside and wait for help to arrive. *Professional* help."

"Yes, sir," Molly said, perfectly willing to make that promise, as John nodded in agreement.

"We'll do that. Let's go, sugarplum, and get out of these nice people's way," John said, ushering her toward the stairs.

Molly turned and said over her shoulder. "Keep your eye out for trip wires. That friend of Sky's seems to be quite the...practical joker."

The man who'd just admonished them stared at her for a long moment, looking bemused. "We'll do that." Turning, he called out to one of the other firefighters, "Carson! I need you to walk these two out."

As Carson escorted them through the house, Molly could barely contain her excitement and the need to share her find with John.

Once they stepped outside, however, and she saw her least-favorite detectives, Bastien and Mill, interviewing Mother Tick, she was distracted from the cell phone burning a hole in her pocket.

"Here you go. The detectives will want to speak with you." He nodded toward the Denver cops.

"Thank you, Carson," Molly said politely, even as she plotted an escape route. The detectives' backs were turned toward the house, so she was pretty sure she and John hadn't been spotted yet.

"No problem." The firefighter tromped back inside, and Molly hustled toward the crowd of onlookers that had gathered to watch the action. John must've recognized the cops, too, since he kept pace without asking why she was basically running away from the house and skipping out on the inevitable police interview. She risked a glance over her shoulder once they were safely mingling with the gawking neighbors. Detective Mill started to turn his head, so she grabbed John's arm and pulled him past the last ring of people.

John's look was distinctive enough that she knew Mill would recognize him if he caught a glimpse. The cops would figure out that they'd been there once Mother Tick described them, but Molly figured they could stop by the police station and find a more sympathetic officer to take their statement. Mill and Bastien would tie them up for hours, just because they had decided she was guilty by association with Jane. She and John didn't have time for that, not when they needed to bring Sonny in.

Once they were free of the crowd, Molly forced herself to slow down to a brisk but not racing pace. John's car looked too far away, and she resisted the urge to glance over her shoulder to see if either of the cops had followed. The normal sounds of civilization—traffic, a lawn mower in the distance, the faint sounds of kids playing—quickly covered up the chatter of the crowd, but Molly still didn't relax until they finally reached John's car.

By mutual silent agreement, they didn't speak until they were both seated and the doors were closed. As John pulled away from the curb, he glanced at her, his anticipation clear. Apparently, her suppressed glee had been obvious...at least to John.

"I found a phone," she said, pulling out his multi-tool but leaving the cell in her pocket. She didn't even want to touch it before Norah could work her magic, in case Molly erased something by accident.

"Sonny's phone?" John accepted the multi-tool

absently as his eyes lit with the same excitement that Molly felt.

"One of his phones. It was under the light-switch plate."

"Nice!" He dropped the tool into his pocket and then raised his fist for a congratulatory bump. "I have people who can take a look at it."

"So do I," she said, although she did bump his fist. "Norah's the best, and she's cheap. She works—at least partially—for street cred and family dinners."

She was braced for him to argue, but he just held on to his wide smile and shrugged slightly. "How can my tech guys beat that?"

The mention of tech guys reminded Molly of their appointment, and she hurried to glance at the clock. She grinned. "Look at that! We survived an explosion, found a clue, and we'll still get back in time to have a security system installed."

"We're just that good," John said solemnly, making her laugh. It hadn't been *that* funny, but the giddy relief that had built up over the past few hours needed to release somehow, and there was no way she was about to cry, especially in front of John Carmondy. Even though she'd discovered that he was an enormous marshmallow mashed inside a huge, muscular package, and that he would most likely be as sweet as pie were she to dissolve into a wet, sobbing mess, she didn't want to reveal that side of herself to him. She wanted him to see her as tough, as an equal partner, someone who would have his back, just as he had hers.

Shaking off her wild thoughts, she pulled out her phone as a distraction. After reading a few texts from her sisters, she sent off a group text summarizing what had happened over the course of the morning...although she minimized the whole explosion thing. They didn't need to know how scared she'd been when she'd thought it was a regular grenade, or that she and John had come inches from being blasted into nothingness.

A buzz from her phone brought her mind back to the present, and she saw that Norah had texted.

Great news! I'll be back at the house in a few minutes, and I'll take a crack at it.

Felicity and Charlie each sent a short congratulatory text, and Cara stayed silent. Concern rose in Molly's chest, but then she remembered that Cara had class until one. Cara, being Cara, would never even consider keeping her phone on—even on silent—during a class.

"Any news on the hunt for your mom?" John asked, pulling her attention away from her phone.

"Nothing solid yet, but they do have a few leads." Charlie had been exasperatingly vague, as usual, but Felicity had filled in some of the blanks. "They're pretty sure they're on the right track."

"Are they going to be gone again tonight?" he asked, his attempt to sound casual failing so miserably that it caught her attention...and her suspicion.

"Why?" she asked. "Did you enjoy sleeping in my bed that much?"

He coughed, sounding strangled. "I just wanted to make sure you had some backup, in case your house gets burglarized again." He put an emphasis on the *again*, as if she wouldn't remember that every Tom, Dick, and Stuart had tried to break in over the past few days.

"Cara and Norah will be there with me. Oh, and Warrant." She glared at him when the dog's name made John snort. "Warrant can be ferocious when he wants to be." Although she tried to think of examples, all she could come up with was that he snored *ferociously*, and that wouldn't deter anyone from breaking in.

"I'm sure he can." From his soothing tone, John didn't actually believe in Warrant's watchdog abilities. Sure, the hairy boy did sleep pretty soundly, and he tended to see all visitors as potential petters and bringers of snacks, but that didn't mean he wouldn't have his moment of save-the-family glory. One day. Maybe.

Shaking off her thoughts, Molly refocused on the point of the discussion.

"Besides," she said, "you're forgetting about Cara and Norah. With this new project, Norah will be awake all night."

"They slept through the last break-in," he said.

"That was a testament to our slick and silent expulsion technique." She wanted to bristle at his implied critique of her sisters, but he wasn't wrong. Unless a loud noise woke them, they did tend to sleep deeply. "Besides, we'll have a security system by tonight. If the alarm goes off, everybody—including the neighbors—will wake up."

Despite her excellent logic, John didn't look happy, grumbling to himself as he glared through the windshield like the oncoming cars were to blame.

His grumpiness was actually sort of funny. "Admit it. You're just in love with my bed and want to sleep there every night," she teased.

The look he shot her was so filled with unexpected

heat that her toes literally curled in her boots. His attention returned to the road, and she took a few moments to get her breathing back under control. She barely resisted fanning her face. "My bed's nicer," he finally said, and the mention of his bed made the molten heat inside her fire up again.

*Stop it,* she commanded her libido. *That was an innocent comment, and you're being ridiculous.* Her self-directed lecture didn't help. Clearing her throat, she decided a change of subject was in order. "Did you find anything in the other two rooms?"

"The one on the end was a sewing room and a bust, but I grabbed this from Tick's room." He pulled a small notepad from one of his many pockets and handed it to her.

She flipped through it. "Tick's not a bad doodler," she said, admiring a sketch of a spider in the corner of one page. Most of the pages had simple drawings or patterns, although there were a few notes interspersed throughout the notepad. One was a to-do list, including "tell Mom to buy Cheetos," but there were some others that had more potential, like a phone number and a scribbled local address. "Nice work, Carmondy."

"Thanks," he said as he pulled up in front of her house. "But the real find is that phone."

"We'll see if Norah can pull anything off it." She was trying to tone down her anticipation, in case the cell was a dud with no usable information. "Should I feel bad that Mother Tick is going to think Sonny's a weirdo who took off all her electrical outlet plates?"

John snorted. "With all the bad things he's done, Sonny Zarver deserves that and so much more."

"True." If all went well, Sonny would be headed back

to jail soon, and Molly kind of liked the idea of being a force for karma.

As they headed toward the front door, she looked around for strange vehicles parked on the street, but it was empty. Somehow, that didn't reassure her. Instead, it felt like people could be hiding in any shadow. She usually loved having the national forest so close, wrapping the west side of their neighborhood like a cozy natural blanket, but now the deep reach of towering trees made her feel uneasy. Whole legions of criminals could be tucked back in the trees, just waiting for their opportunity, and she wouldn't be able to bring them all down with just her Taser and her rudimentary knowledge of self-defense.

With a shiver, she hurried into the house.

"You okay?" John asked as he followed her inside.

She hesitated, debating whether she should share her completely illogical fears with him. Before she could say anything, a huge white ball of fur came galumphing toward them. "Hey, Warrant," she said, bending over to greet him. "What brought on this show of love?"

He breezed by her outstretched hands and wrapped himself around John's legs, his tail wagging enthusiastically. Narrowing her eyes, Molly straightened and glared at the dog thief. John didn't even notice her glare—he was too busy petting Warrant.

"How's my sweetie pie?" John cooed, massaging the dog's ears in a way that made Warrant groan in ecstasy. "Who's the best boy? You. Yes, you are."

Rolling her eyes, Molly walked away from the love-fest to find Norah in the kitchen.

Norah's face lit with anticipation. "Do you have it?"

"Right here." Molly pulled it out eagerly, her sister's excitement at the find feeding her own. She held it out, and as Norah reached for it, the phone vibrated.

They both jerked back, and the phone started to fall. Molly reached out, trying to keep it from hitting the floor. Her fingers just touched the plastic case, bobbling the phone several times before her fingers closed securely around it. As the cell vibrated again, she moved to answer, but then remembered that she didn't sound anything like Sonny Zarver—at least she assumed she didn't. She'd never heard him speak before.

"Carmondy!" she called, dashing for the living room. At her call, John jerked up, his face falling into the stern, *danger's-here* lines that she'd only seen on him a few times before—and all over the last few days. She chucked the phone at him, and he caught it automatically. "Answer! Pretend to be Sonny."

To his credit, he didn't waste any time asking her to elaborate. Instead, he answered the phone immediately. "Yeah?" he said gruffly. After a pause, he said, "It's me. Sonny." As Molly rushed to pull up the recording app on her own phone, she hoped that, unlike her, he actually knew what Sonny sounded like. Once she had it going, she held it up to show John, who immediately switched to speaker mode.

"…sound strange," a male voice was saying.

John cleared his throat but kept his rough intonation when he spoke again. "Just woke up."

Holding her breath, Molly glanced at Warrant, hoping he wouldn't choose this of all times for a rare bark.

"It's almost noon. Glad one of us is able to sleep." The sarcastic voice on the other end of the call sounded

familiar to Molly, but she couldn't place the person.
Filing it away in the back of her mind to think about
later, she concentrated on what he was saying. "Are you
taking tonight's deal seriously? This could make us or
break us, so if you're just blowing it off…"

"I'm taking it seriously," John said. "I've been sick,
that's all."

"Sick or using again?"

"Sick." John flashed a look at Molly, who was still
trying to keep her breathing as quiet as possible. Norah
was frozen in the kitchen entrance, looking as if she was
just as petrified to make a noise. "I'm clean. You know
that, so quit bitching at me and tell me what I need to
know for tonight."

Molly could feel her eyes widening at John's bossy
tone. What if the guy on the other end of the call was
Sonny's boss? She didn't want him to get angry and
hang up before they got any details.

"Watch your mouth." He sounded more resigned
than furious, and Molly relaxed slightly. "It's nothing
we haven't gone over before. The exchange is at eleven,
the usual place. They'll have your new ID papers. Don't
bring that squirrelly kid along this time. I'm serious,
Sonny. Nothing can go wrong tonight."

"Fine," John growled. Although most of her attention was riveted on the conversation, a part of her was
impressed with John's acting skills. He generally seemed
so up front and open that it was always strange seeing
him play a part. "What d'you need me to do?"

There was a pause, and Molly's heart rate took off
like a greyhound after a bunny. "What do you *think* I
need you to do, Sonny? You need to be there on time

with the merchandise. That's it. Think you can manage without screwing that up?"

"Yeah, I'll have it there." John looked at Molly, and she mouthed *where?* at him. "You don't think the usual place is too risky?"

"Why would it be?" the man asked with a snap in his voice. "Have you been running your mouth?"

"*I* haven't, but that doesn't mean word hasn't gotten out," John said, inserting a slight, nasally whine that suited Sonny to a T… At least, she imagined it did. She knew a lot more about Sonny's reputation and the destruction he left in his wake than she did about the guy himself.

"Word better not have gotten out," the other man snarled. "If something happens to wreck this deal, I swear to God, Sonny—"

A loud knock on the front door interrupted whatever threat the guy was going to throw out. Molly jumped a foot before rushing as quietly as possible over to open the door.

"What was that?" the man on the call demanded.

The good-looking Latino man outside had to be Desmond, John's security system friend. He opened his mouth to speak but went still when Molly dramatically thumped a finger against her lips in the international sign for *be quiet*. Before he could do more than frown at her in confusion, she grabbed the front of his button-down shirt and hauled him inside.

"Just my landlady," John lied easily, giving Desmond a wave. "Ignore her."

A loud, exasperated sigh rattled through the cheap phone speaker. "Fine. Just…be there on time. Don't screw this up."

"I'll be there." John's gaze met Molly's, his words a vow, and she felt a spark of excitement race through her. The two of them would be there, and they'd finally bring this chase to an end. Sonny Zarver was in their sights. Together, she and John would finish this, even if they had to drag Sonny by his hair all the way back to the county jail.

They just had to figure out where this exchange was happening, and then they could finally bring down the elusive—and dangerous—Sonny Zarver.

# CHAPTER 17

EVEN AFTER JOHN ENDED THE CALL, THE REST OF THEM were silent until he tossed the phone to Norah. "It's all yours now, genius."

Molly eyed him sharply, but there was no sarcasm in the term, just affectionate admiration. Norah, who was not the queen of activities requiring hand-eye coordination, fumbled the catch, and Molly cringed, too far away to make the save this time. By some miracle, Norah managed to hold on to the phone before it hit the floor. Holding it up in a sort of *I've got this* gesture, she rushed upstairs.

"Slippery skip?" Desmond asked.

"You could say that," John said, greeting his friend with a handshake-hug combination as Molly ended the recording and tucked her phone into her pocket. Already, her thoughts were spinning as she tried to figure out where the "usual place" could be. Dutch's was too busy, and she couldn't imagine that Sonny would do anything at Mother Tick's place, not when he lived there...or at least he had before that morning's events. Unfortunately, those were the only two places she knew that were connected to Sonny. The "usual place" could be anywhere in Langston or Denver or...well, anywhere within an eleven-hour radius.

"Pax?" John's voice pulled her from her thoughts to find both men looking at her.

"Sorry." She grimaced. "Just going over the huge grab bag of possibilities in my head. Why couldn't he have just given us an address? Easy-peasy, Sonny-handcuffy."

Huffing a laugh, John shook his head with mock sadness. "That doesn't flow at *all*. Really, Pax?"

If she was closer, she would've pinched his arm. Instead, she settled for a frosty look before turning to Desmond with a polite smile. "Sorry to grab you and drag you into the house just now. Thanks for coming so quickly."

"No problem." Desmond's wide smile was almost as appealing as John's. "It's not the strangest greeting I've ever gotten."

Her eyebrows shot up, and Molly instantly wanted to hear stories about the even-weirder situations he'd walked in on. Before she could ask, though, John strode over and threw one of his monster arms over her shoulders, distracting her.

"What are you doing?" she asked, baffled by the action and by the fact that she didn't hate being tucked against John Carmondy's side.

"Showing affection." He cuddled her closer, sending pleasure zinging through her nerve endings. "To you."

"Why?"

The puzzled look he gave her made her feel like she was the one out of sync. "I'm an affectionate guy?"

Desmond must've understood something that she was missing, because he was laughing behind his hand.

Wriggling free, she threw her arms up. "Okay! Today is only half over, and I have a shady business

transaction to attend late tonight. I can't afford to have
my brain explode before then, so I'm going to go see
if Norah's having any luck. You guys"—she sketched
circles in the air that encompassed the entire house—
"do your security-system thing. I trust your judgment."
She paused as she headed for the stairs, glancing back
at John. "Just don't make it too expensive. I'd rather not
have to sell this house to pay you for it, not after all the
effort we're going through to keep it in the family."

"We'll get you set up," Desmond said as John fixed
her with a wry look that told her he was well aware she
was running away. Feeling her cheeks warm, she turned
around before he could see the telltale redness. As she
climbed the stairs, she could feel his gaze on her back,
reminding her of a predator patiently settling in to wait
for his prey.

Telling herself that sleep deprivation and an overdose
of adrenaline were taking a toll on her, leaving her a
victim of a too-active imagination, she shook off the
sensation and hurried to Norah's bedroom door. She
knocked and, after waiting for the invitation to come in,
slipped inside, closing the door behind her.

"Any luck so far?" she asked.

Norah gave her a *really?* glance before refocusing on
what she was doing with the SIM card. "It's been, what?
Three minutes?"

"Five." Molly paused. "Maybe. Anyway, it's a measure of your skill that I believe you could have discovered something by now."

"Mmm-mmm." Norah didn't sound like she fully
believed Molly's excuse.

"Fine. John was weirding me out."

That caught her sister's attention. "What do you mean? I thought the two of you were...you know."

Molly fixed Norah with her best basilisk stare. "Why did you think that? Have you been listening to Fifi's gossip again?"

"No." Norah—sweet, innocent Norah—rolled her eyes so hard that Molly thought they would roll out of their sockets. "Anyone who's around the two of you for five seconds knows that you're banging. It's obvious."

"*Banging?*" This was so much worse than she'd expected. Maybe she should've stuck with the guys. At least then she would've been spared this discussion. "We're not *banging*."

"Right."

"We're not. At all." Molly tried to ignore the twinge of disappointment at that fact. "There's no banging. There isn't even any kissing and hardly any cuddling."

Norah's attention, which had drifted toward the SIM card again, snapped back to Molly. "But there's *some* cuddling?"

"Minor cuddling. Extremely minor cuddling."

Norah studied her face. "You sound disappointed. Do you want there to be more cuddling?"

"No." That felt like a lie. "Maybe. How can I tell when we keep getting almost blown up all the time?" Her brain was spinning again, this time with her very confused feelings about a certain rival bounty hunter. She flopped down next to Norah, forced to curl around her sister in order to fit on the narrow bed. "Let's stop talking about that. How do you manage to sleep when Warrant's on the bed? This is so tiny."

"Just used to it, I guess," Norah said absently, already

immersed in her project again. "I'm a deep sleeper, so that helps." After a pause, she lifted her head and looked around her small room. "Where is he, anyway?"

"Still with his crush." At Norah's confused look, Molly clarified, "Carmondy. Warrant's in *looove*. I suspect that there were sneaky, secret bacon treats involved, but I don't have any evidence."

Norah smiled as she turned back to her work. "Guess it's going around."

"What is?"

"John Carmondy love."

"Staaahhp." Molly covered her eyes with her hands. "My poor brain can't take any more. Can we talk about something else? Anything else? Like…if fairies exist, or whether fudgy brownies or cake brownies taste better, or the best ways to destroy the patriarchy, or something besides John Carmondy and his stupidly adorable dimples? Please?"

"Sure." Several seconds of silence passed before Norah spoke again. "I like blond brownies."

Molly smiled as her eyes closed. "Me too."

"And education is the basis of all societal change."

"Mmm-hmm…" Her sleepless nights were catching up with her. Her eyes refused to open. "I'm taking it that we're not discussing fairies, then?"

"Gross."

"What's gross?" Molly blinked at her sister sleepily. "Fairies?"

"They creep me out. If they do exist, I don't want to know about it. I'd never sleep again."

Molly's eyes drifted closed again, even as she snorted. "You're so weird."

"Right back at you."

———————————

A jab to the ribs woke Molly. She sat up, confused by the location and the daylight that filled the room, her mind still half-asleep but her body on full alert. "What is it? What's wrong?"

"Get up and grab John so I only have to go through this once," Norah said, closing her laptop with a click.

Everything about Sonny Zarver and Jane settled back into Molly's brain, and she got to her feet, yawning and wishing she could have another hour—or day—to sleep. A glance at her cell phone showed that she'd been napping for almost two hours. That'd have to be enough for now. "I'm up. Did you find the address for the meet-up tonight?"

"Maybe."

"Maybe?" Molly repeated. "Likely maybe or doubtful maybe?"

Instead of answering, Norah fixed her with a stern look. It would've been scarier if she hadn't been wearing a shirt with *You are dumb* written in binary code. "Get John first. Then I'll tell you everything."

"Fine," Molly agreed through another yawn as she headed for the door. When she couldn't hear any other voices, she wondered if Desmond had finished and John had taken off. She couldn't blame him, since he'd been neck-deep in her crazy, dangerous family drama ever since Jane had contacted him. He had to be behind on his own life stuff.

Pushing away the wave of irrational and unwanted

disappointment, she tromped down the stairs, heading for the kitchen to get some water.

"Good nap?"

She hid her startle at the unexpected question, turning toward where John sat at the dining room table, Warrant's snoozing head on his foot. "Short," she answered belatedly, taking in the sight in front of her. She had to admit that having John around made the house feel even safer and cozier than it normally did, which was impressive considering the excessive number of people who'd been breaking in recently. Her gaze fell to where Warrant was sprawled under the table. "How'd you manage to win the dog over so fast?" Without pausing, she guessed, "It *was* bacon, wasn't it?"

John's smile started slowly, curling up the corners and denting his cheeks until he was grinning broadly, making her heart beat abnormally fast. What John Carmondy did to her nervous system couldn't be healthy. "No bacon. We just bonded. I think he's happy to have another guy around."

She made a *humph* sound. "The five of us spoil that dog like crazy. You should be so lucky to be surrounded by beautiful women who feed you treats, rub your belly, let you kick them off their beds, and tell you that you're the most wonderful being in the universe."

As she'd been speaking, his gaze had heated to a simmering smolder. "He *is* a lucky dog, although five women would be too much for me. Just one feeding me and petting my belly is plenty." The way his eyes raked over her made her wonder, just for a moment, if he was fantasizing about *her* being that woman. She could feel the heat burning her from the inside out, and she knew that if they continued this line of conversation, she would probably spontaneously combust.

"Uh…right. Okay. So…Norah has info for us that she's refusing to share until we're both there to listen." When her heart settled down enough that the roaring in her ears disappeared, she noticed that he had a notepad in front of him. "Did you have something for us, too?"

He grimaced, picking up the notepad and tilting it side to side, as if the paper itself was shrugging. "Nothing concrete. I'm just putting my thoughts down and hoping that something'll jump at me… Useless so far." Dropping the pad onto the table with a slap, he stood. "Let's see what Norah's found."

As Molly led the way upstairs, feeling twitchy with the knowledge that her butt was right at his eye level, she asked, "Did Desmond finish up? Or is he still lurking around here somewhere?"

With a laugh, John caught up to her, so he was right behind her. Because he was so much taller than she was, he still managed to loom over her, even though he was a whole step down. "He's done. I'll take you and Norah on a tour of the system, and then she can tell us what she knows."

Stopping on the top step, Molly turned abruptly. It was only when she came eyes-to-neck with John that she realized what an awkward situation she'd just created. If she tilted her head up, she'd be in the ideal position for a kiss, and that knowledge completely scoured her brain clear of what she'd been about to say. It might've been her imagination, but it seemed as if heat was radiating off him, warming her muscles and bones until she was about to melt into a puddle of goo at his feet.

Frantically, her eyes fixed firmly on the divot at the base of his throat, she rewound their earlier conversation until she remembered what had been so urgent that she needed to tell him right this second. "Thank you." Her voice came out sounding husky, and her gaze darted to his eyes automatically, just in time to see his pupils react. Clearing her throat, she tore her gaze away, this time focusing on a spot just below the collar of his T-shirt, right where the seam was starting to pull apart. Crazily, that tiny hole made her feel protective of him. She felt a sudden need to wrap him up in soft blankets and tuck him away somewhere safe, somewhere he wouldn't get blown up or punched in that too-pretty face of his or shot or—

"For what?" The question ripped her attention away from the small tear in his T-shirt and her thoughts off the weird and unsettling path they'd traveled down.

"What?"

The creases in his cheeks were back. "Why are you thanking me? I mean, I know that I'm an all-around thankable person, but if there's a specific reason why you wanted to tell me what a magnificent specimen of perfection I am, then please share."

Suddenly, Molly regained her ability to think…and to roll her eyes. "You know, you'd be so pretty if you just stayed quiet, but no… You have to open your mouth and ruin the picture." As soon as the words were out, she felt a little guilty, even though he looked extremely— and aggravatingly—amused. "Sorry. That was probably rude. I was thanking you for arranging things with Desmond. I really appreciate having a security system, and I'll pay you back with interest as soon as possible."

"Never apologize, Molls. Your rudeness is one of

my favorite parts of you. And you're welcome. Now
let's get Norah, and I'll show you how this alarm
works." He stepped past her, his body just barely
brushing against hers, and walked toward Norah's
bedroom door. Molly blinked, confused about why he
liked it when she gave him a hard time and weak-kneed
from the full-body contact.

With an almost silent growl, she shook off all her
conflicting emotions and stalked after him toward
Norah's room. She'd figure out her feelings later. Right
now, they had a brand-new security system to learn and
a bail jumper to catch.

"Okay, so you think it's going to be at the Denver
address Sonny had in the notes on his phone?" Molly
asked once John had shown them how the security
system worked and then Norah had given them the
rundown on what she'd found. There'd been a disap-
pointing lack of information that she'd been able to
retrieve. It seemed that Sonny had used the phone for
calls to another burner phone—the mystery caller who'd
talked to John earlier—and not much else, except for the
random address on a note-taking app.

"Like I said, it's a possibility." Norah tapped her
laptop keys a little harder than necessary in obvious
frustration. "It's a vacant building in a commercial area
that's been on the market for over a year. Seems like
a handy place to have a meeting of supervillains. At
eleven at night, there won't be many people around to
see whatever goes down."

Molly yanked on a strand of hair hard enough to sting. "Why do things always have to be hard? Why couldn't Sonny have put the location on the calendar app?"

"He could've at least put up a meeting agenda," John said. Despite his joking words, his fingers were careful as he extricated her hair from her grip and gently tucked the strand behind her ear. Once again, Molly didn't know whether to poke him or thank him for being sweet.

Flapping her hands in an effort to clear her thoughts, she asked, "Wait. What was the address that you found in Tick's room? Do they match?"

"No," John said, even before he pulled out the crumpled bit of paper to check. "It's a Langston address." He held it out so she could see, and her shoulders collapsed forward in defeat.

*No. Not defeat. We have two excellent leads.* "Okay." She sat up as straight as possible while being perched on the edge of Norah's bed between her sister and John. "This is easy. Two possible addresses, and there are two of us."

"Three, actually," Norah said dryly. "Did you know that five out of four people find math to be hard?"

Since that didn't deserve a laugh, she just gave Norah an exasperated look. John, on the other hand, snickered, which would only encourage her. "You're research," Molly said firmly. "You stay in the van."

"What van?" Norah and John chorused, making Molly sigh.

"The *figurative* van." Molly pushed to her feet. "We need you here, not bumbling around with the two of us, trying to get ourselves blown up."

"Hey!" John protested, getting up as well. "I'm not bumbling. I'm a sleek, efficient machine."

"Right." Molly used her driest voice and felt a surge of triumph when he narrowed his eyes at her. "Anyway, Norah, you keep working. Carmondy, let's go check these two places out. We should have enough time before the meeting."

"Let's go *bumble* around, then," he said.

She turned to Norah. "Text if you need anything. My phone'll be on silent."

"Got it." Norah had already dived back into her research.

"Let's start at my house," John said as they made their way to the door. "I need to reload my pockets."

The mention reminded her that she needed to stock up on a few things as well. "Good idea. I'm going to make a stop at my room, too." She turned down the hall in that direction. John followed her into her bedroom as he pulled out his notepad.

"Really?" she asked, her hands settling on her hips. "Do you actually need to be in here, or are you just following me around like a hungry stray?"

"It's my bedroom now, too." His voice was absent as he flicked over to the next page.

"No, it's not."

"Yes, it is." He pointed at her bed. "That's where I sleep."

"*Slept*. Once. That doesn't give you room rights."

"I have an open invitation to stay here whenever I want to. Therefore, I have a stake in it. Like a time-share."

Although she opened her mouth to argue, all that came out was a frustrated sound. Muttering to herself, she gathered the items she needed, tucking them in various easy-to-reach pockets. "You're the most aggravating person I've ever met."

"Thank you."

Her eyes rolled yet again. She was going to have permanently strained eye muscles if she continued to hang around John. Patting her pockets, she went over a mental list of tools and weapons, making sure she hadn't forgotten anything. "Are you hungry? We need to eat before tonight's...thing." She hated her hesitation, her lack of certainty, but the whole mission was a huge question mark. They didn't know what they'd be walking into... if anything. The two of them could be heading to completely wrong locations. She didn't like this, functioning without a plan. It made her itchy in a bad way.

"We can grab sandwiches at my house," he said.

"Sounds good to me." After one final glance around her room—or *their* room, according to John—and one last pat of her pockets, she was ready. "Let's go."

"You sure you have everything?" he asked, and she started another mental checklist, her paranoia kicking in at his suggestion. His dimples were showing, though, and that tipped her off to the tease. "What about a bazooka? Maybe a few anti-aircraft missiles?"

"Let's go," she growled, and his earnest expression cracked as he laughed. "You're one to talk! You have more things in your pockets than I do—and more pockets." He waved her ahead of him, and she headed for the stairs. "Besides, I don't use guns of any kind." Reconsidering that statement, she raised her arms in the air, elbows bent, and made her not-that-impressive biceps pop. "Except for these babies."

He gave a burst of laughter behind her. "Why not? Seems like that'd be a good equalizer when you're tiny and your skip is huge and armed and has some buddies."

Since he'd sounded honestly curious, she decided

to answer him seriously, rather than give him the brush-off she typically offered people who asked that question. "Because if I bring a gun to a knife fight, it suddenly turns into a gunfight. You're right that I'm not a monster-truck-sized person like you"—she ignored his amused choke—"so I use that, take people by surprise, have a plan. If all goes well, there won't be time for them to draw their gun, and everyone goes home safe that night. Well"—she had to pause—"the skip doesn't go *home*, but they're safe, at least."

"Huh." John didn't sound convinced, although he did seem to be chewing over what she'd just said. "Do you mind if I'm armed?"

She checked in with herself, probing at the idea like it was a potential bruise. There was no lingering ache, though, no tenderness at the thought of him carrying a gun. "That's fine. I'd rather you do what you need to make yourself safe. We're both still learning each other's methods. For example, you go blasting in somewhere without a plan, and I'm more thoughtful and smart and successful."

His loud boom of laughter made her smile, but she kept her face forward so he couldn't see how he affected her. As they crossed the living room toward the door, Warrant came running over, straight to John. Molly frowned as she watched her turncoat dog cuddle up to the guy he barely knew. John stroked Warrant's head and massaged his ears as Molly watched, not sure if she was jealous of the man or the dog.

"Seriously, you need to confess. How'd you turn Warrant into your canine love slave?" she asked.

John looked smug as he dropped a kiss onto the top

of the dog's furry head and then straightened. "I'll never tell. That's between me and Warrant." He winked at the dog, and it was sweeter and less weird than it really should've been.

"Bye, Warrant." Feeling miffed, she bent and ruffled the dog's ears. Releasing a happy huff of air at the attention, he flipped over onto his back. His ecstatic reaction made her feel a little better, and she gave his upturned belly a few final scratches before straightening. Setting the alarm, she headed out the door.

The neighborhood was quiet, warm sunlight streaming through the tree branches and mottling the yards. Molly still had the uncomfortable feeling of being watched, however, no matter how idyllic it seemed. There could be that enemy army waiting just inside the cover of the national forest, biding their time until she looked away to charge.

"What is it?" John must've sensed her tension, since his voice lowered and his head turned on a swivel, trying to find the threat.

"My wild imagination," she said wryly, although she didn't lower her guard, just in case. "All the burglars and lurking cars have made me jumpy."

"Understandable," he said as he opened the passenger door for her. "A lot has happened."

As she climbed in, she almost laughed at his understatement. "Yeah. It's been crazy." She waited for him to close her door and circle the car before she asked, "Why are you sticking around?"

"Warrant," he said, looking completely serious. "He'd pine for me."

She actually fell for it, staring at him wide-eyed for

a long moment before the joke clicked in her head and she smacked him on the arm. It was hard to refrain from shaking out the sting in her fingers. The man must've been made of iron.

"You're an idiot," she said, although she couldn't bring herself to put any real heat into it. She knew that she was the idiot. If John Carmondy did rediscover his sense of self-preservation and bailed on them, her dog wouldn't be the only one pining. As much as she didn't want to admit it, she knew that she'd miss him, too.

# CHAPTER 18

As the car started to roll forward, Molly felt her eyes drift back toward the forest. The ever-present wind rustled the tree branches, creating movement and shadows that could easily hide any number of villains—burglars and treasure hunters and criminals who wouldn't hesitate to kill every member of Molly's family in order to get their hands on that necklace. All sorts of ruthless thieves could be sneaking through the woods at this very moment.

The car abruptly veered over and stopped by the curb.

She looked over at John, startled by the sudden stop. "Forget something?"

"Yeah." He put the car into park and shoved open his door.

"What?" He'd only been at her house one night. How much stuff could he have left there? She knew she would have to watch him, or he'd have half her drawers filled with his clothes before she could blink. He was already laying claim to her bedroom, after all. It was becoming more and more apparent that John Carmondy was a nester.

"To check out the forest." He started getting out of the car, but she grabbed a handful of his shirt to stop him.

"You're going into the forest? Why?"

Glancing at her over his shoulder, he raised his eyebrows but didn't try to escape her hold. "Because it's bugging you. I can tell."

She relaxed her grip as she stared at him, touched that he'd not only noticed, but was doing something to make her feel better. Except for her sisters and her dad, no one had ever cared enough about her to bother doing either. It was hard to believe that John Carmondy, of all people, did. There had to be another reason. "That still doesn't explain why you're going to go wandering around in there."

"Sure it does." Taking advantage of her loosened fingers, he stood and strode toward the trees. She blinked after him for a moment, the growing warmth in her chest feeling dangerously addicting, before she jumped out of the car and chased after him.

When she fell in next to him, he cocked an eyebrow at her. "Now it's my turn to ask. Where are *you* going?"

"With you."

"Why?" He gave an exaggerated flex, even as his dimple appeared. "Think I can't handle the forest beasties?"

"Forest beasties?" she repeated, unable to hold back her grin. When he just shrugged, unabashed, she turned to face the trees. Even though her unease about who could be lurking in there was still niggling at the back of her brain, more of her attention was focused on the man next to her. "You might be a big, bad wolf who's able to handle whatever scary things lurk in the woods, but you still might need backup." She could feel his gaze burning into the side of her face, but she refused to glance at him. If she did, then their eyes might meet, and who knew what would happen after that. "I *have* saved your bacon several times already."

"And I appreciate your concern for my bacon." Despite his words, he sounded more serious than usual, and she had to fight the urge to look at him again. "I'll be fine, though. I can handle a few wannabe jewelry thieves if they're lurking in the trees. You don't have to worry."

"We're partners." She stubbornly kept pace with him. "We have each other's back. Bacon buddies, if you will."

He was silent for a beat too long, and temptation got the best of her. Turning her head, she caught an expression she'd never seen on his face before. It was surprised and affectionate and tender and smoldering and a lot of other things that made her skin feel prickly and her insides melty, so she quickly focused on the trees again. It was too late, though. She knew she'd be seeing—and overanalyzing—that expression every time she closed her eyes.

"C'mon then, bacon buddy." His voice had a softer edge than normal, and it made her shiver—and then immediately pretend that he hadn't caused that reaction. It was no use, though. As much as she fought against it, as much as she told herself it was a terrible idea, she was starting to have feelings for John Carmondy.

A twig snapped under her heel, reminding her why they were there. "This is probably a wild-goose chase," she said, her voice carefully low despite her words, "but thank you for doing this anyway."

"You're welcome, BB." He winked at her, and Molly sighed to hide how much she wanted to laugh at his over-the-top flirting. They fell quiet as they walked just inside the tree line. Molly searched for signs that someone else had been there. All she could see were rocks, dry earth, and the first autumn leaves scattered over the ground.

Being in the forest was just as bad as looking at it from the outside. Molly was hyperaware of everything around her—from John's almost silent footsteps to the rustle of leaves and the quiet chatter of a distant squirrel. Every sound tightened her nerves, and even John's reassuring presence wasn't enough to keep her calm. Although she prided herself on being relatively fearless—or at least fear-resistant—something about the shifting shadows and hushed movements of the forest made her want to grab John and run for the safety of the car.

"Is this a shoe print?" John's voice made her jump, and she hid the movement by turning toward where he was crouched down, studying the ground in front of him. Her heart still beating a little faster than normal, Molly bent over his shoulder so that she could see the semicircle mark.

She frowned, leaning closer. "Could be. There's no tread pattern that I can see, though."

Making a hum that sounded like agreement, he shifted forward, still in a crouch, checking the ground for a possible trail. She did the same behind him, looking for any impressions in the dirt that could possibly be prints. After she'd fruitlessly covered twenty feet, she gave up and returned to John's side.

"I couldn't find anything," she said, and he held out his hands in an I've-got-nothing gesture.

"Probably not a footprint, then," he said. Despite his casual words, Molly noticed that John seemed even more alert than he normally was, and she felt a little less silly about her own jumpiness. Maybe it was just that there were too many hiding places in the underbrush, but she was relieved when they returned to the spot where they'd entered the woods.

"Would this be considered a success that we didn't find any evidence of lurkers, or a failure?" she asked as they made their way through the scrubby weeds that edged the forest.

"Success," he answered without hesitating. "We haven't been shot, punched, or blown up."

She gave him a sideways glance. "That's your definition of success? Not mangled?"

"Pretty much, yes."

"I think… Oh, crap." Grabbing John's hand, she dashed the few steps back into the cover of the trees, relieved when he followed her rather than digging in his heels and demanding explanations. Hauling them behind a bushy evergreen, she peered between the branches at the black-and-white squad vehicle parked behind John's car.

His annoyed grunt told her that he'd seen the two Denver detectives, too.

Molly's phone vibrated in her pocket, and she hurried to yank it out, the buzzing sounding nerve-rackingly loud. "Hello?" she whispered.

"Molly?" As happy as she was to hear Sergeant Blake's voice, Molly cringed at the bad timing of her friend's call.

"Hey, Sarge. Mind if I call you back? I'm kind of in the middle of something." She batted at a branch that had caught in her hair, but it stayed firmly stuck until John carefully untangled the strands.

"Yeah, I guessed that, since you're whispering," Blake said dryly. "Does the 'something' you're in the middle of involve a certain pair of Denver detectives who don't know how to stay in their lane?"

"Yep."

"Is that supersized bounty hunter still following you around like a homeless puppy? Garcia filled me in on the gossip."

She glanced at John, biting back a laugh. He mouthed *what?* but she just gave a small shake of her head. "Yes."

"I don't know what the two of you did, but those two sure have it out for you. When I stopped by the station just now, I heard them radio in. They're at your house to pick up you and your hungry puppy."

She made a face, and John flipped his hand in an impatient motion. *Who is it?* he mouthed, and she held up her index finger in a *one moment* gesture. He grumbled but didn't press her for more information, dividing his attention between her facial expressions and the two detectives talking in low voices next to John's car.

"Don't let them pick you up. You need to get your asses to the station and give your statements to one of our friendly local officers, or those two are going to be slapping cuffs on you quicker than you can smack John Carmondy with a rolled-up newspaper."

"Okay, okay. Enough with the dog jokes. We'll be there in fifteen." She reviewed the route in her mind and sighed silently. "Make that twenty. Have the notepads ready."

"Notepads?" Sergeant Blake scoffed. "Okay, Grandma. We use *computers* now for that."

Resisting the urge to say something rude to her good friend who was helping them avoid the Denver detectives, Molly settled for a grunt of farewell and ended the call.

As she tucked her phone away, she saw Detective Mill snap his head toward where she and John were standing.

Molly froze.

Even though she knew she and John were well hidden in the shadows of the trees, disguised by the branches of the evergreen, a pulse of anxiety shot through her. The detectives couldn't find them until after they reached the police station. Even if the detectives didn't drum up some bogus charges to hold them on, they'd still be detained for hours. Sonny would go to his meeting and then disappear again…along with Molly's chance of saving her family's house.

The seconds ticked by agonizingly slowly as Mill's gaze raked over the trees. Finally, he turned back to his partner, and all the air gushed out of Molly's lungs. Her relief was short-lived, however, because both detectives started walking toward the trees, their hands going to the butts of their guns.

This time, John was the one who grabbed her hand as he moved deeper into the forest. She went with him for a few steps before giving him a tug and leading him to their left. If she wasn't mistaken—and she really hoped she wasn't—there was a path in that direction, one of Felicity's favorite routes when she was torturing her sisters by making them trail run.

Now that there were more trees between them and the detectives, Molly couldn't see them anymore. She picked up her pace, wincing at every rustle and crunch her boots made, but needing to move faster. Any second, the detectives could be on them. Her pulse beat quickly in her throat as her fingers tightened around John's. He was right behind her, trusting that she knew where she was going, so she could've released him…but she didn't. The press of his warm palm against hers was the only thing keeping her calm enough to think.

Weaving around a clump of scrubby pine trees, she broke through the brush and stepped onto the path. Relief coursed over her, making her knees shaky, but she ignored that and sped up, her fast walk turning into a jog. The trail was wide enough for John to fall in next to her, making it impossible for her to pretend she needed to hold his hand anymore. She was surprised at her reluctance to release him, but forced her fingers to let go anyway. He jogged easily next to her as she risked a glance over her shoulder at the spot where they'd emerged from the trees.

No one was there—no one she could see, at least.

"Who was on the phone?" John asked a few minutes later, his voice low but annoyingly even. She, on the other hand, was already starting to breathe heavily, thanks to the running and an overdose of adrenaline.

"Sergeant Blake." She paused for a breath before continuing. "Warning us that…the detectives…want to bring us in. Said to…get to the station…and one of the local cops…will take our statements…minus the handcuffing and detaining."

"Nice of her to warn us."

Not willing to waste any more breath, Molly just gave an affirmative grunt, which made John smile fondly at her for some odd reason.

"Are we headed to the station, or are we still running away?" he asked a few moments later.

"The station." When he gave her a raised-eyebrow look, she added, "After backtracking…a little."

Instead of protesting the detour, he just settled in next

to her. She got the impression that he could run at this speed for hours, and she mentally promised herself that she would work harder during Felicity's training sessions. Already, she was dreading it. She loathed running.

They followed the trail as it looped around and joined up with a logging road. The two-track felt too wide and exposed, especially as they reached the edge of the forest. Staying in the trees, Molly checked the area before stepping out onto the paved city street. They were several blocks away from her house, and she was fairly confident that they'd managed to lose the detectives.

The neighborhood was quiet, making the sound of their footsteps seem even louder, and Molly resisted the urge to take John's hand again. That was a growing addiction she needed to nip in the bud. As they approached the intersection, she let her attention stray toward him, noticing how the sweat dampening his hairline just made him look better.

*Stop it,* she told herself firmly. *Not the time to be ogling, even if he is looking even hotter than his usual considerable hotness.*

She swallowed a startled sound as he grabbed her arm and jerked her sideways, hauling her back. Before she could recover her balance, he was towing her with him as he dashed to the side of a small garden shed.

*Detectives?* she mouthed, following his lead and pressing her back against the tiny building. She hoped that the homeowners weren't there to see them hiding next to their shed. That could lead to awkward questions—or a call to the cops.

John gave a short nod just as the front end of a squad car came into view as it slowly rolled past. This time,

Molly was ready when he moved, staying right next to him as he slipped around to the back of the shed and then to the other side, staying hidden from the occupants of the passing car.

After interminable seconds ticked by, he caught her hand again and jogged through the yard. The squad car was out of sight, but Molly still felt exposed after leaving the concealment of the shed. They cut between two houses, and she gave silent but fervent thanks that neither homeowner had a fence that they would've had to climb.

For the rest of the run to the station, Molly didn't let her attention waver, but stayed alert for any sign or sound of the detectives' vehicle. When the law-enforcement building came into view, she swallowed a triumphant noise and didn't let down her guard. They were so close, but they weren't in the clear yet.

As they crossed the parking lot, they slowed to a walk. It was hard not to dash for the doors, but Molly knew that they'd just draw unwanted attention. As they were halfway across the lot, the rev of an engine caught her attention. A squad car barreled down the street toward the entrance to the lot, and Molly knew that the detectives were inside.

"Let's go," John said calmly, but she was already running full out for the door. She didn't look at the squad car again, but she could hear the tires squealing as it made the turn into the lot. Dashing up the stairs, she and John barreled toward the door. He reached it first, pulling it open and holding it while she sprinted inside. Despite everything, she gave a breathless huff of laughter. Even while being chased down by grudge-holding detectives, John Carmondy remembered his manners.

Molly must not have been the only one Blake gave a heads-up to, since Sergeant Garcia was waiting for them, waving them through the lobby like he was their track coach. "Third room on the right," he said, holding the security door open.

"Thanks," she said breathlessly, sweat stinging her eyes as she darted past, followed quickly by John, just as the detectives burst into the lobby.

"Hold that door!" Mill yelled.

Garcia looked all too satisfied as he pulled the door closed behind him, the lock engaging with a click. The detectives could use their key cards, but it would slow them down just long enough for Molly, John, and the sergeant to get to the interview room. The three of them piled into the small space, and Molly dropped into one of the chairs, panting. John looked slightly more composed, but even his chest was heaving as he propped his shoulders against the wall.

"Thanks for this," he said.

With a smug smile, Garcia waved off his gratitude. "The pleasure is all mine. The captain is making us cooperate with those Denver bastards, but I'll do anything I can to make their lives a little more miserable."

The door burst open, revealing two pissed-off detectives, and John quickly moved, putting himself between them and Molly. Although she appreciated the sentiment, he was blocking her view of the fireworks, so she shifted to see around him.

"What the hell are you doing, Garcia?" Mill demanded. "These two should be cuffed and interrogated."

"These two?" The sergeant looked supremely satisfied. "They're innocent witnesses. Heroes, actually."

"They're suspects in *two* bombings."

Garcia blew a raspberry, and Molly was hard pressed not to laugh. "We all know who planted those bombs, and neither of these two go by a name that rhymes with Honey Barber. Now go do something useful and quit harassing the witnesses."

The two detectives glared, but they didn't seem so menacing now that Molly was safe in the interview room, watching Garcia mock them.

"We'll be discussing this with your captain," Mill snarled, finally turning away. Bastien just gave them a measuring look, which made Molly nervous. His quietness seemed scarier than his partner's bluster. The two left, and Garcia swung the door closed behind him.

"That was enormously satisfying."

It had been, but Molly was still worried. "Will you get in trouble for this?"

"I'll get a stern lecture about my attitude from the captain and a pat on the back from every other Langston cop. Probably some free drinks at the bar from Blake, too." Garcia didn't lose his grin as he pointed toward the laptop sitting on the table. "Now statements. I'm assuming you're still chasing Sonny and he's the reason explosions keep following you around?"

Molly simply nodded.

Garcia's smile had disappeared completely the second he mentioned Sonny. "I told you you're going to get yourself killed going after that sociopath. Whatever you're going to make on this, it's not worth it."

Molly's mouth set in a grim line. That was the problem. Her family was worth it. And tonight, they were finally going to bring Sonny in.

# CHAPTER 19

"I DON'T KNOW IF IT WAS A GOOD IDEA TO SEND CARA TO check out the warehouse." Molly tugged off her boots just inside John's door. "There's no chance she'll just do a drive-by like I asked. This is Cara we're talking about. The perfectionist who can't half-ass anything. She'll probably end up presenting us with a full video tour of the interior, including a bunch of security guards with guns."

John patted Molly's shoulder. "She's smart. She won't get herself into anything she can't get out of safely. Besides, if she did do the video, at least we'd know what kind of security is in place."

Molly was too worried to laugh, although she did relax slightly at his reassuring words. He was right. Cara was smart, and they could definitely use any information about the potential meeting place before walking into it blindly that night. She just wished they hadn't been stuck giving statements rather than staking out the Langston warehouse themselves.

"So what's the plan? Are we still each taking a location?" Her frown deepened. There were too many variables—they didn't know where, when, or the majority of who. So much could go wrong, but this could very likely be their last chance. The person on the phone had mentioned that Sonny was getting new identification. If he disappeared, then so did Molly's opportunity to bring him in.

She plopped down onto John's couch. All of her frustration was shoved to the back burner as she fell instantly in love. Pulling up her socked feet, she wriggled around to get even more comfortable. "Oh, John…"

He'd been headed to the kitchen, but at those two words he whipped around.

Molly didn't even care that she'd basically purred at him—and used his first name at that. She was in too much bliss to worry about anything. "Your couch is incredible. Can I have it?"

"Can I have a time-share on your room?"

"Are you trading your couch for occasional access to my bedroom?" Despite her preoccupation with wallowing in her newfound squishy paradise, she was still amused.

"You're right. Put it that way, and you're getting a much better deal." He prowled back over, sinking down next to her. "My couch for full bedroom privileges."

Somehow, the conversation had taken an unexpected right-hand turn, but Molly didn't think she had the willpower to bring things to a halt. Instead, she tilted her head to study him, rubbing her cheek along the silky-soft fabric of his magic sofa as she did so. "*Full* bedroom privileges? What does that entail?"

He leaned closer, stretching his arm across the back of the couch until she felt surrounded—cushions of heaven on one side and John Carmondy on the other. Her heart rate, which had already accelerated, now beat so fast it felt like a hummingbird was hovering inside her rib cage. "Whatever you'd like it to…entail."

Suddenly, she wanted it to entail all sorts of things, but a small part of her brain was still squawking indignantly that this was John Carmondy she was ever so slowly leaning toward, and he was her nemesis—or at least he used to be. Now, he felt an awful lot like a partner…a very hot partner with a great body and adorable dimples and a habit of watching her back and trying to keep her safe.

She realized that she'd forgotten to breathe, too caught up in his closeness to do anything but feel. As she sucked in a breath, her lips fell open just a little, and John's gaze instantly locked onto her mouth.

His pupils were dilated wide with desire, turning his eyes almost black. She couldn't look away. It felt like they were locked in position, turned toward each other on the couch, so close but not yet touching. This was the moment they had to decide: leap over the cliff or back away.

John exhaled, and the stream of warm air brushed her lips, making her viscerally aware of how close they were, that the slightest shift of weight by either of them would bring them together. She wanted that, to touch him, to be touched by him, even more than she'd wanted his couch just seconds ago.

She just wasn't brave enough to take that final step, and she wanted to smack herself for her cowardice. Chasing criminals over fences and tackling them to the ground? Sure, no problem. Kiss a guy who clearly—unless she was reading all the signals very wrong—wanted her? Run away! *Girl, you're messed up*, her brain scolded, and she could only agree.

"John?" she managed to say, needing to do *something*

to break the tension that had wrapped around them like a whole roll of barbed wire.

"Yeah?" The problem was that it hadn't worked—the tension was still there, the wire pulling even tauter, dragging them closer together through sheer desire and, she had to admit, a huge, heaping load of affection that had sprung up completely unexpectedly over the past harrowing days.

Now she'd started a conversation, though, so she had to finish it. "What are we doing?"

"What do you want to do?"

*Very dirty things to you.* "So it's all on me?" She wasn't sure how she felt about that.

His lips twitched up just the slightest bit, although it didn't dim the heat in his gaze. "You know what I want—what I've wanted since we met. The question is if you want the same thing."

"But I *don't* know!" The words burst from her in a panic. "I know you want me to work for you, but I told you that one of us would end up killing the other one if we tried that."

The crease of his dimples dented his cheeks. "I don't think we'd kill each other." His gaze darted down to her mouth again before meeting her eyes. The dark, smoldering depths sucked her in, and she instantly lost track of the conversation. "It'd be…explosive, but not how you're thinking. And I would love for you to come work for me, but that wasn't why I kept seeking you out."

"It wasn't?" Her blood felt like it was on fire as it coursed through her, heating her skin and turning her insides molten.

"No." As if he couldn't help himself, his fingers

brushed across her cheek, tracing her jaw to the point of her chin before dropping away. She immediately missed that featherlight touch. "I like being around you. You wake me up, make me laugh, make me swear." She huffed a laugh at that last one, and he closed his eyes for a moment as if he was in pain. When he opened them again, they were hotter than ever. "You make me *hungry*."

The words burned across her skin, making her gasp. She wanted him more than she'd ever wanted anyone. It had been building beneath their banter and arguments and one-upmanship until just having him in front of her without being able to touch was intensely painful.

"John?"

"Yeah, Molly?"

"Would it be okay if I kissed you now?"

He smiled, but it wasn't like his smirks or his teases or even his jolly grins. This was so sweet that it squeezed her heart, wringing it so tightly that she was pretty sure she'd never be the same again. "It would be very okay."

As soon as the words were out, she tipped her head that tiny distance she needed in order for their lips to meet. She jumped off the cliff without looking down, and even the squawking voice in her head had gone quiet. Pressing her lips against his ever so tentatively, she knew this was right. Even if things crashed and burned disastrously later, it would be worth it. After all, she'd never experienced anything so incredibly *perfect* as the feel of his sweet smile against hers.

Then his hands were cupping her face, and the kiss deepened, going from gentle to smoking hot in a split second. Grabbing his shirt in both hands, she hauled him closer before wrapping her arms around his neck, needing to feel the full press of her chest against his. She always had known he was big—tall and broad and solid as a rock—but it was so much more evident when he was wrapped around her, making her feel like a giant had her tucked securely in his fist.

He burrowed his fingers into her hair and kissed her even more deeply, bearing her back into the couch cushions. His kiss really was hungry, just like he'd said, as if he were a starving man and she was the only sustenance around. She was just as desperate to taste him, and they kissed until there was nothing else in her brain except John.

When he pulled his mouth from hers, she groaned in disappointment, but he simply chuckled hoarsely as his lips found their way to her jaw and then her throat. This time, her moan was from her own hunger, and she could feel him smile against her skin. Her fingers worked on the back of his head, her short nails scoring lightly against his scalp.

She felt it as he sucked in a breath, air drawn against her overheated skin, and she shivered, needing more even while she didn't want anything to change, wanting to keep feeling John's lips against her neck forever. While he was kissing her, everything else disappeared. There were no felonious mothers or dangerous bail jumpers or greedy bondsmen right now. There were only John's mouth and hands and the feeling of his muscles twitching beneath her touch.

Even as incredible as his kisses were, Molly shifted impatiently, needing more bare skin to explore. The barrier of his T-shirt, as thin as it was, was unbearably frustrating. Grabbing a handful of fabric, she tugged it upward.

He understood right away what she needed, pulling back for just a second as he hauled the shirt over his head and tossed it away. She reached for him, wanting to touch, but he held back. As soon as she realized he was tugging at her shirt, she immediately helped wrench her top over her head, making him laugh with delighted surprise.

"This is okay, then?" he rasped, looking equal parts wild and concerned. "It's not too far?"

"We've jumped off the cliff, Carmondy," she said, and her voice sounded just as raw and rough as his. "Nothing's too far."

His eyes blazed as if her words were gasoline on the fire, and her desire rose to meet his. All their inhibitions were burned away, and they tugged and pulled until all their clothes were tossed aside and there was nothing between them. Their kisses grew frantic as Molly tried to feel all of him at once. Even though she hadn't realized how much she wanted him until recently, it still felt as if she'd been waiting an eternity to be able to stroke her fingers across his broad, smooth chest or feel the jump of his ab muscles beneath her lips.

"There's just so much of you," she murmured against the skin of his shoulder. "It's going to take me forever to explore all of this." Without taking her mouth off him, she waved a hand to indicate the full expanse of his naked body—his *beautiful* naked body.

"Sorry?" His laugh was rough and even a little shaky, making her raise her head to meet his gaze. The tenderness there snatched her breath away, and it was several moments before she could respond.

"Don't be sorry for this. It—all of you—is amazing." Unable to stop touching him, she followed the line of his thigh down to the indent of his hip, making him hiss through his teeth as his eyes went dark.

"You're so beautiful." He didn't glance down at her body as he said it. Instead, he held her gaze, making her want to kiss him and squirm and duck her head to hide from the compliment all at the same time. The urge to kiss him won out, though, and it was a long time before they came back up for air. "You're even more gorgeous naked than I'd imagined, and you were pretty incredible in my head."

Her laugh surprised her, bubbling out in an honestly happy stream. "Have you really wanted me for that long?"

"Yeah." He pressed his lips to hers, hard and quick and intense enough to leave her panting when he pulled away. "Forever."

"Why were you so annoying, then?" She nipped at his bottom lip in retaliation for all the times he'd driven her up a wall. By the way he sucked in a breath and then kissed her hard, the punishment had backfired.

"It got you to talk to me, didn't it?" he asked when he pulled back. He dropped a line of kisses across her cheekbone to her ear. He scored the rim with his teeth before nibbling on her earlobe and stealing all her breath away so she couldn't scold him.

She wanted—needed—to explore more of him, so she pushed at his shoulder and wrapped a leg around his hip, turning them so they flipped over. John went along with her silent request, even when they rolled right off the couch onto the area rug. He gave a grunt when his back hit the floor, but he grinned as well, as if every part of the experience, even falling off a couch, was fun and wonderful, just because he got to be with her. That thought touched her at the same time it drove her wild, so she kissed him…hard.

Now that she had her way and could be on top, she took full advantage of her position, exploring every inch of his huge, muscled form, driving him crazy with touches and kisses, until his patience snapped and he took over. He did the same thing to her, discovering every sensitive spot and freckle, learning her bit by bit until she felt as if he knew her body better than anyone. She was frantic and squirming with need long before he donned a condom and slid inside her.

As he moved in her, learning her reactions and how to get her to tighten around him with building pleasure, he watched her face, kissing her and touching her and making her feel so connected to him that she could barely stand it even as she craved it at the same time. Tension built inside her as he watched, quickly finding exactly the best way to move and the best places to stroke and touch until the pleasure peaked and she shattered, her body clutching him as she cried out and dragged him over the edge with her.

He finally closed his eyes as he came, ecstasy contorting his features. It was Molly's turn to watch him, and she hungrily took in his expressions as pleasure washed over him—pleasure that she'd caused. The idea that she'd given this to him, just as he'd done for her, gave her a warm, satisfied feeling that merged with her afterglow into a deep contentment.

As they lay there immediately afterward, their bodies still linked, Molly thought about what had just happened. Making love with John hadn't been like what she'd expected…not that she'd allowed herself to think about it—at least not for long—before now. It had been crazy intense, and completely different from their usual light and teasing interactions.

She wasn't sure why she was so surprised by that, since it made sense. That was how they were together in everything else, after all. They argued and teased and laughed and stole each other's skips, but they also watched each other's backs and took care of each other. No wonder sex had been wild and passionate. They could be fun and silly, but together, they could be more than that, too.

John slid out of her, and she felt a pang, missing that physical connection. He kissed her once—thoroughly—before reluctantly pushing to his feet. As he crossed the room to toss the condom in a small garbage can, Molly moved to a sitting position, feeling awkward now that she was lying by herself on the rug.

"What time is it?" she asked, not really wanting to know. She wasn't ready for reality to roll over them quite yet.

He patted his bare hip, as if his cell phone was somehow attached to him, and she laughed. His dimples appeared as he pretended to frown at her and stalked closer, his eyes narrowing in a way that, along with his suppressed smile, Molly knew meant trouble. With a laughing shriek, she tried to scramble out of his path, but he grabbed her and tossed her over his shoulder.

"Careful!" She was almost laughing too hard to speak, even as she pinched his tight butt in retaliation. "You're like eight feet tall. If you drop me on my head, there's going to be some major damage, and you're going to have to bring Sonny in yourself."

"I've got you." His voice was confident, and she believed him completely. He wouldn't let her get hurt. "And it's just after seven. Plenty of time for a shower… if we share. That would be the most efficient plan, and I know how much you like a good plan."

Although she rolled her eyes at his transparent plot to get his hands on her again, she was still smiling. She wasn't sure if she was going to stop anytime soon. "How can I say no to an efficient plan?"

"You can't." As he climbed the stairs, he gave a dramatic, evil-villain laugh, making her snort. "I know your weakness."

Even as she pinched his bare backside again—or tried to, since there wasn't any give to his buns of steel—she silently acknowledged that he was right. He did know her weaknesses, but she trusted him, both to have her back and with her tender, tentative heart.

───────────

After a shared shower that stretched so long the water ran cold, Molly got dressed in his bedroom. Sitting on the neatly made bed, she pulled on her socks. Now that she was clothed and didn't have anything to do except look around the room and try to wrap her head around the fact that she'd just had sex with John Carmondy, she felt anxious and twitchy. Unable to sit still, she started toward the door as John emerged from the bathroom.

The sight of him, all huge and buff, his upper half bare, made her freeze in her tracks. She felt both justified in the decision to tumble into bed with him—well, onto the couch—and also even more nervous, because seeing him made what they'd just done all the more real. He gave her a slow, curling smile that instantly lit the smoldering fire in her belly, but she firmly stomped it down. That was what had gotten her into this situation in the first place.

He grew serious as he studied her. "What's the matter?"

"Nothing." The denial was automatic, but it felt wrong. This was John, the guy who'd had her back over the past few nightmarish days, who'd protected her too many times to count, and whom she'd just slept with. She could tell him. "Just...this was fast."

He looked stricken for a fraction of a second before his expression blanked. "You regret what we did?" Molly was careful not to look at him, knowing that she couldn't think of how wonderful he was without losing the last of her composure.

"No. Maybe. Not regret." Her thoughts were whirling, impossible to sort through, frustrating her. "I'm just adjusting. I mean, now I know what John Carmondy looks like naked. That's so...weird."

His expressionless look cracked slightly as the corner of his mouth tipped up. "I look weird naked?"

"Of course not." The familiar feel of their banter settled her nerves a little. "You know you're pretty. I just feel like a time traveler who woke up in the future... in bed with John Carmondy."

"I'd watch that movie."

"Me too, but that's not the point." She struggled to pin down what exactly her point was. "It's just not what I expected to ever happen, so I think I'm in shock."

"In shock? My naked body put you in shock?"

"Minor shock." Her qualifier didn't seem to help, judging by his expression. She opened her mouth to say something, who knows what, when she was rescued by the hum of her phone against her leg. Hurrying to answer, she didn't even check who was calling. "Hello?"

"Moo, we need to have a strategy meeting."

She'd never been so happy to hear Cara's voice. "Are you okay? Any problems at the warehouse? You didn't do a video tour, did you?"

"And go inside the spooky, abandoned building? Of course not. How dumb do you think I am?"

"Not dumb, just task-oriented and conscientious," Molly corrected as she noticed that John was watching her closely. Unable to think coherently with his eyes on her—never mind the distraction of that gorgeous naked chest—she dropped her gaze to the rug beneath her socked feet. "You're okay, then?"

"I'm completely unharmed. The warehouse seemed totally empty, actually. No one in or out. Can you and John swing by the house? I'll finish filling you in, and Norah has some stuff to share, too."

"Sure." She snuck an upward glance at John's face, but he still had his blank mask on. "We'll get there in fifteen."

"See you then."

Molly said goodbye and ended the call, feeling both relieved and sad to be leaving John's house. She had too many emotions rampaging around her body, and she was actually looking forward to a good chase to clear her brain of everything except the need for immediate survival. "Cara asked if we could meet at our house. She's fine, but she and Norah have some info for us."

He was quiet for a moment, just long enough to reawaken the jangle of nerves inside her. Finally, he said, "Let me grab a shirt and we'll go."

The drive to her house felt endless and horribly awkward. Everything had been wonderful until she'd started overthinking. Regret filled her as he pulled up to the curb in front of her house.

"I'm sorry," she blurted, turning to face him. John kept his gaze fixed through the windshield, even though they'd stopped moving, showing her his impressive profile and the small muscle twitching in his jaw.

"Sorry for what?" he asked, his voice stiff.

"Making you think I regret it. I don't." As soon as the words were out, Molly knew they were absolutely true. Her wild thoughts calmed down, and she reached for his hand, pulling it into her lap. "Not at all. I just freaked out for a second. It's been a long time since I've cared about anyone besides my sisters, and it scared me how much I want you to stick around."

He finally turned to look at her as his cool expression melted away, leaving the tender, warm look that was quickly becoming her favorite. "As long as you want me to stick around, I'm here."

It was hard to believe, but Molly shoved away the thought of all Jane's husbands and boyfriends who'd been there one day and gone the next. Even Lono, Molly's own dad, had ended up leaving. Cramming all the bad memories into a back corner of her brain, she smiled at John.

"I'll hold you to that."

# CHAPTER 20

CARA WALKED INTO THE KITCHEN AND STOPPED SO ABRUPTLY that Norah bumped into her back.

"Why are you both…damp?"

"We took a shower." Even though Molly was trying to act nonchalant, she knew her face was red.

"A shower?" Cara looked back and forth between them, a broad smile spreading across her face as Norah's eyes widened. "Singular shower? Meaning you shared one? Meaning you're finally doing it?"

"Doing it?" Molly's lip curled even as John laughed. "Are you ten? What grown woman says that?"

Cara offered a fist to John. After a short pause, he tentatively bumped it. "Finally. I'm happy for you two. If you hurt my sister, I'll cut you down the middle and make you wear your own entrails as a scarf."

To his credit, he only blinked once before he gave Cara a serious nod. "Noted." Sending a quick glance at Molly, the corner of his mouth quirked up as he added, "Sister."

"Nope." Molly tried to glare at him, but her usual eye lasers didn't seem to be working. She felt too soppy inside to get up a good basilisk stare.

From John's grin, she knew that he was well aware he'd pretty much obliterated her tough outer shell. "Sissy?"

"I'm going to veto that one," Cara said dryly, leaning

on the counter. "Congrats, you two. Now, time's ticking if we want to crash that meeting."

Norah was still studying them, and Molly felt a twinge of concern. "You good with this, Norah?"

"Of course. I mean, we all knew it would happen eventually."

Molly huffed. "Everyone but me, apparently."

Ignoring her, Norah continued. "I'm happy for you. You're always so busy taking care of everyone else. It's good that you have someone to take care of you."

Molly wasn't sure how she felt about the thought of John "taking care of" her. On one hand, it was an alluring temptation. On the other, it was terrifying. Deciding to deal with that later, since Cara was right about their deadline fast approaching, she cleared her throat. "Thanks, Norah. We'll talk more about this later. Maybe. For now, let's figure out the plan for tonight."

"The warehouse looked dead, although that isn't a guarantee no one was in there. Despite what some people think, I wasn't dumb enough to go inside to check it out." Cara gave Molly a pointed look before continuing more mildly. "Did you find anyone willing to be your backup?"

Molly shook her head glumly, holding up her phone to show a sad lack of return text messages. "No one responded except for Christian, and he just wanted me to know that he wouldn't get within fifty feet of Sonny Zarver. Fifi and Charlie are chasing a solid lead, plus they're a twelve-hour drive away, so they're out." She turned toward John. "How about you? Any luck?"

"Nope. Pretty much the same as you, although more people wanted to tell me that I'm an idiot."

His words made her stomach roil with sudden guilt. "I'm sorry for dragging you into this."

Wrapping his arm around her shoulders, John pulled Molly into a side hug that was almost ridiculously comforting. "You're not. I'm here of my own free will."

When she didn't respond, he gave her a gentle shake.

"Hey. Can you see anyone making me do anything I didn't one hundred percent want to do?" he asked.

"No." Despite that, she knew that she was the reason he'd been in danger—multiple times. Tonight would be the worst of them all. "But—"

"But nothing. I chose to be here, and I want to do this. You never asked. It's all on me."

Unable to come up with an effective counterargument and aware of the ticking clock, Molly let it go. It still ate at her, though, that John was in such danger because of her. She could've convinced him at the very beginning to leave her alone, and he would've listened. She'd enjoyed his company too much to send him away, however, enjoying that safe feeling having him with her created—and loving just having him around. She jolted at the last thought and then immediately banished the L-word from her mind. This wasn't the time to be distracted.

"Fine," she said. "Just…be careful tonight, okay?"

Pulling her in closer, he pressed a kiss on the top of her head. "Always. You too."

Shivers—pleasurable ones—ran from the base of her skull to the bottom of her spine. Cara's throat-clearing finally brought her out of her haze, and Molly dragged her gaze away from John's. "Right. Okay. So one of us will go to the Langston address that Cara checked out this afternoon, and one will hit up the Denver location."

She looked at her sisters, seeing the apprehension Norah was trying to hide. "You'll only be called in as backup if the world is ending, got it?"

Even as her sister nodded, John protested. "No."

"What?"

"I don't want you by yourself."

She gave him a steady look. "Since all of our potential backup is fleeing at the mere mention of Sonny, we don't really have any choice, do we?"

Although he didn't look happy, he stopped protesting. "Fine, but I'm taking the Denver location."

"Fine." In fact, Molly was a little relieved that she wouldn't have to deal with an unknown building in Denver. She rarely went, especially now that the city reminded her of her mom's crime and the detectives who were after them.

Despite having gotten his condition accepted, John still looked unsettled. "You can take my car. I'll borrow my buddy's. He owes me one."

Molly was tempted to argue, but she let it go, telling herself to pick her battles wisely. Besides, she loved John's car. It smelled like him.

Norah placed a tablet on the table. "Now that the logistics are settled, let's talk building plans."

Although Molly was focused on her sister's diagrams, a part of her was hyperaware that John Carmondy was sitting next to her and that they'd just had sex. The word made her frown, sounding too clinical for the incredible experience they'd had together. *Made love*. She immediately shoved the words into a dark box at the back of her mind. She wasn't ready to figure out how deeply she'd fallen for John Carmondy.

After they'd gone over the layouts and set up plans that basically involved watching the buildings and calling the cops if Sonny showed up, Norah and Cara wished them luck before both slipping out of the kitchen, as if there'd been a prearranged signal to leave her alone with John. She moved to leave, but he caught her hand.

"I can't discuss anything remotely deep right now," she blurted out before he could say anything. "Nothing about feelings, either. Not now."

Instead of arguing, he just gave her fingers a squeeze before letting go. "That's fine. Whenever you're ready, I'll be here. Your bedroom's my time-share, after all, and you have equal rights to my couch."

Contrarily, him giving her space made her want to move in closer. "It is a fabulous couch."

"All yours." He gave her a sweet smile and then gestured toward the doorway. "Let's go get Sonny."

As they walked out, emotions swirled around in Molly's chest, and she wished she'd just blurted out how she felt. At least then it would be out, and he'd know how she felt, just in case he…

She didn't allow herself to finish that thought.

They reached his car, and he opened the driver's door for her. Instead of getting in, she took two handfuls of his shirt and shoved him back against the car. As his eyes widened in surprise, she yanked him down and kissed him, putting everything she was feeling, everything that she couldn't say—all her worry and affection and confusion and the love that she didn't want to admit, even to herself—into the press of her lips on his. It all poured out of her in one bruising, incredible kiss.

One of his hands cupped the back of her skull, and

the other wrapped around her back, pulling her even more tightly against him. Not only was he not pulling away from her almost-violent embrace, but he was fully participating. Soon, though, it grew too intense, and she had to pull away, knowing that if she didn't, she'd never be able to leave him.

They were both breathing hard as they stared at each other.

"Do. Not. Die." She gave him a little shake with each word.

"I won't. I promise."

"No getting hurt, either." Reluctantly, she released her grip on his shirt, smoothing out the wrinkles her fists had made, using them as an excuse to touch his ridiculously hard chest.

"Not even a paper cut." His dimple popped out for a moment, but then he quickly sobered. "Stay safe. I don't want to lose you right after you finally stopped snarling at me."

"I never *snarled*—" She broke off when she saw that mischievous dimple reappear. "Brat. Okay. I'm leaving. Stay safe. If you die, I'll revive you in a satanic ceremony just so I can kill you again."

"Molly Pax. Always has a plan, even a post-death one."

"Good thing for you." She forced herself to get in the car. "Otherwise you'd still be bumbling around planless, waiting for me to find your skips for you."

His mock-offended gasp made her roll her eyes and press back a smile. As she drove away, she couldn't keep herself from glancing in the rearview mirror, just to get one final look at John Carmondy.

# CHAPTER 21

MOLLY'S PHONE VIBRATED AGAINST HER HIP, AND SHE quickly glanced at it, pretty sure who it was going to be from and what it was going to say.

I hate this plan.

Holding back a huff of amused exasperation, she quickly texted John back I know before sliding her phone back in her pocket. That was about the tenth time he'd texted her that, and that was after telling her that in person multiple times before they'd headed to their respective spots. She was fairly sure the only reason he agreed to the plan was that he was about ninety percent sure that the Denver address—the location that he was staking out—was where the action was going to be, so he'd figured that she'd probably be safe by herself at the Langston warehouse.

To her, it had been the only thing that made sense. After all, there were two possible locations for Sonny's meeting, and there were two of them. Neither of them was going to try to interrupt the meeting, so they just needed to wait for Sonny to finish whatever nefarious business he was doing before following him and snagging him as soon as he was alone. It was something both of them had done by themselves hundreds of time to hundreds of skips. Sonny wouldn't be any different. Molly had built him up in her head to be something of a white whale, but he was simply another bail jumper... one who liked to blow things up.

Despite her attempts to soothe her nerves, though, she was worrying about John just as much as he was obviously worrying about her. She just couldn't admit it to him, or he'd be speeding back to Langston, plan abandoned.

Dragging her brain back on track, she shifted to a more comfortable position. She was perched on the edge of the neighboring building in the dark shadow of a cottonwood tree, watching the main entrance of the warehouse. The other doors were either the huge overhead kind that semi trucks could fit through or chained and locked, so this appeared to be the only possible way to access the building at night.

She shivered slightly, both from the chill in the night air and from anticipation, wishing John were with her right now. She'd gotten used to being a team, and working by herself again made her feel vulnerable and lonely. The previous hours ran through her head in vivid color— the way his soapy skin felt under her fingers in the shower and the long, intense kiss he'd given her before they'd split up—and she was suddenly no longer cold.

Peeking at her phone, Molly saw that it was just a few minutes before eleven and that John had sent her a frowning emoji. Swallowing a snort before it could escape, she focused on the entry again. Her heart rate slowed back to normal as she pushed thoughts of John out of her mind and concentrated on scanning the front of the building and the space around it. Nothing moved.

As the minutes ticked by, she grew more and more uneasy. Things were too quiet. Even as she watched the door, she knew in her gut that she was alone except for the night bugs and a few bats. No one was meeting at this warehouse tonight.

A chill crept back over her skin. If Sonny's cohorts weren't here, that meant they were possibly at the Denver location with John. The silent buzz of her phone made her jump, and her fingers trembled slightly as she pulled it out. The text was from John, and she relaxed slightly when she saw his name, but the actual words on the screen made her stiffen.

Tell your boy goodbye.

Her heart stalled before stuttering back into motion too fast, like a startled jackrabbit's, her fingers suddenly numb and fumbling as she texted back.

Who is this?

There was no answer.

Her skin went clammy as she stared at her screen, unable to tear her gaze off that menacing text. Something had happened to John. Just as she knew that no one would be showing up at this address tonight, she also knew that John was in trouble. Terror roiled in her gut. She had to get to him.

Scrambling to her feet, trying hard to ignore the twenty-foot drop to the asphalt below, she rushed for the back where a work truck had been parked conveniently close to the building. It was a struggle to descend cautiously, to not just hurl herself onto the roof of the truck cab, heedless of noise or safety. Even though she was terrified that something had happened to John, she shouldn't blindly run right into a trap. She needed to plan.

Slipping from the top of the cab into the truck bed, she jumped to the ground, hardly noticing the sting as her boots hit the pavement. She could barely keep herself from running the few blocks to where John's car was parked.

Not wanting to stop long enough to text, she called Cara once she was in the car.

"They have John." The words spilled out as soon as her sister answered.

Cara sucked in an audible breath, but when she spoke, her voice was calm. "I'll grab Norah. Are you picking us up?"

"I'll be there in three minutes." Cara's matter-of-fact steadiness settled Molly's nerves, and anger at Sonny started to build. It was an effort to keep from gunning the engine as she raced toward their house. She couldn't be delayed, not now.

As she pulled up to the curb, Cara and Norah were waiting. As soon as they'd piled into the car, Molly swung around and took off the way she'd come. "You ready for a rescue mission?" she asked her sisters grimly.

"Not really," Norah admitted, surprising a choke of laughter out of Molly. "It doesn't matter, though. Let's go get John back."

---

The drive to the Denver address felt endless, and it was almost physically painful to keep her speed down. Her sisters helped, offering up plans and reassurances that Molly didn't really believe but was touched by anyway. Her fingers clutched tightly on the steering wheel as she tried not to imagine what horrible things could be happening to John. It didn't help that his car smelled like him, reminding her of every sweet thing he'd said or done. She forced her brain to concentrate on the interstate mile markers, counting down until—to her enormous relief—they finally reached the right exit.

"Turn right at this light," Cara said in her quiet way, although Molly could see how tightly her sister was gripping her phone. After just a few miles, Cara pointed through the windshield. "It's just a half mile down this road."

Molly cut the car's lights and eased a few blocks closer to the address, parking along a line of old, mostly vacant-looking buildings. Shutting off the engine, she turned to look at her sisters. "Ready?"

Even in the pale light from a streetlamp half a block away, she could see that Norah was terrified. Although Cara's expression was tense and strained, she looked a little better. Both of them gave firm, resolute nods, and Molly had to blink back sudden tears as a rush of affection for her sisters hit her hard.

"Thank you for this. I love both of you."

"Love you too, Moo," Cara said. "Now let's do this before I throw up from nerves."

They got out, and Norah slipped into the driver's seat, ready to be the getaway driver if necessary. Molly and Cara hurried toward the address that Sonny had noted in his phone. Except for the distant sound of traffic, the neighborhood was silent, but it didn't feel like the same empty quiet that Molly had felt at the Langston warehouse. This was tense and watchful, as if someone in the darkness was waiting for the right time to strike.

Molly evened her breathing and straightened her shoulders, not allowing her imagination to terrify her even more than she already was. They just needed to get in, grab John, and get back out again. *Easy-peasy*. Once he was safe, then they'd nab Sonny, and everything would be right again. She wished she could call the cops, but she needed to find out more about John's situation first. If the sound of sirens spooked them into killing John, she'd never forgive herself.

Shoving away a wave of hopelessness, she focused on the next step. They needed to see what was happening in the warehouse.

It was much easier said than done, she saw as they reached the chain-link fence surrounding the property. That barrier was eight feet high and topped with razor wire. Unlike the surrounding buildings, this one had several area lights, cutting away the shadows that would be so handy to hide in. Molly scanned the exterior of the building, trying to pick out possible points of entry. It looked to be single-story, with just a few windows in what appeared to be a reception area on the northwest corner. Otherwise, the walls stretched tall and impenetrable.

"No wonder they picked this location," Cara said, barely loud enough for Molly to hear.

With a grim nod, Molly eyed the building again, seeing just as few options as she had the first time. It didn't matter, though. If John was in there, she was going to get him out, even if she had to rip through the steel siding with her teeth.

Motioning for Cara to follow, she slipped along the fence until they reached the far corner, where the shadow of an industrial-sized dumpster darkened a short stretch of the barrier. Without pausing long enough to let herself think and get freaked out at what they were walking into, Molly pulled out her wire cutters and got to work on the chain link, snipping each wire until she could push a section aside large enough to crawl through.

The fencing scraped against the pavement as she squeezed through the hole, and she fought the urge to freeze like a trapped rabbit. Instead, sending out a prayer that the small noise hadn't been heard, she held the cut section back so that Cara could follow her into the fenced enclosure.

Once Cara was through, Molly tucked the improvised door back into place, hoping that it wouldn't be noticed until they were out. She glanced at Cara and then at the stretch of clear, dimly lit asphalt between them and the warehouse. There was no way to keep hiding in the shadows, not if they wanted to reach the building. Taking a deep breath, she sprinted as soundlessly as she could.

With every step, she braced for the sound of gunfire and the impact of a bullet. Her breathing was coming too fast, but she couldn't help it. Between fear and running, her body was demanding more oxygen. It felt like it took an eternity to cover the short distance to the building. As Molly drew closer to the metal siding, she resisted the urge to look behind her. *Just get this part done,* she told herself. *Then you can worry about Cara.*

She finally reached the building and flattened herself against the siding, trying to keep in the shadows without bumping against the metal sheeting and giving away their position. Cara was just a step behind her, and Molly felt something release in her chest at the sight of her sister. Feeling exposed, she moved quickly, staying close to the side of the building as she tried to find an access point she'd overlooked.

There was nothing, though—just a smooth, unbroken wall.

Swallowing a growl of frustration, she tipped her head back and went still. *There*. An access ladder climbed the wall to the roof, the first rung starting seven feet off the ground. Molly pointed, and Cara crouched, linking her fingers together to offer a boost.

Placing her foot in her sister's hands, Molly jumped as Cara launched her upward, her arms reaching for one of the rungs. She managed to catch the third one and curled her body, pulling up her feet very carefully so she didn't accidentally kick the siding and give their position away. Her abs ached from the slow effort, and she sent a mental thanks to Felicity for her core workouts. It was the second time in the past few days that she'd had a reason to be grateful for her sister's drill-sergeant tendencies, and she made a silent vow to never whine during workouts again.

Pressing the soles of her boots against the first rung, she hauled herself to a standing position and then glanced down at Cara, prepared to give her sister a hand up. Cara waved her away, however, gesturing toward the front of the building. Molly interpreted that as Cara intending to look for another entrance, and she frowned. Splitting up was how they'd gotten in this situation in the first place. There was no arguing with Cara, though, and she watched with growing worry as her sister moved away, staying close to the side of the building.

Her stomach tight with fear for both John and Cara, Molly gave up on trying to call her sister back using only vehement gestures and started climbing the ladder instead. Once she could see over the top of the wall to the roof, she paused, checking to make sure it was empty of people. Nothing moved, and she cautiously climbed the last few steps until she could swing a leg over and step onto the flat roof.

Small pebbles crunched beneath her boots, and she tried to quiet her footsteps. The industrial condensing units provided too many hiding places, making her flinch at the tiniest sounds. Trying to see into every shadow, she made her way toward the hatch into the building. She missed having Cara at her back—and she really missed having John with her.

*I'll get him back*, she mentally vowed. *He'd better be in the condition I left him in, too.* It helped to think of all sorts of punishments that she'd rain down on anyone who'd hurt John. Her spine stiffened and her hands steadied as she reached for the opening that led into the building. It was locked from the inside, so she pulled out a set of lockpicks and got to work. Every scratch and click of her tools sounded too loud in the silence, and it felt as if every exhale was a shout. By the time she'd managed to unlock the hatch and swing it open, her blood was buzzing with adrenaline and her nerves were rattled.

The room the hatch had opened into was pitch-black. Unwilling to shine her flashlight into the space and possibly alert someone of her presence, Molly took a deep breath and descended the steps into darkness, silently closing the hatch behind her. Moving quickly and quietly, she reached the floor and blinked, trying to see shapes in the thick blackness, but there was nothing.

Knowing that she needed to see where she was going, she pulled out her small flashlight, pressing it against her hand to muffle most of the light. She looked around, her bones going watery with relief when she didn't see anyone waiting to pounce. It looked like she was in a utility room, judging by the mechanical equipment and the dusty cleaning supplies piled up by the door.

Turning off her light, Molly crept toward the door, pressing her ear against it to listen. There was only silence, so she carefully turned the knob and opened it the tiniest bit. Putting her face to the crack, she peered into the space but didn't see anything in her line of vision except some empty industrial shelves. The light was slightly brighter outside the room she was in, illuminating it enough that she could see shapes without her flashlight.

Taking a deep breath, she exhaled as she slipped out of the utility room. The hugeness of the open space made her feel like she was out in the open and vulnerable, so she stayed in the safety of shadows created by the oversize shelves. She moved through the space, stopping occasionally to listen for voices or to squint through the dimness, trying to see anything—movement or human-sized shapes—but she was alone with the shadows and the empty, dusty shelves.

She started wondering if she'd overreacted. Maybe John was back in Langston right now, laughing about the joke he'd played on her.

*No*. He wouldn't have tried to scare her, not when they were both keyed up and watching for Sonny. Someone else had sent that text. Even though he loved to tease her, John wasn't a jerk, and he cared about her too much to do something that dangerous and hurtful.

Molly cared about him, too—so much that the idea of losing him made her want to curl up into a pain-racked ball. There was no time for that, though. She needed to rescue her man.

Moving through the building with more purpose now, she started looking for a way to divide up the warehouse so she could search each section without missing any parts. As she passed a pillar, she looked to her right and paused. Was the light slightly brighter in that direction? She cautiously headed that way, taking greater care to stay silent and keep to the shadows.

A sound made her freeze, even before she recognized it as the smack of knuckles against flesh. A thousand images of how they could be torturing John, each one worse than the last, ran through her mind, but she firmly shut off that flow. If she wanted to function, she couldn't think about that.

She moved closer to the sound and started to pick up the murmur of voices. The light was brighter, and she moved cautiously, not wanting to make any noise. Picking up her foot, she carefully stepped forward. The slight pressure on her shin made her go completely still as she looked down. A trip wire, pulled taut by her lower leg, caught the faint light. She bit the inside of her cheek to hold back a distressed sound as the grenade at Mother Tick's house flashed through her mind.

Unbearably slowly, she moved her leg back, returning

the wire to its original position. As she stepped over it, pulling her knees up higher than she needed to clear the wire, her heart beat loudly in her ears, even as anger made her hands tighten into fists. *Of course Sonny set booby traps.* She wondered if that was how he'd caught John and gotten hold of his phone, and then she forced herself to quit dwelling on her worst fears. She couldn't wait until Sonny Zarver was back behind bars again.

Placing each foot carefully, she moved to the end of a row of shelving. Peeking around a partition, she saw a small huddle of people looming threateningly over a man sitting in an office chair. Shifting so she was slightly more exposed, she got a better view of the bloodied man.

*John!*

# CHAPTER 22

Aʟᴛʜᴏᴜɢʜ ɪᴛ ᴡᴀs ɴᴇᴀʀʟʏ ɪᴍᴘᴏssɪʙʟᴇ ᴛᴏ ᴅʀᴀɢ ʜᴇʀ horrified gaze off John's swollen and bloody face, Molly forced herself to look at the others. There were four of them: Sonny; a big, bouncer-shaped guy she didn't recognize; a tall man with his back to her; and a shorter, wiry man.

Biting her lip to keep the mental shout from slipping out of her mouth, she watched in horror as the burly guy hovering over John cocked back his fist and then let it fly. The clenched paw swung around, seeming to slow as it headed for John's already battered face. The man's knuckles caught John on the side of his jaw, snapping his head to the side as the punch connected with a meaty thump.

Molly flinched as if she'd been the one hit, and she barely kept herself from running toward John's assailant and tackling him to the ground. She'd see how he liked having a flurry of punches raining down at his face. Her fists were clenched so tightly that her nails dug into her palms, and the tiny pain steadied her thoughts.

Looking closer at the group, she saw that John had been tied to the chair, his legs, arms, and chest gleaming silver with strips of duct tape that circled his limbs and torso. Although his head was bobbing slightly, he looked conscious, and she sent a mental prayer that he stay that way for a while longer. If he couldn't run or walk or even crawl to the car, she had no idea how she'd manage to get him out.

She hadn't called the cops, since she didn't know the situation that John was in. Now, she was still torn. As much as she would've loved some armed backup, it would be too easy for one of these guys to put a bullet in John's beautiful head before anyone could even breach the building.

Her phone vibrated against her leg, and she carefully looked at the screen, taking great pains to hide any flash of light from reaching the huddle of men. It was from Cara, a group text to both Molly's phone and Norah's.

I'm in.

Molly squeezed her phone so hard her fingers ached. Her thoughts spun, bombarding her with half-assed plans and impulses, but she forced herself to focus on just the next step, her fingers trembling as she typed out her text.

John's here. Tied. Sonny +3

In just seconds, a response popped onto her screen.

What's the plan?

After a short hesitation, Molly sent just the word hold. Although she didn't know if her sister had spotted John and the four goons yet, Molly wasn't sure how to direct her to this spot. She hated to see John being hurt, but she knew if she messed this up, then she and John and very likely Cara could be captured or hurt or killed. Her stomach lurched at the thought. It was so much easier to come up with risky plans when it was just her safety on the line. When it was people she loved, it got a whole lot harder. In case Cara disregarded her message, Molly typed Watch out for traps!

Squeezing her eyes closed, she let out a silent, shuddering breath. She could do this. All she needed was a plan. Opening her eyes again, she took in the horrifying tableau in front of her. She needed to even the odds so it wasn't four with guns against two without—plus a taped-up John. As she forced her thoughts into some sort of order, she slipped closer, using the partition to hide her movements from the group and watching out for trip wires.

In her new spot, huddled behind a stack of cobwebbed pallets, she could hear what the men were saying.

"Who are you working with?" the tall guy asked. Molly recognized that voice from the phone, and she peered around the edge of the pallets, trying to get a glimpse of his face. The sliver of his profile was of little help in identifying him, but the familiarity of his form and that voice itched at the back of her brain.

"I told you." Even though John's voice was rough and nasally from what looked like a broken nose, hearing it sent shaky relief through Molly's entire body. "I work by myself. Why would I want to split the bounty?"

"Liar," Sonny spat out, and Molly barely kept herself from surging from her hiding place to tackle him. The explosive-loving bastard was the reason they were here in the first place, the reason John was trapped and hurt.

Sheer willpower kept her still, but she vowed that she'd drag Sonny back to jail if it was the last thing she did. "You and that nosy bitch were working together. I saw you at Dutch's."

John scoffed, the sound wet from the blood that ran from his nose over his mouth. "We don't work together. She tries to steal my skips, that's all."

"If she's your rival," the tall man said, "why were you at her house?"

As he asked the question, he turned his head, glancing at the shorter man next to him. When she saw his full profile, Molly froze in shock, her skin washing cold and then hot again.

*Detective Bastien!*

*I knew I didn't like that weasel*, Molly thought as her shock faded and determination took its place. She didn't dare text from her hiding spot. It was too close, and it'd be too easy for a flash from the screen to catch one of the guys' attention.

"Haven't you heard?" John grinned, but it was a macabre sight with his swollen mouth and blood coating his teeth. "You're supposed to keep your enemies closer."

"Can we just kill him and get on with it?" The shorter man next to Bastien spoke for the first time, sounding bored. "I have other things to do tonight."

"I want to know how he heard about this meeting first," Bastien said. "You don't have to stick around for that, though. Let's just do the transfer and be done."

"Fine." The man looked at Sonny expectantly.

"Let me see the papers first, Lubchek," Sonny said. "Then I'll send you the file."

Bastien stiffened visibly, his head whipping around

toward Sonny, but Lubchek didn't seem to be offended. Pulling a large envelope from his laptop bag, he handed it to Sonny. "The file is complete?"

"Just like we promised," Sonny assured him as he pawed through the contents of the folder. "It has the personal and financial details of every one of LZH Finance's clients."

Molly absorbed that information, a little shocked. She'd expected drugs or weapons or even black-market laptops, but financial data theft was not what she'd thought Sonny would be hocking. The way they were doing this right in front of John was a bad sign. She needed to act before they made sure he could never testify against them.

Lubchek snatched the envelope away from Sonny.

"Hey!" Sonny protested.

"Send me the file, then you get this and the rest of the payment we agreed to."

Now! she texted.

Praying with everything in her that her hastily cobbled together, half-assed plan would work, she lifted a piece of wood that had broken off one of the pallets. Cocking back her arm, she threw it as far as she could to her left, desperately hoping that Cara was not close to where it landed. The wood hit the metal bracing on one of the shelves and clattered noisily to the concrete floor.

All four of the men turned toward the sound, all but Sonny drawing their guns in unison, as if they'd rehearsed it. The burly guy and Bastien took off toward the sound, while Sonny slipped off in the other direction, leaving Lubchek with John. Without pausing to dwell on the utter insanity of her plan, Molly darted out

of her hiding place and sprinted toward Lubchek. His
eyes widened as he swung around, bringing his gun up
as he turned.

"H—!" he started to shout, but her shoulder hit him
squarely in the midsection, driving the air out of his
lungs and bringing both of them to the floor. The impact
clacked her teeth together and sent a jolt through her.
Ignoring that, she grabbed for the gun he still clutched
in his right hand. Grasping the barrel, she pushed up and
twisted, yanking the pistol from his grip.

As soon as she had the weapon, she pushed off him,
drawing another grunt as her knee dug into his lower
belly. She backed up several steps, the gun aimed right
at Lubchek's still-heaving chest.

Keeping the gun in her right hand trained on a glaring
Lubchek, she yanked a folding knife out of her pocket
and used her teeth to open it. Once the blade sprang free,
she sliced through the tape holding John to the chair—
arms, then torso, then legs.

He pulled free of his chair just as Bastien gave a
shout, and he and the bouncer look-alike came charging
back toward them, guns raised. Molly threw the knife
at them, but it flew wide. John grabbed the back of the
chair and shoved it so it barreled toward them, knocking
into the bulky guy and tripping him up. Bastien didn't
slow, his lips drawn back in a grimace as he aimed his
gun at John.

Aiming her own gun toward the cop, Molly fired
twice. The first shot winged his arm, and he dove to the
side, taking cover behind one of the plywood partitions
as the second shot missed him completely. Turning back
toward Lubchek, she saw he was already up and lunging

toward her. She brought the gun around, but she knew she was going to be too slow. He was going to take her down, and it was going to hurt.

Before he reached her, John's booted foot connected with his temple, and Lubchek dropped to the floor. She barely even blinked in reaction before John was grabbing her arm and dragging her behind a nearby toppled shelving unit.

As soon as they were concealed from the others, he squeezed her in the quickest, hardest, most welcome hug she'd ever experienced. "That was amazing. I love you. You're insane, but I still love you. If you ever do that again, I'll… Well, I'll probably have a heart attack, so don't ever do that again." As he continued to mutter, he crouched and ran to the opposite end of their over-turned shelf, towing her behind him with a firm grip on her hand.

"Maybe don't get captured and punched in the face a bunch of times, and I won't have to," she whispered, handing him the gun. "Here. You take this. I love you too, and I'm very glad that you're not dead…yet. Cara's in here somewhere, and Norah's in the car." As soon as he accepted the weapon, she checked her phone, but there weren't any new texts. "I think she's still parked and waiting for us, but she's a horrible communicator. She could be driving back to Langston, for all I know."

"At least my car won't get shot up, then," John said, quickly peeking and then firing twice over the top of the shelf. There was an answering volley of shots, and Molly flinched, hoping that the wooden barrier would at least slow the bullets down a little.

"Always the optimist," she muttered once the

shooting stopped. Needing to know what was happening, she poked her head up just far enough to see. Lubchek was still down, apparently unconscious, sprawled where they'd left him. She couldn't see Bastien, but the burly man was very unstealthily sneaking between the shelves toward them. "Bouncer guy who likes punching at three o'clock."

"Thanks. May I use your Taser for a minute?" John handed her back the gun. Accepting the pistol with one hand, she dug out her Taser with the other. "You're pretty comfortable with that," he whispered as he took the Taser from her. "I thought you didn't like guns."

"Doesn't mean I don't know how to use them," she said. "Now shoo. Go take care of business."

With a bloody, crooked grin, he rushed at the approaching man. Keeping alert for any sign of Bastien, Molly also managed to watch John take down the burly guy. As she grinned, finding a deep satisfaction in watching Mr. Punch-A-Lot writhe on the floor, a movement in her peripheral vision caught her attention. She turned, bringing the gun up, to see Bastien bearing down on her. Aiming squarely at the center of his chest, she ignored the panicking corner of her brain telling her that she could never kill someone intentionally and pulled the trigger.

*Click.*

Horror dawned just as he dove at her, bringing her down to the ground. It felt as if a car had landed on her when Bastien's weight drove the air from her lungs. The empty gun went flying as her arm cracked against the floor. She struggled, but he had her pinned, and no matter how she twisted or tried to turn, she wasn't able to roll them over so she could get the upper hand. Her right arm was numb and unresponsive, so she swung with her left, but the angle didn't allow her to get in a solid hit, and her fist harmlessly glanced off the side of his head. She switched from punches to trying to gouge at his eyes, hoping to hit a vulnerable spot, but he grabbed her left hand in his right and wrenched it down to the ground.

His face was grimly satisfied as his free hand wrapped around her throat, cutting off her oxygen. She kept fighting, but darkness started to edge her vision, and panic threatened to overwhelm her brain. All she could see was his stupid, homicidal face, and it pissed her off like nothing else that it was going to be the last thing she saw before she died.

Suddenly, there was a loud *thump*, and the pressure was gone as Bastien slumped limply to the side. Molly gasped in long, ragged breaths that hurt her throat but still felt incredible. She blinked, clearing the blurry, oxygen-deprived haziness from her vision, and Cara came into clear focus. She was standing over them, a Maglite in her hand and a fierce expression on her face.

"Get him off," Molly managed to wheeze, shoving at the unconscious man's shoulder. "He's freaking heavy."

With Cara's help, she pushed him off far enough that she was able to wiggle out from underneath him. As soon as she was standing, she grinned at her sister. "Thanks."

"Anytime." Although she could tell Cara was trying to sound casual, her voice shook.

"Molly!" John was suddenly there, hugging her hard and then running his hands over her as if checking for injuries. "What happened? Are you okay? I was preoccupied with dealing with them..." He gestured toward the guy he'd just been tasing, who was bundled up in so much duct tape he looked like a spider's next meal. Lubchek, though still unconscious, was lying next to him, also bound with tape.

"I'm fine." She ignored her still-numb arm, glad that at least it wasn't hurting. "We should get this one secured before he wakes up, too." She let herself give him one solid kick to the ribs, figuring he deserved that and so much more. "Did Sonny escape?"

"Looks like it."

Losing Sonny yet again made Molly want to scream in frustration, but she shoved it down. They'd get him. They had to. Her family was depending on her to do this.

"Let's get this guy restrained and then see if we can catch up with him. We still have that new ID that he wanted so badly." John nodded at the envelope that lay abandoned on the floor. He grabbed Bastien's arms and dragged him over to the others, making quick work of binding his arms and legs with duct tape. Molly tried to help, but she was pretty much useless with her dominant arm out of commission.

"Time to call the cops?" she asked with a wince. This was going to be a long night.

"No." Sonny walked out of the shelves, pulling a terrified-looking Norah along with him. Molly's gaze immediately dropped to the belt Norah was wearing, but her brain refused to accept what her eyes were telling her. Those couldn't be explosives wrapped around her baby sister's waist. They just couldn't. She lurched forward, automatically trying to reach her, but Sonny yanked Norah farther out of reach.

"Don't touch her," Molly snarled, unable to look away from the belt that circled her sister's thin hips over her T-shirt.

"What happens to her is up to you," Sonny said, looking disturbingly gleeful as he clutched a cell phone in one hand and Norah's arm in another. "I just want to leave this town. There're people who want to kill me, and I'll be a sitting duck back in jail. You, I'm assuming, don't want this bitch to be blown to little pieces." He cocked his head as Molly vibrated with growing rage. "And all of you, too. This baby'll have quite the range."

"It'll take you out, too. You'll be just as dead as us," John said, moving in front of Molly, to her terrified annoyance. How was it better if he had his face blown off rather than hers? They were going to have a long talk about his self-sacrificing tendencies when they got home…*if* they got home.

She immediately shut down that line of thinking. It wasn't helpful. What she needed was a plan or at least something other than the panicked voice shrieking in her head.

Sonny gave a twitchy movement that might've been a shrug. "If I don't get out of here, I'm dead anyway. Might as well have the satisfaction of taking all you with me." His grin was all wrong, spiking a shiver down her spine. "You would've just kept chasing me if I ran, anyway."

In the tense silence that followed, there was a faint wail of an emergency siren, and Sonny's head snapped up. The sound was both welcome and bitter, because Molly knew they'd arrive too late to do any good. It was up to them to save each other. "Hey, Norah. Remember Brody Knick?"

Before Norah could respond, John was already in motion, taking advantage of Sonny's moment of distraction to plow into him, bringing all three of them to the floor. Grabbing Sonny's wrist, John pounded it against the floor, and the cell phone that he'd turned into a detonator went skittering away from them. Sonny, his expression filled with fury, tucked his legs in and then double-barrel kicked John in the stomach, knocking him back. Twisting back around, Sonny reached for Norah. As his hand wrapped around the belt, Molly knew exactly what he planned. He must've designed the belt to detonate if it was removed, and he was about to rip it right off Norah's waist, dooming them all.

Time seemed to slow as Molly ran toward them, her functioning arm outstretched in a futile attempt to prevent what was happening. As Sonny's fingers closed around the belt, Norah moved toward him and drove her knee right between his legs. Apparently, she *did* remember the Brody Knick incident after all. He screamed, his grip releasing, and Norah rolled out of reach, the belt intact.

Molly stepped forward, preparing to dive on top of Sonny and subdue him, but something tightened roughly around her ankle. Her entire body stiffened with fear as her leg was yanked out from under her, making the world spin. Disoriented, she blindly struggled, her mind filled with nightmare images of impossibly strong men who could flip her so easily upside down, holding her painfully by her ankle as she struggled helplessly like a fish on a line. How could she ever hope to fight back against *that*?

When her shocked confusion cleared and the scene around her stopped spinning, she saw the cord that was wrapped tightly around her ankle. That's what had flipped her and yanked her off the ground by her foot, leaving her dangling upside down. She'd been snared by another one of Sonny's traps.

She could only watch helplessly as Sonny scrambled to his feet and sprinted away. John shifted, as if to chase after him, but then moved toward Molly instead.

"Get him!" She flailed her arms in a shooing motion, but John still advanced, wrapping his arms around her and lifting her so that the rope around her ankle loosened. "He's getting away!"

"We'll get him," John promised. "If not today, then soon. Can you reach up and get that off?"

Despite his words, frustration still coursed through her. He'd slipped away from them again and again. He'd put a bomb on Norah. Molly didn't want to catch him *someday*. She wanted to bring him down now.

Reaching up, she wrestled the snare off her boot. Seeing that she was free, John turned her right side up and set her down. As soon as her feet were on the ground, she took off after Sonny, shouting over her shoulder, "Don't unbuckle the belt!" Norah and Cara nodded, their faces pale with shock, as Molly focused on finding the bastard who'd tried to blow up her sister.

She was done with his nonsense.

Even as she ran, John keeping pace right next to her, she kept her eyes open for other traps and trip wires. As she reached the end of an aisle, she turned the corner, catching a glimpse of movement to the right as Sonny ducked into a deeply shadowed corridor.

"This way," she mouthed to John, who nodded grimly. From the look on his face, he was just as fed up with Sonny as she was. They chased after him, and Molly felt a dreaded sense of déjà vu. Except for the lack of patrons, this was just like the night they'd chased him through the bar, the night that ended in a huge explosion. Who knew how many bombs Sonny had planted around the building? The whole thing could go up, killing them all, and there'd be nothing Molly could do to save them.

Shoving the morbid thoughts out of her head, she concentrated on speeding up as they entered the dark corridor.

"Wire!" John shouted, and Molly jumped, hoping that her timing was right to clear the trip wire that was hidden to her in the darkness. When nothing caught on her lower legs, she let out a breath of relief.

"Thanks!"

His teeth flashed white, even in the dim light, as he grinned at her without slowing down. "Nice jump."

Molly gave an amused snort and was amazed. Only John could make her laugh while chasing a bomb-loving skip. No wonder she loved him so much.

Sonny darted to the left, and Molly sped up, not wanting to lose sight of him. In this maze of a building, it'd be almost impossible to find him again if he disappeared. As soon as she turned down the hallway after him, she dug deep and sprinted even faster. An exit sign lit up the darkness with an eerie green light.

They couldn't let him get outside. Once he'd left the warehouse, there was nothing to keep him from blowing the entire thing to pieces.

John must've had the same thought, because he put on a burst of speed, his long, powerful legs churning as he pulled in front of her. In the dim light of the sign, Molly saw Sonny come to a skidding stop halfway down the corridor. He dug in his pocket, and she flinched, expecting another detonator, but a small flame flared from the object instead. *A lighter*. She felt relieved for a fraction of a second before she realized that a lighter was just as effective as a detonator.

Bending down, he touched the flame to the end of a fuse. As soon as it lit, he dropped the lighter and took off for the exit door again. The fire ran quickly—too quickly—along the length of the fuse, and Molly felt her lungs freeze, refusing to suck in any oxygen. Time seemed to slow as her gaze locked on the flame. It felt surreal that such a tiny thing was going to kill them all.

"Got it." John's steady voice, so confident, allowed her to rip her gaze from the burning fuse, the world reorienting again. Despite his bruises and the blood streaking his skin, he was still the most beautiful person she'd ever seen. Just looking at him allowed her to breathe again.

Diving for the explosive device, John grabbed the lit end of the fuse in his fist, smothering the flame. She swallowed a protest as his unprotected hands wrapped around the fire. As he extinguished the burning fuse, her horror at his injuries was mixed with pride. Of course John Carmondy ignored his own pain to save her and her family. That was John. He was part of her family now. She loved him, just as he loved her, and they'd have each other's backs. Always.

Trusting him to extinguish the fire and save them all yet again, Molly dashed past John and the explosives, putting on one final, impossible burst of speed.

Launching herself into the air, she flew toward Sonny as he reached for the door. For a terrible moment, she thought that she'd misjudged and would miss, but then her arms were wrapping around his lower legs, bringing him down just as effectively as a trip wire.

He hit the floor with an *oof* before immediately trying to crawl away. Filled with adrenaline- and rage-fueled strength, Molly flipped Sonny onto his back and started punching him, needing to punish him for what he'd tried to do to her family. As Sonny weakly tried to fend off the hits, she thought of the explosives strapped around Norah's skinny waist and swung a solid punch.

Each time her fist connected with flesh, at every grunt and protest, she felt a sense of vicious satisfaction. She needed to make him pay in bruises and blood for every hurt her family had suffered because of him, every moment of terror they'd experienced. Her blows continued to rain down onto his body until he went limp, and still she swung, only stopping when John grabbed her by the waist and lifted her bodily off Sonny's unconscious form.

Although she fought to get back to hit Sonny some more, most of her rage had been spent, and she subsided quickly, especially as she remembered the explosives. "Did you get the fuse out?"

"Are we in tiny, bloody pieces?" Although his words were joking, the way he clutched her against him and the slight shake in his voice were completely serious.

"Nice job." Turning, she squeezed him back just as hard. "Thanks."

She pressed against him, appreciating the feeling of security she felt in his arms so much more after coming so close to losing him. Remembering his injuries, she pulled away, even as he tried to keep her tucked against him. Wiggling free, she flipped his hands over and examined the burns as well as she could in the dim light.

"Your poor hands." She peered closer. "How bad is it? Are you in a lot of pain?"

He just shrugged—of course he did—and grinned at her, despite his poor, swollen mouth, looking much too happy for a guy who'd just had his face beaten and his hands fried. "I'm not feeling too much pain right now, but you can kiss them to make me feel better."

Although his tone was joking, she did just that, pressing her lips carefully to the skin of his inner wrists, safely above the burned spots on his palms. His breath caught audibly at each touch, and all humor disappeared from his expression as he intently studied her for a long moment.

"Did you mean it?" he finally asked in a quiet voice. "I'll understand if it was just fear and adrenaline talking."

"Did I mean what?" she asked, meeting his serious gaze.

"Do you really love me?"

She didn't even hesitate. "I do. So much it completely freaks me out."

His laugh was a rough exhale, as if he'd been holding his breath. "Thank God, because I'm completely gone for you." He pressed his lips to hers in an intense kiss filled with love and relief, and Molly returned it, the incredible feel of him blotting out everything else.

As much as she wanted to keep kissing John's miraculously alive face forever, Sonny groaned and the real world returned. Reluctantly taking a step back and releasing John's hands, Molly remembered Norah still had the explosives strapped around her waist. "Let's get back."

She moved toward Sonny, who was still limp despite the sound he'd just made, intending to swing him over her shoulders in a firefighter's carry, but John got there first. Giving her a look, he hauled Sonny over his shoulder with obnoxious ease. "Let's go."

Molly ran back toward where they'd left her sisters, watching for any remaining traps, with John close behind her. As they turned out of the corridor, she stopped abruptly as she almost ran into Norah. Molly's gaze immediately dropped to her sister's waist—her wonderfully explosives-free waist.

"You got it off!" Grabbing Norah in a hard hug, she saw Cara beaming behind her. "How'd you manage that?"

"It involved taking off my pants and some careful maneuvering," Norah said, squeezing Molly just as hard as she was being squeezed. "For once, I'm really glad my butt is nonexistent."

"We need to let the cops in," Cara said, shooing them toward the corridor they'd just left.

"Not that way," John said, sounding slightly out of breath, but not nearly enough for a guy who'd just sprinted after a killer, put fire out with his bare hands, and then carried a full-grown, unconscious man over his shoulders. "Explosives."

"This way, then." Norah did an about-face and led the way around some toppled shelving. "The northeast corner. I checked out the blueprints on file with the building department while I was waiting."

"Of course you did," Cara said, raising her phone to her ear. From her side of the conversation, she was telling the dispatcher where the cops should meet them.

"Watch for trip wires. And who called the cops?

You, Norah?" Molly followed her sisters, glancing back to make sure that John was doing okay with his burden. As soon as they were out and somewhere with better lighting, she was going to check the burns on his hands again.

"In a way." Norah lifted her arm, letting her sleeve fall to reveal her medical alert bracelet. "I pushed this after Sonny grabbed me, and then Cara called them once we got the belt off to tell them not to just send an ambulance."

"Good."

Hurrying after her sisters, Molly snuck another glance to check on John. Her concern must've been obvious, because he grinned at her.

"Worried about me?" he asked.

"Making sure you didn't drop the skip." Despite her teasing words, she couldn't help but smile back. "You know, just because you're the one who's carrying him out doesn't mean you get credit for bringing him in. Quit trying to steal my skips."

His laughter boomed out, making her smile, her heart full of love and triumph and sheer relief. Her plan might've been hastily concocted and gone a little sideways in the middle, but they'd done it. They'd gotten their guy, and no one had been blown up.

It was a good day to be a bounty hunter.

---

It was just two hours before dawn when they finally made it home. Warrant rushed to greet them, first making a beeline for John. Molly took one look at their bedraggled group and said, "Showers and bed. Everything else can wait until tomorrow."

Cara and Norah didn't offer any protest, instead murmuring their good-nights as they headed wearily up the stairs.

"What about you?" John asked, scratching Warrant in just the right spot behind his ear so that the dog's hind paw paddled in time with the motion of John's fingers.

Ignoring the question, Molly frowned at his hands. "Careful of your burns."

He made a dismissive sound. "These are barely first-degree. They can hold up to a little petting, especially for such a good dog. Isn't that right, Warrant? You're the best puppy in the world, aren't you?" Warrant's tail beat a happy tattoo on the floor.

Although she wanted to protest, the sight of John fussing over their dog was too cute, and it robbed her of her ability to be stern. Besides, she was too tired to get worked up about anything, even if the thought of John in pain made her heart hurt. She made her way to the kitchen, swallowing a groan at the thought of staying up to finish what had to be done.

"What happened to showers and bed and nothing else?" John asked, following her.

"I just have one thing to do, and then I'll happily go unconscious." She opened her laptop and blinked the blurriness from her eyes.

He frowned. "What's so important that it can't wait until after you sleep?"

"Barney's invoice." Despite her exhaustion, saying those words made Molly smile.

John grinned back before plopping down on the chair

next to her. Warrant immediately stretched out under the table, laying his head possessively on John's foot. "You're right. Making the cheap bastard pay up will be deeply satisfying."

As she opened the bookkeeping program, her smile faded. "I just hope he keeps his word about not pushing to move up Mom's hearing."

Reaching over, John took her hand, his bandaged palm scratchy against hers. "He will. We'll make sure of it. And we'll find Jane. Now that Sonny's locked up again, we'll be able to concentrate on searching for her."

"Thank you." She gave his fingers a gentle return squeeze before extricating her hand so that she could type up Barney's invoice. Now that the life-threatening part of the night was over, her anxiety was starting to build again. There were so many problems literally banging down their door. "It's not just Barney who's a threat. Everyone thinks the necklace is hidden in the house—including the Denver cops." That reminded her of Bastien. "Do you think Detective Mill is dirty like his partner?"

"I don't have any proof, but I have a source who's heard whispers about him."

Her fingers went still as she looked at John. "What kind of whispers?"

"Gray-area whispers."

"What does that mean?"

John stared at the dark kitchen window, his gaze pensive. "I don't know anything concrete yet, but I have a feeling he's not on the straight and narrow."

It wouldn't surprise Molly at all if Mill turned out to be as crooked as Bastien. Before she could ask for more details, her phone buzzed with a text from Felicity.

Well, that lead was a dud. We're going to crash and then head home. See you in a few days.

Molly replied with a simple Sorry it didn't work out. Drive carefully. Disappointment that they were just as far from finding their mom as when they'd started swept over her, adding to her exhaustion. John leaned over to read the text and then curled his arm around her shoulders, leaving the comforting weight there until she'd finished emailing Barney his invoice and scans of all Sonny's paperwork.

As they climbed the stairs, Molly turned to look at John. "This means you're staying here tonight...well, this morning?"

He waggled his eyebrows in a way that made her laugh, despite her exhaustion. "Of course. Your bedroom is part mine, remember? I can't neglect it."

"You can't neglect my room? *That's* what you can't neglect?" She loved how his teasing always made her feel lighter.

"Well...and Warrant. I also can't neglect my sweet puppy dog." His voice got syrupy-sweet as Warrant slipped past them into her bedroom.

"Mmm-hmm." Once again, she tried to fix him with a cool stare, but it was hopeless. She couldn't hide the way he turned her to jelly, especially when his adorable dimple was peeking out as he suppressed his smile. She tried to muffle a yelp as he snatched her up with an arm around her waist, pulling her tight against him.

"Can't neglect you, either." His lips were so close to her ear that she shivered at the feeling of his warm breath against her skin.

She leaned into him, drunk on the feeling of warmth and safety, her eyes closing sleepily even as she wished he'd kiss her.

His chuckle was warm against her neck. "Let's go to bed before you fall asleep on me."

She barely made it through her quick shower, falling asleep as soon as she hit the mattress. When John joined her after his own shower, she blearily snuggled closer to his enormous, warm shape. She'd been worried that the terrifying events of the past evening would replay in her head, keeping her from sleep, but somehow John's comforting presence blocked the nightmares. It felt like nothing bad could happen while he was there in bed with her.

Fully content, Molly drifted off again.

A blaring sound ripped her out of a peaceful sleep, and she shot up to see John bounding out of bed. Warrant, who'd somehow wiggled his way between them, groaned and burrowed his head into the comforter.

"What is that noise?" she shouted over the piercing, continuous shriek.

"The security alarm." John looked much too happy for a guy who'd just been yanked out of a well-deserved sleep. "Want to go tackle some wannabe jewel thieves?"

Molly shoved her hair out of her eyes and stared at him for a moment before a smile tugged at her mouth. His enthusiasm was irresistible. "Yes." She scrambled out of the bed, wide awake and ridiculously, unexpectedly happy. "You know," she said as she grabbed for her Taser, "life with you will never be boring."

His smile turned tender. "Ditto, sweetness. And I can't wait."

# CHAPTER 23

WHEN MOLLY BLASTED INTO THE BAIL-BOND OFFICE, SHE didn't even let Ashton say a word before shoving open the inner door and striding right inside Barney's private office.

"Where's my check?"

He only looked startled for a fraction of a second before plastering on his usual smarmy smile and gesturing to the chair in front of his desk. "Molly Pax. What a pleasure. Have a seat. I can't wait to hear more about your adventures. How exciting that must've been! And who would've thought that one of the detectives on your mother's case would be on the wrong side of the law?"

"Nope." She crossed her arms over her chest. She disliked Barney on a good day, and she'd been up for half the night before, thanks to the wannabe burglars. She was in no mood to play. "We don't need to chat. All I need is my check and confirmation that you're not going back on your word. I emailed you our bill early this morning."

"Well, fine. If you're going to be *unsociable*..." He hunted and pecked at his computer keyboard as Molly restrained the urge to tap her foot impatiently. "Despite your lack of manners, I'll admit that I was impressed you managed to bring in Sonny. I could use someone of your talents working for me full-time."

"No."

"You might want to consider—"

"No." When he opened his mouth to argue further, she waved her hand sharply, not even caring anymore that it was her mom's mannerism. "You blackmailed me into this, and Sonny almost killed me and the people I love. You're going to print that check, hand it to me, and give me your word that you won't make any other attempt to move up Mom's court date."

He eyed her, and she stared right back. Enough was enough. She wasn't about to let Barney bully her into becoming his lackey. She remembered Norah's pale face as she stood wrapped in explosives, and it steeled her resolve. Barney must've seen her determination, because he dropped his gaze to the computer screen and clicked the mouse button.

The whir of the printer kicking on sent a wave of triumph and relief crashing over Molly, but she tried very hard to keep her emotions from showing. She waited in silence as he signed the check and slowly, very slowly, extended it toward her. After snatching it from his grip, she quickly glanced down, confirming that he had actually made it out for the full thirty percent plus their expenses.

"Now your word that you won't try to move up Mom's court date."

"I'd never—"

"Your *word*, Barney." It wasn't worth much, but at least it was some kind of promise.

"Fine. I give you my word that I won't try to move Jane's court date." He said the words easily—too easily—and she didn't trust the smug way he leaned back in his chair. She knew it was all she was going to get from him, though, and she was ready to get out of this grubby office and away from its slimy inhabitant.

"I'll hold you to it." With a short nod, she turned and strode away, ignoring Barney's attempts to get her to stay. She strode to the main door and threw it open, stepping out into the fall sunlight just to slam head-on into a broad chest that smelled wonderful.

John caught her, not releasing her even after she'd regained her balance. Although she tried to scowl, her ability to frown seemed to be on the fritz whenever she was around him. "You did that on purpose," she scolded him. "What are you doing here?"

"I wanted to reenact our last encounter outside Barney's office," he said with absolutely no shame as he tucked her hand into the crook of his arm and headed across the parking lot. "Which answers both questions. Oh, and your Sergeant Blake called. She couldn't get hold of you, but she wanted to let you know they found your car."

"They did?" Molly's voice rose to an excited high note, making him wince even as he laughed.

"They did. Want a ride to the station?"

"Yes! Please." She couldn't contain her excitement and gave a little hop that made John laugh again and hug her against his side.

"You're so cute, Pax."

She pretended to frown at him. "You meant stunningly gorgeous."

"Of course I did."

"I got Barney to promise we'd have the month to find Mom. Oh, and I also got our check." She held it up for his inspection. By the way his eyebrows flew up, he hadn't expected Barney to pay the full amount, either.

"Ours?"

"Well, duh." She carefully tucked the check into one of her pockets and zipped it securely closed before climbing into the passenger side of his car. She sent a quick text to Cara, letting her know that she didn't need a ride home, and waited until John had gotten in before adding, "We're partners."

"So I got my way. We're working together." He sounded way too smug for her to let that pass.

"I still say this will end in bloodshed and tragedy."

"Probably."

"Although I'm shocked by how much less you annoy me when you're supplying me with regular orgasms."

That made him choke before he roared with laughter. "Same," he said once he was able to speak again.

Glancing over at that adorable dimple, she gave in to the urge to poke it with her fingertip. Gently grabbing her hand, he kissed it before returning it to her lap. She studied him as he drove, looking wildly happy, which, in turn, made her just as happy.

"I really do love you a ridiculous amount," she said as they turned into the police station lot. She was shocked by how quickly the drive had gone. Apparently, staring at John Carmondy with googly eyes really killed some time.

His look was both hungry and incredibly tender. "I've loved you since I first saw you chasing that woman through the mall."

"Doreen the scam artist? She was a really fast runner. If Charlie hadn't cut her off at the south exit, she would've gotten away that day." Molly frowned at him as he parked. "That was weeks before we met."

"Yeah, but I saw you tearing through the food

court, looking all determined and hot, and that was it. I was yours."

"You couldn't have loved me." Even though she denied it, she adored the idea. "You didn't know me then."

"Didn't matter. I loved you from that second, and I know you now." He opened the door and got out, and she hurried to do the same, needing to hear the rest of what he was about to say. He waited until they were climbing the steps to the entrance to speak again. "The more I get to know you, the more I love you."

Lieutenant Botha stepped outside, so Molly couldn't hurl herself into John's arms like she wanted. She had to limit herself to merely squeezing his arm for a moment before releasing him and smiling at the cop.

"Hi, Lieutenant. I heard my car was found."

"It was." A strange expression flickered across Botha's normally stoic face, and Molly felt a twitch of nerves.

"What's wrong?"

"It's…" When the lieutenant's voice trailed off, Molly really started to worry. "I'll show you. It's in the garage."

Shooting John an anxious glance, Molly followed Botha along the outside of the building to an overhead door. The lieutenant hesitated for just a moment before using her key card to open the door. As it slowly rolled up, Molly's imagination flashed through all sorts of horrible possibilities. What had happened to her beloved Prius? It had to be bad to fluster the otherwise unflusterable Lieutenant Botha. Had it been trashed? Smashed? Stripped?

Molly couldn't take it anymore. As soon as the door was high enough, she ducked underneath and looked frantically around, scanning the rows of squad vehicles

for her car. When her gaze landed on it, her heart sank
down to her toes. She vaguely heard John trying to
muffle his laughter.

"Oh…no."

———————————

"Keep your eyes closed."

Molly snorted as she stumbled over the bottom of the
doorframe. "Why does it even matter when your ham of
a hand is covering my entire face?"

"I have to keep my hand over your eyes because I
know you'll try to peek." Before she could respond to
that, he continued, "Ready?"

"As I'll ever be." Despite her dry tone, she was actually excited about John's surprise.

He dropped his hand to reveal a gorgeous porch swing.

"Whoa, you made this?" She ran her hand over the
back before plopping down on the cushioned seat. "It's
amazing. I'm so impressed."

He grinned his sweet, happy grin, the one she'd been
seeing more and more of since they'd brought in Sonny,
and plopped down next to her. The bench vibrated but
took his weight without complaint. "I am impressive."

"You are. Thank you for this." She glanced over at
the far side of the porch swing to see Warrant settling
happily on a dog bed she didn't recognize. "And for
Warrant's, too."

John's smile turned a little sheepish. "I couldn't leave
him without a place to sit."

Molly kissed him on the cheek in a spot that wasn't
swollen or mottled with bruises and cuddled in closer as

he wrapped his arm around her, careful with her still-sore arm. In all the time she'd known him, she wasn't sure how she'd missed what an absolute sweetheart this man was. As they gently swung, they watched as Mr. P next door glared at them suspiciously through the window before snapping down the blinds.

"Not only is this the perfect spot to enjoy a sunny fall day," she said, leaning her head back so she could see John's face, "but we also get to annoy the neighbors. It's a win-win."

His loud laugh triggered her own. They were still smiling as they watched a car pull up to the curb in front of the house. Felicity and Charlie climbed out, looking a bit bedraggled. Tail wagging, Warrant jogged down the steps to greet them.

"Welcome home!" Molly called as her sisters scratched Warrant's upturned belly.

They trudged through the yard and up the porch steps. Warrant followed and resettled on his new bed. "Thanks. What the heck is sitting in our driveway?" Charlie asked, plopping down next to Molly, who gave her a sitting half hug in greeting. "Did you start a new family business?"

Felicity dropped down onto her sisters' laps, turned sideways so she could eye the way Molly was tucked against John. "Finally. Took you long enough, Moo."

"Yeah, it did." He held up a fist for Felicity to bump, and Molly elbowed him—although not too hard, since he had just made her this very nice porch swing.

Molly ignored them and answered Charlie instead. "That's my car. It was not returned in the condition in which it was taken." After the initial shock, however, it was kind of growing on Molly. The neighbors were universally horrified by it, so that was a plus. "Apparently, Mom's friend sold it to someone who has a marijuana delivery business, and they had it custom painted. Just wait until you smell the interior. I'm worried I'll get a contact high just driving to the grocery store." She glanced at her beloved Prius and winced, just a little. A jungle of pot leaves stood out against a bright-blue background, with *Weed on Wheels* printed in huge hot-pink bubble letters on both sides.

"I think it's kind of pretty," Norah said as she came outside, letting the screen door swing shut behind her. "Very green and nature-y. Hey, Fifi, Charlie." She started to perch on the arm of the swing, but Felicity pulled her into her lap, making Charlie and Molly groan from the added weight.

"Let's not break the swing on the first day," Molly protested, but John just waved a hand, dismissing her concern.

"I made it strong enough to hold the whole family."

That made her heart squeeze with affection, and she smiled up at him. He grinned back, adoration clear in his expression as he hugged her closer.

"Speaking of family," Felicity said, "where's Cara?"

"The library. She said she had to work on a group class project." Molly tried to keep the doubt out of her voice. Cara had been gone a lot over the past few days, using the "group project" excuse every time someone asked where she'd been. The problem was that Cara was a terrible liar. Molly made a mental note to talk to her sister and make sure that everything was okay. This shady behavior wasn't like her.

"Heads up," Charlie said quietly, drawing everyone's

attention to the unmarked sedan rolling slowly down their street. They all fell silent as they watched it. As it crept past their house, Molly saw the bitter face of the driver.

"Detective Mill," John said, a hard note underlying his tone. "Looks like he's going to be a problem."

"Yep." Molly felt her stomach twist with renewed worry as the sedan followed the turnaround at the end of the street and sped away. Between detectives with grudges and a still-missing mom and unscrupulous treasure hunters and possible lurkers in the forest and a bail bondsman holding the title to their house in his money-grubbing fingers, they were still in a boatload of trouble. John squeezed her shoulders, and some of her tension slipped away. By bringing in Sonny, they'd gotten some breathing room and had at least a month to find their mom. They had time to save their house. She'd worry about it later. Right now, she just wanted to enjoy being with her family on their new porch swing.

"So what'd we miss while we were gone?" Charlie asked.

Molly and John looked at each other. She smiled, loving that they could communicate without saying a word, just like they were an old married couple. She settled in more comfortably against him. Telling the whole tale was going to take a while.

# EPILOGUE

CARA TRIED TO ACT CASUAL AS SHE WALKED ALONG THE cracked, weedy sidewalk in front of the motel, but she knew she looked exactly like what she was: a kindergarten teacher—well, almost—who was scared out of her mind. For the thousandth time, she mentally chided herself for her pick of bail jumpers, especially since she was solo on this job. If she told her sisters who she was tracking, they'd yank her home and tie her to a chair to keep her safe. Now that their home and business were threatened, however, she needed to do more to help. As the nape of her neck prickled with the feeling of being stalked, she decided it would've been smarter to choose a jaywalker or someone who cut tags off their mattresses for her first skip.

Of all the cases to take, why did she have to pick a killer?

Even as she asked herself that question, she knew why. Henry Kavenski had the highest bond. The dangerous ones always did.

Stopping at Room 87, the green door with a suspicious dark-red substance splattered over it, she took a quick glance around before pulling her lock-pick kit out of her pocket. Her fingers trembled, making her fumble the picks.

"Stop it," she muttered. "You're good at this. You

even beat Charlie's best time by eight whole seconds on lock-picking test day. Quit being a chicken."

This was her chance. She'd watched Kavenski get on the one-ten bus, but she wasn't sure how long he'd be gone. She needed to plant the tracker in his things before he returned. The thought of him walking in on her while she was still inside his hotel room made her shake even harder. Finally, though, the dead bolt released with a *click*, and she exhaled hard, relief and a fresh surge of nerves coursing through her. She'd done it. Now she just had to go inside and plant the tracker.

She reached for the door handle, the metal cold and slightly greasy to the touch. It gave under her hand, and the door swung open. Her heart thumping in her ears, she peered into the dim space, the smell of mildew and stale cigarette smoke tickling her nose.

A hard hand clamped down over her shoulder and shoved her into the room before she could even suck in a breath to scream.

**READ ON FOR A SNEAK PEEK AT THE
NEXT BOOK IN THE ROCKY MOUNTAIN
BOUNTY HUNTER SERIES:**

# RISK IT ALL

A HARD HAND CLAMPED DOWN OVER HER SHOULDER AND shoved her into the room before she could even suck in a breath to scream.

Her fingers tightened around the lock pick in her right hand and the tension tool in her left. She spun around, the soles of her shoes catching against the worn scruff of the carpet, and held the two tiny steel tools up in front of her as if they were a weapon. As Henry Kavenski—who looked even more enormous close up than he did from a half-block away—shoved the door closed, she locked her knees to keep them from shaking. Cold sweat prickled along her hairline as her brain frantically scrolled through all the things she had done wrong. She wasn't prepared. She should've brought a Taser or even some pepper spray or, better yet, backup. Her sisters were going to be so pissed if she got herself killed in such a stupid way.

From the hard set of Henry Kavenski's mouth, he wasn't feeling particularly merciful.

They stared at each other without speaking, the only sound Cara's heart thundering in her ears and the rapid breaths she couldn't seem to slow. She couldn't help but notice the details that she'd missed during the weeks she'd been tracking him from a distance. The scruff on his face was just slightly darker than the sun-bleached, tousled hair on his head. His jaw was solid, almost blocky, his nose and his mouth drawn with aggressive slashing lines, but the tops of his ears came to the slightest point. That elven detail didn't fit with the rest of his solid form and rugged features. Henry Kavenski was more of an ogre or giant. Despite those unsuitably adorable ears, he could never be mistaken for an elf.

She blinked, pulling her thoughts back in line. He still hadn't said a word, and she wasn't sure whether that meant she should be more or less terrified. Their mutual silence did give her a chance to come up with a plan—a fairly dumb plan, but at least it was something that might give her a chance to get out of this alive.

"Who are you?" Her voice shook, but she figured that was only natural.

His scowl deepened. He still didn't make a sound.

Her trembling worsened, her fingers tightening around the lock-picking tools. She tried to tuck them behind her in a way that looked natural, but his gaze followed the movement. His eyes met hers again, and she fought to keep from quailing beneath that stone-cold glower.

"What are you doing in…" she mentally grabbed for an imaginary friend's name, "Martin's room?"

His head cocked just slightly in question, although those eerily light eyes didn't soften.

Cara cleared her throat, using the sound to take a precious few moments to scrabble for her composure. It helped slightly, but she knew that all the time in the world wouldn't magically give her nerves of steel. She'd never envied her twin sister's badass-ery more. "I came here to surprise him. Uh…Martin." Why was her brain working at turtle-slow speed? She knew she'd think of all kinds of credible stories as soon as she left the room—if she managed to leave. The reminder that these could easily be her last minutes alive made her talk faster. "I passed my test—my..." She held her hands in front of her, forcing her fingers open to reveal the slim tools. "My locksmith test. Martin gave me some tips when I was practicing for it, and I thought we could go out to celebrate. Mexican. He loves Mexican." She made herself stop adding made-up details about her nonexistent but very helpful friend. "This is his room."

Kavenski still didn't say anything. He didn't even twitch. Instead, he continued to stare at her with those chilly eyes that reminded her what he was...a killer. A pro. As he stared at her, he was most likely contemplating the easiest way to dispose of her body with less emotion than he'd feel stepping on a spider.

Her imagination raced, her heart pounded, and she struggled to swallow with a suddenly dry throat. The air in the musty room felt thicker as dread filled her.

His considerable bulk blocked the one and only door, and the window was covered by the heavy polyester drapes. Even if she took him off guard with a dash to the window, there wouldn't be enough time for her to open it—if it was openable.

Tension twisted her insides until it was difficult to breathe. She had to say something, or the silence would smother her.

"What are you doing in Martin's room?" she demanded. Even though she was positive he knew her story was a complete lie, it was all she had.

When he shifted his weight, she flinched, but he just

leaned back against the door and pressed the heels of his
hands against his eyes. Before Cara could do more than
twitch toward the window, he dropped his arms to his
sides. She froze, her gaze never leaving his face. The chill
in his eyes was still there, but there was a slight droop to
his mouth that made him look extraordinarily tired.

"Are you okay?" The words were out before she
realized how ridiculous the question would sound. Even
after it penetrated, her mouth kept moving, as if it were
separate from her brain. "Have you been sleeping?"

He blinked at her.

"Not that it's any of my business if you did or not."
Why are you still talking??? her brain screamed at her,
but it was no use. The freight train of awkwardness
had left the station and was hurtling down the tracks.
"Now, if it were Marvin, my friend, then it would be my
business, but you're not Marvin. You're a stranger. A
stranger I don't know. Not that you'd be a stranger if I
did know you, so, um, you don't have to answer that, if
you don't want to. Don't feel obligated."

"Martin." His voice was unexpected. Deep and
smooth and perfect for narrating adventure movies or
candy commercials.

"What?" That unexpectedly delicious timbre threw
her off. It didn't match what she'd expected a killer to
sound like.

His chest lifted with a silent sigh as he straightened
away from the door. "Martin. Not Marvin."

She tensed at his movement, but he just stepped
sideways, opening a path to the door. "Right. Martin."
She couldn't believe that she'd messed up her fictitious
friend's name. It was a stressful situation, sure, but

surely she could keep track of her made-up lock-picking study partners for five minutes.

"You need to stop following me."

She jolted again. Not only had he caught her breaking into his motel room, but he was aware that she'd been tracking him across town. Her sisters were right. She was not cut out for field work. If she managed to survive this encounter, it'd be best if she just stayed home and researched. That was what she was good at, not the chasing, tackling, and wrestling parts of bounty hunting.

Then she realized he was eyeing her with the slightest hint of amused resignation, and she realized she hadn't responded to the accusation.

"Following you? What are you talking about?" It was weak, she knew, but everything about this interaction was throwing her off. She didn't know if he was going to kill her slowly and painfully or give her tips on shadowing fellow criminals. It was disconcerting. "I'm here to meet…uh…?"

"Martin," he offered helpfully.

"Right." She eyed the door and then snapped her gaze back to him. It was so tempting, having the path to the exit clear, but she worried that he was just setting a fun little trap for her. Still, she dared take a step forward. When he didn't grab her, she edged forward again. "Since Martin isn't here, I'll just go find him."

Despite those icy eyes and the hard line of his mouth, she was pretty sure he was amused. Strangely, she wasn't as terrified of Kavenski as she'd initially been, and she wondered if she was in shock or, perhaps, under the effect of a fast-acting strain of Stockholm Syndrome. Telling herself to wait until she was safely outside the motel room to analyze her emotional state, she took another cautious step toward the door.

Then he moved, and she froze, her mind clamoring that she should've known it was too good to be true. Of course the brutal killer with the ice-cold stare wouldn't just let her walk out after catching her breaking into his room. She'd fallen into his trap, and now she was in grabbing distance, and she was going to die.

When his hand grasped the doorknob instead of reaching for her throat, she stared at him. With a hard twist of his wrist, he yanked the door open and then looked at her expectantly. A hard breath shuddered into her lungs. Had she not been breathing this whole time? It was an easy thing to lose track of while waiting to be murdered.

"Oh…um." She took the final step to the now-open door. "Thank you? Sorry for…ah, intruding." Slipping through the opening, she hurried away from the room, jumping as she heard it close behind her with a loud snap. It was only after she'd reached her car and was cocooned in the familiar safety of the driver's seat that the danger really hit her, and her breathing sped up until she was taking in short, rapid puffs of air.

That was the closest she'd ever come to dying. What a failure of a bounty hunter she was. If it had been Molly or Felicity or Charlie trapped in the room with Kavenski, her sisters would've had him tackled and cuffed before he could even glare at them. It was mortifying that the only reason Cara managed to escape was because a known killer had stepped aside and opened the door for her.

As her breathing gradually slowed, she started the car, her fingers trembling just a little now. "It's okay," she told herself out loud. "You just need to walk before you can run. Work your way to the upper levels, rather than jumping right into them." It was clear, now that she'd seen him in all his close-up power and glory, that Henry Kavenski was not a skip for a beginner bounty hunter. He'd known that she'd been following him, and he'd obviously set her up to catch her breaking into his room. She needed to find a skip who was a little less deadly and a lot dumber.

Remembering to bring her Taser would be a good idea, too.

As she pulled away from the curb, she felt a strange curl of disappointment in her belly. She should've been relieved by her decision to leave Henry Kavenski to other, braver, more experienced bounty hunters, but a part of her didn't want to give him up. After following him around and learning everything she could about him, she'd become, oddly enough, a touch possessive.

She firmly quashed the thought. It was time to focus on a new skip, one whose worst crime was jaywalking or tearing tags off mattresses.

Pressing down on the accelerator, she left the run-down motel and Henry Kavenski behind.

———————

Two days later, Cara was regretting her decision to leave Kavenski to the professionals…well, the more professional professionals. She clicked through the pile of jobs she'd lined up and made a face. None of them were even close to the bail bond he'd skipped on, and the fifteen percent fee seemed paltry compared to what they'd get for bringing Kavenski in.

"That's the problem, genius," she muttered to herself, tapping the side of her laptop with an anxious fingertip. "You'd have to actually bring him in."

With a Taser or her sisters' help, she probably could manage that, but the real issue was that she honestly didn't want to. There weren't a lot of killers—or criminals of any sort—who would've just let her walk away unharmed. It made her wonder if he really was the vicious killer he was accused of being.

"You're such a sucker." With a sigh, she shut down her computer. "You just think he's pretty."

"Who's pretty?" Her twin, Charlie, charged into the kitchen, heading directly to the fridge. Warrant immediately hopped up from his sprawl under the table to follow her, obviously hoping for snacks.

Trying to disguise her guilty jump by standing up and slipping her laptop into her backpack, Cara blinked innocently at her sister. "One of the skips." It wasn't a lie.

Charlie frowned at the contents of the fridge before closing the door and grabbing a banana. "Whose turn is it to get groceries? Things are looking a little desperate in there." Leaning her hip against the counter, she raised an eyebrow at Cara. "Speaking of desperate... A skip? Really?"

Despite her discomfort about talking—even indirectly—about the mess she'd made of her encounter with Kavenski, Cara had to laugh. "Come on. You can't tell me that, of all the hundreds of skips we've handled, you've never found any remotely attractive?"

Charlie grinned around her bite of banana, conceding the point without saying a word.

Zipping her backpack, Cara hauled it over her shoulder and glanced at the time on her phone. "Got to get to class. And it's your turn."

"My turn for what?"

"Getting groceries. Don't bring home only junk this time, or Felicity will make you run extra laps." Cara headed for the door as her twin gave a dramatic groan.

"Fine, but I'm still getting Lucky Charms."

"It's your funeral," Cara called as she stepped outside and closed the door behind her, rather proud that she'd managed to wiggle out of what could've been an awkward conversation. As she headed toward where her car was parked on the driveway, she felt an uneasy prickle on the back of her neck. Trying to look casual, she glanced down the street, but there weren't any parked cars in sight. Her gaze roamed over the neighborhood, but it all looked quiet. Even the ever-present breeze had settled, leaving only the scuff of her shoes against the concrete to break the eerie silence.

"Stop it," she ordered herself. "You're getting paranoid." Just to be on the safe side, though, she scanned the trees next to the house, looking for anything suspicious. Since they'd gotten an alarm system installed, the attempted break-ins had dropped significantly, but there was still the occasional treasure hunter trying their luck. Thanks for that, Mom.

The forest was still and dark. Despite the lack of any suspicious figures hiding in the shadows, the prickle of unease intensified, and she hurried back to yank open the door.

"Charlie!" she called.

"Yeah?" Charlie stepped into view.

"Make sure to set the alarm when you leave." Still unsettled by the odd stillness of the forest, she frowned. "Or if you stay. And lock the door."

Charlie straightened, meeting Cara's gaze steadily. "Trouble outside?"

"Nothing I can see. Just a feeling."

"Got it." From Charlie's sober tone, Cara knew she wouldn't blow off the warning.

"Thanks."

Dropping her serious expression, Charlie made shooing motions with her hands. "Now get to class before you're late."

Cara gave her a mock salute before closing the door and hurrying to the car. She hoped that they'd find their mom soon—as well as the valuable necklace Jane had stolen—so that their lives could go back to normal. Maybe it was wrong to hope that her only surviving parent would be back in jail, but Cara didn't care. Jane had really screwed them over this time. If she hadn't stolen the necklace, used their house for collateral on her bail bond, and then skipped town, then Cara would be happily attending classes and doing her usual research. Instead, Cara was scanning the bushes for danger and breaking into murderers' motel rooms.

Accused murderers, her brain corrected, and she sighed. It was probably a good thing she'd sworn off chasing after Henry Kavenski. As far as he was concerned, she had a hard time staying objective. He hadn't killed her, after all.

Plus he really was incredibly pretty.

# CHAPTER 2

HER CHILD DEVELOPMENT THEORIES CLASS WAS A GOOD distraction from the utter chaos of the rest of her life. The two hours flew by, and she was disappointed when it ended and all her worries crashed back down on her. Not wanting to return to dealing with skips and the possibility of burglars lurking in her backyard, she dragged out the process of packing up her bag.

When she was the last one in the classroom, she knew she couldn't delay any longer. It was time to dive back into the less-fun parts of her life. Heaving her backpack over her shoulder, she headed for the corridor. The classroom was on the third floor of Meyers Hall, an ancient brick building that was stiflingly hot in the summer and as cold as a walk-in freezer in the winter. The majority of the students had already made their way outside, and the few remaining were making their way toward the stairs.

Cara followed slowly, still reluctant to get home and have to think about which skip she would choose to take the place of Henry Kavenski. The soles of her tennis shoes squeaked slightly against the highly polished floor, and the sound echoed through the hall, making her realize how quiet it had become. The classrooms had emptied and the rest of the straggling students had disappeared, leaving her alone.

Even as she told herself she was being silly, she couldn't help but tense. Her pace quickened, the sound of her hurried footsteps making her even more aware of how horror-movie-like her situation was. She tried to be amused by it, but it was hard to laugh at her very real apprehension as she rushed toward the stairs. All the crazy and dangerous things that had been happening to her and her sisters lately made her see menace in everything.

"Hey, Cara Pax."

She whirled around, a shriek of surprise trapped in her throat. As soon as she saw who'd spoken, she was glad that the startled sound hadn't made it out. The little weasel had intentionally tried to scare her, and she would've hated to give him the satisfaction of knowing he'd succeeded.

"What are you doing here, Stuart?" she asked, wanting to keep walking toward the stairs but not trusting the creep enough to turn her back. Moving backward away from him felt too much like running, and she wasn't scared of the little punk. He'd been one of the many who tried to break into their house. Since Molly and John had caught him in the act, he'd been popping up around campus wherever Cara happened to be. He seemed to have a mistaken impression that she knew where her mom had hidden the stolen necklace.

"Why are most students in a campus building?" He really did have the most punchable smirk in the history of the world. "What do you think I'm doing here?"

Irritation surged at the question, and she pivoted toward the stairs, too annoyed to be worried about what he'd do if her back was turned. "Quit stalking me."

His low laugh followed her, and she straightened

her shoulders, fighting the urge to glance back. She wouldn't give him the satisfaction of knowing just how creepy she found him. He was trying to frighten her. What he didn't realize was that she dealt with scarier people every day. She'd faced down Henry Kavenski. After that, Stuart seemed like small potatoes.

Still, Stuart's mocking laugh did make her uneasy, as much as she tried to hide it. Campus was her escape from the stress of her sisters' bounty hunting business, and knowing he was lurking around her, following her, ruined that feeling of safety.

Anger filled her as she rushed down the stairs, her shoes thumping on each step, creating enough of a clatter that she couldn't hear anything else that Stuart tried to say. When she reached the ground floor, she couldn't keep herself from glancing up to see if he'd followed her. The stairs were poorly lit, the steps quickly disappearing into the gloom, and she felt the prickle of goose bumps ghost down her spine.

That's what he wants, the reasonable part of her brain said. He wants to freak you out.

Despite knowing that, she still had to hide a shiver as she shoved through the door out into the late afternoon sunshine. As she strode toward the parking lot, pretending that she wasn't relieved to see the clusters of students scattered around the area, Cara set her jaw. No more chickening out. She was going to bring in a skip and show her sisters that she could be useful in the field. That way, Charlie and Felicity could focus on finding their mom and bringing her back.

Cara was going to do whatever she had to in order to get their lives back to normal. She only had to be a badass for a short time, and then she could go back to worrying about normal things, like class projects and finding a student-teaching position next semester and whose turn it was to clean the bathroom.

Her cell phone dinged, the ringtone telling her it was a work call, and she pulled it out with brisk motions, caught up in a wave of determination. "Pax Bail Recovery."

"Hey, there." Barney's slimy voice made her wrinkle her nose. Between him and Stuart, she was getting a full dose of creeps today. "Which pretty Pax sister am I talking to?"

"This is Cara. How can I help you?" She put on her best professional tone. Before everything happened, she would've blown him off as quickly as possible, but now that he held their mom's bail bond—which meant he'd own their house if she didn't show up for her next hearing—she had to be polite to him, which just about killed her. That was another thing that needed to go back to normal as quickly as possible. She was going to relish being able to hang up on Barney again.

"I have a job for you."

She had to bite her tongue to hold back a groan. The last skip Barney had wanted them to bring in had almost killed Molly multiple times, and Cara and her sisters had almost been blown up.

At her silence, Barney hurried to add, "He's nothing like the last one. This one'll be easy. A walk in the park. I'm actually doing you a favor by telling you about him."

His protestations were just making her more wary. "What's he being charged with?"

"Tax evasion. He owes enough that the judge set his bail high."

That was promisingly non-violent. "Send over his file, and we'll consider it."

Barney's grunt didn't sound too happy that she wasn't accepting the job immediately, but he just said, "Fine," and hung up.

Cara had barely gotten into her car before her phone alerted her that she had an email. Still suspicious why Barney was so desperate to have them bring in a simple tax-evading skip, rather than siccing his own bounty-hunting dogs on the guy, she opened the file on her phone. After scanning the information, she was frowning more deeply. The skip, Geoffrey Abbott, appeared to be an easy job on the surface, but the name teased her brain. It sounded oddly familiar.

Setting down her phone, she turned on her car, eager to get home and research the guy. He might be just what she was looking for to replace Henry Kavenski as her first successful capture. Her mood lifting for the first time since Stuart had popped out of the shadows, she backed out of her parking space and headed home.

━━━━━━━━━━

Climbing out of her car, she paused, pretending to check her phone as she fought to push away the urge to jump back in and drive away as fast as she could. She'd only been to Dutch's Bar once, but that had been in the middle of the day with Molly. At night, it was exponentially creepier. The warehouses surrounding the bar seemed to loom over the space, creating shadowed places where any number of dangerous people could be lurking. The bar, which had looked nondescript and slightly dingy in the full sunlight, now gave off a menacing air, making Cara sure she wouldn't be welcome or safe there. That didn't matter, though. She was determined to follow through on this job, and that meant checking out his possible hangouts…including Dutch's.

She slid her hand over the lump the Taser made in her jacket pocket. The presence of the weapon gave her courage, and she pulled up the photo of Geoffrey Abbott, getting his image freshly lodged in her brain. Slipping her phone back in her other pocket—the Taser-less one—she pulled back her shoulders and strode toward the entrance.

Her confidence wavered as the bouncer eyed her suspiciously, his sharp gaze running over her as if he could see the Taser despite it being hidden in her jacket pocket. She hoped that he wouldn't conduct a pat down, and then wondered if that would be legal for a civilian. Making a mental note to look up the Colorado statute as soon as she had a quiet moment, she focused on the big guy in front of her.

His hand extended, palm out, and Cara offered her driver's license, bracing herself for what she knew was coming. Even though she was legal by almost four full years, she was used to the disbelieving squints. Her small stature and baby face—including dimples—made her appear younger than she was. She'd pulled her dark hair back into a severe bun, to keep it out of grabbing range as well as to make her look more like a serious professional, and she hoped it didn't make her look like a teenager playing dress-up.

The bouncer's gaze flicked between her and the license several times, and his frown deepened.

Cara sighed as she dug out her wallet. "That really is my authentic, legal license. See? The same birthdate as my student ID."

"Why are you here?" the bouncer asked in a warning rumble.

"Uh..." She didn't expect to be questioned about her motives before she even got inside the place. What kind of dive bar was this? "To have a few drinks, maybe dance a little. Do, you know, bar things."

"Bar things," he repeated expressionlessly, and she nodded too quickly.

"Bar things."

His sigh was deep enough to make his enormous shoulders sag for a moment, and she was pretty sure she was about to be sent away. To her surprise, he handed back her IDs and motioned toward the door. "Don't blow anything up."

"I'll do my best." She would've made a comment about how that was a strange thing to say, except that a skip Molly was chasing had blown a hole in the bathroom wall just a few weeks ago. Besides, she was just glad the bouncer hadn't searched her and found her Taser.

Slipping inside before he could change his mind, she looked around, getting her bearings. The bar wasn't as intimidating as she'd expected. It was smaller than the building it was in would've suggested, with a fairly good-sized crowd. Loud old-school rock pounded through the space, and the usual beery, sweaty bar smell filled her nose. She'd half-expected the music to screech to a stop when she entered as everyone turned to stare, but no one even seemed to notice her entrance.

She took a few deep breaths before moving toward

the bar. After the whole motel-room incident, she'd planned better this time. This was simply a reconnaissance mission. Even if she spotted Abbott, she wouldn't try to make contact. The most she'd do was follow him to his car and get his plate number.

The bartender, a redhead who resembled Jane a little too much for comfort, gave her a suspicious look but handed over the beer Cara ordered without any fuss. Clutching the cold bottle a little too tightly, she wove her way through the throng toward a shadowed booth in the back. From there, she'd be able to watch the crowd while staying somewhat hidden.

Preoccupied with not running into anyone while she scanned faces for one that matched Geoffrey Abbott's mugshot, she was right in front of the booth before she realized that it was already occupied.

"Oh! Sorry. I thought this was empty." Even as she apologized and started to turn away, she recognized the man sitting in the corner of the booth where the shadows were the deepest, and her head snapped back around. Her first thought was that the gloom was playing tricks on her eyes, because there was no way that was Henry Kavenski. It had to be her mind messing with her.

As much as she blinked, though, the face in front of her did not change. It was indeed her first attempted skip. She continued to stare, unable to process the fact that, now that she'd given up on bringing him in, Henry Kavenski just happened to pop up right in front of her. He looked back at her, expressionless except for the slight tightening of his lips.

"Hi." Of course she said that. "I didn't expect to see you here."

"Didn't I tell you to quit following me?"

Maybe it was because there was more long-suffering exasperation in his tone than anger, or maybe it was because she was relieved to see a familiar face in this intimidating bar—even if it was his face—but once again, her mouth worked before her brain could stop it. "Mind if I sit down?"

He blinked at her, his face poker-straight and his lips compressed, but he didn't say no. Cara slid into the booth next to him, careful to leave space between them so she didn't intrude on his personal bubble. "What are you doing?" he asked.

"Sitting." A part of her was impressed with her audacity, while the rest was just screaming a warning that she was going to get herself killed.

"There's an entire empty bench over there." He flicked his hand at the other side of the table.

"I can't see anything from over there." Her tone was apologetic, but she settled more firmly on the battered vinyl seat. This was perfect, once she got used to the idea that she'd plonked herself down next to an accused killer.

"So find another table." That tone was back—the annoyed yet resigned one that was starting to become so familiar. It was oddly reassuring, which made her wonder if she was right in the head.

"This one is perfect for watching the bar, though." She pretended to take a sip of her beer and scanned the crowd. Unless Abbott was wearing an excellent disguise, she was pretty sure he wasn't in the main room.

A heavy sigh drew her attention back to her booth-mate. "Who are you stalking now?" he grumbled.

"Geoffrey Abbott." She watched his expression as

she said the name, but he didn't even twitch. Even if he did know Abbott, she wasn't sure why she'd expected Kavenski to show any reaction. He had his poker face down pat. "He's a tax evader."

The amber liquid in his drink caught the light as he rotated his glass. He hadn't taken a sip since she'd joined him, making her wonder if he was pretending to drink, just like she was. "A tax evader with connections," he grumbled.

"What do you mean, connections?" Even as she asked, her stomach sank. She'd known it was too easy, especially coming from Barney.

"You don't want that mess," he said, rather than clarifying. "Find another target."

"But he was perfectly non-violent and seemed kind of dumb. That's just what I was looking for." She allowed her head to thump against the back of the booth. "I should've known he was too good to be true."

Kavenski stayed silent as she worked through her disappointment. It made sense, now that she thought about it. After all, weren't mobsters traditionally brought down by tax evasion? She stared at the crowd as she mentally ran over his file again. Organized crime ties fit, she had to admit to herself.

As if to mock her, her gaze caught on the profile of the very man she'd come to Dutch's to find. He worked his way through the crowd, as if intent on finding someone. The someone turned out to be a woman who looked to be in her fifties, with light brown hair, strong features, and a wide, mobile mouth that came together into a striking whole. They had an intense, low-voiced discussion before Abbott turned away abruptly, his mouth pinched with anger. As intently as he'd made his way into the bar, he now worked his way toward the exit.

Cara slid out of the booth. Even though Kavenski had warned her about going after Abbott, she couldn't let him leave without at least getting a plate number. It'd be simple and danger-free, and that bit of information might soften the blow when she informed Barney that they wouldn't take the case.

"What are you doing?"

Cara gave him a sunny smile. "Nothing dangerous. Thanks for letting me sit with you."

She turned away and slipped through the crowd, keeping her eye on the back of Abbott's head, thankful that he was taller than most of the other bar patrons. By the time she'd worked her way to the door and stepped outside, he was nowhere in sight. She paused, waiting for one of the parked cars to start, hoping that he hadn't parked it in the lot across the street or, even worse, walked to Dutch's.

Glancing at the bouncer, she saw that he was watching her grimly. "I didn't blow anything up," she said.

Before he could respond, she saw red brake lights illuminate on a car in the far corner of the parking lot. It was too far away to see the plate, so she hurried across the lot. He was already backing out of his spot, and she moved a little faster, not wanting to attract attention by running, but also unwilling to miss her chance.

The back end of his car drew closer as he reversed, and she squinted at the license plate. He started to pull forward toward the lot exit, moving the car away from her, and she trotted forward, hoping to catch it as he paused before turning onto the street.

A loud squeal of tires behind her made her spin around, startled. Bright headlights blinded her as an engine revved loudly. A car was coming at her—fast, too fast. She dodged to the side, but the lights followed her, steering toward her as if to intentionally run her down. Pivoting in the other direction, she ran toward the row of parked cars, hoping they'd at least take some of the car's impact, but a glance over her shoulder showed that it was too late.

The car was going to run her down.

# HOLD YOUR BREATH

JUMPING INTO A HOLE CUT IN THE FROZEN RESERVOIR WAS A stupid idea. In fact, of all the questionable decisions she'd made since abandoning civilization for her tiny mountain cabin seven months ago, this was probably the worst.

At least, Lou mused wryly, it was a beautiful place in which to do a dumb thing. The sun lit the snowcapped mountains circling like sleepy sentinels around them, and the wind chased powdery snow across the frozen reservoir. Despite the cold, it still smelled strongly of fish.

"Ready for some ice-rescue training?" Derek bumped his neoprene-covered arm against hers. He seemed much too cheerful for a guy about to dive into glacial water.

"No."

"Aww, Lou." When he tried to pat her head with one of his bright blue gloves, she ducked out of reach. "Nervous?"

"Of course not. Why would I be nervous about

jumping into a hole in the ice and swimming around in thirty-two-and-a-half-degree water? Why did I join the Field County Rescue Dive Team and not the Jamaican Whatever again?"

"Because I would not be on the Jamaican Dive Team," Derek answered. "And I make it worth the cold."

"Yeah, not really."

"Hey!" He smacked her arm, she laughed and whacked him back, and then it evolved into a full-fledged slap fight. The blue-nitrile shade of their gloves made them look like life-size cartoons, and Lou couldn't hold back another laugh.

"Sparks!"

Callum's bellow froze her in place. She shot Derek a wry glance before turning to face their team leader. She took careful, deliberate steps in the clumsy dry-suit boots, as humiliation was better served in small doses. Being caught goofing off was bad enough. She didn't need to fall on her ass, as well.

"Yes?" She eyed his scowling face. It was too bad about his surliness, since Callum was a joy to look upon otherwise, in a gladiator-meets-drill-sergeant kind of way. His blond hair was military short, and his eyes were a startling and beautiful blue against tanned skin. His jaw was square, and his body... Taking a deep breath, she carefully did not check out the neoprene-wrapped perfection below his neck.

Because...damn.

"What are you doing?"

Somehow, answering "Fooling around with Derek" did not seem like the best idea. "Uh...nothing."

He stared at her, heavy frown still in place. "It

didn't— Never mind. You're like a terrier with ADD.
Why can't you stand still for five minutes?"

"Because…" She shot a glance at Derek. The traitor had taken several steps back and was pretending to
examine a seam on his dry-suit sleeve. "He… I just…
Um, the gloves…"

Callum let the silence hang for several seconds.
When he eventually turned away from Lou, she let out
the breath she'd been holding and shuffled over to rejoin
Derek. Once there, she punched him lightly—well, sort
of lightly—in the kidney.

"Ouch." He gave her an injured look. "What was
that for?"

"Why am I always the one who gets in trouble?"

"Because you're the one who starts it."

"Do not," she protested, realizing she'd gotten a
little loud only when Callum's eyes focused on her
again. Dropping her gaze, she studied the half-frozen
puddle in front of her boots. It seemed as if every
single time she did something embarrassing, Callum
was there, watching her with the look—a mix of exasperation and irritated bafflement. The sad part was that,
even after three months of getting the look, Lou still
wasn't able to smother the obnoxious butterflies that
fluttered in her belly whenever she was the center of
his attention.

"You done?" he asked. At her nod, he jerked his chin
toward the icy reservoir.

Lou fell in line with the six other divers, taking
slow, exaggerated steps to avoid tripping over her own
neoprene-wrapped feet or slipping on the ice. As they
reached the large opening that had been carved out

earlier in the day for the training exercise, Lou peered at the water, frowning.

"What's wrong?" Derek asked, stepping up beside her and following her gaze as if looking for the answer to his own question.

She shrugged. "All that ice around the edge makes the water look really cold."

Bumping her with his elbow, he snorted. "It is cold, genius. It's literally freezing, which explains all the hard stuff we're standing on."

Lou elbowed him back. "Dork," she grumbled.

He smirked at her.

"The ice is just under ten inches here," Callum announced in his schoolteacher tone—the one that always made Lou want to act up like a contrary third-grader. "Is that thick enough for a group of people to walk on?"

"Wouldn't it have been better to confirm that before we left shore?" Lou muttered, making Derek snicker. Callum sent a sharp look her way.

"It's thick enough," Chad answered, taking a step toward Callum. "It'd even be okay to drive on it."

"Drive what?"

"A car or light truck," Chad said quickly. "For anything more, twelve inches would be better."

"That's what she said," Derek whispered loud enough to make everyone except Callum laugh. Even Chad grinned before dropping his chin to hide it.

Callum let his gaze fall on each person in turn. The chuckles died, replaced by awkward coughs.

"So this ice is safe?" he finally asked when silence had fallen over the team members.

"Yes." Chad was the first to speak up again, and Lou winced. He'd obviously already forgotten the four hours they'd spent watching training videos that morning.

Wilt gave a slow, sad shake of his head. "No ice is safe," he said in the Arkansas drawl he held on to even after forty years in Colorado. Lou liked Wilt. He was a soft-spoken man who kept quiet unless he had something important to say. When he spoke, everyone shut up and listened. Wilt was in his sixties, with a thick mustache that drooped over his mouth, giving him a perpetually mournful expression.

"Good, Wilt," Callum said. "Glad someone was paying attention this morning. We have to be especially careful of weak spots after the warm spell last week. Even though it's been cold the past couple of days, the ice probably hasn't recovered yet."

Chad's shoulders sagged. Knowing all too well how it felt to be under the heavy weight of Callum's displeasure, Lou shot him a sympathetic glance. He avoided her gaze.

"Okay!" Callum clapped his blue-gloved hands together. "Everyone in the water. First time in is the hardest, so it's best to get it over with."

Lou eyed the water doubtfully, shuffling a little closer to the edge of the hole. She had a lot of scuba diving experience, but most of it had been in tropical locations. This was new to her.

"What if my suit has a leak?" Chad asked. Lou whipped her head around to stare at him. Hell. She'd never thought about a leaky suit. Her newly panicked gaze flew to Callum's face.

"Your suit is buoyant enough that it won't matter,

even if it fills with water to your armpits." Callum waved a dismissive hand. "You'll still float."

Slightly relieved but trying not to think about how freaking cold thirty-two-degree water up to her armpits would be, she turned her attention back to the opening in the ice. Derek had already taken the plunge.

"C'mon in," he said, letting his legs float to the surface and leaning back as if he were in an easy chair. "The water's fine."

Deciding to just get it done, Lou took a breath and jumped in. When her head went under, she instantly realized her mistake. Once the shockingly cold water hit her face, her lungs clamped down, squeezing out all her oxygen. She didn't even try to figure out which way was up but just let her suit float her to the surface instead.

She felt a tap on the back of her hood and yanked her face out of the water. Callum was close enough for her to see the deep creases between his eyebrows.

"You good?" he asked.

"Y-yep."

After examining her face carefully, he shook his head. "Never do anything halfway, do you, Sparks?"

Since she didn't know if that was a compliment or an insult, she kept quiet. Her legs kept wanting to float to the surface behind her and tip her onto her front as the others climbed in more carefully. Scowling, she tried to force her lower half down but ended up flailing unsuccessfully.

"How are you staying upright?" she asked Callum, craning her neck to keep her face out of the water as her legs headed for the surface again.

"Tuck them to your chest and then push them straight down." He swam toward the icy ledge as she struggled to master her buoyant suit. She finally managed to shove her legs down so her body was more or less upright.

"Ha!" she crowed, slapping the surface in victory. "Got you down, bitches!"

"Did you just call your legs 'bitches'?" Derek asked from directly behind her, making her jump. Her upper body tilted forward, but she got herself back under control.

"Yep. Occasional evidence to the contrary, I am in charge of all my body parts."

"Glad to hear it."

"Everyone out!" Callum bellowed, levering his body onto the ice with ease. "Exit the water on your front like a seal and then roll away from the edge. Remember, the more you can distribute your weight, the less likely it is you'll go through the ice."

Lou flattened her hands on the ice and tried to hoist her body out of the water, but it looked a lot easier when Callum did it. Her legs, damn the rogue bastards, floated forward and up, catching under the ledge. She managed to slam the edge of the ice into her belly, driving out her breath.

"Nice, Lou," Derek mocked as he slid gracefully onto the solid surface. "You're like a special seal."

"Oh, shut up," she muttered, panting, as she hauled herself out of the water.

This, she could tell, was going to be one hell of a day.

―――――――――

"Sparks!" Callum bellowed. "You're up!"

She sighed, relinquishing her spot on the rope where

she'd been helping to pull the "victims" and their rescuers out of the water and across the ice. It was like a lopsided game of tug-of-war—all brute strength and teamwork—and she'd actually been getting to like that part of training, despite the hard work. But now that she wasn't pulling, she noticed her eyelashes had frosted over, and her neck and the top of her chest were clammy from the water that had leaked into the suit after her full-body plunge.

Trudging over to Callum, she lifted her arms so he could wrap the end of the rope around her middle. Although she'd watched three of the guys perform an in-water rescue, she was still nervous. The ice-rescue veterans had made it look easy, but she had a feeling her first time wouldn't go so smoothly.

Callum handed her the victim's harness, which looked like a skinny pool noodle. It was attached to her rope with about six feet of line. That way, the victim would be first out of the water, and she'd be behind him, in a position to help lift him onto the ice.

"When you get to the victim, carabiner should be in your right hand," Callum instructed. "The other end goes in your left. Get control of your suit before trying to save anybody. Approach the victim from the side or back, talk to him, harness him up, signal the guys to start pulling, and lift your knee to help boost him onto the ice with your thigh. Once you get your hands on him, do not let go of your patient. Got it?"

"Yes." Her voice sounded a little uncertain, so she firmed her jaw and tried again. "Yes."

Callum's mouth quirked up on one side. If it had been anyone but Callum, Lou would've thought he was holding back a smile.

Okay. Okay, she could do this.

She approached the edge of the ice, crawling when she was ten feet out and then moving to her belly and sliding across the last yard. Swinging her legs around, she dropped feetfirst into the water, careful to keep her face above the surface this time. She looked back at where Callum stood on the ice. He bumped his closed fist on the top of his head, the signal for Are you okay? She answered in the affirmative with a matching fist-to--head bump before heading toward her "victim."

Holding her face out of the water, she swam toward Phil, who clung to the ice on the other side of the opening with melodramatic panic. Lou had to bite back a groan when she saw how he was putting every ounce of community-theater experience into his role of drowning victim.

Coming up next to him, she tried to get her legs underneath her as she spoke. "Hang on, sir. I'm Louise Sparks with the Field County Dive Team. We're going to get you out of here."

Phil's pretend struggles increased, and his thrashing hand slapped the water, splashing it into her face. Air left her lungs again at the breath-stealing cold, and her legs floated up behind her. Damn it. When she could move her body again, she drew her knees up and pushed her feet straight down, glaring at her grinning victim.

"Oops," Phil said. "Sorry, Lou."

"Uh-huh," she muttered as she moved around behind him. "I'm hooking this harness around you, sir, so the team on shore can pull you out."

She struggled to reach around Phil's wide girth, wishing she'd gotten skinny Wilt as her victim instead. The dry-suit gloves made her fingers thick and unwieldy, and she fumbled with the carabiner. To make matters even more silent-swear-worthy, Phil had resumed his melodramatic struggling.

"Don't make me drown you," she snarled, jerking her head back so his flapping elbow didn't connect with her eye.

"Where's your compassion, Lou? I'm a panicked, hypothermic tourist here." The bastard sounded as if he were about to laugh.

"I'll show you compassion," she muttered through gritted teeth. "And if you're hypothermic, shouldn't you be getting tired and sluggish?"

"That sounds threatening." Phil was definitely laughing, the ass. "As soon as you save me and I get out of the hospital, I'm going to file a complaint with your superior."

"That's where you're wrong—there is no one superior to me," she said, letting out a relieved grunt when she finally succeeded in hooking the carabiner through the metal loop of the harness.

Phil laughed and then wiggled several feet sideways, pulling his slick, neoprene-covered body free of her grip.

"Never let go of your patient!" Callum yelled. "Once you put your hands on him, you do not let go until he is being lifted into the ambulance, understand?"

With a heavy sigh, Lou tried to maneuver behind Phil again, but he was surprisingly agile for such a big guy. Plus, the training had been tiring, and she still had to help hoist Phil's bulk out of the water. Clenching her jaw, she lunged toward him, managing to latch her arms around his waist.

"Got you!" she crowed, but her satisfaction was

quickly overruled by irritation as her legs floated up behind her again, curving her spine into an awkward partial backbend. With Phil's body in the way, she couldn't pull her knees up very easily. After several unsuccessful attempts at getting her legs underneath her, she kicked out in frustration. But instead of passing through unresisting water, her booted foot hit hard against something.

"What the hell?" she mumbled, looking over her shoulder. She couldn't see whatever it was through the murky water. It had felt fairly firm, although it had moved with her kick. She was tempted to thump it with her boot again, but reconsidered.

"What?" Phil had finally realized she was ignoring him. He quit his fake struggling, twisting his head around to follow her gaze.

"I kicked something." She kept staring at the water, as if she'd suddenly develop X-ray vision. Her arms were still locked around Phil's middle. No need to get yelled at for making the same mistake twice.

"The Mission Reservoir Monster?" he asked in his best spooky voice.

"What's taking you so long?" Callum called from the ice. "For Christ's sake, Sparks, your victim would be dead by now. Just complete the recovery, and let's get his body out of the water so we can notify his next of kin."

"You gave up on me so quick, Cal," Phil whined. "Aren't you even going to start CPR?"

"No way," Derek yelled back. "He knows where those lips have been."

"What's the problem?" Callum didn't sound amused. He did sound annoyed.

"There's something under the water. I kicked it."

"Shark?" Chad suggested.

"Seriously?" Derek scoffed. "In a freshwater reservoir?"

"Maybe," Chad muttered with a shrug.

"Well, it didn't bite me, so hopefully that rules out both the Reservoir Monster and all woman-eating fish."

Moving a few feet closer, Derek peered at the water. "If it's anything valuable, I call dibs."

"No way!" Lou protested. "I'm the one who kicked it. Finders keepers!"

Callum expelled an impatient sigh loud enough for Lou to hear, even across the twenty feet that separated them. He moved to the edge of the ice and slid gracefully into the water. As he swam toward them, Lou turned back to scan for the unidentified object.

At first she thought she was imagining it, but she could definitely see something down there, and it was getting larger and more distinct with each second. She wondered if her kick had knocked whatever it was loose, allowing it to float to the top. As she stared, holding her breath, the faint shape got closer and closer, until a large, gray mass bobbed to the surface. Lou gave a muffled shout, her arms tightening around Phil. A part of her knew what it was as soon as it surfaced, but a larger portion refused to accept it.

No. No way. No way.

"Is that a body?" Derek yelled from the ice.

"Yep, that's a dead guy," Phil said, his voice as casual as if it were a beer can floating next to them and not the waxy gray back of a corpse.

"Huh." Derek didn't sound too freaked out about it, either. "Lou, I'm good with finders keepers, then. You can have it."

She couldn't respond. For once, no words would leave her mouth. All she could do was cling to Phil's middle and try to breathe. It wasn't working.

As he pulled up next to them, Callum looked at the peacefully bobbing mass of flesh. "Fuck."

Lou's lungs had locked up again, and she felt as if her face had been dunked back into the frigid water. She couldn't tear her eyes away from the bloated body.

"Hey, Cal?" Phil still sounded much too calm. "Where's the head?"

## ABOUT THE AUTHOR

A graduate of the police academy, Katie Ruggle is a self-proclaimed forensics nerd. A fan of anything that makes her feel like a badass, she has trained in Krav Maga, boxing, and gymnastics, has lived in an off-grid, solar- and wind-powered house in the Rocky Mountains, rides horses, trains her three dogs, and travels to warm places to scuba dive. She has received multiple Amazon Best Books of the Month and an Amazon Best Book of the Year. *Run to Ground*, the first book in her Rocky Mountain K9 Unit series, was a 2017 *RT Book Reviews* Reviewers' Choice Award nominee. Katie now lives in a 150-year-old Minnesota farmhouse near her family.

# SEARCH AND RESCUE

In the Rockies, lives depend on the
Search & Rescue brotherhood. But this far
off the map, secrets can be murder.

**By Katie Ruggle**

### Hold Your Breath

Louise "Lou" Sparks is a hurricane—a
walking disaster. And with her, ice
diving captain Callum Cook has never
felt more alive...even if keeping her
safe may just kill him.

### Fan the Flames

Firefighter and Motorcycle Club
member Ian Walsh rides the line
between the good guys and the bad.
But if a killer has his way, Ian will
take the fall for a murder he didn't
commit...and lose the woman he's
always loved.

### Gone Too Deep

George Halloway is a mystery. Tall. Dark. Intense. But city girl Ellie Price will need him by her side if she wants to find her father…and live to tell the tale.

### In Safe Hands

Deputy Sheriff Chris Jennings has always been a hero to agoraphobe Daisy Little, but one wrong move ended their future before it could begin. Now he'll do whatever it takes to keep her safe—even if that means turning against one of his own.

---

# ROCKY MOUNTAIN K9 UNIT

These K9 officers and their trusty dogs will do anything to protect the women in their lives

**By Katie Ruggle**

### Run to Ground

K9 officer Theo Bosco lost his mentor, his K9 partner, and almost lost his will to live. But when a ruthless killer targets a woman on the run, Theo and his new K9 companion will do whatever it takes to save the woman neither can live without.

### On the Chase

Injured in the line of duty, K9 officer Hugh Murdoch's orders are simple: stay alive. But when a frightened woman bursts into his life, Hugh and his K9 companion have no choice but to risk everything to keep her safe.

### Survive the Night

K9 officer Otto Gunnersen has always been a haven: for the lost, the sick, the injured. But when a hunted woman takes shelter in his arms, this gentle giant swears he'll do more than heal her battered spirit—he'll defend her with his life.

### Through the Fire

When a killer strikes, new K9 officer Kit Jernigan knows she can't catch the culprit on her own. She needs a partner: local fire spotter Wesley March. But the more time they spend together, the hotter the fire smolders… and the more danger they're in.

---

For more Katie Ruggle, visit:

**sourcebooks.com**

**ALSO BY KATIE RUGGLE**